Aliens on a holiday

AF281365

Friedrich S. Plechinger

by Friedrich Severin Plechinger

Production and publishing:

BoD - Books on Demand,

Norderstedt

ISBN: 9783759768063

MIX
Papier aus verantwortungsvollen Quellen
Paper from responsible sources
FSC® C105338
FSC
www.fsc.org

Table of Contents:

1) Foreword

2) A day in Lontzen

3) The family from another planet

4) Men in Black

5) Aliens on vacation

6) Patosh on the road

7) The aliens are coming

8) Patosh and Mary

9) Aliens know no stress

10) Patosh and the Pyrenees

11) Aliens in search of clues

12) Santiago de Campostella

13) We have lost them

14) The High Council is not pleased

15) Mr. Gonzales has disappeared

16) Hard times for Patosh

17) UFO Delusion

18) The trail

19) And the world stood still

20) Back to Lontzen

21) The universe is seething

22) Escape

23) Vacation lockdown

24) A Land Rover drives through night and fog

25) Day zero has arrived

26) Between heaven and earth

27) Nothing is as it seems

28) Earth is not a vacation spot

29) The Red Door

30) Back to Connington on the Shyre

31) Hell is empty and all the devils are here

32) Star war is possible

33) The Arrival

34) Invisible War

35) Abyss

36) New Earth

Foreword

After a short break, it was time for me to write again, or thanks to the lap top, to type, because restless as I am, my life would otherwise be boring. Naturally, the question arose as to what I should put on paper this time and yes, the Middle Ages, the time period in the sixties and seventies, as well as the present, I had already used for my novels and my biography. That left a journey into the future mixed with the present. The idea was born during my stay in Luxembourg, where I occasionally stay in a hotel and use my free time to write. A good Luxembourgish friend, named Patrick Gafron, who is called "Patosh" for short and is also one of my readers, motivated me to write something new during one of the various pub visits and yes, since we often talked about UFOs, moon landings and moon landings that didn't happen, I decided to write a science fiction thriller and since Patrick is a good listener, I call the main character in this thriller Patosh. I deliberately left out the "c" in Patosh because I also want this book to be published in English and the "c" in Patosh doesn't fit in. The question now is to whom I will dedicate this book. First and foremost, my loyal readers, as well as Patrick Gafron (Patosh) and all new readers who will enjoy this journey.

Everything told in this thriller is NOT true and all the characters in it are fictional. In this case also Patosh, who has nothing to do with my real buddy Patosh from Luxembourg. One last thing for all Duden fanatics. I still like to use the "Scharfe S" (ß). Telepathy or the word "telepathic" is also used repeatedly. This is intentional. So please don`t get annoyed.

Have fun reading.

Yours

Friedrich S. Plechinger

A day in Lontzen.

Loud thunder, caused by two low-flying fighter jets, made the dogs in a small village, close to the German-Belgian border, bark and the citizens of this village called Lontzen rushed out of their houses to see what was going on. The dogs looked up at the sky and more Belgian Air Force fighter jets shot past the roofs of the houses like arrows. Tens of fingers pointed upwards as they all saw it. Elliptical lights moved in a zigzag pattern from left to right and then from top to bottom at an unprecedented speed. Some watched in fascination, but others showed panic on their faces and when the lights suddenly disappeared, the usual dead silence returned. But not for long. They, who all saw it, met at Patosch's (short for Patrick in French), who ran a pub in this otherwise very quiet village and his establishment was about to burst as more and more forced their way through the narrow pub door. All the tables were taken within minutes and those who weren't lucky enough to get a chair were scattered around the room. Noise and cigarette smoke filled the room, as Patosch thought nothing of the smoking bans that were otherwise imposed on the world. In his opinion, everyone was free to choose the way they wanted to die, whether by nicotine, alcohol, colesterol or a constantly nagging wife who made one's life, at least for him, a living hell. Patosch stood at the tap and the beer flowed in the mugs like never before.

"Five more Stella and four Orval Patosch!" shouted Georgette, a waitress who had moved here from the western zone of Belgium.

7

"Coming right up!" beamed an overjoyed innkeeper, as the rouble was rolling like never before on that particular day.

"What do you say to the lights from earlier Patosch?" asked one of the many farmers in the village, who was standing right next to the bar and looking into the crowd.

"What do you want to hear Gerome? Those lights can show up every day for all I care, if it brings me such a profit..."

"Yes, but what were those lights? I've never seen anything like it in all the years I've spent in the fields, plowing the land with the tractor..."

"The end of the world is near!" suddenly shouted a fatter woman from the corner

"Oh shut up Francine!" shouted another, laughing.

"More beer..." shouted an elderly citizen of the village, holding up his right hand to make himself heard and the noise continued into the deep hours of the night until Patosch had had enough and moved the last guest out of the pub called " À la cruche dòr " (To the golden jug) shortly before midnight.

"Just one more Patosch..."

"No, no Thibault, off home now. Tomorrow is another day." And with a gentle shove, the innkeeper pushed the stubborn guest through the door and locked it immediately. A shock ran through him when he turned around and saw the mess. Full ashtrays, empty and half-full glasses and jugs on the tables. Some standing, others tipped over. Plates with gnawed chicken bones and other leftovers. But even more unpleasant was the crunching sound under his shoes and when he looked at the floor, he noticed shards of glass from broken glasses, caused by the excessive alcohol consumption of some of the guests and its consequences.

"Holy shit." Patosch whispered, cursing.

"Not today. I'll clean up tomorrow." He said to himself, yawning, and disappeared into the bedchamber on the second floor of the house. Dead tired, he put on his pyjamas, went into the bathroom and brushed his teeth, and as he looked at himself in the mirror, he wondered what the lights that everyone in the village saw were all about. They were elliptical and constantly changed position. Sometimes they hovered horizontally, but then the light turned vertical and shot back and forth like one of those rubber balls you had as a child. He drank water from the tap, gargled briefly and spit the foam into the basin and when he couldn't find a towel, he simply brushed his right sleeve over his mouth.
She lay there snoring, the wife called Camille. Once the beauty of the village and the daughter of the local gendarme, and now a nightmare of a walrus who only scolded and nagged constantly. "Patosh do this, Patosh do that..." as if he didn't have enough to do with all the shopping and preparations. She just vegetated, too sluggish to contribute productively to the household or the pub.

9

"Oh you lights, whatever you've been. Come back and take me with you." he thought to himself quietly.

Meanwhile, two hundred and thirteen million kilometers from Earth, another scenario was playing out. On Venus, to be precise. Everything harmonized with divine precision and the inhabitants there, we would call them aliens or extraterrestrials, spent their "existence" carefree and emotionless simply because they were thousands of years ahead of the earthlings, i.e. us. They differed in appearance and could not exactly be described as beautiful, but they would think the same if they saw us for the first time, which they did several million years ago. Their language is telepathy, their food is from another world and their philosophy is unconditional charity and tireless service to others. They were, evolutionarily, in a different density and were thousands of years ahead of the earthlings. No wars, no religion, no governments, no taxes and no mendacious media could poison their lives. There was no boss, no president, no king or emperor. There was a council that consulted constantly, but always under the telepathic eyes of the venusian population, and the transfer of datas of any correspondence thus determined was transmitted in this way. They also had no names. They just looked at each other and the exchange of thoughts and communication began. Why did they need a name when everyone was equal? Their reproduction was also telepathic. If they thought they were compatible, the mating was carried out in this way and after just one week, they received a cosmic, extraterrestrial bundle of joy. But what the Venusians (that's what we call these beings from Venus for simplicity's sake) love most of all is traveling. All they have to do is make a telepathic request and, if approved, they are allowed to choose a spaceship of their choice. Borrowed, of course. Just like the usual car rental service but without payment, because money or other foreign currency did not exist on Venus. And so our story begins.

The family from another planet

On Venus there are no buildings or houses as we are used to, but telepathically furnished and imaginary living spaces, if you want to describe it that way. No walls that can be touched or felt. You experience everything there in your mind and in your consciousness, but you can arrange it the way you want it without restricting your connection to family members. The father may be in one of his imaginary homes at the same time as he is talking to his son, who is in a completely different imaginary environment to the father, but they are still close to each other. You have to imagine it like this. The father, who is a lover of books and old artifacts, has imagined in his mind a private mixture of a library and a small museum and at this moment he lives in such a room, while the son at the same moment imagines an ice cream parlor, which does not exist on Venus. Nevertheless, the conversation between father and son takes place telepathically. In the same way, the mother can imagine her living space according to her taste etc. etc. This is just an example.

On one of these Venusian days (the Venusians do not use a unit of time or a calendar because, as I said, they are thousands of years ahead of us), the father of a Venusian family of three decided to go on a cosmic vacation and discussed it with the compatible unit, we would call her wife, and the resulting offspring, in this case the son.

"Where should we go this time, my dears? Last time we weren't very happy with Orakium (Pluto) and Mastonius (Mercury)." Said the Venusian father.

"Yes, my compatible and the food was downright unpalatable on both planets. I had terrible gas from all the mangaria salad. (A vegetable not worth going into further)."

"True, but I made a lot of friends there. I really enjoyed it and the mangaria salad was delicious. I could never have eaten enough of it." Said the son.

"Oh my little offshoot. You still have a lot to learn, but yes, it's nice that you've made friends on both palnetes. This is essential for your cosmic development. Still, the Mangaria salad was disappointing this time and too much of it was quite unhealthy. So? Where should we go next?" asked the father, let's call him Jonathan for simplicity's sake.

"Oh, oh, how about one of the many moons of Corantio (Saturn)? The moon called Sorio has a great adventure park and my friends will be there too. A telepathic call is all it takes. Please dad, please mom!"

Here, too, the earthly title for the parents was chosen so as not to confuse the reader too much, because who can do anything with the cosmic titles? That would drive us "telepathically" mad, make this book unreadable and annoy my readership. That's why we call the Venusian boy Fred and the cosmic mom Martha in this story. We've already called the father Jonathan.

"Corantio, hmm? Good idea Fred, what do you think Martha? It would be something new and our boy is already driving me telepathically crazy with his sad eyes."

"Corantio. Yes, why not. My sister Sybilla (compatible with Martha) has already been there and told me about a very relaxing spa facility. I could do with a telepathic massage. And you, my husband (telepathically compatible chosen one) could improve your Sorana (cosmic golf) skills there."

"Indeed, I could Martha." Jonathan smiled telepathically, because the facial features of these aliens didn't move an inch and they would win at any poker game imaginable on our planet called Earth, as they had an unfathomable poker face.

"However, I would suggest making several stops." Father Jonathan said cheerfully.

"Exosauro, for example, has an infinite archive of knowledge and a large educational database. If not the largest. Our little treasure could stuff himself with all that data and learn more about the history of the universe..."

"Oh no, how boring...."

"Fred! Listen to your father. You should have fun on Corantio, but education is a basic requirement, my cosmic angel," Martha persuaded her defiant son.

"It's definitely fun too. An educational trip with games and excitement. I'm all for it." Jonathan agreed.

"And what else? Which other planets should we visit?" asked Fred, bored, because no child goes to school voluntarily. Even less so during a vacation trip.

"Sybilla told me about a planet called Earth. At least that's what the aliens who live on it call it. We know it as 'Terrarion'.

It was supposed to be pretty wild and she had a lot of fun. Her spaceship was chased and hunted by what they had down there, also known as fighter jets, and Sybilla always won that game..."

"MARTHA?" Jonathan suddenly admonished sternly. „Think of the boy. He deserves to know the truth about Terrarion. What goes on down there is not a game and the inhabitants are stubborn and backward. They have hardly evolved. Fighter jets. Don't make me laugh. They're stuck in their ways."

"Oh yes, oh yes. That sounds like fun!" rejoiced Fred, who only saw the game in it.

"Can I also pilot the spaceship on Terrarion and play tag with the Earthlings?"

Jonathan made clacking noises in response, which meant NO.

"No Fred. Terrarion is a dangerous place and yet it's the most beautiful planet in the whole universe. The inhabitants of this planet have emotions, are fearful, uncommunicative and unwilling to open up spiritually in order to enable better coexistence and cooperation with other species. All they want is power and our knowledge to enrich themselves and in the process their planet is becoming more and more endangered. It was different thousands of years ago, because back then the humans, as the race on Terrarion calls itself, were more attentive, open and willing to learn from us. Also grateful for the knowledge we gave them. We helped them to found a civilization that focused on love and cohesion. We helped build monuments that also facilitated our presence there. But there was one thing we hadn't considered and we are still feeling the effects of this mistake today."

Martha knew what Jonathan was talking about, but little Fred had not stored this knowledge in his telephatic database.

"What mistake Dad?"

"A bug that is unique in the entire universe my boy and only occurs on this planet. It is known as greed, power, money, envy, jealousy, resentment, fear and the worst of all is called hate. In a word, "evil". Our ancestors had completely disregarded these characteristics, partly out of naivety, because as I said, we too had to evolve. The people there have a chronology that we do not use and so, for the sake of simplicity, we will use their unit here for this example. This started millions of their years ago, but the heyday of our work on Terrarion was 8000 Earth years ago. They, the humans, were very primitive, but as helpless as they were, they were innocent and loving as well."

"Innocent? What does that mean, Dad?" Fred asked curiously.

"Well. I can't explain it like that son and that's why a trip to Exosauro, before Terrarion, would be highly recommended, because there you can telepathically receive, process and understand all the data. Another dangerous quality they have is called emotion. I could apply all of this to you in a nutshell, but to really understand it, you have to experience it for yourself."

Fred made a clacking sound that we on Earth would understand as an affirmative nod of the head.

"So should we plan it like this? Corantio first, then Exosauro and finally Terrarion? Suggestions are welcome." Jonathan asked the group.

"Let's start with the most distant planets first. Exosauro. Fred can pump himself full of knowledge there. Then Corantio for a well-deserved rest and finally Terrarion to save the best for last."

Martha's suggestion made sense and they agreed, and Jonathan immediately took care of reserving a spaceship. Telepathically, of course.

"Hello? Yes, this is Jonathan. I wanted to inquire regarding a reservation for a spaceship..." .

"Yes... for three people. Destination Exosauro, Corantio and Terrarion....what? Do I have a special permit for Terrarion? No, why?...Aha...Aha...Aha. Okay! Can I apply for it through you? Well, that's fantastic! Which model? What do you suggest? The Orion Deluxe?...no, I already had that. It always runs out of breath quickly. Galaxia Supreme? What can it do?
Aha...Aha...Aha...we'll take that one. When should we start? Yes, as far as we're concerned, right away! Fantastic. So you're bringing the spaceship over? Excellent."

Men in Black

Back on Earth, things were not so relaxed, because Patosch had a strange visitor. He wasn't the only one in Lontzen, because there were many who saw the spaceship or spaceships that day, were bothered. Men in black suits and dark sunglasses, reminiscent of a sixties cliché, appeared like ghosts.

"What am I supposed to do?" Patosh shouted at one of these strange men.

"I'm supposed to deny what I've seen and never speak of it again? Can you actually still be saved? The whole village has seen it and probably the surrounding villages too. We're not in Hollywood you morons and while we're at it, what's that accent you're using? It's neither English nor American. If I didn't know better, I'd bet my head on a Slavic one."

"No, we're not Slavs and where we come from doesn't matter here. You forget everything and don't give any interviews, otherwise you can close the place down...." One of the two said cheekily.

„You know what you assholes? Get out of here before I get my shotgun and blow several holes in your airless skulls. This is Europe and things run differently over here. You can't seal the mouths of hundreds of citizens. I've seen the spaceship and that's that.

Now piss off before I forget myself!" shouted Patosch, beside himself.

"That wasn't the last word Mr. .....what's your name?"

"Napoleon and now get out of here."

Annoyed but not responding to the outburst of anger, the two men left the "Golden Jug" and Patosh followed them to the door. But as he looked after them, he noticed that they were not the only men in dark suits. There were more of the same kind walking around outside. There must be around fifty of them. Shaking his head, he locked the door and muttered curses under his breath. He had to open the inn in an hour. It was not easy for him to get his mind back under control after this incident, because he had to listen to the threat over and over again in his mind: „...otherwise you can close the place down...How dare these foreigners and non-belgians make such threats here in his country? Weren't the Nazis the best example of what that feels like? The new world powers did nothing different here. Invading, stealing oil and minerals and imposing their false democracy." Patosch continued to curse to himself, not realizing how quickly the hour passed.

All the tables were clean and only the floor needed a wipe and as he followed his train of thought and mopped, his wife, Camille, slipped past him.

"I'm going to the hairdresser. It may take a while,"

she said. But Patosch didn't react, because he hadn't had anything to say to her for a long time. This marriage only existed for economic reasons, because he no longer had the strength to lose his house and farm through divorce at the age of fifty. Starting over after all these years was not an option for him. It was better to close his eyes and be done with it than to find himself on the street again, because the divorce law in Belgium was not very man-friendly. The first guests entered the pub and the room filled with noise and cigarette smoke within minutes and Patosch visibly felt the tension and anger caused by the appearance of these unfriendly gentlemen in dark suits that day.

"They told me to keep my mouth shut or they'd block my son's scholarship. Can you believe that? What do these idiots think they're doing?" Gerome complained, holding a glass of pastis in his right shaking hand.

"They threatened to revoke my cab license. I think we've had enough of this bullshit. Our own government hates us because they allow such measures by third parties. The Germans could have stayed right here. At least they were Europeans."

"They still are, you idiot!" said Gerome.

"I'm just saying. What's the difference?"

"Don't take it all so seriously. It's all just empty threats."

Patosch tried to calm the men down, but this seemed to be no easy task. The ladies of the village were also talking loudly and complaining amongst themselves, but the beer and wine continued to flow in streams, just like on the day the UFOs were sighted. However, the UFO sightings brought with them another problem. The sensation.

Now UFO fanatics and so-called experts flocked to Lotzen as if on a pilgrimage, and they too found Patosch's pub, behaving far too loudly for the taste of the actual citizens of Lontzen. Economically, it was a blessing for Patosch, because now he could rent out rooms on his farm, which stood three kilometers away and empty. He had no animals or tractors there. It was passed on to him after the death of his aunt and now this opportunity presented itself to rent rooms to these UFO pilgrims and the prices would be "salty". Without wanting to, Patosch became almost wealthy overnight and, clever as he was, he knew how to book the income so that his wife didn't notice. He transferred most of this income discreetly and securely to a private account in Brussels. If she asked any questions, it was because of the necessary expenses that nothing remained in the actual joint account at the end. Why share the income with someone who no longer loved and respected you and was just lying on the lazy side?

She disappeared without a word to Patosch when she came back from her visit to the hairdresser. It didn't hurt him anymore, despite the fact that they were once happy and in love together and she was beautiful and willowy. But then she got pregnant and the baby died in childbirth. The world ended for both of them.

But she suffered the most and she has not been able to come to terms with it to this day. She also blamed him, Patosch, because he was a drunkard and he had filled her with his sick drunkard genes. Patosch hasn't drunk since then, because there's one thing women do best. Burdening men with guilt until there are only two options left. You either accept these feelings of guilt or you break away from them and thus also from your wife. Divorce is only one consequence that Patosch did not take for the reasons mentioned above, and if anyone thought this marriage could still be saved, they were very much mistaken. Love turned to hate and that was the end of it. Nevertheless, the UFO pilgrims became a nuisance for everyone after a while, as they left behind garbage and blocked parking spaces. The village, which had only eight hundred inhabitants, was now bursting at the seams with just under three thousand. The village police couldn't cope with the problems this caused, and it was also becoming too much for Patosch, who used to be able to close the pub at midnight, but now this privilege was delayed by two hours. He was exhausted and, despite the profits generated, he cursed the UFO fantasists. Then the constant harassment from the military and police and by then the UFO issue had been forgotten by the villagers had they not been confronted with this nuisance over and over again. The rescue finally came in the form of an order issued from the highest level, directly from the Brussels Presidency, to all the police and military services. This matter had to be taken off the table once and for all and an end had to be put to it.

The media received an unconditional ban on reporting on the case and the "UFO-Experts" were more or less kindly expelled from the village. Peace returned to Patosch and its inhabitants and the old habit was restored, like a long-awaited liberation. They never spoke of it again. What Patosch needed now was a vacation. He didn't want to fly because he was afraid of flying and traveling by train was also out of the question because he hated crowds, both on the train and at the station. So the only option was a car vacation. But where to go? A round trip around the south of France, Portugal and Spain wouldn't be bad, he thought. You could stop along the way, visit restaurants and sleep wherever you wanted. His old Peugeot wouldn't survive such a trip, so he picked up the phone book and searched and searched until he found what he wanted. He picked up the phone, dialed the number and when a human voice answered, he was pleasantly surprised, because he didn't want to talk to a machine.

"If you prefer English, press two, if you want to book a short vacation, press three...etc, etc."

"Montfort, how can I help you?" came the voice on the other side.

"Bonjour. My name is Patrick Van de Brog. I would like to rent a motorhome."

"That would be no problem Mr. Van de Brog. Do you have something specific in mind?"

"Something small. For two weeks. Maybe a Mercedes Sprint, for example..."

"We would have something like that. But not a Mercedes. A Montana, would that be OK?"

"Hmm... I've had one of those before. Wasn't very happy with it. Would you have something else?" Patosch asked.

"A Citroen with a Hymer bed. Space for two, fridge, sink, two cupboards and a mini shower..."

"That's all right. How much would it cost?"

"You said two weeks? May I ask where you're going?"

"Why?"

"So that I can calculate an approximate total mileage. The first 1500 kilometers would be free, every additional kilometer costs forty cents."

Patosch thought about it and gave the agent the information he needed. In the end, three thousand kilometers were calculated as total distance.

"That would give us a total of 1996 euros, including insurance, Mr. Van de Borg."

"That's all right. Send me everything by email and I'll make a firm booking." Patosch ended the conversation with satisfaction.

No ten horses would hold him back, because what he needed was distance and time with himself.

Time to think about everything he had done wrong, everything he had missed out on, why he wasn't spending his time with someone who really loved him and who was happy to be there and didn't make him feel guilty like Camille did. He realized one thing at that moment. He couldn't go on like this. He deserved better and if God didn't help him, then maybe someone from another world who had more power than God. But first he wanted to book the trip and simply disappear.

Aliens on vacation

The compatible family (let's call them that) went to the spaceship rental company and pulled small suitcases on wheels behind them that looked very similar to the earthly suitcases. The strange thing was that the Compatibles were walking around naked as God (or whoever) created them and you wondered what they were carrying in their suitcases. The spaceship renter greeted them and showed Jonathan what the Galaxia Supreme vehicle was all about.

" Here is the gravity compensator. Please only use it on Terrarion and just before landing. The magnetic field converter impresses with its simplicity and redundancy. Sixteen of them are installed. But we are particularly proud of the flex transformer."

"Oh. And what can it do?" Jonathan asked curiously.

"It makes the spaceship invisible if it is noticed and pursued by frightened terrariens. An unpleasant matter if this happens, as this species is one of the most underdeveloped in the universe and everything that appears alien is categorized as hostile at the same time. It's best to leave the switch on "AUTOMATIC"."

"Is it the way they say it is?" Martha asked the landlord.

"What are they saying, ma'am?"

"Well, that it could be dangerous on Terrarion."

"Let's put it this way. It's by no means boring and if you find residents who are in favor of the new, then it's the best trip and the best vacation you've ever taken. I can say that from experience. And it's good that we're talking about this, because I'm going to give you a folder that you should inprolate before the trip (study telepathically in Venusian). This does not apply to Corantio and Exosauro..."

"That goes without saying." Jonathan said dryly, because he wanted to speed up the briefing on the ship and not prolong it unnecessarily. Martha was surprised by this behavior, because she didn't know Jonathan like this.

"Can this ship also automatically activate the rescue unit in an emergency so that we don't get stranded and forgotten somewhere?"

"Each of our spaceships has a homer. If it is not triggered automatically, it can also be activated manually. It's right here, under the control panel."

"How fast is it? That's the last question and then we want to get going."

"9 scal!"

"That's very impressive. Thank you for the briefing. Let's get going." Jonathan urged and Martha was taken aback, because he seemed totally alien to her at that moment. A behavior that was not at all noticeable on Venus and yet seemed worrying. The agent left the ship and said goodbye with the usual clacking sound. The entrance to the spaceship closed and the Galxia Supreme and its ET contents disappeared silently and in a flash.

"Corantio, here we come!" clacked little Fred and Martha rejoiced with him, emotionless yet galactically moved.

Jonathan sat at the "wheel" and pressed buttons with his long, slender and bony fingers, probably on the cosmic navigation system and when everything was set, he relaxed too. Corantio was only 13 human light years away and with "9 Scal" the journey will seem short. As said before, aliens have no time calculation and therefore no sense of time, but the scal measurement is necessary to hit the spectrum portal correctly to get to a different dimension faster.

"I'm hungry!" said little Fred.

"What, already?" called Martha motherly.

"I'll unpack the Mangaria salad..."

"Don't we have anything else? No Milky Way bars?"

The reader should know that although the cosmic Milky Way bars have the same name as the earthly ones, they have nothing to do with each other and that the similarity of the names is purely coincidental.

"No Fred. Too much of it is unhealthy and you overindulge yourself every time with this unhealthy stuff.

I wonder how the kids on Terrarion eat. Probably more sensible."

A mistake that Mama Martha would soon learn. There were hotels on Corantio just as there were on Earth, but they were different in their structure and because the rooms of these establishments were separated by stone walls on Earth, this was not the case on Corantio. The room had opaque walls and you could see the cosmos as if you were outside in space and yet privacy was maintained because guests could not see each other, not even telepathically, except for family members who traveled and belonged together. Little Fred had a blast and Jonathan played Sorana every chance he got. This extraterrestrial golf game had the feature of having to put a ball in a hole, just like on Earth, only the ball had to hit a hole on one of the many surrounding, uninhabited moons for which the game was designed. The ball had a kind of GPS, so you could see exactly where it was. If it hit one of the holes, you were sent a congratulatory note and a Mangaria salad coupon for one of the restaurants on Corantio. Jonathan played so well in those days that he already had quite a few coupons and the Mangaria salad was hanging out of his ears. The same happened to little Fred, who made new friends and played everything imaginable with them. They also thought the Mangaria salad was a puke and would rather eat the lava dust of the of the surrounding hills than stuff another purple leaf of this vegetable into themselves. When everyone had had enough of Corantio, Exosauro was set as the next target. Three spectrum portals had to be penetrated for this, as this planet was several light years away (by Earth measurement) from Venus and Corantio. It now came to

30

one`s attention, why this cosmic family was carrying suitcases. Like the Earthlings, the Venusians loved souvenirs, so it was understandable that they needed a container to store and carry them.

"I think we'd have to get two extra suitcases on Exosauro, otherwise we won't have room for the souvenirs from Terrarion." Martha said.

"Don't worry. There's nothing worth taking with us on Exosauro apart from knowledge." Fred protested.

"But you're getting smarter, son." Said Jonathan.

"What's the point? I'm already clever..."

"You can never acquire enough knowledge Fred and you don't have the knowledge that will take you to the next level in your development. You're still a long way off." Martha said firmly.

Fred was not convinced and made a not quite intelligible clacking sound.

"There. We're reaching the First Portal. What a traffic jam..." clacked Jonathan.

"Seems like everyone's taking a vacation. And look where they're coming from. Isn't that the spaceship of our neighboring compatibles?" Martha asked, delighted.

"Indeed, Hubert, Sonia and little Tamara. Who knows where they'll end up." Jonathan said.

Again, the names are made up to avoid using far more complicated names such as: X//&((((.

"I'm not hoping for Exosauro. Would only continue to spoil my vacation if that smartass Tamara..."

"FRED!!! What's got into you boy? We don't use such thoughts on Venus and yes, take an example from Tamara. She's been on Exosauro four times and has acquired a lot of knowledge. How I would love to have her as my future daughter-in-law." Martha exclaimed, but Jonathan also mentally allied himself with his son when Martha said this.

"What? You don't agree with me my husband?"

"Why did you get into my thoughts? You don't do that." Protested Jonathan.

"Sorry, you're right." Martha apologized.

"We have to let the boy have his free will, dearest. This is and remains Venusuain law and I don't know if Tamara will be compatible. Fred should be allowed to find out for himself."

"You're right Jonathan. Something is disturbing my senses. Ever since the spaceship rental. We've all been behaving strangely since then."

Jonathan also had to realize this. The mental balance, should aliens have such a soul, was unbalanced and this could be seen in the quality of the conversation. More rabid and sometimes more irrational than usual on Venus.

"Hand me the vibescanner son. Let's see what it shows, because I've noticed this change too." Jonathan said, not quite sure if the scanner was any good. Fred handed him the vibescanner and Jonathan scanned the entire interior of the spaceship. When he was finished, he had the results analyzed and sure enough, the scanner showed something irregular. Jonathan tried to get hold of the results, but the scanner reported "access denied". This made Jonathan suspicious, as there were no secrets on Venus. So what was that all about? He couldn't make any sense of it and let the matter rest.

"What does the scanner say?" Martha asked.

"Nothing."

Martha left it at that and the journey continued as the first portal was crossed. The next, or second, portal was now the destination and Jonathan stepped on the gas. Scal 9 showed up on the cosmic speedometer and the Galaxia Supreme delivered what it promised. Jonathan even overtook his neighbors' ship and Fred couldn't contain a barely visible alien grin.

"Bye bye Tamara." He thought to himself quietly and Martha turned to face him. Fred didn't like it at all and kept quiet during the whole flight.

Martha felt guilty, but in the end she was just a woman and very concerned about the welfare of the cosmic family. She knew that she had no right to interfere telepathically in the family's thoughts. She fetched a Milky Way bar from somewhere and handed it to little Fred. He thanked her and everything was forgotten. Soon the second Spectrum portal was crossed and the third was not far away. Shortly before the third portal, Jonathan reduced the scale number to 5 and finally the planet Exosauro was reached. The family got out of the spaceship and Papa-Alien stretched because his bones were aching. Yes, extraterrestrials also have the same maladies as earthlings, only these come much later, as ageing is delayed by centuries according to the human calendar. Fred helped unload the suitcases and Martha negotiated the registration with the hotel receptionist. The rooms here differed from those on Corantio. Here, the walls were solid and the facility was reminiscent of one of the many motels that have proliferated in the United States, only more well-kept.

"I'm going to lie down. I'm exhausted." Jonathan said, but Martha wanted to check out the facility and perhaps indulge in a spa. Fred just wanted to look for new friends and get up to the usual nonsense with them, like on Corantio. He was very disappointed when he didn't find any children and Martha delivered him to one of the study places so that she could undergo massages and the steaming benefits of the geysers in peace. Fred was horrified. Hundreds of children were sitting in front of screens, inprolating (studying).

"Ah. You must be Fred." An exosaur called out in a friendly manner and directed the little alien to his screen. All the other children paid no attention to him because they were telepathically paralyzed while studying.

"This is your place, my boy."

"What do I have to do?"

"Just look into the circle and shout 'I am Fred'. That's all." Smiled the usher whose smile showed in contrast to the Venusian.

Fred did as instructed and a microsecond later was also paralyzed telepathically. Like a movie, data, images, videos, cosmic hyroglyphs and much more streamed through his little head, as if he had several memory sticks that could hold trillions of gigabites. Nevertheless, he was fully aware of his senses and could finally converse, again telepathically, with the others while all this knowledge was being transmitted. The only thing he couldn't do was move, and that was set up by the system so that none of these galactic kids could fuck off and go on adventures, which in itself was part of education.

"What's your name?"

"Fred, and you?"

 "Rudolf. Have you just arrived?"

"Yes. What else can you do here but sit and get stuff introduced?"

"Nothing. But it's relaxing. You'll see."

"Hey. Hello everyone. I'm Karin. I've just been logged in too. It's cool, isn't it?"

"Hello Karin. I still need a little time to settle in." shouted Fred.

"At least they don't know any Mangaria salad here on Exosauro!" exclaimed Rudolf happily.

"You're wrong!" suddenly came from a corner.

"Who's that?" asked Karin and Rudolf almost simultaneously.

"My name is Tamara. I've been here four times and the Mangaria salad is flown in here. So no chance of getting rid of this torture."

Fred mentally pulled the rug from under his feet, even though there were no rugs on Venus. He had completely forgotten about her and to put a good face on it, he greeted her politely.

"Tamara, you're here and not on Varalios (Galactic Hollywood). Nice to meet you here."

"You've lied better than that Fred." she just said.

Everyone laughed and Fred felt embarrassed.

"Not OK Tamara. No mind reading. It's forbidden without prior agreement!"

"Not on Exosauro and there are no prohibitions in the universe. Only free will. You should know that." Tamara shot back, causing everyone to suddenly shut down telepathically. Fred knew he had no emotions, like the Earthlings on Terrarion did, but Tamara was awakening frequency fluctuations in him that he didn't find pleasant and he desperately wanted to erase them from his system. They grew up together on Venus, but one thing was clear. They were not compatible and never would be.

"What are these disturbing fluctuations I'm registering?" the observing mentor admonished without showing any emotion.

"Continue without interruption, otherwise you'll have to repeat everything."

"Don't!" thought some.

"That's what I thought and Fred is right. You mustn't interfere with other people's thoughts without prior agreement and yes, we also have prohibitions Tamara and you should know that. Now get on with it or it'll go off!"

Everyone immediately immersed themselves in the knowledge upload without ever being distracted telephonically again.

"What kind of break-in was that? ...or it`ll go off.... never heard of it before. Strange guy, this observer." Fred thought to himself secretly, but nothing escaped the mentor.

"I know that you and your parents are traveling on to Terrarion. I was there myself and did research for the High Council and believe me, I came back changed. So be careful and try not to investigate the humans, as they call themselves, for too long and it's best to look at everything from a distance, otherwise their habits will be transferred to you and they'll be hard to get rid of. Believe me, you don't want to store them in your system." Said the mentor, who had nevertheless logged into Fred's mind without prior consultation. The good thing was that he did it in a way that the others didn't notice. Fred wanted to know more, but the Menteor refused. All Fred needed to know was in the upload.

"Everything you need to know can be found in the data transmissions. Now, no more interruptions." And with those words, he left the room. Fred carried on, not allowing himself to be distracted again, and after he had made himself powerful with all the knowledge, he searched his repertoire for the data regarding Terrarion and its inhabitants. Without a doubt, he was fascinated by what he learned about this planet and the "humans" living on it. Yes, they were retarded compared to the rest of the universe, but that made them even more interesting and multi-faceted, because they had to use their brains and activate their minds. For Fred, it was like turning the crank on a spaceship. And how they were mostly controlled by emotions. He wondered more and more how this species was able to survive on this planet at all. But then came what had to come. The negative side and that horrified him telepathically, although it shouldn't be described in earthling words, because as I said, the Venusians had neither emotions nor pity or compassion. They had logic and that was all. Of course, reason was one of their main assets and that was all that mattered. Good and evil was not an element for them as it was on Earth, because good and evil did not exist in the universe. There was unconditional love and a sense of duty to serve the universe so that it would continue to function harmoniously and healingly. But what Fred found in his studies made no sense. This lust for power, this craving for control and the insatiable desire for foreign currency just to burden oneself with all kinds of crap amused him, even made him giggle cosmically, which sounded like a loud clacking. "How stupid is that?" it shot through his galactic skull. But he suddenly felt this instinctive urge to save this earth and the "sheep" living on it. Yes. There are no sheep on Venus, but you know what one means. He was just thrilled that nothing on Earth was like on Venus, Exosauro or Carantion and probably nothing like the rest of space. To him, this Earth, as it is called, seemed like an adventure or a theme park where the duty to save it would even be fun. And all the things they wear that they call clothes. No wonder the state of this planet is not at its best with all the chemicals to do eight billion people's laundry. Even aliens have to sleep and Fred's eyes fell shut after all that study and research. He was already looking forward to Terrarion.

Patosch on the road

While aliens hundreds of light years away were preparing for their vacation on Earth, the earthling Patosch was heading south in a rented camper van. He wasn't traveling alone, however, because he was taking his dog along, who constantly had to be around his wife Camille, although Patosch always suspected how much the dog preferred to stay with him. Patosch simply radiated a better mood and the dog sensed that. He would have died with Camille if Patosch hadn't taken his four legged friend with him. "Mr. Gonzales" was the name of the Jack-Russel Chihuahua crossbreed and "Mr. Gonzales" loved Patosch more than anything, because he could always get a piece of sausage from him, while Camille ate everything herself and tormented the dog while she chewed looking at him and didn't give up any of her sandwich. Mr. Gonzales was not a moocher, but a gesture of sharing was a sign for him that he belonged to the Van de Brog pack. Camille never saw it that way. So they were both in high spirits on this spontaneously arranged journey and the two friends drove swiftly past Paris towards Lyon. Patosch had changed his plans the day before and wanted to take a detour to explore certain cities along the way. He loved French history, even though he was Belgian in heart and soul, but even as a child he was a passionate reader of books about knights and castles and "Mr. Gonzales seemed to share this passion, as he ran everywhere without complaining and waited outside for his master wherever he wasn't allowed in.

Everyone loved this dog and wanted to stroke him all the time, which he allowed and which delighted Patosch.

In Lyon, the two of them took a break. They easily found a campsite with happy people who greeted each other in a friendly manner when they met while shopping in the small supermarket or when having a walk along the camping area. Mr. Gonzales was also greeted by other dogs at the campsite, sniffing amongst themselves without barking at each other. Neither size, sex nor breed disturbed the harmony between the four-legged friends and so Mr. Gonzales also quickly made friends. Patosch felt better than he had for a long time and bought two bottles of red Bordeaux, some ham and Brie cheese, as well as six eggs and two bottles of water for dinner. A little chat with the cashier about this and that brought Patosch up to date on the campsite rumors, which he showed no interest in at all, but for the sake of politeness he nodded understandingly and was finally able to turn away from the gossip. Back at the camper, Patosch set up three camping chairs and a table. One chair would have sufficed, but if someone wanted to sit down to join in a more sensible conversation, Patosch only had to point to the chair.

Mr. Gonzales was exhausted in the meantime, because his little legs marched a lot over this short distance. For every step taken by a larger dog, he had to take three. He was so tired that he wouldn't even accept a piece of bologna and only ate it at the constant urging of his master so that he could get some rest.

The baguette was cut in two with a rather blunt bread knife and generously smeared with butter before the ham was allowed to bed down on it and the bottle of Bordaux was opened with a corkscrew with a loud "plop". Patosch smelled it with relish and didn't wait. He poured himself a full glass and took a big sip.

"Ahhhh. That's not bad Mr. Gonzales, is it?"

But Mr. Gonzales was already in his deep dreams, dreaming of the poodle lady at number 43. She was arrogant, but not even such a beauty could resist a Chihuahua with Jack Russell genes for long. Patosch took a big bite of the smeared bread and washed down the chewy mass with the red Bordeaux, letting his taste buds do the rest. What a relief. The ringing of his cell phone left him cold. He was on vacation and had just forgotten to switch it off. One look at the display was enough. It was Camille. She probably wanted to know how he could just drive away and close the pub without saying anything. If he had taken the call, the wine would have turned to vinegar and so he switched off the cell phone. He leaned his head back and looked up at the night sky, which was cloudless and starry, and a shooting star that shot from right to left caught his attention, but he wished for nothing, because at that moment he had everything. But what if it wasn't a shooting star, but one of those spaceships like the one in Lontzen?

What the hell. Tonight was beautiful as it rarely was for him and the universe was kind to him. He treated himself to another sip of the delicious wine and allowed himself to immerse himself in this "moment". A moment without the hustle and bustle, without the aroma of smoke and alcohol, without bills, taxes and shopping. Without visits to the bank to rearrange loans that were due. No, that night he felt freer than ever and he suddenly understood what wealth actually meant. Owning nothing but nature, the starry sky and a good companion named Mr. Gonzales by his side. That was all he needed. After the second bottle, he finally fell asleep on the camping chair and only the barking of his dog brought him back to his feet.

"What's the matter Mr. Gonzales? What are you barking about?"

But all the dog wanted to know was whether his master was still alive, because despite his snoring, which woke up half of Lyon, Patosch didn't make a single movement and his master felt it as soon as he got up from the chair and stretched. His bones ached and the smell in his mouth tasted bitter and foul. What Patosch needed now was coffee and lots of it. An aspirin would also have done the trick, but he had left the small first-aid kit at home in Lontzen. In the meantime, Mr. Gonzales was lovingly handed his breakfast and all was right with the world again.

"Let's find a pharmacy, my friend. Daddy needs aspirin and Alka Selzer. Let's see. Maybe there's a small pharmacy here at the campsite." Patosch and Mr. Gonzales trotted along the grounds, but far and wide they couldn't find a pharmacy and all the small supermarket had to offer were pills that never had any effect on Patosch and were more likely to help people with a placebo effect.

"Merde!" he cursed quietly to himself. His head was threatening to burst, the Bordeaux had given him such a hard time and that was all he drank. On the way back to the camper, the little dog suddenly ran off, barking its head off.

"Mr. Gonzales...stay here...Mr. Gonzales!" But he was gone and now Patosch was allowed to search for him. After about 500 meters he found him on the back of the poodle from place 43, with his tongue hanging out and scolding the poodle owner loudly, but Mr. Gonzales didn't notice anything and the poodle lady brazenly let it go.

"Is that your dog, sir?" The woman shouted at Patosch.

"That depends." Patosch said with a laugh, proud of his little Don Juan, who simply took what he wanted. He was just following his natural instinct.

"Do something!" the lady shouted.

"What do you want me to do? Would you want to be bothered?"

"Well, that's the height of it. How dare you?"

"Do you have a water hose connected somewhere?"

"Yes, I'll get it." She just said and ran off.

"Well, go ahead and splash if you want to free your poodle from that sinner, you spoilsport."

The woman just stared angrily at Patosch and squeezed the tap of the Gardena system that was connected at the end, but no water came out.

"Have you turned on the main tap too?"

"Help me, you moron!" yelled the woman, but Patosch just shrugged his shoulders, went to the tap and turned it on. It was too late, however, because Mr. Gonzales dropped onto his back with satisfaction. He got what he wanted. A shag with the canine beauty from his dreams.

"Now you don't need the hose any more." Patosch said, but the woman, as angry as she still was, simply sprayed and hit both dogs. She was particularly targeting Mr. Gonzales, so Patosch snatched the hose out of her hand and screamed.

"That's enough, ma'am. You must be out of your depth."

"Really? If Jenevieve is pregnant, I'll report you."

"Oh yeah? Your bitch put up with it, didn't she?"

"You men are all the same. You only want one thing."

Patosch only laughed even harder, because this woman seemed beyond good and evil to him.

"Of course we are. We men are all pigs but you keep spreading your legs and remain innocent. They're dogs, madam. Do you notice anything at all? They follow their instincts and let's face it, if we were more like these dogs, we'd have fewer wars. Your mutt is not pregnant. Mr. Gonzales is neutered, but he still likes to ram. He thinks he's still a full male, poor guy. However, I am happy that he seems to have had his fun. Now, let me take my dog and get out of here."

The woman stared at him in horror searching for words, but she couldn't find them. She had never come across such a lout before and no one had ever dared to speak to her in such a tone. With a whistle, Patosch ordered his dog to start moving, who kept pace with his master, his head hanging down. The number 43 shone out of a sign nailed to the tree, marking the parking space of this very upset lady.

"Oh, may I ask you for something, ma'am. Would you happen to have two aspirin for me?"

As if remote-controlled, the lady ran to her mobile home and returned a short time later, speechless, with two aspirin tablets.

"Thank you very much. And again, I apologize for the impertinence of my Mr. Gonzales. He just stormed off on me."

"Again? You've now apologized after I went out of my way to bring you the two aspirin tablets. What the hell. I think I overreacted a bit. Jenevieve is not usually so approachable with males. Your Mr. Gonzalez seems to know how to handle female dogs."

"I didn't know he was such a heartbreaker either. I have to say... thanks anyway and have a nice day."

Patosch turned around with a smile and went on his way without thinking. She looked after him for a long time before she too retreated into her caravan and closed the door behind her.

"Mr. Gonzales. No sausage for you tonight. Shame on you."

But the dog looked at him with those googly eyes and knew that Patosch didn't have the heart to deny him the sausage. Patosch also sensed his dog's thoughts and laughed.

The two of them were in no hurry and stayed at the campsite for another two days, as Patosch didn't have the heart to separate his Mr. Gonzales from his newfound friends and so what? You take your time on vacation. They went for long walks and explored the area. Patosch also drove to Lyon twice to visit museums, but there he left Mr. Gonzales waiting in the caravan, with the windows slightly open, of course. The joy of seeing him again was always nice.

"So my friend. Pappi has brought you something nice and you'll only get it at the campsite."

An hour later, the camper van drove through the driveway and an oncoming smaller camper van almost blocked his way. He wanted to scream, but he noticed the lady poodle owner at the wheel and her dog sitting in the passenger seat. A surreal image that left him in a state of mild horror.

"Bon jour madame. Well? Going into town?" he called to her through the open window.

"No. We're going further south. Let's see where the road takes us, monsieur."

"I wish you and your darling a safe journey. Who knows, maybe the road will lead us back...."

"I don't think so. Bon jour monsieur!" she interrupted him with her nose upturned and drove on, almost tearing off the wing mirror.

"What was that?" Patosch thought to himself, "I thought we had made up, but who can understand women, right Mr. Gonzales?" But Mr. Gonzales didn't care in the end.

Patosh parked the camper in the usual spot and noticed a new neighbor. A tent was pitched on pitch 23 and a strange woman of a difficult-to-estimate age was settling in. Her hair was dyed a greenish blue, her mouth smeared with black lipstick and fingernails that could have come from a vampire and were also painted black."

"Good morning monsieur...OH I am terribly sorry....I hope I didn't make a mess of your place. I borrowed the tent from reception as I'm traveling as a hitchhiker. What a handsome dog. What's his name?

"Mr. Gonzales is his name and no. You're not messing up anything. You're in spot 23 and I'm in spot 22, everything's OK, madam."

The Englishwoman, Patosh realized, laughed out loud when she heard the name.

"No how funny...hahaha...Mr. Gonzales, how original."

"Why don't you come in? I'll make us a coffee." Patosch offered and she accepted without hesitation.

"My name is Patrick Van de Brogg." he said, holding out his hand to her.

"I'm Mary. Mary Mitchell from England."

"Pleased to meet you. Sugar and milk?"

"Yes please." She called out and something stirred in Patosch, because this woman was so different from the women from Lotzen and not at all comparable to Camille, who was an iceberg compared to this Mary here. A fat, cold iceberg. Mary, however, was refreshingly cheerful.

"How long have you been here?"

"Oh, I hitchhiked all the way from England and only arrived here an hour ago. I just find this way of traveling so much more exciting."

"Isn't it dangerous?" Patosh asked, slightly puzzled.

"NO, not at all. I usually talk the drivers' ears off and they're glad to have got rid of me at my destinations."

They both laughed out loud and looked at each other.

"Where were we...oh yes...you're hitchhiking. So you don't think it's dangerous?"

"Let's cut the crap, Patrick, I'm just Mary and the 'you' is a hindrance. Yes, sometimes it's dangerous, but pepper spray and my fingernails have helped me get out of awkward situations from time to time. But it has rarely happened so far. Do you have any wine? Red would be good?" she asked with a smile.

"Uh.... yes, of course. Didn't the coffee taste good?"

"Yes, it was excellent, but I like our conversation and wine breaks the ice better than coffee."

"Indeed, Mary, indeed." Patosh exclaimed, looking for the wine on one of the shelves.

"Ah, there we have it. A Pommerol from 2018, let's enjoy it then." With a loud PLOP, Patosh uncorked the bottle and poured two glasses of the red delicacy. They clinked glasses and looked each other in the eye. The mascara on Mary's eyelids would have struck fear into Patosh earlier, but on Mary they were more "SEXY" due to the prominent black shade, as it brought out her eyes more intensely, which were maroon and gave off a warmth that made Patosh squirm. She noticed and had to smile cheekily.

"Well, Pat, tell me about yourself."

"About me? By the way, my nickname is Patosh..."

"Not possible. It sounds so, how shall I put it, demeaning, almost insulting," Mary said, grimacing as if she had swallowed a spoonful of vinegar.

"No, no. It's quite common here in Belgium and in France, but Pat is fine too."

"I call you Pat and I call Gonzales Gonzi. Can I do that?"

"Of course you can. Gonzi. Why not?"

"So shoot, Pat. Are you married? Do you have children? Are you a pensioner or are you even running away, perhaps from the police or from a lover?" Mary urged, taking a big gulp of Pommerol.

"No, no. I'm not on the run, just on vacation. My life isn't that interesting Mary and yes, I'm unhappily married. In that sense, I am on the run and from her. I own a pub in a small town in Belgium called Lontzen. It's enough to live on, nothing special. I just need to get out, especially with what's happened recently. Strange events that I can`t explain."

"What events? Sounds exciting and, by the way, I find you and your life interesting."

"Oh, I can't tell you. You'd think I was crazy and I don't want to talk about it either. I don't understand what's happening around me any more and I sense a change coming where I don't know whether it's good or bad. Let's just enjoy the wine. Do you fancy veal's liver with onions and mashed potatoes?"

"Yes. Sounds good and I'm hungry."

"Good, then go ahead and start slicing the onions." Patosh smiled at her and handed her a board, a knife and two large onions. Confused by this sudden spontaneity, she just nodded in the affirmative and started peeling the onions. No doubt she had never done anything like this before, because she was clumsy. Patosh shook his head with a smile, amused by her loss of self-confidence and her feigned self-assurance. She was probably a spoiled brat from a rich family, tearing herself away from home to discover life outside a golden cage.

"Well then? I don't know anything about you. Go ahead. Tell me," Patosh urged, almost commandingly. He was not a gentleman in the usual sense, but straightforward, honest thereby transparent, also shy and reserved towards the ladies.

"What are you doing with that poor onion, my child?" Patosh shouted in horror as he saw her almost cut her fingers.

"No, not like that, but like this. See?" and their hands touched causing his heart almost to burst. Everything around him seemed colorful and bright and he experienced a love that was not of this world. Not a sexual love, but a pure, true, human and, if he believed in God, divine love. Shocked by these feelings, he let go of her hands and apologized as if he had done something terrible. Mary, however, was confused.

"What do you want me to forgive you for, Pat?" she laughed out loud.

"I want you to show me how to do it right. I want to learn."

"We hardly know each other and I'm not treating you hospitably. Forgive me. Let me cut the onions." He asked, ashamed.

"No. I'll cut them because I enjoy it. You're a good bone Pat." And when she said that, even Mr. Gonzales stopped playing at the word "bone." Patosh let her continue cutting and in the meantime seasoned the veal's liver.

"A little salt and pepper and sauté tarragon and sage with butter in a pan. That's how I make it for my guests in the pub."

"Sounds delicious. What about the potatoes? Do they need ten minutes to cook?" Mary said anxiously, as the butter was already steaming.

"Don't worry. I pre-cooked the potatoes yesterday. A little hot milk and warm butter, salt, pepper and a little nutmeg and the timing is just right. Like this. Pass me the onions Mary....Thank you."

The pan hissed and smoked and the first aroma smelled a little penetrating, but over time a wonderful aroma developed, especially when Patosch poured a cup filled with Chardonay over the sizzling liver. Another sizzle filled the cramped room and both Mary and Patosh didn't realize how quickly time was passing. They ate and drank and told each other stories and Patosh was surprised to find out how right he was with his guess. She came from a good family and was wealthy, but she was bored with her life. She was unmarried and in her mid-thirties. Too old in herself to wear make-up like a gothic monster and walk around like a hippy, but despite all this masquerade, there was something about her that made Patosh's heart beat faster. He couldn't get enough of her, but he had to keep his composure because he was several years older.

"I'm supposed to inherit everything one day, but I don't want Daddy to croak. He's such a great guy, you know? Not one of these stuffy and poshy lords who come in and out through our house. Sure, Daddy's a lord too, but he's different. I love him very much and I don't want his legacy. I want him to grow old as a stone." Mary said with a sigh. Patosh found her touching and smiled and was amazed at how much this slim girl could eat, because the calf's liver was not enough. The cheese still had to come out of the fridge and so did the pudding cup.

"My God, Mary. You're completely famished." Patosh said with a laugh.

"I haven't eaten for days. I left my wallet at one of those highway gas stations and by the time I realized it, I was already in Lyon. I couldn't buy anything and I had my credit card blocked by phone."

"Why don't you call your daddy? I'm sure he can help you."

"I don't want that. I want to pass this test of my own survival without an American Express or Visa card. It has to be possible without."

"Respect. What's next for you then? What's your next destination?" Patosh asked curiously.

"I'm traveling to wherever you and Gonzi want to go. I'll go with you and keep you company."

Mr. Gonzales was the one who was happiest about it. He liked her and barked at them and Patosh turned his head.

"Shshhhh Mr. Gonzales. Enough already!" he yelled in confusion

"I don't know Mary. We don't know each other well enough and..."

"Oh papperlapap. The matter is settled and it's two to nothing. We've outvoted you." She laughed out loud.

There was no longer any doubt about what a strong character this Mary possessed and if she hadn't been so refreshing and full of life, Patosh would probably have thrown her out by now, as he sometimes did with his drunken guests. But Mary was not one of those guests. She was a little drunk, but not to the point of losing control. Patosh nodded and said:

"All right, then. Welcome aboard Mary. But I have rules. You will take part in the work that needs doing. Cleaning, ironing and things like that, okay?"

"I can cook too..." she exclaimed enthusiastically.

"Naahhh. You English better keep your hands off it. We Belgians do it better. I'm a trained chef, by the way."

"Oh. A real chef in a camper van."

"I wouldn't call myself a chef, but I can cook and you don't look like a chef. So, now it's time to tidy up and then it's time to sleep. The folding bench will be your bed." Patosh said seriously.

"Yes, boss!" Mary shouted with a laugh and was visibly happy to have found a new home on her quest.

The aliens are coming

Our alien family, who were preparing for the onward journey to Terrarion and were looking forward to it, received a telepathic message from the high council on Venus.

"Jonathan, Martha, Fred! Greetings. We understand you are still on Exosauro?"

"Yes, we do. We're about to save the coordinates for the flight in the navigation system and then we'll be off."

"Why aren't you using the existing ones?" asked the High Council.

"We've looked everywhere in the on-board computer, but it seems to have been deleted. We'll re-enter it."

"Don't do that. I have a reason for notifying you. Your spaceship was used by a Venusian to escape from Venus. The fugitive was my daughter and I have an urgent request for you when you arrive on Terrarion. Look for her. Use your vacation there to track her down, for she cannot be allowed to linger on Terrarion. She is a member of the High Council here on Venus and must not adopt the habits of this "vacation planet". She must return and your task will be to find her and report her current location to us. We will do the rest.

I am sending you her details and the list of her currently known earthly appearance. Program the list into your Vybe scanner, because I think she will constantly change her appearance. Is the mission understood?"

"We understand, High Council."

"Good my loyal friends. Our blessing will accompany you. By the way, we deleted the file for Terrarion so that we could telepathically track the escape in the High Council. I am returning her escape route to you as she used it and would like you to follow it exactly. Enjoy your stay on Terrarion and don't let yourself be led astray."

The conversation ended and the new route was stored in the system.

"Well, who says so. The adventure begins with a mission." Jonathan shouted and Martha and Fred were beside themselves with excitement, although such emotional outbursts do not exist for Venusians. At least not in our earthly sense.

"Boarding stairs retracted and locked...cheked...magnetic field transformer on full power...checked.....fusion converter on half power checked...family on board...checked. Let's go then." Jonathan let the spaceship ascend vertically until the fusion converter displays authorized full power and when the necessary symbols appeared on the display, Jonathen set the fusion converter lever to full power and the "GALAXIA SUPREME" disappeared.

One wonders why they couldn't control the ship telepathically. They can, but not on rental spaceships. Telepathic control was only possible on ships belonging to the Confederation, because the High Council was the only one allowed to pilot these ships. How fortunate that the fugitive daughter did not use such a ship for her villainy, although on Venus such a term did not exist in the vocabulary.

"Terrarion is only 26 light years away (earthly measurement for simplicity's sake)" Jonathan said and slowed down a little.

"What's for dinner?" asked Fred, who was hungry and didn't care about the distance to Terrarion.

"I've got exo slime paste, rotvril salad and raborautesandwiches." Martha exclaimed delightedly.

"YYAACHHH. I'd rather have Mangaria salad and I already don't like it." Protested Fred.

"Say something my compatriot!" Martha asked Jonathan for help.

"So Fred, listen to your mother. You can't go on like this. You haven't been compatible at all lately, my friend, and that's not acceptable. Then take something from the vending machines..."

"But that stuff doesn't taste good..."

"I don't want to hear any more. You've become unbearable since your stay on Exosauro. What's wrong with you?"

"Maybe I should take a scan with the Vybe scanner. Not that you're making us sick," Martha said worriedly.

"Oh no. I just want to go back to eating what we ate on Venus. What I wouldn't give for a Matesa sausage. The Vybe Scan is superfluous, Mom."

But Martha would not be turned away and took the scan.

"Lo and behold. Our son has formed compatible conception. Who is it? Tamara? Because I've been watching you on Exosauro. I am convinced that Tamara thinks you are compatible."

"Don't!" Fred shouted in horror, although he no longer fully understood his inner frequencies. Was there something to it? Then why weren't the signals between him and Tamara understood?

"So what? Our baby is now becoming a man!" Jonathan exclaimed in amusement.

Fred was stunned and his clacking grew louder and louder until Martha touched him on the shoulder where the compensatory nerve was located and Fred calmed down again. Not wanting to talk about it further or attract attention, he took a Raborautesandwhich. Martha sat down next to her compatibles and a sort of telepathic snog ensued between her and Jonathan.

"Not now dearest. I need to concentrate and the little one might notice something."

"Oh where from. I put him to sleep." She said with a smile.

"You incorrigible one. You're not allowed to do that. The compensatory nerve is not meant for that..."

"Calm down, my husband, or should I grab you by the balancing nerve too?"

"What I wouldn't give for that, my shooting star." And since the autopilot was switched on (yes. This development is thousands of years old), Jonathan let his compatible wife telepathically glide over him in a concert of orgasms. She sat on top of him head-on, obscuring the navigation display, and a clacking sound began to make the transistors glow. Just a figure of speech, because of course there were no transistors on board.

"That was wonderful, my cosmic angel. There. But now I must continue navigating." Jonathan said.

"Do that."

A few exoskeletons and Raboraut sandwhiches later, because making galactic love makes you hungry, Martha came back on the Vybe scanner.

"No wonder we registered such irregularities during the first scan, remember? On our trip to Exosauro?" said Martha.

"Yes, I can still remember. Also the message: Access not permitted. What are you getting at, my darling?" Jonathan asked curiously.

"What if we run a hologram with the data we've been given to get a better picture of the fugitive?" Martha asked eagerly.

"I think that's an excellent idea and a lot more helpful than just tracing the route. Do you think you could make a hologram so that we can't see it telepathically, but transmit it to one of these screens? That would make me feel safer and less observed." Jonathan rightly remarked.

"I can do that, and I can do it in such a way that it can't be transmitted elsewhere and can't be accessed by third parties."

"Sounds almost a bit treacherous, but it's our mission alone and who knows what's behind this escape. After all, we don't want to be sabotaged by anyone in the process."

"Give me the Vybe scanner, my love."

Jonathan handed her the scanner and she began her work. The entire interior of the Galaxia Supreme was scanned and Martha telepathically channeled the data provided by the High Council. She had now stored a hologram program in the scanner.

"There. Hologram is ready. I'll insert the chip into the empty screen."

"Well done, Martha. Let it run." Jonathan asked, turning his chair to face the screen. Martha sat on his lap and they both watched the movie. The first scene was of a female alien figure who was in a hurry and was still looking around the spaceship somewhat awkwardly. She touched the inner wall and as if by magic, all the instruments lit up and the ship began to come to life. She used telepathy and as she was a member of the High Council, she could make this spaceship fly and steer it in this way.

"To Terrarion via the Saronto Belt. Full fusion conversion...Now!" said the fugitive.

Jonathan and Martha continued to watch and were dead silent, eager to see what came next.

"Entry in the High Council log. I, KLTXK, compatible daughter of KLTXG, have decided to fly to this planet, which we call Terrarion, to land there and explore it. The peculiar behaviors of the inhabitants who call themselves human have put this planet in danger of irretrievable self-destruction and since our High Council has not responded to my pleas to do something to stop this galactic genocide, I will be the one to do something about it. To sit, watch and do nothing until a confrontation would eventually arise that could cause further planetary interventions between confederates of other galaxies, Venus and eventually Terrarion, is upsetting the balance of the universe. We must re-inhabit this planet as we once did and found this species to lead them as they are about to destroy themselves.

This secrecy between the High Council and the military of Terrarion must stop and we must make ourselves visible to the rest of the population. Nobody buys the lie of our non-existence anymore, because our ships have been spotted too often, even by those we didn't have on our list. I know, dearest father, that we must not interfere, but should this planet called Earth be removed from the Galactic Atlas, the entire cycle of this solar system will be jeopardized. Please do not seek me out and let me do something meaningful for the universe. Think of me as a traveler. One of many who have returned. My love is assured to you my father.

Your daughter KLTXK

Martha and Jonathan looked at each other and clicked telepathically.

"I think now we know why she did it." Martha said less enthusiastically and almost disappointed, because she expected more.

"I don't know Martha. This escape doesn't strike me as a teenager running away from home to save the world. My intuition tells me there's something else behind it. The whole thing is too simple for me. If she hadn't made an entry in the logbook, I would agree with you, because if someone wants to save the world, he, or she, doesn't openly state his intention by making an entry in the logbook. The whole security squadron would be sent out to find her and who knows what she might do on such a solo run.

No, no, my shooting star, I smell a rotten fish (according to Nasa, there are no fish on Venus), because the High Council alone gave us the mission. Why would the High Council do this? It needs an inconspicuous observer and that's us. She is on a mission and I don't think it's an escape."

"You mean it's just supposed to look like a teenager's prank? You're a genius, my compatible."

"I know. There's just one catch. The High Council has asked us to track her down and give her location to bring her back home. That would interfere with a mission, don't you think?"

"But if the whole thing is to be as you say, perhaps this remark is also an excuse, or a deception, to make us believe that the High Council has nothing to do with this matter."

"True. We make a good team, my little moon-pie. But maybe I'm just imagining things and it's just like the entry says. I need to have my senses defragmented again. The journey is more exhausting than I thought."

Terrarion now appeared on the display and it was getting closer and closer. The Galaxia Supreme was programmed to make a landing in a lake at night, when all the earthlings were asleep. Lake Büttgenbach in East Belgium was chosen. Why? The answer was to be found in the hologram, because the refugee's spaceship was also located there. The only problem was that Jonathan and his family had never been here on Terrarion before and, as the saying goes: "All beginnings are difficult", even for overdevelopped ETs.

The lake was wide and deep enough and the ship, like an octopus, was able to adapt to the conditions. But landing in a lake was something new for Jonathan and perhaps he should have been briefed in the simulator by the rental company beforehand. Now it's too late to worry about it, because this strange planet, which shone so uniquely in all kinds of colors in front of them, captivated the alien family and their attention left something to be desired.

"I think we're going too fast, dearest." Martha called out a little worriedly, but Jonathan clacked out "I'll rock the child." Meanwhile, the Galaxia Supreme broke through the atmosphere, stratosphere, troposphere and all airspaces on Earth.

Their spaceship appeared on a radar screen, stationed at a military base.

"What's that, Captain?" a lieutenant from Swedish Air Control shouted nervously as he recognized an echo on his radar, but as quickly as the echo appeared, it disappeared again.

"Probably just a fake echo, lieutenant. Continue."

The same thing happened in Danish, German, Dutch and finally Belgian airspace.

However, the lieutenant in Sweden was able to create a so-called snapshot and what he read from it made his blood run cold. "38 km altitude and 35,000 kilometers per hour fast. That's not one of ours." The lieutenant thought to himself and decided against the captain's assertion to save and print this snapshot. So that his superior wouldn't notice, of course.

"I really think you're going too fast Jonathan." Martha shouted and Fred was also starting to worry. Jonathan finally reacted to the frequent resonance in his wife's voice, which also made his blood run cold, and reduced the speed. But it was a little too late, because although the approach steered the ship exactly to the entered coordinates, the spaceship crashed into the lake at excessive speed.

" Well good that we were strapped in, weren't we?" said Jonathan jokingly.

"What seatbelts, you joker. We have gravity dampers in case you didn't know." Martha remarked, a little bitchy and annoyed, which shouldn't have been the case, because as I said, there were no emotions on Venus. However, they were now on this planet called Earth and immediately after diving into Lake Büttgenbach, their DNA changed in relation to the location. They took on a human appearance and developed side effects that they could not explain.

"The Galaxia Supreme is a piece of junk. How are we ever going to get out of here Jonathan?"

"We have a different problem. Take everything we need to survive, including the Vybe scanner, and let's get out of here. We have a leak and the water will drown us if we don't get out of here fast." Jonathan ordered and they left the ship through an evacuation hatch, which fortunately was on the ceiling, leading outside of the ship. Another fact also proved that the Venusians were ahead of the humans on Earth. They could breathe underwater and inflate their lungs like life jackets. As soon as they reached the surface, they swam to the nearest shore. Every man for himself.

"We are naked. According to the guidebook, the people here walk around dressed in robes. It's a good thing your cousin lent us the clothes she bought on her vacation here. Also good that we have something in your size Fred."

"They're girls' clothes!" Fred protested

"What's the problem, son?" Jonathan asked in astonishment.

"Hello? I'm standing in front of you as a human boy. Don't you think it might be a bit of a problem to let me walk around in girls' clothes?"

"That's right. Martha, give me the gender changer."

Martha handed him the little device and in no time at all Fred was a girl.

"HEY!!!"

"Just until we get you the right clothes Fred, now don't be like that."

They got dressed behind some bushes and moved towards the road. Of course, the crash was noticeable because half the highway was flooded with water and hundreds of fish were gasping for breath."

"We mustn't kill anything Jonathan..."

"Yeah, all right!" and the fish were back in the lake. Telepathically transported back into the water.

"Quick, we have to get out of here."

"Why do we have to, Dad? We look like them now."

"Yes Fred, we do. Only I have to delve into my archive first and see how to proceed."

Every Venusian, as well as most aliens in the universe, has a soul archive with an automatic survival procedure for alien planets. We would call it survival instinct. After Jonathan had consulted his archive, he mastered the English language and looked for a hotel. However, the nearest hotel was 23 km away in a small town called, yes, you guessed it right, Lontzen.

"We need to hail a cab somewhere." Jonathan said and after a 2 km walk, a cab came towards them. Jonathan stretched out his right hand and stopped the vehicle, which appeared purely by chance, because the luck of finding one on a main road is pretty slim.

"Where are we going?" asked the cab driver.

"To the OX Hotel in Lontzen."

"Well, get in then. It's by taximeter, is that OK?"

"Yes, of course."

When they had driven about three kilometers, the driver was startled when he noticed the mass of water on the road.

"What in God's name has happened here?"

At the same moment, dozens of police and fire engines came towards them, stopping at the flooded area and cordoning it off. What luck that the cab had driven past them first, otherwise the alien family might have been caught in the mess.

"Didn't you forget to set the spaceship to invisible?" Martha asked, as if they had forgotten to turn off the stove before going somewhere.

"I did. Have the Vybe scanner produce some currency for Terrarion Martha. I think you have to pay with bills here.

It said so in the guidebook."

Martha just typed in foreign currency and the Vybe Scanner asked how much it should be. Martha simply pressed a symbol and five hundred euros in various denominations appeared on her lap. The Vybe scanner responded to location mode, no matter which planet you were on. On Exosauro the currency was fixed in crystals, on Corantio in precious stones and on other planets it could be precious metals. Depending on their wishes, the Vybe scanner could produce these currencies as soon as the location mode had registered where and on which planet they were. Three quarters of an hour later, they arrived exhausted in Lontzen. Jonathan paid the cab driver the requested amount to the penny and the driver drove off in a huff.

"It's a strange species, these people." Martha said.

There they stood in front of the entrance of a hotel, which was a better inn and a competitor to Patosh's Golden Mug, except that Patosh did not rent out rooms. Somewhat wavering the family entered the hotel, pretending to be English tourists. But why Lontzen, where nothing was going on, would have been difficult to explain, because no tourists strayed here, except the UFO freaks. But they were long gone again. The real reason was only for the family from Venus to know and because the fugitive UFO landed not far away.

"What can I do for you, sir?"

"I would like a room for three Venu...excuse me, people."

"How many nights?"

"Two nights, please."

"Pets?"

"What do you mean?"

"Whether you bring pets. Dog or Cat, that costs extra."

"No, no pets."

"That's 60 euros per night including breakfast and WIFI. Sign here. Room 314."

Jonathan took the pen and didn't know exactly what to do with it. Telepathically, he consulted his archive, which showed him what to do with it and with a flourish he drew what looked like a signature.

"I see. I almost forgot. I'd still need a passport or some kind of identification like a driver's license. From one person is enough." Said the receptionist with a grin and again the Vybe scanner had to be used secretly so that Jonathan could produce an English passport.

"You are English. Well then. Your accent doesn't exactly sound English." Said the man behind the counter.

"It's Welsh. Hardly understandable even to the English." Said Jonathan as if shot from a gun.

"I hear you. We have that problem here in Belgium too. Flemish, Valonian and even German are spoken not too far from here. Have a nice stay. Oh yes. Breakfast is from six to ten o'clock."

"Thank you." replied Jonathan without smile, because he somehow couldn't switch his lip to "Earth" and so they remained locked in Venusian.
In the room, which looked more suitable for long range truck drivers and where the wallpaper was coming loose at the corners, the alien family unpacked their things from the suitcases they had brought with them.

"Well, that went well once again. We have to acquire a real English accent. Welsh is apparently not the right one." Jonathan said.

"Which one do you want?" asked Martha.

"Let's run through the accent samples and maybe we'll find something suitable."

Several examples were called up on the Vybe scanner and in the end the one from Birmingham was chosen.

"I like that one. We still need a name. Which one did you give to the receptionist?"

"What does it say on the passport?" asked Fred, positively astonishing his father with this idea.

"Look at that. The education on Exosauro has payed off after all." Jonathan said proudly.

"Jonathan Basil Wilson says on it." the alien father replied with a laugh, as he was called by his middle name after an herb.

"Those Englishmen. Good thing I don't have parsley as a middle name."

"We're the Wilsons from now on." rejoiced Martha.

"It's all very exciting here despite this strange species. They're not exactly friendly, but they're kind of funny."

"I can only agree with you Martha."

"But how will we ever get home again? Our ship is destroyed and...."

"Please don't talk about it. Let's just just sleep on it for now. We'll think of something." Jonathan said, yawning, and fell asleep immediately.

Patosh and Mary

Patosh's trip has now turned into a completely different adventure to what he had previously planned or even imagined, as he now had a travelling partner at his side. Mary Mitchell, as the lady is supposedly called, and as she had left her handbag and purse somewhere, her travel documents were of course also missing.

"We'll go to Perpignan first, buy things there, because you need clothes and underwear. You're a strange Lady I must say. How can you be travelling around like a hippy?" Patosh shook his head incomprehensibly.

"I've got underwear in my rucksack and I can wash it at the next stop," Mary whispered a little shyly.

"Anyway, we have to do the shopping. Food, too. Then we'll head west to Carcassonne and take a two-day break there. I want to see the castle. I don't care what you do until then. Just remember the car park and we'll meet back there before we drive to the campsite and put up."

"I like castles. I can just walk around with you and look after Gonzi." Mary said and Patosh liked the idea.

Once in Perpignan, Patosh stuck to his plan and bought clothes, underwear, toothpaste, towel, shower gel etc. for Mary and the two of them even had fun doing it. She acted childishly silly and Patosh was always delighted by her freshness and youthfulness.

Then they bought fresh food in the local market hall, where there was a riot of screaming fish and vegetable vendors and Mary was thrilled by the whole show. She had never seen anything like it and Patosh couldn't hide a fatherly smile.

"Can you buy some of that salami and some of that cheese? Oh and baguettes. Lots of baguettes..."

"Yes, that's all right Mary. I'll do everything. But it all has to be eaten, because I don't like it when food goes mouldy or bad in the fridge. We also need meat, then we can have a barbecue at the next campsite."

"Oh yes, barbecue!" Mary shouted enthusiastically, dragging Gonzi into the supermarket even though dogs were not allowed. But Gonzi felt comfortable in the hustle and bustle and didn't mind in the slightest that thousands of feet were zigzagging in front of him as he skilfully dodged them.

"Hey there. No dogs allowed in here." Shouted a butcher from one of the stalls.

"If you stop grumbling, I'll buy meat from you too." Patosh shouted back.

"Well, if that's so, then I haven't seen the dog.

Patosh didn't like this butcher. He was fat and pink as a pig, but to avoid trouble he bought from him because he also had good meat on offer.

"Four Chops, four grill- sausages, two of the Florintener, 200 grams of salami and if you have a soup bone, that would be all."

The butcher weighed and packed the meat, took a soup bone from the vetrine below him and also a piece of sausage for Gonzi.

"That's 56 euros exactly and here's a small piece of sausage for your Waldi."

"Gonz is his name." Mary protested, but Patosh intervened, annoyed.

"He's actually called ....oh what the hell." Patosh paid and was annoyed at the steep prices, as meat was much cheaper in Belgium.

"What prices. How can people here afford anything at all? Let`s get the Cheese, potatoes, lettuce, tomatoes and that`s it."

"Cucumbers too, please," Mary asked.

"Yes, that too in the name of God."

"God? You need his permission first to buy the cucumber?"

Patosh looked at her in disbelief and burst out laughing, and the shoppers looked at him since his outburst surprised them.

"You're killing me Mary..... I haven't laughed like this for a long time. Come on, let's do the rest of the shopping and then get out of here. I'm getting a terrible backache from all the walking."

Once they'd bought all the shopping they needed, they walked to the car park where the camper van was parked and Patosh noticed two teenagers tampering with the door lock. With a loud shout, he left the shopping bags on the ground and ran towards the two burglars. Of course, Mr Gonzales also ran after them, growling and barking, who also knew what was going on. The burglars were not intimidated, at least not immediately, and even dared to attack Patosh, but two punches were enough to put the first on the ground and the second preferred to run off with Mr Gonzales still hanging on to his trouser leg.

"Please let me go. No police or my father will beat me to death." Shouted the one on the ground.

"Let him, you lout. Instead of looking for a job, you'd rather steal the things of hard-working people. You should be locked up, my boy."

"Pat. If you call the police, I might get in trouble too. I don't have any documents." Mary said.

"What? Oh, yes. That'll only get you into trouble." Patosh let the boy go and shouted a few more curses behind him.

In the mean time, Mr Gonzales came back with his tongue hanging out and a hero's look on his face.

"We sure showed them, didn't we boss?" he wanted to shout, he could only speak like a human, but the first was Mary, who stroked him and said. :

"Yes, little one. You are indeed a hero and you showed them."

Gonzi, as he was affectionately called by Mary, just looked at her perplexedly, but really enjoyed being stroked.

"Come on. Get in, you two. We still have a few kilometres to drive."

Once everything was stowed away in the fridge and cupboards, they set off again and left Perpignan. Patosh favoured the country road and they drove past the Cathar ruins of Peryperthuse and Queribus, where he didn't want to stop and when Mary asked him why, Patosh became melancholy and told the story of the Cathars, but was interrupted by Mary who already knew their story.

"The Albigensian Crusade of 1209-1229 ordered by Pope Innocent the Third. Thousands were burned at the stake by him. I can just imagine what happened there. How terrible." And Mary clapped her hands to her face and tears ran down her eyes. "What beasts you humans are!" She suddenly shouted and immediately recognised her Fopas.

"Hey, hey, hey. Slow down, my lady. You know your way around very well, my dear, and what do you mean by beasts? You`re a human too. Calm down Mary, what's going on in your head I wonder?" Patosh called out to her and tried to get her relaxed.

"Forgive me Pat."

"There's nothing to forgive. It was a terrible time and I'm glad I'm alive in this decade, but tell me. How is it that you know so much about history?"

Mary tried to find an answer and replied.

"Oxford."

"Oxford what?"

"I studied history and politics at Oxford."

"What for?"

"Oh Pat, you do ask questions sometimes. I wanted to be a journalist...."

"Journalist? Yes, I can really see yourself doing that job."

"Yes? Thank you," Mary said with a smile.

"With that chatterbox, it's the right job for you."

"Oh gosh!" Mary hit her little fist on Patosh's upper arm and laughed.

They left the castles with their sad history behind and saw before them this rugged, natural and glorious landscape stretching out so near and far at the foot of the Pyrenees and if Mary had her way, the journey could have gone on for days without stopping. With a bag of potato crisps in one hand and a salami baguette in the other, she savoured what she saw before her. Sipping loudly, she sucked on the straw stuck in the can of cola so loudly that even Patosh turned to look at her. Her big, brown eyes radiated only childlike love and joy and his heart warmed. He had always wanted to have children, but Camille had turned her back on life after the death of her baby, and every time Patosh offered her the chance to try again, she refused. How he would have loved to have someone like Mary as a daughter, but life had other plans for him. Mary was no longer the youngest at 37, but her appearance could fool anyone into thinking she was 22 or 23 years old. Her nature was also very playful and youthful, Patosh blew this thought away and called out.

"We're here."

"What? But we've only been driving for a few hours."

"Look ahead Mary. This is Carcassonne," and Patosh pointed to the castle with his finger. A city walled by the Middle Ages, only to be surrounded by the concrete blocks of the twenty-first century. Now she saw it too and the straw fell out of her open mouth.

"We'll find a car park and walk through it," Patosh said. In the meantime, Mary tidied up everything in the motorhome and left behind a clean camping hall on wheels. With screeching brakes, the HYMER box on a FIAT chassis came to a halt and all three of them left the camper.

"Have you got Gonzi on the leash, Mary?"

"Yes."

Patosh locked the door and they walked towards the entrance to this medieval town. The streets were paved with cobblestones that had been laid who knows when.

Tourists everywhere you looked and languages you never heard. Other dogs were also on a leash and so they barked at each other. Mr Gonzales was the loudest, of course, as the saying goes: "the smaller the dog, the more hysterical its nature." But Patosh had noticed this characteristic in people rather than the four-legged friends. Cars tried to adapt to the narrow streets and drive through, but the tourists slowed them down. They must have their shops here, or they were just vendors delivering more souvenirs and kitsch. Americans, Japanese, Chinese, all led by a guide holding an umbrella upside down with a sort of a licence plate stuck to it so the group wouldn't get lost. Patosh had his Pentax around his neck and took his time taking pictures and Mary browsed through the dozens of shops with their tempting wares.

Spices here, incense there, rose crosses, Cathar crosses, knight's armour, Templar flags, books, goat's cheese, various oils and much, much more, but she was spoilt for choice and couldn't decide what to buy. She finally decided on a bottle of yasmine perfume, which smelled rather strong. After hours of walking around, taking photos and shopping, they found a cafe where they could sit outside and enjoy a refreshment. Mary had a cup of tea and Patosh a quarter of an ice-cold Chably. It was a relief and the sun was shining, which added to the atmosphere and Gonzi was exhausted and sought shade under the table.

The next campsite was only three kilometres away and as Patosh's legs and back were aching, he paid the bill and they headed back to the motorhome. This time there were no teenagers trying to break in. All aboard and off they went. They found the campsite and were lucky as there were only three pitches available. Mary helped Patosh connect the water hose, the toilet drain pipe and the power supply through an electric cable. Gonzi sniffed around and picked up the scent of various female dogs but look and behold, one scent seemed very familiar. The poodle was here. Without anyone noticing, Gonzi set off in search of his old friend, who he found and soon the shouting started in the square.

"Funny, I recognise that voice!" Patosh exclaimed, not wanting to guess what he had in mind.

"Where's Mr Gonzales!" he shouted and looked reproachfully at Mary. She looked back and just shrugged her shoulders.

"Let's follow the shout. I know the lady." And when they arrived at the scene of tragedy, Mr Gonzales was still working on the poodle lady.

"YOOOUUUUU!!!!"

"I can say the same for you, madam. Are you stalking me?" Patosh shouted at her and a verbal argument began, causing several people to surround the scene laughing.

"Take your Jigolo of dog from my Jenevieve, you ogre."

"What do you want for the poodle? I'll buy it. No dog should suffer the agony of your servitude. And don't call Gonzi a Jigolo you spinach quail you!"

Patosh's head turned red and his veins thickened on his forehead as the poodle owner continued to shout at him in an extremely high soprano, yes, it was like a dramatic opera and Mary just watched in fascination. Nobody noticed how Gonzi and Jenevieve had finished their passion and were also watching the whole spectacle in amazement. If anyone didn't know better, Gonzi, AKA Mr Gonzales, seemed to think: "Humans, what a species!"

Patosh grabbed Mr Gonzales and scolded him. Something Patosh had never done before until Mary intervened and silenced him. He then angrily threw his dog to the ground and ran off, while Mary took the dog, still trembling with fear, by the leash and tried to keep up with the running grump.

"Pat, slow down. What are you doing?" Mary called after him, but their distance grew and Patosh disappeared from her field of vision. When she arrived at the caravan, she also noticed his absence, but exhaustedas she was, she refused to look for him and decided to stay in the camper, drink tea and wait.

Hours passed but there was no sign or sound of Patosh and as night fell, Mary lay down on the folding couch and fell asleep. She was woken early in the morning when Gonzi started growling and someone outside seemed to be struggling with his balance as they could hear the camping table and other objects falling over. It was Patosh, but he didn't come in as he tried to sit down in one of the chairs. He was stinking drunk and when he finally managed to sit down, his head tipped back and the snoring started. What luck that it was still warm outside. Gonzi wanted to go out to him, but Mary prevented it.

"We'll let him sleep it off first, Gonzi." But Gonzi only made a pitiful noise felt with guilt.

Hours passed before Patosh decided to enter the caravan. Staggering and scmolling, he climbed the small steps and leant on the door frame.

"I want to apologise. I was just angry because, to be honest, I'll never understand women and I'm developing an inexplicable aversion to this gender, which I don't want. However, I have never had any luck with women in my life and am constantly treated by them as if I have leprosy. They seem disrespectful, presumptuous and arrogant to me and I get lonelier by the day. All I want is some love, tenderness and affection. Am I asking for too much? We were so much in love at the beginning, Camille and I, and when our baby son died, I've been going through hell ever since.

I should have divorced immediately, but this fucking pity that is eating me up from the inside and holding me back from new happiness is driving me crazy. I just want a second chance, but I'm not getting it. I'm just being cheated on, used and ripped off. I'm so fed up with these snobbish monsters and yet I won't give up hope. I'm sorry Mary. You were a breath of fresh air for my soul and sometimes I thought you were sent to me from heaven to give me hope again. But that's not the case. Instead of supporting me, you shouted at me. I want you to go. Take the dog with you and leave me alone. I'm not in the mood for fake friends, pets and other disappointments who just laugh at me. I want to be alone. Take your things and get out. I'm sure you'll find another ride. Maybe the poodle witch will give you a lift and Mr Gonzales can fornicate the coiffed bitch until the curlers explode, what's it to me. I don't need anyone so go....GET OUT!"

Without saying another word, Mary packed up her things and left the caravan. She didn't take the dog with her because she knew it would destroy him.

"Take care of your master, Gonzi. He needs you now more than ever." She whispered to the dog, stroked its head one last time and left. Patosch didn't even look back at her, but dragged himself, drunk as he was, to his bed and simply dropped onto it. He didn't want to know anything more and tears ran down his cheeks as he finally fell asleep.

Aliens know no stress

In Lontzen, our alien family went for breakfast in the meantime. They were not familiar with Earth food and the inner soul archive could not provide any satisfactory answers as far as the flavours of the food on this planet were concerned.

"What do scrambled or fried eggs taste like? Or fried bacon? People seem to love these foods especially for breakfast. I think we're about to find out." said Jonathan as they made their way into the lobby and the receptionist simply pointed the way to the dining room.

"What an unfriendly creature." Martha complained, but she immediately apologised, wondering why she was suddenly upset by such a triviality. Yes, yes, our dear earth. It's just as if the air we breathe in consists not only of nitrogen, hydrogen and oxygen, but also of other nasties that can significantly manipulate the mood of the inhabitants on it. Even that of the aliens. The family took a seat at a table and were surprised by a friendly waitress.

"Good morning madam, good morning monsieur and good morning to you young man."

"Oh, there are still friendly beings on this planet." said Jonathan and this time he was even able to grin sarcastically without tensing up.

"Why, we're all friendly here." the girl replied in surprise.

"But not that one." Fred pointed in the direction of the reception and the waitress laughed heartily.

"Oh him! That's Rene. He's always like that, but believe me, he's otherwise as harmless as a lamb. He just doesn't like to talk."

"Good to know." Martha simply said, "Let's get down to business. What do you recommend for breakfast?"

"Well, that depends, Madame. We usually recommend the American breakfast. Scrambled eggs, bacon, hash browns and Mexican beans. But as you are English, judging by your accent, I recommend the English Breakfast. Two fried eggs. Bacon, two sausages, baked beans, black pudding, grilled tomatoes and toast. Then there is the "Continental Breakfast". Two rolls, two croissants, butter and strawberry jam and, for the less hungry, corn flakes with milk. I can also bring yoghurt and fruit on request."

"Please bring us one of each and we'll have a look round." Said Jonathan with a very suspicious smile that even the girl seemed a little voulgardly.

"Of course. Would you like coffee or tea and orange juice with that?"

"Yes. Just bring us everything."

Jonathan still had to work on his facial features, because the grimaces he made were out of this world and gave apparently wrong signals. Meanwhile, the girl brought breakfast and the mess began, for this was the first time this cutlery, which consisted of a fork, knife and a tea spoon, had been used. A few experiments later, however, they had found out how to turn it and lo and behold, it tasted excellent.

"Delicious. I didn't think it would taste so good. And these funny colours. Yellow and white and red. When I think of our food, everything is just grey," said Martha enthusiastically.

"Indeed, dear. It tastes delicious. What do you think Fred?"

But Fred was deeply immersed in his fried eggs and sucked in a strip of bacon. The table turned into an abstract Kokoshka painting, that's how messy it looked and the other guests stared at them in horror and disgust. Jonathan, however, used his repertoire of smiles, which caused even more excitement. The alien family didn't mind, because here on this table they were doing research and slurping and smacking was part of it.

"These baked beans remind me a little of opraso slime. Don't you think Jonathan?"

"Hmm. I was thinking more of kambariut puree."

They experimented with their breakfast until the waitress arrived and had to kindly point out to them that it was already a quarter past ten and that they had to leave the dining room. It would be open again for lunch at twelve o'clock.

"Ah lunch..." but before Jonathan could say anything else, he received a telephatic call from the High Council and while they cleared the table and walked into the lobby, the conversation continued.

"Yes, I have understood. I'll hire a car and continue the search. By the way, our spaceship is badly damaged and I don't think we can return with it."

"We'll talk about it when you've found my daughter. You can use her spaceship to return."

"I'll call you as soon as I know something." and the conversation was over. Jonathan arranged for a taxi to take the family to the car hire company, the only one in town. They hired a Volkswagen Passat and Jonathan got the hang of it straight away. Driving licence and credit card were produced and presented by the Vybe scanner and when Jonathan signed the rental agreement, everything took its course. Back at the hotel, they packed their things with the calmness of a lobster as the aliens know no stress.

"We'll just follow the route as programmed in the hologram," suggested Martha and Jonathan agreed.

"What else is there to do?"

"But before we go, let's go to the pub there. It looks fun. And what a delightful name. The Golden Jug."

"What do you want there, Jonathan?" Martha asked.

"According to the guidebook, there's a drink called beer. Well? How about it? After all, we're on holiday."

Martha couldn't refuse Jonathan's wish because she couldn't have stopped him. That was against the rule of free will and you can't violate that. So she nodded in the affirmative.

They found the pub open, even though Patosh had closed it for his company holidays. Camille, however, reopened it purely out of anger and revenge for Patosh just leaving her without a word. Her female ego was bruised and woe betide the man who made that ego glow, because whether Camille loved him or not, she was a selfish and self-indulgent creature. She had clawed away the income in her pocket without a receipt. The Golden Jug was not as full as usual, however, because Patosh brought excitement and humour to the shop, Camille did not. Her rough and inhospitable manner tended to scare the customers away.

"Good afternoon, a table for three please." Shouted Jonathan as he came in and the family was greeted with quiet laughter.

"Sit somewhere where it's free!" Camille yelled from behind the counter.

The alien family was gaped at, not because they were aliens, because you couldn't tell, but because of the strong English accent, or rather the Birmingham accent and their clothes. If you hadn't known better, this family was still in their sixties. Camille approached their table with a smouldering cigarette in the corner of her mouth and the long ash fell on its way to the floor. Martha looked at her motionlessly and just wanted to leave.

"What can I bring you?" she asked more or less friendly.

"Three beers please." said Jonathan.

"How old is the kid? I'm not allowed to serve beer to children, or is he eighteen?"

"What would you have for a child to drink?"

"Coke, Fanta, Sprite, mineral water."

"Let's start with Coke and then we'll see."

"Which beer would you like? Stella Artoise, Orval, Jubile, Heineken?"

"Let's start with Stella Artoise." Said Jonathan with a grin that still needed practising.

"Wow. Looks like you've got plans if you want to start with Stella. Fine by me."

"I don't like the atmosphere here Jonathan. Let's leave after the beer."

"Patience, dearest. Let's just behave like them and cosy up. If they're unfriendly, so are we. It's as simple as that."

"Well, it's finally getting exciting." Fred said. "I'm still bored to death."

"Don't worry, my boy. You'll have your fun. Let's telephatically record the conversations of these guests and hear what they say."

"But that's against the free will law." Martha protested.

"Nonsense. We have a mission and so it's not an offence."

"Oh yes. That'll be fun!" Fred exclaimed, wringing his hands.

"But no matter what you hear or what they say, you have to back off, OK?" warned Jonathan.

"OK." Martha and Fred replied with amusement, looking forward to the game that was about to ensue.

The guests were seated at different tables and Gerome, who was sitting next to Clautilde and Jean, was talking the loudest. All three were farmers from the neighbourhood and met almost every day after work at the Golden Chalice. At the other tables were Guilomme, Robere, his wife Matilde, Jaques and Katrine. Most of them were pensioners and had nothing more to do than hang around and gossip, even though gossips can be dangerous if it reaches the wrong ears.

"What are they, and their clothes? Englishmen, that's what they are." Said Gerome.

"A strange bunch of tourists. Seem to have money. That's what Jean said."

"Look at that woman. Elegant and stiff as a pompadour," whispered Clautilde. When Martha heard this, she began to shake, but Jonathan held her hand and calmed her down again. Nothing was said about Fred, because you don't gossip about children. He can't help having parents like that, who dress him up like a conservative schoolboy.

"I wonder where Patosh is. His old lady is no fun here and neither are the prices. Charging three euros for a beer now is outrageous. Two was always OK, but three....no, no monsieur. That's just going too far," said Guilomme.

"Indeed it is. Patosh has always been a good man. Taking more from the tourists is fine, but the regulars, no. Patosh has always been decent to us. It was those fucking UFOs that got us into this mess. The thousands of UFO freaks and the press got us into a lot of trouble. Camille, that old lizard, naturally got the revenue back then and now she treats us like tourists. We who were born here and will probably be buried here too." Jaques said.

Jonathan wondered what they meant by Patosh, UFOs and UFO freaks and checked his soul archive and when he got the answer, he pricked up his ears. Well, Patosh is an abbreviation for Patrick, that was now clear, but UFO automatically meant that this city was visited by aliens and this was indeed exciting. They continued to listen and took notes telephatically.

"Just two days ago another UFO was sighted, some say it crashed into Lake Butgenbach. The main road was flooded," said Robere.

"He must be talking about us right now." Jonathan thought to himself, looking at Martha and she just nodded in agreement.

"So, have the police gone looking for this spaceship?" asked Katrine.

"No. Of course not. It's all just fantasy. The police aren't doing anything on orders from the top and our tax money is being wasted elsewhere. No divers or other units combing the lake. We're taken for fools. For drunken pensioners who have seen white mice. It's a big dog, that sort of thing."

The guests sitting at the other table just shook their heads, while the farmers at their table continued to whisper to themselves.

"I still have a piece of metal from the spaceship that was chased by the hunters. It fell in my field not three metres from my tractor," whispered Gerome.

"Did you give it to the police?" asked Clautilde.

"Rubbish. How much money do you think this thing will earn me? I won't give a damn to the police. It fell on my field and not at the police station." This was followed by loud laughter and Gerome ordered another round.

"Three Orval Camille."

"Coming right up."

"How much do you think this piece of tin is worth? Maybe it's radioactively contaminated?" Jaques said rightly.

"Everything still works on my side, doesn't it Clautilde? I haven't noticed any damage. I have no idea how much the part is worth. It's a pity our fighters didn't shoot down the whole UFO. He got away with it."

"How do you mean shot down? Did the lunatics actually shoot at the spaceship? My God. What would have been the consequences if they had hit it. We would have had a war with aliens."

"Of course they shot at it Jaques. I saw it with my own eyes. How else did this thing fall? I saw the bullets ricochet and if I were to comb the field with the metal detector, I would also find the projectiles."

"Oh Gerome. You're bullshitting us as usual. What if an F16 lost a piece of metal and not the spaceship? Let's have a look at the part and I can tell you with reliable certainty what kind of part it will be." Shouted Guilomme from the other table, who had overheard the conversation.

"Stick your nose in your beer glass Guilomme. I'm not showing this metal plate to anyone. Only the person who buys it from me gets to see it." Gerome replied back, slightly annoyed.

"You're just a gobshite, Gerome."

"Oh yeah? How about if I smash your face in, then you wouldn't throw such reckless insults at others anymore."

"HEY you two. Stop it or I'll throw you out." Threatened Camille.

Jonathan found it all very interesting because part of the hologram was missing. Could the attack by the fighters have been lost for some reason just before the fugitives landed, or was it a completely different spaceship? To find out, Jonathan had to get hold of this metal disc. But how? He was not allowed to steal it, as such a trait was not found in the DNA of the Venusians, so he had to buy it from Gerome."

"Sir. Forgive me for interfering, but I would buy the metal plate. Give me a price.

The room went dead silent and Jonathan was gawped at from top to bottom, but Jonathan stood upright and this time with a successful smile.

"Well, what is it? How about five thousand euros? I'm such a UFO freak, as you call it, and that's why we travelled here. We are UFO tourists."

Gerome got up from his table and walked over to the alien family.

"Can I sit with you?" Gerome asked, a little intimidated.

"Yes, but of course. Have a seat. What would you like to drink?" Jonathan gentlemanly insisted and signalled to Camille for another round of drinks. Camille just looked at him with a dismissive look and thought to herself: "What a show-off."

"You really want to buy that metal plate?" Gerome asked uncertainly.

"Yes, I would like to. Provided it belongs to the spaceship you described earlier. When was that exactly? I mean the incident."

"Did I talk about it so loudly that you heard everything? Clautilde, my wife, is right. I'm not being discreet right now. It happened a few months ago. Maybe four or five...."

"They were seven." Shouted Guilomme from the other table.

"I said don't get involved." Shouted Gerome back.

"When could we examine this disc? I would bring cash. Does 5000 euros meet your expectations?"

"Oh yes. Of course. May I know your name?" asked Gerome.

"Of course. I'm Jonathan Basil Wilson and this is my wife Martha and Frederik Wilson."

"Pleased to meet you. How about right away? I have time?" urged Gerome, who could already see the 5000 euros in his hands. He hadn't expected that much and would have been happy with 500 euros, which was already a lot of money for him.

"We'll be ready after this round, but let's enjoy the beer," said Jonathan calmly.

Gerome drained his beer and wiped his mouth with the sleeve of his old jacket. Fred already had three Cola, two Fanta and two Sprites and was burping around like an ill-bred boy, but he thought it was fun and laughed to himself. There was no farting or burping on Venus, because the food there was boring, pathological and too healthy compared to earthly food. On Earth, pretty much everything tasted good. Martha was already tipsy and couldn't stop herself from giggling.

Jonathan paid the bill and gave a good tip, because the visit had been worthwhile and not just for Gerome. He followed Gerome's old Renault Clio for about 3 kilometres until they had to drive through a courtyard entrance. An old, almost dilapidated house was visible in front of them and several barns filled with mooing cows, squealing pigs and cackling chickens running around freely amazed them and especially Fred couldn't close his jaw. He just found it too fascinating.

"Can I have a look at all this?" he asked the farmer.

"Yes, of course. Choose a chicken. A gift from the house." But Gerome paused and chose the chicken for Fred himself, not wanting the lad to get himself another good laying hen.

"Here she is. She's yours."

"WHAT??? REALLY?" Fred exclaimed enthusiastically.

"It's included in the price." Gerome grinned because the hen, called Gerogette, hadn't laid any eggs for a long time.

"Her name is Georgette."

Fred took her carefully and stroked the mite-filled fowl lovingly.

"But that wouldn't have been necessary!" Martha said delightedly with a hiccup, as the beers fermented in her stomach and made gurgling and growling noises.

"So, show me the metal plate, good man, because I'm sure you want to get back to the pub and your wife Clautilde." said Jonathan a little impatiently, which is unusual for a Venusian.

But Earth, as I said, has its own ways of dealing with its inhabitants and for the remaining "holiday time" the alien family was one of them. Gerome walked to a barn and asked the others to follow him. He pulled on a dusty green tarpaulin covering an old crate and opened the two locks, which opened the lid of the crate with a metallic "plop". The disc was wrapped in a sackcloth and Jonathan, as well as the other two, could feel an incredible energy radiating from the disc. The humans could not feel this energy because they have not reached a certain universal maturity.

A sign of how underdeveloped they are compared to the aliens scattered around the universe. They would have been at the same stage of development if they had followed the teachings of their cosmic visitors thousands of years ago, but instead the teachings were ignored and they opted for the material, which only brought short-lived qualities of life. However, if they had followed the more or less well-intentioned teachings, they would have moved on to another layer that would have improved their BEING a thousandfold. They decided in favour of door C, where the main prize was a dishwasher and a years supply of soap, if you want to describe this human crror of judgement in a sarcastic way. Gerome carefully handed the metal plate to Jonathan, who read the inscription on the plate quietly with piercing eyes. It was a different ship and not that of the fugitives. Nor was it a Venusian spaceship, but one belonging to a different species. A species known to the Confederation, but which did not belong to it, and which stood out in an unpleasant way in the universe for its self-serving missions. She belonged to the Orion-Clan, a gang under observation by the Confederation. Not too big, but comparable to the so-called Hell's Angels gang on Earth, in a cosmic way. Jonathan took the metal plate, paid the promised amount, took Martha, Fred and now Georgette the chicken into the car and drove off without looking back.

"Where are we going, my compatriot?"

"To Lyon."

Patosh and the Pyrenees

Patosh could see the last of Carcassonne in the rear-view mirror of his camper van getting smaller and smaller until this colossal castle of a town disappeared completely. His head ached and all he could think about was Mary. His heart was pounding like it had in his teenage years, when he was fifteen and young Francine had turned his head at school. He was really in love with Francine back then and it was because of her that he stayed behind in his last year at school. He could still feel his father's beatings during these thoughts. Francine, however, had eyes for someone completely different. A big bully who was bullying and blackmailing the younger pupils. Today he is a policeman in Lontzen and married to Francine. Both are getting on in years, fat and living on the breadline, not to mention regulars at the Golden Jug. He, Patosh, had only really been in love once and then Camille came along. It wasn't the same, but there was still a loving energy between him and his wife and perhaps they had been in love at first. Patosh didn't have many women in his life. A couple of 'runaways', as he called them, including a few hookers from the neighbourhood, but this was between the times of Francine and Camille. From that point of view, his life was not full as far as love and it's experience was concerned.

Then Mary came into his life and he went through an illusion that ate him up inside. His shyness had always been a drag, but that was how he was brought up. Bourgeois, Catholic and fearful. I wonder where she is? He thought to himself and opened a Coke while driving with an uncertain destination and Mr Gonzales lying in the passenger seat, who forgave his master everything. Dogs are what they are. Living creatures full of love and mercy towards their masters.

"Where are we going, Gonzi?" he asked the mongrel, who looked up at him briefly but put his head down again, as he had no idea what Patosh wanted from him at that moment. Was Mr Gonzales perhaps thinking of the poodle lady Jenevieve and going through the same hell as Patosh? Who knew for sure. Patosh left the motorway and decided to take the country road over the Pyrenees because, after all, he also wanted to enjoy the scenery and the magical mountains, which would have a lot to say if they could talk. But the mountains were always talking and only the worthy could hear what was being said. Small villages, old monasteries and serpentines swept past the caravan and it started to rain. It even thundered and lightning struck in the distance. The horizon turned dark, as did the daylight, despite the early morning.

"This doesn't look good my friend and now it's hailing." Patosh whispered, not knowing if what he said was meant for him or Gonzi. The pattering grew stronger and more menacing and Patosh looked for a place to park where he would be safe from this hailstorm and he thanked the heavens because a covered subway, which might once have been a bridge, gave them shelter. It was high time, as Patosh realised with horrified eyes how large the hailstones had become, and they were no longer grains. They were eggs of solid, hard ice. Suddenly, lightning struck less than a hundred metres away and Gonzi began to howl fearfully.

"It's all right dog. We're safe." Patosh comforted him lovingly.

After half an hour, the spitting stopped and Patosh drove on, but the roads, which were covered with rubble caused by the mud lavas, made them difficult to drive on and farmers from the neighbourhood helped the police to push the masses of earth and stones to one side. They continued at a crawling pace and Patosh cursed. He should have taken the motorway to Biaritz and then continued south. Now he was in a mess. It was also suddenly cold, as he was 3000 metres above sea level, but there was no turning back and finally he found himself on a country road that was reasonably clean and passable. The sun was shining again and when he opened his window, he could even hear the birds chirping.

A paradise opened up before him and revealed itself. He stopped just few miles before the Spanish border and breathed in this incredibly fresh and uncontaminated mountain air and felt the energy that this mountain radiated at him and made him smile.

"If there is a God, then he lives here." He heard himself say inside and Gonzi completely agreed with him as he sniffed through everything in front of him and marked it with his urine. Patosh spotted a ruined monastery less than a hundred metres away. He got into the campervan, took two sandwiches from the fridge, a can of beer and then took them to the ruins of the monastery, where he found a stone block and sat down on it. The view made him hungry and made him forget everything that had been weighing him down an hour ago. His mind was empty and his worries erased. A lizard perched on one of the crumbled pillars, bobbing its head up and down and spider webs hung from plants and ferns wet with morning dew caught his eyes. There was even an inscription on the stone next to him that could have been a thousand years old. It was difficult to read, but Patosh could make out the word Albrechtinus and next to it was a cross scratched into it that looked like a Templar cross. No doubt this monastery had a lot to tell, but Patosh didn't feel worthy to be able to decipher the message. The beer was finished, the bread eaten. Time to move on. Next destination, Bilbao. Fifty kilometres further on, the landscape changed drastically as they reached Spain at midday.

However, Patosh did not stop in Bilbao or Santander. He wanted to reach La Coruna while he was still fit to drive, so that he could spend two days exploring this city with all the fish restaurants and botegas that he only saw and heard about on television and that made him dream, as he loved fish dishes more than anything. The car radio was on full blast and Patosh sang along to some of the songs and Gonzi was also in a great mood, letting his tongue flutter in the wind as he stuck his head out of the open windows.

They arrived in La Coruna in the evening and set up camp in a nearby campsite, where hundreds of tourists were spread out. Patosh ordered a taxi, wisely realising that he wouldn't be able to find a parking space at the harbour with the monstrous vehicle, he also wanted to drink wine with the fish and driving with a drunken head wouldn't have been a good idea. Gonzi, however, was tired and just wanted to sleep and Patosh, almost relieved, agreed. And so our friend made his way to the harbour in the evening hours and decided on a small but cosy restaurant. From gambas al ajillo to octopus salad and oysters, washed down with a quarter of local white wine, he tucked into these appetisers. Grilled prupunias and sea bream followed and his heart began to sing when a paella bowl was brought, which he washed down with another bottle of wine. For him, this was a holiday and far away was his pub with all the negative side effects that he experienced on a daily basis.

A prawn almost got stuck in his throat when he suddenly saw Mary, who was walking around side by side with this horrible woman and who made his life hell on every campsite. She didn't have the poodle with her either and now, for the first time, he was glad he hadn't taken Gonzi with him. The evening would have been ruined. He would have recognised Mary and started barking immediately. What a traitor, he thought to himself. Women can't be trusted and he felt that stab in his heart after all he had done for her. Yes, it didn't seem like much at first, but she had issues and he took her in and let her be a part of his life and now this. Patosh lifted the menu higher and looked at the two of them. "I hope they keep walking and don't get the idea to choose this place." He thought to himself and he was lucky. They kept walking and the evening that was shaping up so nicely turned into a nightmare. He only hoped that they were staying at a different campsite, as he couldn't imagine them staying just yards from him. It all suddenly seemed very suspicious to him, because he didn't believe in coincidences. What was going on there? His imagination never played tricks on him and his intuition had always saved him from problems that arose. It was the third time they had met and he wondered if this poodle owner had been following him since Lyon. He ordered the bill, paid and decided to follow them. The crowds overwhelmed him, but he kept up well with the two women in pursuit, only stopping when one of the ladies suddenly stopped herself and turned round.

They walked on, comparing the menus of several restaurants and stopping at some stalls to look at souvenirs. So far he could see nothing suspicious was to be noted and it looked as if Mary had only joined this woman to be taken along on her journey as a hitchhiker. But for some, the eye only sees what it wants to see. Patosh calmed down a little and was inwardly relieved that nothing else seemed to be going on between the two of them. He learnt just how wrong he was when Mary and her companion entered a Tappas bar and took a seat by one of the windows. His mind was on the verge of going blank when he saw the poodle owner suddenly lean forward and kiss Mary passionately and he, Patosh, couldn't get out of his amazement. "No!" he shouted, because he didn't want to believe it and luckily the two women couldn't hear it. Then it started to rain. A summer downpour that suddenly came out of nowhere and made the hot cobblestones steam with its coolness. People started running to find a dry place, but not Patosh. He stood there and continued to look through the window. The water ran down his body as if he was standing under a shower. His clothes were sticking to his skin and he hoped that lightning would strike him. He wanted to puke out the meal he had enjoyed half an hour ago and had paid dearly for, but he pulled himself together and decided in favour of reason, for where did he get the right to judge Mary? She was a stranger and possessed the freedom of free will and was allowed to choose her own friends, because after all he, Patosh, had chased her away.

Where did this sudden urge to possess her come from? Yes, he wanted to possess her, but that would be wrong. What actually goes on in a man's head when he falls in love? Probably not the same as with a woman, or maybe it is? He turned round and walked back to the taxi stand to be taken back to the campsite. Hopefully Mr Gonzales had at least been able to sleep peacefully in his absence.

"Al camping del Valle de San Sebastian por favor."

"Si senor."

It stopped raining and the streets filled up again with people crawling out of their hiding places like crabs. The first thing he would do is take an aspirin and then get a good night's sleep, but he changed this plan immediately because Mr Gonzales had to be taken for a little walk on a lead, after all, he had left him alone for hours. The taxi stopped in front of the driveway and Patosh paid the requested amount.

"Wow, 35 euros for a six-kilometre journey. Pretty steep prices, amigo."

But "Amigo" didn't understand French and just said: "Muchas gracias. Asta luego." and off he went. It was about a two hundred metre walk to the motorhome and the night revealed a starry sky that would not normally appear. The Milky Way was bright and clear and the Orion constellation was clearly visible, as were the Little and Big Dipper. The fresh air he breathed in would perhaps replace the aspirin, as he felt better and his head no longer throbbed as it had at the harbour. As he approached his mobile home, he could already hear Mr Gonzales barking, who was waiting passionately for Patosh and had probably already noticed him at the entrance gate. Jumping and cheering, he greeted his master and Patosh was just as happy to see his faithful friend again.

"So my friend. I'll just get the leash, but don't worry, you can roam free," and the mongrel didn't need to be told twice. Patosh locked the door and followed his dog, who poked his nose everywhere to find out what was new in the campsite. It must have been 10 p.m. when Mr Gonzales caught a whiff of something. Something that seemed familiar. Something that would make his heart rage, but Mr Gonzales would behave himself that evening and set priorities, because he felt Patosh's grief. No, today he would trot past the car park without a care in the world and pretend that nothing was wrong, and he succeeded, because Patosh didn't notice the caravan, whose owner was still enjoying herself in the port of La Coruna. Patosh woke up early the next morning and decided to take a decent shower and the campsite had a large shower room for campers not far from the swimming pool. He showed the lifeguard his plastic wristband and chose a locker in the changing room. Dressed only in his swimming trunks, he walked to the shower room where other men were washing themselves and standing under the hot waterblast.

Patosh immediately felt at ease and let the hot jet of water pour over him. The hair shampoo stung his eyes a little, but it was a small price to pay to finally not have to stand in the camper's tiny shower. When he finished, he dried himself off, said goodbye to the friendly bath attendant and went back to the campervan.

"Hello Pat. How are you?" called a female voice behind him. A voice that he recognised well and made his heart vibrate. He turned around slowly and recognised Mary, who had apparently also come out of the women's changing room.

"You here?" "That means the poodle dachshund is here too. I'm all right."

"We saw you at the harbour yesterday, but I didn't want to disturb you. I also saw you standing under the rain. Please Patosh. Let me be with you again. I can't continue travelling with her. She kicked me out because I did not agree to her urges. Please Pat...." she begged and thick tears rolled down her cheeks. Patosh was Patosh and he took her back. Not because he was in love with her, but because he was human through and through. He couldn't see any suffering and so he agreed. Mary jumped for joy and hugged him. A kiss escaped her lips and touched his, making his blood boil.

"I'll take you with me, but I'll tell you the truth. You have to know that I have fallen in love with you and I don't want to play hide and seek anymore. You don't have to feel the same and don't worry. I will never get physical or harass you in any way Mary. You should just know."

She looked at him with a smile and just said, "Thank you Pat. I've taken note." and then she laughed with delight.

"Where are your things?" asked Patosh.

"Behind your caravan. Since last night. I put them there while you were asleep."

"But Mr Gonzales must have scented you."

"But he didn't."

Patosh had to laugh as well, because she was something special, his Mary. Full of mysterious secrets and an energy that immediately mesmerised you. They walked hand in hand to the caravan and when the mongrel recognised them and saw them from afar, his little tail wagged like a windscreen wiper on high.

"Gonzi, my hero!"

Aliens in search of clues

In the meantime, our alien family reached Lyon, but they had missed the refugee by less than a week, which didn't upset Jonathan, but frustrated him inwardly. It was a feeling that seemed completely new to him and he didn't like it. Martha felt the same way. Fred didn't care because he was playing with the hen, Georgette, who suddenly laid eggs again. The High Council on Venus received Jonathan's report about the metal plate they had found and bought and this was noted with a note to scan every Orion species they encountered and transmit the data to the High Council headquarters. This species had also been a thorn in the eyes of the Venusians, metaphorically speaking, for thousands of years, as they sneaked into the nature of every alien being they encountered, including humans, in order to manipulate them, and not exactly for the better. They educate the weak characters to become egoists, advantage-seekers, exploiters, self-servers and ultimately serious criminals. You could say that everyone in the highest position today has been influenced by this Orion Clan so that these beings feel no love, no passion, no compassion and no mercy. A price one has to pay to become a billionaire and control the world. To this day it is horrifying to realise how venal some beings are and especially those of the planet called Earth.

"She was definitely here and according to the Vybe-scanner, she's in company.

Unfortunately, I can't create a hologram from here, which will of course make things more difficult," said Jonathan, somewhat irritated.

"How is that possible?" Jonathan wanted to know.

"Don't forget, she's a member of the High Council and therefore able to switch her aura on and off as she pleases. I had also wondered before the trip to Terrarion why she hadn't switched her aura off. She was probably in a hurry and careless at the time. From that point of view, it contradicts your theory that she might be travelling on a secret mission. It looks more and more as if this escape was undertaken for personal reasons. We may never know," Martha replied.

"You could be right, my compatible one. But we won't be swayed by speculation. Let's enjoy Lyon first and maybe we'll find out more telepathically."

On the way to Lyon, they stopped at a petrol station because they received a so-called cosmic hint, if you want to call it that. There they found a trace of the fugitive in the form of a cheap wallet containing travel documents needed on Terrarion, or Earth, but no cash. It was located directly under the drinks shelf in front of the till. In fact, Jonathan also asked the petrol station attendant, who remembered a very strange woman who did not appear to be from this world.

She paid him with crystals that looked valuable, but he couldn't sell them anywhere, as this type of crystal wasn't on any earthly gemstone list and gave many an expert a headache. Jonathan then bought the crystals from the petrol station attendant. It must have been the fugitive's, because these crystals were only found on Venus and it was also very risky to pay with them, but she probably couldn't find the wallet at that moment and just wanted the goods. It was two bags of crisps and two bottles of Coke Zero. If the petrol station attendant knew how valuable the crystals were, he would close the petrol station and retire early.

They stayed in Lyon for two days, strolling through market halls, narrow streets, shopping centres, old churches and monasteries and finally a cemetery, which was more for research purposes only. They could still detect soul vibrations at the fresh graves, but probably only a residual breath before the deceased ascended to the next "density", or volunteered again as a "traveller" to provide service to others, because yes, this was part of every being's mission in life. If he had no desire to do so, he entered the next "density", where the soul was "upgraded" one level higher, if you like. If the deceased was an Orion manipulated person, he entered either the "Crusaders" or "Orion" clan. His mission would then have been to travel to various planets and manipulate the species for the worse, thus becoming a manipulator.

Here, Jonathan collected data for the High Council, but there wasn't much. To be precise, there were only two.

Jonathan then looked for a restaurant because, as always, Fred was hungry. However, it wasn't easy to find a restaurant that allowed a family with a hen on a lead and Fred ended up putting Gerogette in his rucksack with her head hanging out. He just thought people were "STUPID". Gerogette, however, apparently loved being put in the rucksack, because she clucked happily from time to time, in Fred's judgement.

"So, spaghetti Bolognese for the young man, Chateau Brion for Madame and half a chicken for Monsieur. But don't let your hen see it otherwise, Oh LaLa. Bon Appetite." said the waiter with amusement and went to the next table. The Alien family enjoyed their meal and yes, they still needed some practice with their cutlery. It goes without saying that the other guests noticed them. Some laughed and some found it outrageous, but they didn't let it bother them, and they smacked and sipped their food with relish. The shirt and tie smeared with sauce, it was now the desert's turn. Coffee and even more wine flowed in streams and the murmuring of the staff and other guests never stopped.

"Waiter, the bill!" shouted Jonathan and it sounded like a relief for the waiter to finally get these barbarians off the table, but this calmed him down again after he received the tip.

"Oh monsieur, that wasn't necessary..."

"Yes, it was, young man, we really enjoyed it here and we'll be back. You can count on it." Jonathan said almost arrogantly, as if he belonged to the noblesse oblige. This forewarning made the waiter swallow, but with a tip like that they would always be welcome. As the family and Georgette left the restaurant, the waiter turned round and looked at the guests. "Yes, I hope they come back, you cheapskates, just to annoy you." He thought to himself, because most of them didn't leave a cent as a tip.

The alien family had to make a decision, because the two days were over. Where to now?

"I can't get a signal by telephatic means, dear. It's as if she's disappeared from the scene forever...."

"I've got her. She's in the direction of Perpignan, then Carcassonne."

"How do you know, Martha?"

"Feminine intuition, my husband."

"Let's try logic, please." Jonathan asked.

"It's quite simple. She switched her aura back on."

"What? Quick, we have to create a hologram before she switches it off again." Jonathan shouted excitedly. A behaviour he would never display on Venus. This Earth is scary, he realised more and more.

"Already done. We have to hurry. I've been able to track them all the way to La Coruna in Spain."

"Then let's waste no time and be on our way immediately."

"Wouldn't it be better to hire a caravan? Who knows where this journey will take us and the car won't have room for all the souvenirs we've bought."

No sooner said than done. The small car was exchanged for a camper van at one of the car hire companies based in Lyon and the journey resumed with a direct destination, La Coruna. Here too, after around eight hours, the Pyrenees were crossed, but Jonathan didn't take any detours and took the shortest route. As beautiful as the view was, there was no time to lose.

"Do you know where they are, my cosmic angel?"

"At a campsite called San Sebastian."

"Very good. I think we could make it there by tomorrow morning."

"What about sleep Jonathan? You need to rest."

We'll just take turns. You go and lie down. I'll call you after six hours love. Is that OK?"

"OK!" she replied.

A word that didn't exist on Venus, but according to the soul archive, a word

that is used billions of times a day worldwide and so Jonathan accepted it as well. Martha nodded in the affirmative and went to sleep in the back and Fred joined his father in the passenger seat.

"Where's Georgette son?"

"She's sleeping and laying eggs. How funny."

"Is that even possible Fred?"

"Apparently yes. Something to do with love. She's accepted us and she's laying eggs for the joy of it. What a chicken." laughed Fred, who loved his hen just as much. After about five hours of driving, Jonathan's eyes closed and Fred screamed his head off.

"CAUTION!"

Just in time, Jonathan managed to turn the steering wheel to the right and pulled over to the hard shoulder.

"Wake up your mum...."

"She's already awake because you threw her out of bed." whispered Fred.

"Ouch."

"We'll have to practise that again." came from behind and seconds later Martha was at the wheel.

Jonathan flopped down on the bed and fell asleep immediately and Fred got tired and did the same.

Night fell and the roads in the Pyrenees were poorly lit or not lit at all, making the journey a little challenging for Martha, but she persevered and reached La Coruna early in the morning. Jonathan brought her a cup of coffee, which she had bought in abundance so that she could bring the rest back to Venus, as there was no coffee there.

"We're actually here and the campsite is over there on the right."

The camper slowly drove in through the driveway and stopped in front of the reception where they had to register. They were lucky as they found a parking space only three spots away from the fugitive. Thus the hologram. Martha mastered the camper and parked the long vehicle in reverse with ease, which made Jonathan smile.

"You're the best, my darling," he said.

"You think?"

As they settled in, they wanted to take a walk around the campsite to find and recognise the fugitive. They only had the cosmic image of her and not the one she had taken here on earth, so the whole thing had to be done telepathically so that the fugitive wouldn't notice, otherwise she would switch off her aura immediately.

They had to manage a snapshot before she realised she had been found. Gerogette had already caught the full attention of Mr Gonzales, as Gonzi was barking his head off.

"Gonzi, what's the matter with you, you crazy dog? Patosh cursed from the bed and yes, Mary was lying next to him. Naked and happy. What happened between the two of them in the meantime that we didn't realise? The wine was to blame and she was head over heels in love. But back to Gonzi. As I said, he barked and barked and forced Patosh to get up from the bed and put a towel round his abdomen. When he looked through the windscreen, he had to laugh heartily, because he had never seen a hen on a lead before in his life.

"What are they?" he thought to himself, shaking his head, and went back to bed, where Mary was still lying on her stomach, asleep.

"What was that?" she asked sleepily.

"Our new neighbourhood. A strange couple with a child and a chicken. They're out for a walk and the chicken is on a lead. What's happened to this world?"

"All is right with the world Pat. You humans are...." and she immediately noticed the Foppas.

"We humans? Yes, you're right about a lot of things, but this is the second time you haven't included yourself as a human.

Should I be worried Mary? You are human, aren't you?"

"Of course my lover and wild stallion. What a night. You mounted me inhumanely."

"Oh yeah? How about another special treatment?" Patosh teased and less than three seconds later they were at it again. Patosh didn't believe his luck and rocked the campervan violently and Mary moaned and screamed her head off, making some people at the campsite envious.

The Alien family bought groceries in the small market inside the site and Fred and Georgette had to wait outside as pets were not allowed here. When all the errands were done, the family made their way back to the camper and as they approached the Patosh's motorhome, Mary realised what a strange couple they were, when she looked through the windscreen. The chicken made her laugh so loudly that the coffee flew out of the cup. But what was that? An alarming feeling ran through her body. The alien family had already arrived at their camper, but there was one thing they couldn't do. Switch their aura off or on like the High Council could. Mary knew immediately that she had been discovered and a panic ran through her veins.

"We have to get out of here now Patosh. I'm begging you."

"What? Why? We have it good here." But not only Mary, also Gonzi confirmed Mary's concern with loud barking. Patosh, freshly enamoured as he was, did not disappoint his new-found princess and packed up everything he could and set off. New destination?

"Santiago de Campostella."

Santiago de Campostella

When everything was asleep, a caravan crept out of the San Sebastian campsite at night. Patosh drove slowly enough to avoid hearing the pebbles crackling under the tyres. They had paid when they checked in, so there was no sense of guilt. There were also two cameras installed at the gate, which registered all entries and exits. Patosh only switched on the lights of his vehicle at the gate and drove off a little faster. Mary switched off her aura before the unplanned escape, because yes, she was the fugitive.

"Would YOU please explain to me what this panic attack means and why we have to flee like criminals?"

"Oh Pat, you wouldn't believe me anyway and you might break up with me after I tell you."

"Try me. You should trust me, even if we haven't known each other too long. I don't care what you've done and I'd swallow a murder with a worried feeling."

"No Pat. I haven't done anything bad. Practising crime is not in my DNA. I'm on the run and I don't want to go back home and these strange people with their hen are looking for me to get me back."

"Why do they need the hen? Is it their secret weapon or even a drone in disguise?" Pat asked sarcastically, as he always did in his pub, but Mary laughed her head off at the comparison.

"You're cracking me up Pat, where do you get such sarcasm from? I can't explain the thing with the hen, but my gut feeling never fooled me."

"And what about the boy? Is he also a disguise so that they can be seen as a loving family? So using a child in such a matter is definitely going too far. It can't be that."

"It isn't either. It's a nice family on holiday who received an order from their superiors on the way. To find me and bring me back."

"Bring you back where and how do you know they're a nice family? You're confusing me and I can't shake the feeling that you're lying to me. What are you doing?"

"I'm not lying to you, I'm just not telling you everything for security reasons and also because you wouldn't believe me and send me to hell afterwards, even if I don't believe in the devil."

"If you and I are going to make it work, there can't be any secrets. I don't accept bullshit. I never have. So? Speak up."

"Can you wait until La Campostella? I promise I'll tell you everything, but you have to prepare yourself and you can only do that when there is absolutely nothing going on around us. No movement, no light and no noise. "Santiago is not far away and you can wait the two hours."

"OK. Then let's do it like this," said Patosh with a queasy feeling in his stomach that made him doubt Mary's presence of mind. A very surreal situation arose during the journey and not another word was spoken. In Santiago de Campostella, all the campsites were full. Pseudo-pilgrims, who didn't want to make the long journey on foot and preferred to visit this pilgrimage site of St James after a barbecue and a few cans of beer, blocked the pitches months in advance. Nothing worked here without a reservation. So what now? The only thing they could do was drive to a motorway service station and spend the night in a car park, although it would certainly be noisy. Mary was not happy with this option. According to the map, there was a village ten kilometres to the south and there was a monastery there. Perhaps they could spend the night in the courtyard of this monastery for a small fee.

"What the hell. Ten kilometres more or less doesn't matter. Let's go there and give it a try," Patosh said with a shrug. Once there, they rang the bell at the gate of the monastery and a voice rang out in Spanish. Mary, who, how could it be otherwise, answered in the same language.

Lo and behold, the good Lord apparently had a thing for money too, because the gate opened and they drove into the courtyard.

They were greeted by Domenican monks and the prior, who was less than fifty years old, greeted them just as warmly. Mary, who looked more like a punk with all her black fingernails and black lipstick, didn't impress the prior. He had seen it all in his life and nothing could surprise him anymore. As a missionary in Central Africa, he had learnt that it was not a person's appearance that mattered, but their heart. He had also served in Santiago de Campostella and Mary was one of thousands who used such make-up. No, nothing could shock him.

"Yes, of course you can spend the night here. There's a water supply and a power socket where I'm pointing. But if you want to use the toilet, please use the one behind the shed there. Don't worry, it's a proper toilet. We don't have a waste tank, so don't empty the campervan's toilet tank anywhere in the grounds."

"Of course not Prior. How much do we owe you for your kindness and hospitality?"

"You owe us nothing. If you would like to make a voluntary donation, we would be grateful."

"Of course, is a hundred euros right?" asked Patosh.

"God will thank you, my children. Make yourselves comfortable."

And with these words, the prior left the place where the caravan was parked.

"Here we are also safe from our pursuers, Pat. Thank you for your understanding."

"I'd be ready...."

"Let's wait until night falls. Because we need the darkness."

"I didn't mean that my darling." Patosh said in a way that couldn't have been more unmistakable.

"But Pat, this is a sacred place," Mary replied with an even more ambiguous grin. A minute later they were both in bed and the reader can imagine the rest of the story . If only Patosh knew who he was doing it with and what hot cup of coffee he was dipping his biscuit into, metaphorically speaking. He had to put his right hand over her mouth because she screamed, which turned him on even more.

"I hope no one noticed," she finally said after they finished.

"I don't think so. And if they did, the confessional isn't far away."

Mary laughed to herself. Although the monks couldn't hear them doing it, they could see how hard the caravan was rocking at the back of the courtyard, and certainly not because of the curvature of the earth and it`s rotation.

Night fell and so did the darkness.

"I'm ready," Mary said quietly and Patosh nodded. He realised the fear that was spreading through him. What will she tell him now and why will she use these methods? This uncertainty made him insecure and nervous.

"Sit down, my darling, close your eyes and think of nothing. Stay relaxed and when you feel my hands on your temples, don't move. Just let everything flow in and accept it."

This only made Patosh more nervous, but he wanted this relationship more than anything in the world and so he surrendered. Mary placed all ten fingers of her hands on Patosh's left and right areas and said:

"Relax Pat and don't say a word."

Patosh suddenly felt something warm flowing through his veins. An unprecedented energy that filled him with images. His mind, conscious mind and subconscious mind were set to "snooze mode" since they block the flow of information through the human mind's weakness. It was as if floodgates were opened and masses of water drowned him. He wanted to fight back, but he couldn't, and even though this sudden feeling of warmth and love turned into agony, he let it happen. He wanted to scream, he wanted to cry, he wanted to plead, but nothing worked.

Paralysed and overwhelmed by what was happening inside him, he now knew that Mary carried a deep secret inside her and that he didn't necessarily want to know this secret anymore. Not knowing how long this ritual was going on, Patosh had to lie down after Mary took her hands off him. Now he could scream, now he could cry and whimper, but not because he was being tortured, but because he would not have thought such universal love possible, which he had to experience during the procedure and which made him realise how badly people treated themselves and this planet. How disturbed everything seemed and how unimportant everything is. You can own billions or nothing. In the end, the one without possessions is the happier one. What shocked him more was the greed of the people on his planet. Everything that had to do with money, gold, possessions and power attracted people like cow shit does to flies. He wept because he now knew how far wrong people were and how much knowledge and understanding they had given up for money and gold instead of working with the energies of nature and the universe. Those who were rich had enslaved themselves and sold their souls to the devil, because they couldn't sleep at night for fear of who might want their fortune. Patosh also saw how needlessly people died in wars, whether civilians or soldiers. He was also shown a kind of film of what the earth would have looked like if humans lived as nature intended and how the earth was now in self-destruction mode simply because it could no longer cope with the ingratitude of these creatures, despite all the love and natural abundance given to them. Earth cried out for help and it came from the other Planets in the form of regular visits from extraterrestrials. Humans had been lied to, exploited, bled dry and then thrown away for nothing more than a pittance for millennia by the few who call and called themselves elitists. Patosh felt guilty. Guilty of being one of these creatures, even though he was one of the most innocent of the race. Mary let him cry and waited. When Patosh calmed down and wiped his tears with his sleeves, he looked at Mary, who showed neither pity nor compassion. Her face didn't move at all.

"I'm so sorry Mary. I still don't know who you are, but you've opened my eyes."

"That was just foreplay, my darling. Now comes my story. I'll tell it to you."

We have lost her

There was great surprise when Fred returned from his morning walk with Georgette and reported back to his parents.

"They're gone, they're gone....." cried Fred, gasping for air.

"Who's gone?" asked Jonathan, reading the paper and sipping his coffee, without giving Fred a glance.

"Well, the fugitive and her companion. The caravan is no longer there and another one has taken the space."

Only now did Jonathan react and Martha also looked at her son in horror.

"What a load of rubbish!" Jonathan shouted, slamming the newspaper on the table. Day after day, these three Aliens took on the features of the Terrians, or humans, and now they were cursing as well.

"Jonathan! What's got into you? When whe get back home you should undergo a soul cleansing. What kind of habits are these?" Martha was outraged.

"Oh, shut up. Everything is getting out of hand on this planet. Nothing is coordinated, nothing harmonises and one shouldn't swear with all this happening?. And you know what, darling? Maybe I don't want to go back at all. I really like it here on Earth. The food tastes good, camping is more fun here and, above all, we're so far ahead of those idiots that we could go a long way here. I'm on holiday and the High Council can kiss my arse!" Jonathan finished

"Darling…kiss my arse? I think I'm going to faint." Martha breathed in disbelief at what she was hearing.

"Oh yes. That would be awesome." Fred rejoiced.

"Awesome? You too now Brutus?" Martha couldn't believe it. They had everything and more on Venus and these two compatibles were becoming less compatible by the day.

"That's out of the question. We have a home and a mission. Pull yourselves together."

"You know where the spaceship is parked, my angel. If you don't go with me, then goodbye." Jonathan sipped his coffee as he said this. Fred thought it was a bit over the top and said, "Dad no. If mum doesn't stay, then I won't either."

"Dad? Mum? What have I done wrong? You're no longer Venusians."

"That's right!" said Jonathan with a smile. "And it's fun not being one. Now I understand why there are so many 'travellers'. They want to go back to earth after death to serve, because it's more fun here. Indeed it is. This planet needs to be saved and I agree with the fugitive. So leave the Vybe scanner and enjoy your holiday like I do."

"It's just a shame we're not able to switch off our aura like the High Council can. They can get on our nerves telepathically every day...Oh my God. Did I just say that?" Martha exclaimed in shock.

"Yes, YOU did and also "Oh my God". Wellcome to the club my love."

"Stop insulting me Jonathan. I'm neither your sweetheart nor your darling."

"Oh dear. So that's what an earthly marriage looks like. An annoying wife who just nags and nags. You'd better get me two more rolls and calm down, wife." Jonathan now exaggerated and felt it painfully, because Martha took the thickest volume of a book that was a standard decoration in the caravan and threw it on Jonathan's head. Title: "The Holy Bible". An argument began that even attracted the attention of the High Council on Venus.

"Jonathan? What's going on?"

"Just don't get on our nerves any more, understand? We're going on holiday. Mission accomplished and by the way. We've lost her. See how you find her yourselves. Bye, bye amigo." And Jonathan stopped the telephatic communication with a very traitorous laugh.

"They could beam us up and send us to a soul cleansing planet." Martha whispered in horror.

"They won't do that, because they would be breaking every law. Free will. Have you forgotten?"

"Oh Jonathan. What are you doing? We can't stay on this planet." Martha said, dabbing Jonathan's head wound with cotton wool.

"Let me ask you a question. Do you like it here on this earth?"

"I do very much. But we have obligations."

"Hogwash. We don't. Let's please stay here and try a new life. It's just so much more fun being here. All the delicious wines, beers, spirits and food. My goodness this food.

Yes, the people are totally crazy here and they are in desperate need of help. Let's help them like the fugitive wants and settle down here."

"But the High Council...."

"I'll tell you what dearest. Call them by phone and tell them we're staying to serve here. Just say that these idiots here need help. Not necessarily in that tone, but you understand what I mean. I don't want to talk to them anymore, otherwise they might change my mind and I don't want that. I want to stay here."

Martha no longer understood anything, but yes, Jonathan was right. This planet with all these beautiful colours and the crazy inhabitants also appealed to her desire to reside on Earth, and not since Jonathan suggested it, but almost from the beginning. So she agreed and all three of them shouted with joy.

They stayed at the campsite for a whole week before travelling on and yes, Martha spoke to the High Council, but as on earth, everything still needed to be discussed. They would come back with an answer. Meanwhile, Jonathan was preparing a programme for his new life as a Venusian human. He would set up an institute to help people live better lives in an academic way, educating them about how wrong they had been living all those thousands of years after the Transition happened. That is, after humans sent the aliens away and opted for a material and consumption-orientated life.

Wealth and possessions had always bribed and seduced humanity and only the poorest of the poor still had a remnant of an ancient quality they called "humanity". This institute will not be a scam, because he will claim it as a course of study and offer this subject at universities. Martha also liked her husband's idea and would support him.

In the meantime, the other caravan set off again and, unfortunately, they decided not to visit Santiago de Campostella. Mary wanted to avoid an encounter with the three Venusians, or compatriots, at all costs. She had nothing against the hen, for she was only a sacrifice and even if Georgette was in good, loving hands, she had no other hens to enjoy socially and her clucking became less and less. However, she still laid eggs. Patosh was happy to have found a new love and instructed his lawyer in Lontzen to prepare the divorce between him and Camille.

In fact, Patosh filed for divorce by telephone. Mary was beside herself with joy, because for her it was a proof of love, but unfortunately for Camille it was just another stab in the heart. She received a letter by mail and when she read the letter from the lawyer, everything inside her died a second time. But she understood the reason only too well. She had tormented him mentally for years and she knew that because he was suffering before her eyes. She often thought about trying to make a new start with him, but she couldn't. When the baby died, he, Patosh died in her heart too. Who understands women?

Proud as Camille was, she showed Patosh greatness in this case. She wrote to his lawyer that the will of a divorce was noted and that she agreed to it. She just wanted her share of the pub transferred to her bank account and Patosh could start his life again from scratch. She would also close the pub during his absence and move in with her mother in Antwerp. Patosh agreed to everything and why protest? Half of the pub belonged to Camille and he would discuss her share, which was 42,000 euros, with the bank and possibly take out a new loan. Why hire more lawyers when one could do it? The main thing was to put an end to this nightmare. In Salamanca, Spain, Patosh received a DIN A4 envelope in the reception mail-box of the camping site. The divorce papers arrived. Mary and he read the ten pages and Patosh, signed at the end with trembling hands and tears in his eyes.

It didn't leave him cold, but with any luck the marriage would be divorced within a month and with less fuss than expected. Of course he felt guilty and a suffocating sadness, but what no longer worked didn't help. He was also worried about the pub and didn't know if he should sell it, but Mary recommended to wait until after this holiday to make a decision, as she would be part of his life now.

"You still owe me your verbal story and you've avoided it long enough. I want to hear it now. The mental and telepathic ones are noted, but you should honour your promise now. I'm all ears."

"Have we got another bottle of red wine? We're going to need it, my darling."

Patosh took a Bordaux from the cupboard and uncorked it. Plastic cups had to do as there were no glasses left behind by the car rental.

"You're from Lontzen, aren't you Pat?" she asked him with calm eyes.

"Yes. Born there, but I can die somewhere other than Lontzen."

"You experienced strange sightings in Lontzen some time ago, didn't you? You call them UFO sightings, am I right?"

"You are, Mary, and yes, you can call them that. Why?"

"These UFOs, or spaceships, have been coming to your planet for thousands of years. Some to explore, others to test and then there are the holidaymakers. Yes, the universe loves your planet because it is so varied and colourful and they are trying very hard to ensure that your planet is always preserved. Earth is so wonderful that many from other planets even come here on holiday. We are among you and you don't realise it because we have the ability to change our molecular structure and take on your appearance when it is deemed necessary. We can also quickly adopt all the languages you speak here to communicate...."

"You keep saying we. So you're an alien too?"

"Yes Pat, I am," Mary said softly.

But Patosh's blood froze in his veins. So he had been having sex with an alien the whole time. Yes, those were his first thoughts, because he couldn't imagine what she would look like when she revealed her true form. What would be standing in front of him then? He couldn't form a picture and that unsettled him.

"I come from the planet you call Venus and we have no names. We don't have numbers or letters in our alphabet either, but symbols. My symbols, to get a kind of identifier, can be compared to your letters like this: KLTXK which of course makes no sense. Mary is the name I chose after I landed and I think you like that name too."

Patosh just nodded nervously and wanted to hear more.

"The 'UFOs' you saw back in Lontzen weren't holidaymakers, explorers or examiners. That was a search party to find me again and bring me back to Venus, because I escaped from there. My compatible creator, you would call him father, is a member of the High Council, which I am as well. We are peaceful and our religion, understand me correctly Pat, we don't have religions because we think they are superfluous and very dangerous, but I use that word to make it more understandable. So our religion, or faith, is based on unconditional love and coexistence with the universe. The universe is our nature and our essence. With us there is no greed, no hate, no need except to serve. By serving I mean helping you and other planetariums with difficulties that arise. But the problem with you is, you have reached a state where you can no longer be helped because your governments do not follow our advice. They only want to use our knowledge for military purposes, they don't care about anything else. Energy problems, environmental problems, famine, education, etc., none of that matters to these ladies and gentlemen, and why? They were manipulated by the Orion clan for their own self-interest and that is how they became powerful and control this planet. They became the scum of the universe and your masters, because you are nothing but slaves. Your energy problems should not be solved as long as they can profit financially from them and build a position of power for themselves.

You would not have needed oil a hundred years ago and you would not have needed gas as well, but oil and gas are for sale, not our planetary quantum energy, because we offered it for free. Your environmental situation is on the brink of collapse. Deforestation of the primeval forests in Amazonia, Africa and Asia is destroying the balance and natural equilibrium. Animals are being forced to seek new habitats and are being driven from their territories. Oceans are being polluted and fished out to such an extent that whales, turtles and others can no longer navigate the oceans and end up on foreign beaches, let alone find food, because the sushi plates have to be topped up with raw fish. Your research is only of limited benefit to your species. Rather, it serves the pharmaceutical industry and how appalling are the hoaxes with your "Comet" Virus and your vaccine, which kills rather than protects. You are being murdered on a grand scale. I could tell you more about what goes on behind closed curtains, but that would take us years, so let's leave it at that. Your business here on earth has become so bad that we are on the verge of giving you up. People in the universe are turning their backs on you. But I'm not giving up and that's why I fled Venus. I am a fugitive and a member of the High Council. My absence is dangerous as it is a violation of our laws. Interfering in other worlds is not allowed and neither is manipulating free will. We may only assist in an advisory capacity. That said, the humans are not taking our advice..."

"Wait a minute. A small percentage of humans Mary. Most of them would give the shirt off their back to be helped." Patosh protested vigorously.

"Maybe they would. You're not doing anything to fight this oppression. You do nothing to free yourself from the chains that take away your breath. You have to get rid of this monster called the Elite, or Cabal..."

"Oops. I thought you were peace-loving etc."

"We are, because we are already in the seventh density of the life cycle, but you are still floating around in the third and have these side effects of violence. We were also in your third layer 75,000 years ago, but every 25,000 years you are either raised or not, depending on how we behaved and developed before the harvest. We call our promotion "harvest" because we are nothing other than the seed of the universe. You, however, are far from it and if you are not careful, you will slip back into the second layer. The one of the animals. You have to do something if you want to experience the promotion and save your planet. Eliminate the evil that rules and controls you and eliminate the Orion Manipulated. I will not return. I will stay here and do my utmost to serve and help. Your planet also has the ability to repolarise alien beings who have resided here on Earth for too long. Although you lose nothing in terms of knowledge and cultural maturity, you reappropriate your customs, which are undesirable and difficult to eliminate. This is all about your planet called Earth. You inhabit it, so you must protect it and manage it properly, for it is nothing else. I

143

love you Pat and want to stay with you. But I want you to know that I am not one of your species. Can you live with that and, above all, will you let me do my job?"

"I can Mary, because I love you too. Yes, I even want to support you in this difficult task as much as I can."

Mary looked gratefully at Patosh and they hugged tightly. She felt a pain and a sadness that she had not known before but knew about. A side effect of the humanity of the third layer or density. In the seventh density, such feelings no longer exist. You recognise those in need of help and you help them without selfishness, emotions or demands for thanks. It is the side effect of unconditional love. Mary, however, had already been on Earth for some time and with Patosh by her side, who sometimes cursed and was filled with emotion, she became infected along the way. But what about our other family? Jonathan, Martha and Fred?

The High Council is not amused.

While Jonathan, Martha and Fred were still in Santiago de Campostella, having a great time, an extraordinary meeting was held on Venus. The High Council was "not amused", so to speak, with the behaviour of some of its citizens. The disappearance of the council chairman's own daughter was declared unacceptable, as was the desire of the other party to settle on Earth for good. After all, where would we end up if we simply turned our backs on Venus with all the knowledge, wisdom and abilities that are far beyond the imagination of humans? Chaos in the universe was therefore at the gates of all reason. Yes, you want to help and advise people, but only if they want it themselves. Forcing the issue was and will never be on the agenda of a Venusian. The decision was made to bring the holidaymakers back to their senses, but to use harsher means to get the fugitive back if necessary. Jonathan received daily messages from the High Council to come to his senses and return after the holiday was over, but Jonathan switched to stubbornness and did not respond. He sucked on his Pinia Collada by the pool and waved to Marthe and Fred, who were swimming in the same. Georgette was in a meadow at the campsite, picking at worms and bugs.

This went too far and the High Council decided to send three starships and additional search personnel immediately. The Jonathan Family would have been easy to find, as they had limited aura-cancelling abilities, but KLTXK was another matter. It had the fullest programme of a Venusian. There were four per spaceship, so twelve aliens, who were now heading for Terrarion, which we also call Planet Earth, and since the current location of the alien family was known, there was no hesitation. The exact coordinates were entered into the UFO sat nav, if you like, and if they had been on autopilot all the way, the three UFOs would have landed in the swimming pool, which of course would not have been possible given the size. Georgette's meadow would do.

Martha suddenly had an intuition and she left the pool immediately. Fred also got strange vibes and so did Jonathan. These vibes did not bode well and, quick-witted, they made the right decision. To get away from Santiago de Campostella, but where to? Mary also felt these vibrations and she knew immediately that a search party had been sent in greater numbers to fetch them.

"We have to get out of here now!" she shouted commandingly as Patosh's coffee flew out of the cup.

"Why?"

"They're after me for it. But I'm getting strange telepathic holograms as well. Can you remember the hen and its owners Pat?"

"Not in that order, no. I can remember a family walking a hen..."

"I don't have time for your jokes Pat, put on some trousers, grab the hose and the power cord and let's get out of here. I'm serious."

"Okay, okay. I'm already on it. How much time do we have left?"

"Maybe three to four hours. No more. They're still 450,000 kilometres from the moon."

"How do you know all this?"

"You wouldn't understand anyway, my darling. Let's go now!"

Patosh packed everything up and they left Salamanca. New destination, Seville. As luck would have it, this was also the destination of the Alien family, but they were travelling a different route. The journey was to take them to Seville via Portugal and, by the Almighty, all the speed traps on the motorway were triggered because Jonathan stepped on the gas and the car hire company could pay the speeding tickets using the credit card he had created himself. It's just a shame that this credit card was created by a bank that didn't exist.

Yes, the income and expenses were digitised and paid virtually, but not realistically, only virtually. The car hire company then received a positive certificate even if it wasn't true. And yes again, you could call it fraud, but Jonathan wanted no part of it since there was no cheating on Venus. He called it SURVIVAL. Escaping while enjoying the scenery, what an adventure this holiday was. The camper, packed with beer, wine, bread, cheese and ham, was only left to refuel. After that they continued their journey and, as they had now decided not to return to Venus, they were able to use the coffee they had bought, which was intended for Venus. The sun was shining and burning hot and Martha thought of a way to disguise all of them by using DNA deception. If successful, this would be tantamount to switching off their auras and making it more difficult to find them. But Martha had to hurry, because the search command had registered their escape and entered their position into the UFO sat nav. Yes, I know, I should have chosen a better name than UFO sat nav, but what the hell. On-board computer sounds boring.

"How far are you Martha? Have you found a solution?"

"I'm very close. Don't push me Jonathan and drive more carefully. One hundred and fifty kilometres per hour in a motorhome isn't exactly safe, you know."

"Just let me know and apply it immediately."

"All right."

Jonathan switched on the radio to hear some of the earthy music, however, breaking news suddenly came on all channels.

"Three UFOs have been spotted over the south of France, flying in formation over the Pyrenees towards Spain. Hundreds have seen it ladies and gentlemen and to deny it would only prove the unseriousness of our government or even their fear, who knows. After several interviews with witnesses, they resembled silvery frisbies that could change their position in a jagged shape and yes, our Armee de L`Àire (Air Force) was put to the test as Mirage 2000 fighters were observed hunting them. What kind of lies will we hear tomorrow from the government offices we don`t know, because weather balloons can't fly like that and why would Mirage fighters be chasing balloons. But that's the way it is ladies and gentlemen. The Prime Minister will be working on a reconstructed excuse as we speak. Let's stay tuned. And now on with music on RADIO 24, blah, blah, ..."

"I've found a method!" Martha shouted out loud and laughed.

"Is it being used?"

"Yes, Jonathan. You can slow down. I used Gerogette's DNA in the Vybe scanner and so we're all chickens now."

Jonathan choked with laughter and Fred couldn't hold back the tears either and finally Jonathan was able to step off the pedal a little, because rocking at high speed can make even aliens vomit.

"I'm tired, my angel. Please take over for four hours. I need to lie down."

Martha was happy to do so, as she was already bored and instead of drinking beer and wine during the journey, she preferred coffee. Jonathan didn't like coffee, but he could hold ten times as much alcohol as a human could, so his tolerance for drunkenness was never exceeded, even in a breathalyser test. Fred was now sitting next to his compatible mum and holding the hen.

"Mum? Don't you think people would be surprised to see four hens driving at one hundred and twenty on the motorway?" Fred asked justifiably.

"Don't worry my darling. I've got them all under control. We're still in the same meadow where Georgette was looking for worms. I've set it up like this. I've set our position to freeze with the coordinates of the meadow."

"Freeze?" Fred asked, confused. Martha just laughed aloud and replied

"I know. The longer I'm here, the more human slogans I use. It's stupid. Freeze means to freeze. Our position "froze" in the same place in the search scanner of the searchers when we disappeared. Only this time we're chickens." Martha laughed, not knowing whether she should switch to beer.

"Oh, I get it now. You're brilliant Mamy."

"Thank you Fred."

Both caravans had the same destination and if you were to follow their journey on a screen, the Alien family had the longer route to cover. Portugal was a diversion, but a nice one. Jonathan zigzagged along his route. First Porto, then Tomar, followed by Lisbon and finally Beja, Faro and Huelva and from there he didn't take the direct inland route to Seville, but drove along the coast to Cadiz and finally Seville. Jonathan took his time since Martha had managed to trick the search party. He would have liked to visit the small town of Palos on the last leg of the journey, as the first sea voyage of Cristopherus Columbus began there in his soul archive, which interested him greatly. He had respect for such adventurers who dared to do great things, even if the consequence of this journey meant the death of many natives.
For Jonathan, the universe was also an ocean and, compared to the distance of the Genoese's voyage, an infinite one. He sensed the dangers of these sailors, who for weeks saw only the sea and no land for miles around. Columbus was on the verge of being lynched when suddenly a cry was heard from one of the other ships. It came from the Pinta. Land in sight. After ten long weeks of lies and slogans, they had arrived.

But Columbus was not a fair man, because he himself collected the gold doubloon that he nailed to the mast of his Santa Maria. This was promised to the first person to see land. He claimed that he had noticed the light of fires the night before. Ce la guerre as the French say in such a case. The captain is always right.

But back to the present. Jonathan simply drove past Palos, as Martha urged him to go straight to Seville. She was fed up with the rocking and Georgette was also starting to lose her feathers. In Seville, they dropped the caravan off at one of the hundreds of rental agencies and Jonathan decided to buy a car. It had been an unforgettable journey, but now he just wanted to settle down, rent a flat for Martha, Fred and him and start settling into life on earth. He bought an old Peugeot 504 and put himself and his family up in a three-star hotel and started to think like a human being, something he had previously thought impossible. Fear was his new discovery. The fear of being discovered by the search party and taken back to Venus. How much calmer it would have been if the High Council had simply let him work from Earth as an ambassador. His stay would be legitimate and everything would run more smoothly. On this point, he did not understand the High Council's behaviour. He could provide valuable services on behalf of the Venusians in this way. Martha, meanwhile, was becoming more and more independent on Earth and went for a daily stroll as the Vybe scanner could display all the currencies, while Fred made friends with other boys his Earth age and played football.

Georgette, meanwhile, pecked around and didn't let the game bother her. Only once did a dog have a go at her, but the owner was able to prevent a bloodbath. The days went by and Jonathan couldn't find anything to rent in the newspapers, but one day a barista told him that a finca was for rent. He could arrange a visit as the owner was none other than one of his many cousins. Jonathan agreed and when the appointment took place and the family was delighted with the finca, the contract was signed. This is where Jonathan would finally set up his institute to help people lead a better life by educating them. A new life began. Meanwhile, the newspapers reported strange sightings and jet fighters patrolling loudly every day until the sightings suddenly disappeared, but not the search party. They were left behind on Earth, took on human form and went about their job of searching for the fugitives and only when the job was done would the spaceships come back to pick them up. Martha had achieved one thing then. Freezing the position and declaring the family as chickens so that they would be searched for elsewhere, but the one thing she could not do was to switch off the aura so that it would remain switched off once and for all. If a Venusian was actually in the immediate vicinity, he would recognise them, but the family was lucky because the search party was still left in the dark and searched around Santiago de Campostella.

Back to Patosh and Mary. They arrived in Seville twelve days before the alien family and Mary remained in the switched-off aura position. This would remain switched off until her compatible father finally left her alone. Compared to Jonathan, Mary had absolutely no plan for how to save the Earth and Patosh was also planning to settle down in Seville for the time being, as his holiday was slowly turning into an adventurous nightmare. They both needed peace and quiet, but where to settle down? Patosh was also worried about the pub in Lontzen, because closed as it was, there were empty and half-filled bottles standing around and the taps would also have to undergo a thorough cleaning. Camille had already moved out and of course had done nothing to at least leave "The Golden Mug" clean. If she had had her way, she would have smashed everything to bits with an axe, but she was a lazy person, much to Patosh's delight. They, Patosh and Mary, also gave up the caravan and bought an old Land Rover, which was built under licence in Spain as the SANTANA. Mary also had a Vybe scanner, so at least there was no shortage of money. However, for understandable reasons, they didn't want to attract attention.

"We need to get out of this bed and breakfast Mary. We need a flat," Patosh suggested.

"We'd be stuck here and no longer mobile Pat."

"Why don't we just go back to Belgium? I have to take care of the pub."

"We'll do that when some grass has grown over this case...."

"When will that be the case Mary? I'm fed up with all this fleeing. This is not my home. I have to go back." Patosh shouted resolutely, feeling inferior to her by now and already proving much more willing to compromise than Mary.

"Please Patosh. Give us a month. If we can't find a way out then, we'll go to Belgium. I promise."

That was the first time Mary didn't call him Pat, which showed that she too was tense and worried. One day, something happened that would change everything for them, because on a grocery shopping trip, Patosh and Mary found themselves in the same supermarket as Jonathan and Martha. Fred stayed at the finca to look after Georgette and by now thirty other chickens, five goats, two sheep, two cows and three ponies. Yes, the Alein family had fully settled in. Mary and Patosh, who was pushing the shopping trolley, rummaged through the shelves and lo and behold, Mary picked up an aura that could only have come from Venus. Suddenly she turned white as a sheet and looked around nervously.

"What's wrong, my angel?" Patosh asked anxiously.

"I'm picking up auras. Maybe the search party is already here."

Jonathan and Martha couldn't pick up Mary's aura, however, as Mary's was switched off. The excitement subsided a little when she recognised the family with the hen, but she couldn't guess whether they were friendly or hostile, as she didn't know why a couple would be pushing two full shopping carts in front of them if they were on a search patrol. And anyway. Where is the boy with the hen? They were missing. Jonathan and Martha turned to the wine rack when suddenly their eyes met and they almost froze to stone as they recognised Mary. Not a word was spoken for seconds until Mary began.

"What do you want from me? Why are you following me?"

"We haven't been following you since Santiago KLTXK. We are also on the run. We decided to stay here and this was not authorised by the High Council. Now they're looking for us too."

"How is that possible? You can't switch off your auras like I can. They should have found you by now." Mary asked incredulously.

"Well. We've tricked them so far. But only regarding our position. If they were here in Seville, they would have found us by now like you did. But they're not and by the time they get the idea to come to Seville, hopefully they'll lose interest. We have settled not far from here and I have set up an institute to educate the people. You look as if you haven't found suitable accommodation. Why don't you come and work with us? I need help, because it's very exhausting on my own. New people come to us every day and want to take part in our seminars," Jonathan suggested.

"That would be very helpful and nice for me too. What I miss is communicating with a Venusian friend, or now here on earth girlfriend. Please come and join us. We have a lot of space and we could help each other keep the search party at bay." Martha said euphorically.

Mary stood there and let it go over her head, but Patosh helped.

"It would be a temporary solution Mary. We need a home and some stability. Please."

Mary agreed and everyone cheered, even though Mary still carried an inner mistrust since she didn't know these Venusians. The exhaustion caused by the escape had finally won out.

"We'll just buy the rest, then we'll follow you to wherever you're staying now so you can pack. Then we'll lead the way to the finca."

No sooner said than done, and how else could the finca have been called but "Finca Venusia"? In itself a hint if the search party would appear in Seville. But Mary was able to help the family by switching off the aura once some trust had been built up. They were given a large room and could move freely around the living space together and use everything from the bathroom, kitchen, garden and pool. They had, at first, a home.

On Venus, however, the High Council had initiated a special meeting, and species from other planets who were members of this cosmic alliance also took part. If one were to describe it in human terms, one could call this alliance the Green Peace of Space, but with the use of diplomacy, not the use of rubber boats and harsh protective actions. The situation regarding the fugitives was taken seriously and the consequences of sending more spaceships to retrieve the fugitives were considered risky. Nine aliens from the search party were left behind on Earth and three of them brought the spaceships back to Venus to convince the search personnel of the importance of this mission. If they wanted to go home, then only with the fugitives, and if this was also unsuccessful, then a final option was considered and this would not be in the interests of the High Council. One would now wonder why the fugitives were not left alone and simply allowed to continue with their self-imposed mission, which had always been the intention of the Covenant. Enlightenment. Mary's father, however, immediately put the brakes on this proposal on the grounds that there are already thousands of aliens on Earth who are working on behalf of the Federation and who have a precise mission to carry out.

However, these fugitives are rebels and the consequences of a mission not carried out according to plan could trigger chaos on Terrarion (Earth for the forgetful) with incalculable consequences. Part of the covenant refuted this excuse, saying. "Earth is already in chaos and perhaps the fugitives would be the salvation". For thousands of years they had only watched and sent down observers to keep all the events on Earth in balance, but they had taken the disadvantages of this human species too lightly and done nothing to keep the Orion manipulators in check. Countries are ruled without consideration by banks and organisations and puppets are placed in positions as presidents and prime ministers who only do what the upper elite decides and this elite even plays God with the universe as they consider themselves untouchable and omniscient. Perhaps one should finally intervene in the free will of these manipulated terrarians (humans) and change the laws accordingly so that it does not degenerate any further. This was countered with the fact that it would lead to a war against the Orion clan, the consequences of which could not be imagined. This again, was immediately counter-argued with the fact that it was time to get this clan out of the world once and for all, which of course would break all peaceableness and the law of unconditional love in every instance. Mary's father finally decided that he would give his daughter and the other renegades an Earth year to prove themselves, but only if she was under direct observation by the search personel already on Earth and for that he would have to get the permission of all members of the High Council to initiate his daughter's aura-switching procedure, which would only be used in the case at the highest emergency level.

"Let us reconvene tomorrow to get a result on this matter. Retire for consultation." Mary's father said, relieving the company of their duties for this time.

Should the High Council vote in favour of the aura deactivation procedure, it meant that Mary would lose all her privileges as a High Council member and that she would be traceable and accessible at all times, as this would be the only way to give her the option of an Earth year to prove herself and even though the Venusians felt no emotion, KLTXG (compatible father's name through symbol translation) did not like the vibrations he was picking up. He was worried about KLTXT, Mary, whom he loved very much, emotionlessly.

"The High Council has made a decision. We approve your proposal for the one-year probationary period and agree to the aura deactivation procedure."

KLTXG felt guilty in every way about having to initiate this law, but Venusians feel such guilt very differently from humans.

Having transgressed the law of unconditional love and untouchability of free will through the aforementioned procedure, the one who had proposed it had to leave the High Council and return to an ordinary Venusian existence. In this case, KLTXG.

Mr Gonzales has disappeared

Patosh and Mary felt at home on the finca "Venusia" and helped Jonathan and his family considerably, so that the seminars ran at full speed, while meanwhile KLTXG (Mary's father) tried to persuade and inspire his daughter for the programme he had created. However, he fell on deaf ears, as Mary wanted to stay on Earth forever, which was out of the question for the High Council.

"I have offered you a compromise that seems reasonable for both of us and you are behaving like a being from a completely different star system that we don't know. You have always been my top priority, but now that I realise painfully how much you dislike, even hate, your father, I have no choice but to take other measures. The balance of space takes precedence over everything, including my own compatible family. I am sorry my daughter." and the telepathic conversation ended with these words. In the end, KLTXG was not sorry because, as mentioned several times, emotions do not exist on Venus or on other planets. But of course KLTXG was not a monster spreading terror and horror from outer space, as is suggested in popular Hollywood films. He used a different method, which was no less painful for his daughter and especially for Patosh. He gave the position of the fugitive daughter to the search personnel with the order to kidnap the dearest thing her companion, Patosh, had, so that a rift would develop between Mary and him. Let's see how far the daughter's stubbornness would go.

The order was carried out one night in typical alien fashion. One of the search personnel transformed his molecular structure into a hot bitch, which lingered and prowled around the finca. Mr Gonzales, a cavalier among males, followed his natural instincts and sniffed his way unnoticed through the large garden of the finca to outside the courtyard, sensing something seductive. There she was, this Jack-Russel beauty, turning poor Mr Gonzales' head and, as anywhere in the life of a living creature here on earth, female seduction can spell doom for any masculine gender. In this case, the meeting of the two dogs did not lead to a "happy ending", as the strange creature turned into something that was not of this world and almost caused a cardiac arrest. A scrawny, grey figure with an oversized head and slanted, elliptical black eyes suddenly stood in front of Gonzi. The white of the eyes was completely missing and Gonzi was in the zombie's grip in a single movement. In the meantime, they were getting ready for dinner at the finca and Mary was helping Martha in the kitchen, while Patosh was talking passionately to Jonathan, who was leading him into a world of verbal unbelievability.

"Where's Gonzi?" Mary asked as she spread the crockery on the table.

"I don't know. He was here earlier. He'll come when he smells the food."

Patosh said unconcernedly and gave Mary a smile. A little later, Martha carried a tray into the dining room, filled with all kinds of food, such as bread, sausage, cheese and eggs.

"Fred, look for Gonzi. He's usually the first one to run between your legs when it comes to food. Where is he?" said Martha, who had become very fond of Gonzi and Fred in particular had become the dog's best friend. Georgette no longer showed the slightest interest in Fred, as she was the head hen in the henhouse, which was now inhabited by over sixty hens and chicks, as well as a cockerel called "Godzilla". Why this name? Because he attacked everything that approached the henhouse and struck fear into everyone. A giant of a rooster with a macho figure and a very colourful plumage. But back to Mr Gonzales. Fred returned half an hour later and his face revealed that Gonzi had not been found and now Patosh was worried. After the second sandwich he decided to look for his dog and meanwhile Mary and Martha cleared the table, Jonathan being unpleasantly persuaded to do his share of the housework, which he groaned at.

"Are you coming with me Fred? You can carry the torch too." Patosh offered and Fred nodded in the affirmative, even though he didn't need such a primitive, earthly utensil.

"I even used the Vybe scanner, but not the slightest trace registered, which is quite unusual. Normally I would have found Gonzi in thirty seconds at most, but so....?"

"But that would mean something terrible could have happened to him. I mean, your Vybe scanner records everything and you can use it to create a hologram. Have you tried it?" asked Patosch, who immediately regretted this question when he saw the look on Fred's face.

"That was the first thing I did." came back in an unmistakable tone.

"Sorry. Let's look outside the finca. Maybe he's just after a hot bitch again and, knowing him, he'll come back exhausted with his tongue hanging out," Patosh said with amusement, hoping to have amused little Fred, who apparently had no sense of humour that night. Fred suddenly stood still as if turned to stone and didn't move a limb.

"Fred, is everything OK? Fred, what's wrong?" Patosh called out, quite irritated by this unusual behaviour. He shook the boy, but he stood coldly and as if cemented to the spot where Gonzi had last been. Patosh began to panic and didn't know what to do. In his desperation, he picked up his mobile phone and called Mary, who answered the call immediately.

"Please come straight away. Something's wrong with Fred."

"Where are you?"

"Outside the grounds, by the gate. Please come quickly," he pleaded in a shaky voice and not seven or eight minutes later they arrived, only to scare Patosh even more, because now Mary, Martha and Jonathan were standing just as stiff and lifeless in the same place as Fred. They were staring at something that only they could see, because Patosh could see nothing.

"What the hell is going on here?" Patosh was now screaming at the top of his lungs and every shake and rattle brought no sign of life. Something was going on here far beyond his imagination and it scared him. Suddenly, however, he also realised that he could no longer move and telepathically heard a creature in front of him reaching out a claw-like hand and touching his forehead.

"Listen to me Patosh. I am a Venusian and I am here to guard you. Have no fear. Our intentions are peaceful and your dog is fine. You won't get him back until you bring Mary to her senses and she communicates with her father again. She must obey his orders, otherwise you will never see Gonzi again and Mary and the others will be forcibly returned to their planet. She has one year and then you must part. Enjoy these twelve months and think of Gonzi. The peace of the Creator be with you."

Gone was he, or she, or it, and Patosh had his freedom of movement again, as did the others.

"What on earth was that?" he shouted at Mary and the others. My dog is gone and is being used to blackmail you. This is surreal. A very bad fucking film..."

"Calm down...."

"No. I'm not calming down. I want to get Mr Gonzales back, otherwise it's going to blow. Do you Martians understand that?"

"Venusians." Fred corrected him.

"I don't give a shit. I've been given the task by this alien, who is apparently your compatriot, to bring you to your senses. So? Make a deal with your father and that's that, because everyone has to be prepared to compromise."

"Patosh please hear us out. If we do that, everything here will have been for nothing and you won't see me again after a year. What is more important to you?"

"How dare you ask me such a question Mary? You come here on this planet and take away a loyal friend I've had by my side for eight years and you want me to give him up? Talk to your father and be reasonable. You are guests here on earth and nothing more, so behave yourself and to your one year I have an answer. I'll come back with you if you want, but bring Gonzi back to me. How can you be offended by a dog? Is that your unconditional love?"

"Nothing will happen to the dog Patosh and you can buy a new one....." said Jonathan, who fully realised his faux pas (foppas for the sake of simplicity) when Patosh tried to grab him by the throat after this remark.

"Forgive me, my friend. That was very insensitive of me. We must find another solution."

Mary didn't know Patosh any more and felt this sudden anger that was transferred to her. Had she lost him because of this mongrel? What kind of strange and illogical creatures are these people who put up with such outbursts because of a creature from the second density (animals). But he looked at her with pleading eyes and she gave in.

"I will speak to my father. I'm only doing this for you. I'll try to get him to agree to three years and maybe we'll think of something during that time. A one-year ultimatum would be too short to accomplish what I came for. Leave it to me Pat. Gonzi will be back with us tomorrow. But now I'm exhausted from all the theatre here."

"Promise me, Mary," Patosh urged.

"I promise."

It was difficult for them to embrace again after this incident, as an icy cold caused a rift between them. Was this the end for them both?

Hard times for Patosh

Mary kept her promise and talked to her father, but they
agreed on an ultimatum of two years. Mary also
understood, after this very detailed conversation, why a
permanent stay on earth had consequences for the future
of this planet and for the entire universe, because the
High Council had much more important plans for her if
she were to take over her father's office one day. She
only realised her responsibility after the conversation
with her father and even an ultimatum, as had now been
agreed, could delay her development by a few more earth
years, which ultimately caused her remorse. A peculiarity
that now gnawed at her nerves in agony. Nothing seemed
simple and logical the longer she stayed on earth and
more and more human traits crept into her. Could she get
rid of them one day? The argument between her and
Patosh was also an eye-opener, as she now realised how
unstable compatibility between partners on earth could
be. Feelings had become too much of a factor in making
a relationship falter and now this had happened, which
neither of them thought possible. Patosh wanted to go
back to Lontzen as soon as he got Mr Gonzales back and
see what was going on. The last experience had simply
left him with too many questions that he had to process
first. This holiday should not have happened like this and
a three-week camping trip turned into an almost four-
month odyssey with an alien outcome. A distance that
could not have been more painful for both of them and
when "Gonzi" suddenly appeared out of nowhere and

sniffed his way through the garden into the yard, the joy of reunion was indescribably great.

Everyone was happy to have him back in their circle, but Mr Gonzales had changed. Whereas he was once a social and affectionate mate, this time he was no longer willing to be stroked without further ado and barked at anyone who tried. He only let Patosh get close to him and nobody else. The days went by without anything really meaningful being achieved and the seminars, which had started out promisingly, were only attended by a few. Patosh decided to head north again on the tenth of April. An EasyJet flight to Brussels took him first to Belgium, where he sat down on the train and finally reached Lontzen after changing trains twice. There was no one to welcome him or pick him up and it was as if he had never lived here before. Everyone seemed strange to him, at least at the small railway station, even though he had just been away for four months. He hoped that he would at least catch Guillaume as a taxi driver, who did his driving in the neighbourhood on the side, but he had no luck. An African from the former Belgian Congo, who had only recently moved to Lontzen, drove Patosh to the small town centre and when the taxi parked in front of the "Goden Mug", he was gripped by sadness and the bitter reality that Camille was no longer there. Although the separation was in itself the best thing that could have happened to him, the old feelings and memories appeared and they couldn't be erased for nothing.

"The rest is for you. Have a nice day." and without a thank you, the taxi driver drove off.

"So Mr Gonzales. Here we are. At home. Let's see what we'll find."

With shaky hands, Patosch put the key in the now rusty lock and, heart pounding, he opened the door, suspecting nothing good and his premonition did not deceive him. Dust, mould, cobwebs and leftover food everywhere he looked and the disgusting stench of rubbish that had not been put out that was beginning to ferment in the kitchen bin. Now, in this moment, he was glad that Camille was gone from his life for good and maybe this holiday had done some good in the end. He had his freedom back. Patosh filled a bowl with water, which at first splashed out of the tap in a brownish colour before it ran clear and pure from the pipes, and handed the water-filled bowl to his dog, who accepted it gratefully.

"We have a lot of work ahead of us, what do you think Mr Gonzales?" and Gonzi barked twice in agreement, happy to find his basket again and stretch out in it after this adventure, which ended up being a strain for both of them.

Patosh didn't hesitate for long and when he found the broom in the room, he got to work. Within two hours, the pub had at least been swept clean and when the door of the "Golden Jug" was found open again, the first curious people came in to see what was going on.

"You here Patosh? What a joy. What a desolate place it was without you!" cried a delighted Gerome, who was followed by old Francine and later by Guillaume, and within a very short time half the village was already standing outside the door to greet Patosh, who had almost been declared dead, as rumours of his demise had spread like wildfire during his absence. They hugged each other and many a tear was shed, because yes, Patosh missed his old guests just as much, as they had once brought a lot of meaning and joy to his life.

Apparently Camille had not let a good word grow about him, because the reports from his old customers annoyed him immensely.

"What a witch. Let her rot in Antwerp for all I care. Anyway, I have to clean this place up and I can't promise when I'll open the Golden Jug again. I also need a waitress and have to find Georgette (not to be confused with the hen). Maybe she would start here again, because she was good."

"We'll all help you. Tell us what to do and we'll do it. Give us a mop or a broom and we're in." Guillaume shouted euphorically and meant it. In fact, they all helped and Patosh couldn't contain his joy.

Three days later, the restaurant was up and running and the "Golden Jug" was fully booked to the last table. Georgette, his old waitress, was informed on the very first day and of course she agreed. Mary, Jonathan, Martha and Fred were quickly forgotten. At least for the moment, because work didn't allow for any distractions and Patosh had a lot to tell the guests when they pressed him to tell them about his adventures. However, he didn't tell them everything, but only the parts that were mentally useful for this audience and it was only when he told them that Mary and the others came back to his mind.

"Two Orval, two Stella and four Heineken!" Georgette shouted from afar.

"Come at once!" Patosh shouted back happily.

"When you were away, we had UFOs like that flying around here again and the military were going in and out of Lontzen pretending it was part of a manoeuvre. Just recently Chinese weather balloons were shot down over Alaska by the Americans and I think they are lying to us. Weather balloons...pah...don't make me laugh. Why would the Chinese risk such a provocation? They have been keeping a low profile all these years, observing the mistakes made by the West. They are clever, the Chinese. No, no. I think they were UFOs," Gerome said half-drunk as he chatted with Francine, Jaques, Guillaume and Patosh at the bar.

"Oh, I don't believe in that shit any more. Anyway, I haven't seen any more UFOs here over our area and you might want to question your mind as to whether you were dealing with a top-secret NATO technical development after all. I just want peace and quiet in this town. Have you forgotten what those masses of UFO fanatics did after all the channels reported on these incidents?

No, no. This town doesn't need any more excitement."
Jaques protested and showed Patosh his empty jug,
indicating that he should refill it.

"What do you mean Patosh? You're not going to say
anything?"

"What do you want me to say? These UFO fanatics aren't
bad for business. I had a full shop here and made good
sales. It's all a show anyway, if you ask me. Maybe even
orchestrated by our governments to screw us like they
usually do."

"I haven't seen it like that yet. There could be something
to it..." Guillaume said, belching, and was met with
approval from his group, who called for more beer, as
they had been standing in the dry for months.

Patosh was starting a new life here and nothing would
ever take him away from Lontzen again. No romance and
no alien invasion.

Domestic bliss had returned to him and Patosh ran his
business better than ever. He happily took "Gonzi" with
him when he went shopping, which of course
strengthened the relationship between man and animal
even more. The mongrel also seemed to have regained
his inner peace, as his aggression towards strangers had
subsided. A new car was bought and this proved to be
useful for the business.

A panel van for daily errands that was not too comfortable, so that any temptation to travel was nipped in the bud from the outset. But all that is well and good is unfortunately not permanent. Camille made trouble and wanted more money, now that she knew how well Patosh was suddenly doing. Letters from a law firm in Antwerp filled the box and Patosh had no choice but to consult his lawyer about the matter, who immediately calmed him down.

"She had already signed an agreement that was notarised and declared legally binding by the court, so she has no claims whatsoever. I wouldn't worry about it."

His lawyer was right about this, but he didn't know the methods of the one wife. When her lawyer also declared the matter unappealable and thus dismissed the case, Camille resorted to other measures. What suddenly goes on in the mind of such a person can only be explained by a sick mind, because she paid a gang known in Antwerp to destroy Patosh's life, starting with his newly purchased car burning to the ground in front of the inn one morning and almost destroying the "Golden Jug" to rubble. If it hadn't been for Mr Gonzales barking his heart out, worse would have happened.

"Who could be so sick as to do such a thing?" wondered the pub's patrons, even though they already knew. However, there was no evidence to establish a connection with Camille. Witnesses only reported a motorbike gang that had never been seen in Lontzen before and who had caused a lot of trouble the night before when they rode through the streets on their loud Harleys, but again there was no proof that they had anything to do with it. The police had been informed and had recorded the damage and that was all they would and could do, which naturally caused disappointment and anger in Lontzen. Patosh even had to reassure his customers when they threatened to pay Camille a private visit in Antwerp.

But then something happened that was no longer acceptable. In a car park next to a supermarket, Patosh was attacked and brutally beaten up by the gang and Mr Gonzales was not spared when he, brave as he was, attacked the attackers and was cowardly stabbed several times. People immediately came to their aid, but for Gonzi all help came too late. He died on the spot and Patosh, who lost a lot of blood, was immediately taken by ambulance to the nearest hospital. As soon as the news of this hyopsy made the rounds in Lontzen, the chase was immediately resumed and the gang, who were taking a break at a motorway service station and thought they were untouchable, were indeed recognised. However, they didn't count on the Lontzeners, because this time witnesses were present and recognised the drivers and their vehicles. Guillaume, Gerome and Jaques blocked the exit of the petrol station and other Lontzners blocked the entrance, so that there was no escape for the eighteen lunatics. Gerome was the first to grab the leader and beat him up with a baseball bat he had brought with him, then the others came along, their knives suddenly twitching, but they didn't reckon on the wrath of the Lontzeners and were literally beaten half to death. Their motorcycles were ablaze, which was of course very dangerous for the petrol station.

"That's for Patosh, Patosh's van and for the death of Mr Gonzales, you bastards!" shouted Gerome as he kicked the beaten gang-leader lying on the ground. It was only now that the police were shaken awake, as the flames could be seen almost as far as Brussels and a large-scale operation was launched. They were all arrested and became famous overnight on radio and television and fortunately, apart from a few broken ribs, nasal bones and destroyed motorbikes, nothing more was recorded at the police station. Of course, the knife attack by some bikers was reported as a criminal offence by the Lontzeners, as was the fact that an attempted murder had been committed on one of their citizen who was fighting for his life in hospital. This time the police had enough material to book Camille as well, because this happened immediately when two bikers revealed the name of the client, which did not justify a lynching campaign.

"You scumbags of police officers can't get your act together. We can pay taxes, but only we as civilians can protect ourselves, no thanks to you assholes!" shouted Guillaume in rage, which earned him another 24 hours in custody. Lontzen had made the headlines again, but this time it didn't attract fanatics, but rather kept them away. A small town fell into disrepute overnight and Patosh became the protagonist of this affair, although he was in fact only a victim. He took Gonzi's death hard and cried for him every day.

After four days he was discharged from hospital and picked up by his friends. He was able to open the pub again and tried to forget what had happened as quickly as possible, although everyone knew that this could never happen. Gonzi's basket was now empty and so was Patosh's heart. Cold and turned to stone in the face of so much evil that inhabited people's hearts, but so did the love and solidarity of true friends who stood by one another in their hour of need. Patosh went one step further and made an appointment to visit the women's prison not far from Antwerp, because he wanted to face Camille and give her the rest. It wasn't enough to burden his life for years with her depression, her laziness, her meanness. Now she wanted him dead as well, and so he felt no more pity for her, especially since her hatred took away the dearest thing he had. Mr Gonzales, who never hurt anyone. No, he could no longer forget and forgive and could no longer see the point of simply accepting and letting such unpleasantness pass. He wanted to look her in the eye and tell her how disgusted he was. He was accompanied by Georgette and Guillaume that day, as he still felt weak. Weak from the attack and from the human disappointment. They took their seats in the waiting room and although she refused the visit, Camille had to go anyway, as she didn't seem to make any friends in prison and especially not among the guards, who quickly recognised who they were dealing with. Handcuffed, she sat behind a pane of glass and stared ahead, waiting. Waiting for the line-up that would bring her shame and embarrassment and as Patosh was led into the visiting room with the others, Camille had a screaming fit that made your blood run cold.

"Yes, look at me you witch. I'm still alive!" Patosh shouted at her and laughed to himself, because it did him good to see her suffer. At last he could take revenge on her and this revenge tasted sweet. So sweet that it made Guillaume and Georgette uneasy and they tried to calm him down, because he couldn't and wouldn't stop.

"You shall stew, do you understand me? I'll wait for you out there when you've served your sentence, because I won't rest and I'll haunt you for the rest of your life until you die. I will see to it that you will sit for a long time and perish here. Greetings also from Mr Gonzales, who is hopefully watching the whole thing from dog heaven. You shall rot and the day will be cursed when our paths once crossed...."

But now the guards had had enough of the screams and led the delusional Camille back to her cell and Patosh was ordered to leave again, as visiting hours had just ended. Sweaty and exhausted, Guillaume and Georgette accompanied the laughing Patosh from the prison back to the car, which was parked in a car park. When they arrived in Lontzen, however, the pub remained closed that day because Patosh was not the same. He felt bad and became ill and when the doctor was called in, he diagnosed a stroke, which was not recognised soon enough and he, Patosh, probably contracted it during the visit.

"He needs urgent rest and must not work for the next few weeks." the doctor ordered, but Patosh would have none of it.

His pub had to keep going, because he owed it to the people of the town. "The Golden Jug" had become a home for many and the lonely were no longer allowed to feel lonely here, because they met there to feel like family. No, that was out of the question for Patosh.

"You stay in bed, my dear. Guillaume and I will run the place, don't worry." Georgette reassured him and waved the doctor to leave so that his patient could finally calm down. No sooner said than done. Gerogette took on the task and Guillaume kept the accounts and the purchases in Patosh's absence. The days passed and Georgette kept her promise. Everyone wanted to be there and find out how their local hero was doing. It was weeks before Patosh finally showed his face in the pub again, even though he was walking with a cane, but he had colour in his face again and could make jokes, which gave the visitors hope, because it would be unthinkable if Patosh were to retire for good. The old good humour quickly returned and the room filled with laughter, cigarette smoke and the smell of hot food and, as always, some had to be asked outside when closing time arrived and no one wanted to leave. The old routine returned and Patosh's mind was freed and cleansed of the old memories. At least for the next few months.

UFO mania

UFO sightings have been reported weekly in America and these reports have spread around the world via social media, resulting in thousands of theories being invented and created again without actually publishing a reasonable explanation for all the sightings. But what the world needs is the truth, because explanations sound like flimsy excuses, especially after the first videos were admitted by the Americans, which should lead to clear evidence that one was dealing with so-called UAPs. The new term for UFO (unidentified flying object) was changed to UAP (unidentified aerial phenomena). The word "phenomena", however, is disturbing insofar as it is supposed to represent what the word means and a phenomena is something "untrue" or "inexplicable". An object, however, is something "tangible" and "solid". The videos showed footage taken by onboard cameras of some US Navy F-18 fighters and as always the footage is blurred and minimalistically small. What is the American government trying to achieve with such publications? Do they really want to prepare mankind for the fact that aliens exist and that they live among us, or is it another hoax to distract us from something else that is currently going on behind hidden curtains? To what extent are people prepared to recognise the truth and able to distinguish between deception and fact? As is so often the case, citizens are the victims of fake news and believe most of what they are told, and this was also the case in

Lontzen, as people in Patosh's pub returned to the topic that they no longer wanted to address. UFOs!

Robert, a farmer from a neighbouring farm, came into the pub one day carrying a square piece of "tin" with him. At first the plate seemed to be just a piece of tin, but Robert told how it suddenly fell from the sky and almost hit him while he was harvesting potatoes. He surmised that it might have fallen from an aeroplane, as you often read these days how often touristic holiday flights lose wheels and other parts, and as his farm is right in the flight path of Brussels and Liège, it can of course happen that you get hit in the skull by a piece like that at some point. However, he realised that this piece of metal was unusually light and that it was covered with strange and inexplicable symbols. In his opinion, it could not have come from an aeroplane.

"You've been looking very deeply into your bottle of Schnapps again, Robert. You're just trying to make a fool of yourself now that you've got this rubbish on the telly every day. Leave it at that!"

"I swear on my Josephine's life that I'm telling the truth. That metal sheet almost hit me and crashed into the field less than two metres from my tractor. Do you think I would joke about something like that, Guillaume? You should know me better than that. Those F-16 fighters were also flying very low again, as were two helicopters that were apparently looking for something. Why here of all places, I ask you?" Robert shrieked, almost in tears.

182

Patosh believed him, but didn't want to give him the slip if he was wrong.

"Let me see the tin." he asked Robert kindly and yes, at first glance he knew that Robert was telling the truth, because Patosh knew the symbols only too well. Jonathan had once explained them to him at the finca when he, Patosh, was still with Mary. What they were doing now, he thought to himself, and without wanting to, he felt this longing for her. The symbols told the story of their origins. The one of the Venusians and no doubt this was proof that more "visitors" had apparently landed nearby. Robert was right about one thing. Why Lontzen in particular? What is so special about this place that aliens would choose such a place to make their presence felt, at least in Western Europe? Was it once again extraterrestrial tourists, or an additional mission of the "High Council"?

"What do you say to that Patosh? Surely it can't have come from an aeroplane?"

"I don't know Robert. These days the military has materials that aren't meant for mere mortals. Maybe it's just titanium or something like that. I've read that super-fast aeroplanes have materials like that to contain or at least resist frictional heat...."

"Hogwash. The symbols say otherwise, or are they just "graffiti" painted by the squadron's mechanics? I know what I'm talking about because my son is a mechanic in the Belgian Air Force and when I showed him this sheet metal, he knew with absolute certainty that it wasn't from

183

one of his aircrafts. He had also never seen such symbols before."

"Why don't you take it to the police? Let them deal with it?" suggested Francine, who had just finished her sixth beer.

"I was going to, but I don't trust our police. It'll just end up in the scrapyard. Maybe I should sell it on the internet...." and as Robert was about to finish this sentence, three strangers entered the pub.
They looked awkward and lost and when they finally sat down at a table, Georgette tried to take their order. But they spoke in a language that made no sense and sounded more like a clacking sound without any actual words that could be categorised as a foreign language.

"Are you pulling my leg?" protested Georgette, who didn't find it funny. Then, finally, one of the guests took a device out of his pocket that looked familiar to Patosh. It was a Vybe scanner and seconds later he spoke in perfect French and placed the order.

"We would like something to eat and drink. On the table outside you offer the soup of the day and half a chicken. We'd like three of that and three beers." said the older of the three.

"And which beer? Stella, Orval or Heineken?"

"One of each. We'll try out which one we like best."

"Fine by me," said Georgette, annoyed.

She threw the note to Patosh and shook her head, saying, "Holidaymakers. Why don't they drive or fly to Ibiza?"

"I don't know. Let me do it. I'll take these three birds."

"Whatever you say boss."

Patosh asked Robert to leave him the tray because he wanted to try something. When the drinks were ready to be served on a tray, Patosh took the drinks to the three strange guests. The tray, however, was nothing more than the flat piece of tin that Robert had brought and the symbols appeared on the top for everyone to see.

"So gentlemen, here are your beers. Who gets what?" Patosh asked hypocritically, holding the tray, or in this case the tin, in such a way that it drew the attention of the three men to them.

"I get the jug with the Stella," said the eldest, not taking his eyes off the plate.

"Then I get the Orval and my friend here gets the Heineken." The centre one called out and he too stared at the plate.

"That's an interesting tray you've got there." asked the older man.

"Do you think so?"

"Yes, indeed. Is it for sale?"

"That depends. If you can explain the meaning of the symbols to me, then this tray is yours for, say, five hundred euros."

"Five hundred euros? Quite a hefty price if you ask me. Where did you get it?"

"It was found in a field and brought to me by the gentleman standing there. Do you know what these symbols mean?" Patosh asked, almost demanding. The older of the three just looked at him kindly and said:

"No. Unfortunately not. But I still find it very interesting."

"It means: We come from Venus and are on a peaceful mission. Anyone who gives us their help on this planet will be richly rewarded." Patosh said this in a whisper so that the other guests couldn't hear, and he astonished the three guests with what he said.

"How do you know what's on the disc?" the older man asked more forcefully.

"I've had contact with the Venusians and I know that you are. Your Vybe scanner gave you away. Are you on holiday here or are you looking for someone?"

"Can we talk somewhere else? We attract the attention of the guests. We don't want that."

"Good, after dinner. Which hotel are you staying at?"

"Hotel? We've only just arrived and had to land in the river to escape your primitive fighters. There are already two of our spaceships lying there, we realised. One of them completely unusable. Do you know the owners?"

"Too many questions. One thing at a time. So stay here and I'll join you later. Most of them will be leaving in an hour, as they still have to work..."

"Work? Most of them are blotto blue. Skunk drunk if you ask me."

"Well, what can I say? To each his own, right? So, stay here and we'll talk some more. " Patosh walked back to the bar and pretended it was nothing special, but he was no good at lying.

"So, what are they?" asked Georgette.

"Holidaymakers from Switzerland."

"Oh, that's why I couldn't understand them so well. But you've been talking to them for a while."

"What's it to you? I'm trying to be a friendly landlord, is that wrong?" Patosh shouted at Georgette, who was now looking at him in horror.

"No, no. I only asked. I was just asking."

"You'd better bring them the food before it gets cold and quickly," Patosh ordered in no uncertain terms. Two hours later, most of the guests left the pub, leaving Francine, Gerome and Guillaume behind. But they sat at the usual regulars' table in a far corner. Patosh brought a bottle of pastis to the three strangers' table and poured them each a glass.

"On the house, gentlemen." he said kindly, but curious about what he was about to learn. He grabbed a chair and sat down.

"So? Out with it. What are you doing here?"

"We're just here on holiday. We're not looking for anyone. We had planned two of your days. We wanted to buy coffee, cheese and beer and then get back. It's not our first trip here on earth, but your unfriendly behaviour is really getting on our nerves. Always these chases and they usually end well for us. But we have also lost some of our own in this way and all we want to do is enjoy the diversity of this planet. You humans are really still very primitive in your attitude and instead of making progress, you are regressing. Not much longer and you will belong to a dying species. The universe won't be watching you for much longer and will take appropriate measures, but that shouldn't be our problem. Can you help us with the shopping? We pay well."

"Of course. I'll even make you a lucrative proposition. In future, you tell me exactly what you need before you get here and I'll get it for you. For an extra charge, of course.

I can also rent you rooms for the duration of your stay. What do you say to that?"

"Tempting. It's a matter of price."

"You have your Vybe scanner. It shouldn't be a problem for you to make enough money."

"That's not the point, my good man. We must not further damage your character with money and other things, for you are already so afflicted with this disease that further acceleration will rid this earth of your kin forever."

"What disease are you talking about, man?"

"Greed and insatiability."

"I must be allowed to live from something. It's just a business. You need coffee and whatnot and I'll get it for you. You don't need to clatter around the supermarket like a couple of excited chickens. You'll only attract curious glances. Send me your orders telepathically or whatever and I'll do the shopping for you. In the meantime, you can spend the night at my place. I have rooms available. One hand washes the other. Well? How about it?"

"Agreed. You do the shopping and we'll wait in our rooms."

"So what do you need?"

"A tonne of coffee. The same in cheese. One thousand litres of beer and six hundred kilos of bananas..."

"Wait a minute. You're joking. You can't fit all that in your spaceship and it'll take you more than two days."

"Exactly. I just wanted to see how long it would take you to realise this joke. Do you seriously think we Venusians need such earthly food?"

"What the hell...." cursed Patosh, who saw a huge chance vanishing to make a deal here. Had he really become so naive as to believe that these beings had come here to make purchases? What on earth had got into him? Jonathan, Martha and Fred were holidaymakers, but these were something else. Not holidaymakers and they've come for something completely different and Patosh won't like what the reason is.

"Then what do you want?" Patosh asked more forcefully.

"Your help. Mary, Jonathan, Martha and Fred have to go back. That's what they call themselves here on this planet, isn't it? Mary has to go back because she has to take her father's place and the other three because they know too much. With Mary as head of the High Council, maybe your planet can still be saved, because she wants it. Please don't misunderstand me. We all want it, but she is special because she took such a risk and upset the balance of the universe with her action.

That is why the things that are happening on this earth right now are happening. You no longer understand the connections that are happening around you. Her appearance has alerted the aliens, who are not exactly friendly and helpful. They feel threatened and are manipulating your earthly leaders with more power and possessions even more so that all morality and humanity will soon disappear. These aliens are from the Orion layer. They are not known for helping planets. Quite the opposite. Unfortunately, they also have the same abilities as we do, at least for the most part, and are part of the balance. Necessary to influence the decisions of all beings between good and evil. We then choose our own destiny, but at this moment a negative change is happening on your planet, caused by Mary's appearance becoming known. She has to go back, because here she can only cause more damage. From Venus, however, she can take the necessary steps...."

"If she's so powerful, why can't she just take out this Orion clan?"

"Because that's not how it works Patosh. May I call you Patosh? For thousands and thousands of years, this has been the course of events in our universe and you humans are in need of enlightenment. We have tried to do this every time and have been just as successful. In the beginning. But we left your planet because we had to fight a war ourselves and it took a long time. When we came back, our presence was no longer wanted. Our knowledge and our technologies were no longer needed.

We had a lot to learn ourselves at that time, when we
realised that the war between the Orion group and us was
just a distraction. During this time of our absence, they
settled on Earth and manipulated the minds of the people
to such an extent that it was irreparably damaged. A pity
in itself. You must bring Mary to her senses Patosh. We
don't want to use unnecessary measures that contradict
our principles, but your planet and our balance are on the
brink of an Abyss that will have consequences far beyond
our imagination. Will you help us?" The eldest of the
three said this with an unmistakable facial expression,
leaving no doubt in his mission. Patosh thought about it
and believed the Venusian's words, because there was
one thing they couldn't do. Lie. Their DNA didn't allow
it, as they were several layers more advanced than the
Earthlings.

"You guys repeat yourselves so often. Yes, we humans
are backward…blah, blah…The Orions are coming
…blah, blah! How am I supposed to do that? I don't even
know where she is and we didn't exactly part on friendly
terms...."

"She longs for you. She thinks about you every day
Patosh, because you have also infected her mind with
your earthly habits. It's not even your fault, because this
planet has such a power to cast a spell over every being
and therefore we must not leave it in the hands of evil.
We must do everything we can to avoid it. We know
where she and the other three are, because her father took

the grave step of interfering with his daughter's free will and thus gave up his position as head of the High Council, because this step was a forbidden one. But he did so for noble reasons. His daughter must take his place."

"OK. I will help you, because I also long for her. Give me the details of her whereabouts and I'll be on my way. What is your name anyway?"

"Our names don't matter, because they would only be for a short time. The use of our identifier is also not for your knowledge and you are not ready to understand it. We thank you for this promise. The metal plate that you are holding in your hands as a tray comes from our "spaceship" as you call it. We dropped it on purpose to draw your attention to our landing. I see now that it was not in vain. Be assured of our gratitude Patosh. We are leaving you now, but before we go we will give you the Vybe Scanner. I don't have to explain to you how to use it and what will happen if you misuse it to your advantage."

"You don't have to. I know all about it, thanks to Mary and Jonathan."

"Good, if you fulfil your mission, you will know your reward."

And with those words, the three strangers left the pub and disappeared forever.

For Patosh, it was not a dream, but a bitter reality. Why HE? he asked himself but who knew the path of one`s own destiny. He would see Mary again and that alone was worth the mission.

The trail

Patosh had all the information he needed to at least set a target and to his great surprise the trail led to London and not Spain as first thought. He also remembered Mary telling him when they first met what a good house she came from and that her father was a lord. Patosh wondered to himself why he didn't press her to ask when they were still together why she was using such a lie as a Venusian, as it contradicted her etiquette. Had the influence of this planet taken over from her in the early stages, or had she simply used this lie voluntarily and for self-protection? He, Patosh, had never spoken to her or asked her about it again. Perhaps he now had the opportunity to find out more, as he booked a British Airways flight from Brussels to London Heathrow for the next day. Georgette was put in charge of the pub in his absence, which she was only too happy to do. She had always enjoyed playing the boss, even if the role didn't suit her. However, he could trust her unconditionally and he knew that, because in the end Georgette had her heart in the right place. She was honest and believed in God and her fear of ending up in hell had paranoid characteristics. So Patosh took the train to Brussels, where he travelled on to the airport on a feeder tram. His head was threatening to burst with thousands of questions tormenting him as he took the corridor to the flight counter to get checked in and without even giving him a glance, the lady behind the counter handed him his boarding pass and passport.

Patosh ignored the icy and inhuman coldness that was becoming more and more widespread these days and wondered why people had become like this. He had already noticed this change a few years ago and he thought of the words of the one older Venusian who had visited him in the pub the day before. "....This is why things are happening on this earth right now. You no longer understand the connections that are happening around you....". Patosh couldn't get these words out of his head and yes, people behave like they're being remote-controlled. Like robots who only live to work and survive for a meagre wage, while the rich get richer and richer. Is this the reason for this change? For this dissatisfaction? Nobody goes out without holding their smartphone in their hand and nobody communicates directly with each other anymore, but only digitally. Wherever Patosh looked, people around him were staring at this bewitching, square device they called a mobile phone, regardless of whether they were sitting, standing or walking. Everyone was busy with it or with the iPad they had brought with them and woe betide you if you were approached from the side by a stranger. Yes, this world has become cold, lifeless and already doomed to die. His thoughts were interrupted by the sudden loudspeaker announcement that his flight to Heathorw was delayed by another hour. Patosh took this opportunity to treat himself to a sandwhich and a beer in one of the bars inside the terminal.

"That'll be 18 euros," said the barman, which caused Patosh to short of breath. Eighteen euros. For that, his guests would get a whole menu and several beers, but this isn't Lontzen, it's Brussels Airport. Horrified, Patosh paid the requested amount and chose a seat behind a large glass vestibule with a view of the airfield, where he could watch the planes taking off and landing. "I wonder where they're going?" he asked himself. What drives people to sit like ants in these flying metal and aluminium tubes and shoot through the sky at almost a thousand kilometres per hour? The whole terminal is full of them and languages he had never heard before envelop Patosh. People from all countries, consisting of men, women and screaming children, wandered around looking for their "gate". The hustle and bustle was driving him mad, so mad that he ordered another beer, no matter how much it cost, just to block out the noise. The hour dragged on like chewing gum and finally the passengers for the flight to Heathrow were called to make their way to Gate 35, as the embarking had already begun. Patosh had an aisle seat, which suited him just fine. He would use this short flight to take a nap, but this thought was short lived as a woman woke him up and asked him to make room so she could sit in the window seat with her well-bodied husband. What the heck. It was only a short flight, and when the B737 finally took off and the landing gear retracted, Patosh counted the minutes as the flight turned into a nightmare. Not because of the strong turbulence, but because of the marital quarrel that developed next to him and he had to listen to the curses of these quarrelling birds. He, Patosh, started to laugh, however, as he could not have taken these jokes put upon him from the universe and simply accepted them. How unimportant everything suddenly seemed to him and how stupid people were to make their lives a living hell over trifles, like the two sitting next to him. Trivialities to prove who had the bigger ego or penis and, in the case of the wife, the greater raison d'être. His laughter became so loud that the couple stopped arguing and wordlessly turned their attention to him. Both looked at each other and shrugged their shoulders and the flight continued quietly.

"Ladies and gentlemen, this is the captain speaking. We have begun our approach to Heathrow and will land in about twenty minutes. The weather, as you can already see from the window, is rainy and gusty, so the approach could be a little bumpy. I would therefore ask you to keep your seatbelts fastened and follow the instructions of our cabin crew. Have a nice day at London Heathrow and thank you for travelling with British Airways."

Patosh hadn't taken a suitcase with him, just one of those cheap shoulder bags. That way he would save time and walk straight to the taxi rank or one of the many bus connection counters. It all depends on the price, because London is not cheap and certainly not the airport. The plane touched down hard and yes, the captain was right because it was quite gusty during the approach and Patosh couldn't help but grin every time the woman sitting at the window shrieked loudly as soon as the plane made a hop. However, the husband behaved like a gentleman and lovingly comforted her and encouraged her. Was there really any humanity left and perhaps not all people had become robots after all? Patosh, who had come to like the chubby man next to him, was pleased.

But the nightmare was not over just yet, because as soon as the plane came to a standstill at the gate, all the passengers jumped up and behaved as if they had to evacuate the plane, even though there was no emergency. Everyone tore their luggage from the overhead bin and rucksacks and falling bags threatened to crush them. The couple next to Patosh also urged him to finally stand up so that they could get out, even though they had dozens of passengers in front of them who were behaving as if they were involved in a Viking battle. With a lot of pushing and shoving, he finally got out of this alluminium tube and followed the herd to the exit, whose passage was interrupted by passport control.

"What is the purpose of the journey? How long will you be in England, ect, ect..." and after all the answers Patosh got his passport back. By now annoyed and soaked with sweat, he looked for a bus counter where a queue of people was already waiting. Where did he have to go anyway? Connington on the Shyre was written on the description, but the lady behind the counter knew nothing about it.

"I can't do anything with this information sir, can't you give me some more details? North, south, east or west? Then I could at least point you in an approximate direction." But Patosh couldn't do that and had no choice but to apologise, take out his smartphone and ask Google.

But Google didn't know either and he, Patosh, was now worried. What to do? Then it came to him as sudden as a flash. He had the Vybe scanner, which didn't stand out anywhere because this alien device couldn't be found by others, at least not through earthly security checks. The Vybe scanner spat out the answer within seconds, in the form of a display replay. The destination was east of Northampton, not far from Bedford, and the better airport would have been Luton rather than Heathrow, which annoyed Patosh no end. At least he now had a direction and ran back to the bus counter.

"To Bedford please, direct if possible."

"Unfortunately, you'll have to change at either Luton or Northampton. I would suggest Luton. It's much shorter and cheaper."

"Luton then, please."

"That's £35 sir. How would you like to pay?"

"By credit card. And that £35 is to Bedford?"

"Indeed sir. As far as Bedford. Here's your ticket, stand 13. The bus will show Luton. In Luton, take the bus to Bedford from station 4. Have a good journey."

Patosh thanked the friendly lady and was visibly pleased to have found a solution. In Bedford, he would first stay in a hotel to prepare for the reunion, as his heart was already beating with excitement when he left his pub in Lontzen. How would she react when he suddenly stood in front of her unannounced? Would she be happy or reject him?

How would he react when he saw her again and how would he react if, in the worst case, she no longer wanted to see him? He boarded the bus to Luton, which then made its leisurely way along the M4 to the northbound feeder. The bus was full to the last seat, but this time there was a slim, older gentleman sitting next to him, who didn't spread out and sucked the air out of him like the fat man on the aeroplane before. Patosh looked out of the window and was fascinated by the vehicles travelling on the wrong side of the road. It was now evening, but there was still enough light as it was summer and he completely forgot why he was actually on the bus as he read the names on the road signs, which sounded old and historic. The hum of the engine and the swinging motion made him tired, but he was also hungry and thirsty. It would have to wait until Bedford, he thought to himself, hoping that the prices there were at least a little more civilised. Time flew by and he reached Luton. "Stand 4, stand 4..." Patosh muttered to himself and when he found the bus stand, he was startled. An elderly woman was waiting, sitting on a bench, and she had a dog with her that looked just like Mr Gonzales. He almost shouted "Gonzi" with joy, but reality caught up with him and he sadly caught himself, smiling at the old lady who was lovingly looking after her little darling. The bus arrived and before anyone was allowed to get on, those travelling to Luton had to get off first. At last the journey continued and night fell. In Bedford, the bus stopped at a regular bus stop.

This was the final station in Bedford and because the "gods" or the "aliens" meant well for Patosh, a hotel stood directly on the other side of the road called "The Red Lion Hotel" and without any further hesitation he initially checked in for two nights. A hot shower followed and although he was very tired, he went down to the lobby, where he asked if he could get something to eat in the hotel's own pub, which the friendly hotel owner confirmed with a yes. Strange. Another friendly human and not a robot at all, he thought to himself secretly. Are the robots only to be found on the mainland? Perhaps this alien was not quite right in his assumption and he, Patosh, should only believe what he experienced himself. He took a seat at a table, but what he didn't know was that you weren't served in England. You had to place your order at the counter yourself and after a quick glance at the menu, he ordered a portion of fish and chips and a pint of dark ale. He gratefully took his first sip and no matter how warm the beer was, it quenched his thirst with its unmistakable bitter, malty flavour. He also enjoyed the fish fried in beer batter and his soul was back on cloud nine. Tomorrow would be another day and after a hearty English breakfast, he would set off to look for Mary, for now it was time to get rid of all the stress from this short but devilish journey. After the second beer, Patosh's inner life calmed down again and the landlord, who was also the hotel owner, asked Patosh about his well-being. A little chat ensued, prompting the landlord to sit at the same table when he learnt that Patosh was a fellow pub owner.

They had a good chat about the current difficulties of being a restaurateur, imposed by the EU and also by their own government, which had caused prices to skyrocket and which was noticeable in the number of customers visiting. A few beers later, the landlord asked what the real reason for the visit to Bedford was, as this town was not exactly a tourist attraction. Patosh explained the reason and surprised the landlord when he mentioned the name Connington on the Shyre in passing.

"You're not going to visit the old lord, are you? You're too late. He died six months ago and left everything to his eccentric daughter. Her name is Mary. Good luck, then, my lord."

"Is it easy to get there?" Patosh asked cautiously.

"Well, yes. It's not difficult, but only by taxi or in your own car. There's definitely no bus driving there. I can drive you, but not before breakfast," offered the landlord.

"It would never occur to me to bother you with such a favour. No, no, I'll take a taxi..."

"Oh, nonsense. We're colleagues. I'm happy to help. You'd just have to come back yourself."

Touched by the willingness to help, Patosh agreed and they arranged to meet at eleven in the morning the next day. And so it happened. After a very rich and greasy breakfast, the two of them set off for Connington on the Shyre.

The landlord, whose name was William, drove an old Land Rover pick-up and turned the journey into an adventure, because Patosh would have expected anything but a journey that took them for kilometres along very poorly used country lanes and muddy paths. What he saw before him at the end of the ride was anything but a castle or chalet worthy of a lord, but rather a dilapidated ruin of an oversized farm. William noticed the shocked look on his Belgian guild brother's face and almost laughed.

"So, here we are. This is Connington on the Shyre. Ancient English nobility. Impoverished but respected...."

"Mitchell is not exactly a noble name!"

"No. His lordship was also called Archibald, Basil Wellington. A distant relative of the real Wellington. His daughter, Mary, was not allowed to take the name, however, as she was conceived, how shall I put it, out of wedlock. Her mother, Anne Mitchell, was one of several maidservants when this house was still doing well. His Lordship, however, had a very expensive passion. Gambling, and this is what was left of it. Well, I must be on my way. A taxi will be difficult to get here. If there's no other way, just give me a call."

"First of all, thank you very much for your efforts," Patosh said, hardly believing what he saw before him. Patosh hadn't seen Mary for three years and much has been forgotten since their last reunion. But not her face.

Those eyes that were deep and full of life and could mesmerise anyone. He turned round once more and saw the Land Rover drive away and just at that moment, a dog barked out of the house. It must not have been a big dog, because its bark was not deep. It was more like from a border terrier or a boxer. Patosh knew that much, because dogs had always been his friends. But what surpassed the barking was his racing heartbeat, which seemed to be out of control. Slowly and with unsteady steps, he walked to the old, rusty iron gate. A brass bell tarnished with pattina hung from a poorly attached bracket and a chain invited him to pull on it. Now the barking became even louder and after what seemed like an eternity, the door to the main house, which was also in need of intensive restoration, opened, but the woman who emerged from the door was not Mary.

"What do you want?" called an old voice that must have been through several litres of whisky and umpteen cigarettes, because this lady must have been around 65 and not in the best of health."

"Good afternoon, madam. My name is Patrick van de Brog and I would like to speak to Mrs Mary Mitchell. I've come a long way..."

"You do, I'm Mary Mitchell. What can I do for you young man?"

Patrick had to organise his thoughts for a moment, because the woman standing in front of him was not his Mary.

Not the one he knew, missed and still loved. This woman was old, dressed in black and, to put it modestly, rather unkempt. He still tried to keep his composure and wondered if the Venusians had played a joke on him when they gave him this address, but Venusians don't usually have a sense of humour, especially not if their stay on Earth didn't last several months, because only then did the earthly energies kick in and influence these beings considerably.

"I don't want to be rude, Mrs Mitchel, but the Mary I knew was in her early forties. Here, I have a photo of her in my wallet, perhaps you could take a look at it. Maybe you know this woman...."

"I don't know you young man and I would advise you to get out of here. Not even here in this shitt- hole can you get away from peddlers and dodgy salesmen, make sure you get away or I'll call my nephew. He's the constable in Bedford...."

"But Madame, I can assure you..."

"Behold. A Frenchman. That's all I need..."

"I'm Belgian!" Patosh shouted back energetically.

"Not much better. The same bunch. All you can do is blabber on and take women's knickers off with your drivel. Get out of here."

"Fine, I'll go. Could you at least call me a taxi? My driver has already left and I don't know how to get back into town."

"There's no taxi coming here, you Belgian. Who drove you here anyway?"

"William. The landlord of the Red Lion Hotel." Patosh replied desperately, already suspecting the worst. He was wearing the wrong shoes for a long walk and it looked like rain.

"William? That cut-throat. He owes me money for three geese, five pounds of home-made bacon, twenty pounds of potatoes and five gallons of cider. If you see him, tell him he should be ashamed of ripping off an old woman like that. He owes me 348 pounds sterling and 36 pence. Now get on your way. It's only eight miles and it looks like a thunderstorm."

"What if I pay you the bill. I'll give you an even £400 sterling, madam, if you'll just listen to me and maybe we can find a way for me to reach Bedford by car or by any other reasonable means."

"Have you got the money with you?" screeched the old woman, who had nothing noble about her, even if she was the bastard of a lord.

"I have it here, with me. There, let me show you."

Patosh took out his wallet, which was filled with freshly produced hundred pound notes that he had made the day before with the Vybe scanner, and waved the notes at the old woman.

"I'll open the gate. You'll have to push a little harder, because the hinges aren't what they used to be. Wait a minute..."

Patosch heard the whirring of an elctric door opener and with concentrated strength he opened one of the gates, which was really difficult to open as the frame dragged along the poorly paved floor. Patosh approached the front door with cautious steps and suddenly there was this dog that he had noticed at the bus stop in Luton and who looked exactly like Mr Gonzales. Now he suspected that something was wrong with this woman and, looking at her more penetratingly, he recognised her exactly as the old lady from the bus stop in Luton.

"I saw you in Luton. At the bus stop at the airport...."

"You're suffering from halucinations, young man. Give me the money, otherwise there'll be no tea. You look like you could do with a cuppa."

"I do indeed," Patosh replied, confused.

Again he froze in astonishment as he entered the interior of the house, for it completely contradicted the exterior appearance of the building.

Expensive Persian carpets lay on the floor, everything was gleaming and every suit of armour standing at every corner was polished. Swords and shields hung over an oversized fireplace and valuable paintings hung on the walls. Yes. This is what a lord's residence looks like. Wood and marble, as well as brass and pewter, largely outshone the material from which the interior of this building was constructed. Noble polish odours and expensive leather armchairs convinced everyone who entered this house of its British nobility. But Mary was only the lord's bastard daughter. Was she the sole heir? Patosh remembered only too well how much "his Mary" fancied "Daddy". But this lady didn't exactly look like she had another ten years to live and she didn't look like a gothic punk either. Meanwhile, the dog made himself known to Patosh and wagged his tail happily, as if he wanted to tell him a story. Patosh really missed his Mr Gonzales and this one looked like his doppelganger. Suddenly Patosh's breath caught in his throat as he stroked the dog's head and noticed a scar running behind his left ear. "Gonzi" had exactly the same scar in the same place. This could never be a coincidence, but Patosh's inner voice urged him to keep his composure. It was already hard enough to gain entry to this house.

"What's your favourite tea? Darjeling? Ear Grey? Orange Pekoe?" asked the "Lady in Black" and yes, Uriah Heep probably couldn't have written this song more aptly, because the lyric fit like a glove. Mystical and impenetrable, she moved her slender, still flexible body towards what appeared to be the kitchen.

"I don't really drink tea, but a darjeling would be nice, madam." Patosh called to her from behind.

"How much sugar? Milk or lemon?"

"None of the above. Pure as from the kettle please."

"A minimalist. Like me, I like that. But a few shortbread biscuits would do you good after all that travelling."

"I've already had a very big breakfast. It's still a bit heavy in my stomach, madam."

"Well then, I know a remedy that would help. A good glass of sherry!" she shouted loudly from the kitchen. Patosh chose a leather armchair to sit down in.

"I wouldn't mind that." he shouted back and looked around again. Maybe he would find something that could lead to a clue, like the scar on the dog's head. On the east-facing wall hung a large painting, probably of "Daddy", as it depicted an officer of the British Army. This figure stood proudly with medals on his left breast, creating a colonial atmosphere reminiscent of Queen Victoria's time. However, the red skirt of the uniform deceived the observer, as this soldier was clearly wearing a Rolex watch on his left wrist. There were no such watches in Victoria's time, so it could only be Mary's "earthly" father, which led to even more confusion. His Mary already had a father. He was the head of the High Council on Venus.

How did Mary come to tell him, Patosh, about this "daddy" back then? Did she have to do that to avoid being recognised as an alien? And why did she choose these people in particular? Patosh had one more attempt to add to the confusion before the old lady returned from the kitchen.

"Mr Gonzales. Come to me. Yes, come to me, my dearest," he whispered softly. So softly that he couldn't be heard, but the dog didn't react. It remained lying in its basket and only the food bowl at its side revealed its name. "HARRY" was written large and unmistakably. Patosh leaned back, almost relieved, because if "Gonzi" had responded to his call, it would have been proof enough that his suspicions had not yet been fully confirmed. Venusians could change their appearance molecularly and it would have been easy for Mary to do so. Now it was time to play the game and perhaps this old woman was telling nothing but the truth, because the whole town of Bedford apparently knew her. A name like WELLINGTON would have no connection at all to any aliens in this regard, because that would be like saying the Queen was a reptile. Perhaps his Mary, who bore the identifier KLTXK on Venus, although these letters did not exist there and only served earthly purposes in her megalomania to save the world, had simply stolen this identity. This was not logical. Venusians don't do that. He had been told plenty of times, even at the finca in Spain. Patosh couldn't make sense of this whole story, but now he had been sent here by the very beings who should know better. Had to know better.

"So, here comes the tea young man." she called out, friendly and smiling. Quite the opposite of what she had been before.

"Thank you."

"So you're from Belgium and you're looking for a lady who happens to be called Mary Mitchell. That's strange. And who gave you this address anyway? No one has been coming to visit here for ages. Not even when my father was still alive, may he rest in peace. That's the way people are. If you're in a bad financial situation, you're forgotten. In the end, there's not a single person who turns out to be a friend. Father died six months ago. Pneumonia. He had to repair the fence in the rain. Our staff had left the sinking ship years ago, if you know what I mean, so now we have to do all the work ourselves. The pension just about keeps us afloat and the sales of the farm, consisting of potatoes, cider and other things, provide an additional source of income to cover various costs. As you can see, Mr Van de Brog, I am only allowed to live here because my father passed on the entire estate to my daughter. I am a Mitchell and not a Wellington for reasons which, knowing William, you have already learnt. My father was not the favourite of the Wellington clan, rather the black sheep. What you see here is only a fraction of the fortune of that noble name and he, Archibald Basil Wellington, got the smallest share of it, which was in the order of 5000 acres of land. However, father had gambled away most of it. We only have 2000 acres left and part of it is leased...

"You mentioned your daughter. Why did she inherit everything and not you? The biological daughter, even if not from marital conception." Patosh asked curiously.

"We had agreed that at the time. Father initially wanted to leave everything to me, but I persuaded him that that would be stupid. Paying inheritance tax twice made no sense, because if I died as sole heir, my daughter would have to pay it again. I know what you're asking Mr Van de Brog. Didn't my father have any children from his marriage to Jane? That was his wife's name. No, his marriage was childless, partly because Jane couldn't have children. Allegedly hereditary. So my father gave it a shot with my mother, since he was , never the less, a womaniser, if you know what I mean. My mum, Ashley, liked him because he was always friendly to the staff, unlike Jane, and so one day what had to happen, happened. Mum and Dad fell in love but had to keep it a secret. The scandal was great when Jane found out who the father of one of the maids' children was. Father tried to transfer the family name and title to me after the divorce, but this is not allowed in Great Britain. It's a law from the Middle Ages that still applies today, so I'm glad that he at least loved us enough to stand by us so that we didn't end up on the streets."

"So your daughter is also a Mitchell."

"Yes, Roselyn Margereth Mitchell. That's my angel's name."

"Does she live far away from you? I think she's a great help with such a large household."

"She lives here. With me. She came back from Spain about three years ago, heartbroken. I didn't recognise her. Men are all the same and I know what I'm talking about."

"I'm very sorry about that Mrs Mitchell. I try to be a good man, but in these times it's getting harder and harder. I left my wife not so long ago too. She stopped loving me after the death of our son, which happened after he was born. We lived together for years, but in the end the only thing that helped was separation. As life sometimes goes. And what about your husband? Roselyn's father?"

"He ran away. That scoundrel from Aberdeen, but my father had warned me about the good-for-nothing. He doesn't even want to see his daughter. Roselyn doesn't know her father."

Patosh tried to build up a picture of all the family relationships laid out here, but how could aliens fit into all the drama? Without a doubt, his KLTXK (Mary) was an alien, as she had abilities that no normal human possessed, and the address he was given was this one. Connington on the Shyre. What exactly was going on here and as he was still trying to count one and one together, the door of the house opened and a loud, cheerful voice rang out.

"Hi MUM. I'm back. Oh, there's tea...."

And the world stood still

How does a person react when a ghost suddenly appears in front of him or her? A long-lost, beloved ghost who was thought to have disappeared forever and then suddenly appears out of nowhere? That's what happened to Patosh, because standing in front of him was "Mary", who in this case was called Roselyn. He slowly put down his cup of tea and struggled to get up from the armchair as his legs trembled at the sight. Repressing is easy, forgetting is all the harder, but even Roselyn, who once called herself Mary, froze when she saw him and turned pale as chalk. The old woman, meanwhile, watched this spectacle from the leather sofa and her expression betrayed tense confusion, as thousands of questions arose in her brain at that moment, like a matrix. As we all know, it doesn't take long for a woman to understand what pain means, especially when it's the pain of love. This guest who was drinking her tea must be the heartbreaker who was causing her Roselyn so much grief. However, she was also an experienced woman who could recognize that he was also suffering and therefore could not have been a heartbreaker, but both were just victims of unfortunate circumstances.

"Pat," Roselyn called softly and she struggled inwardly not to show any weakness, proud as she once was. Her human side, since she had left Venus, was showing itself in an extremely pronounced way.

215

"Mary...I'm sorry....Roselyn...." stuttered Patosh, not as strong as one would expect from a man such as he was, for his eyes moistened reddishly.

He walked slowly towards her and took her hands. They looked at each other for a long time until she, too, became weak, shed tears of joy and sorrow and embraced him passionately. Old Mary couldn't have had a better OPERA in front of her, because she didn't let the two of them disturb her, continued to drink her tea and also smiled with delight. Her Roselyn had her Patosh back and it seemed that he had his Roselyn. But why did he ask for a Mary Mitchell when he arrived and not for a Roselyn? This needed a good explanation.

"You have no idea how happy I am to see you again," Patosh said, hugging her tightly once more.

"What are you doing here?" Roselyn asked, equally happy but puzzled.

"A long story, but we can't talk here."

"Where are you staying?"

"The Red Lion Hotel."

"You can't stay there. William is no friend of the family. He bankrupted my grandfather. You're moving here and we can talk in peace. Do you still have your things there?"

"Yes. I still have to pay my bill."

"But I'm not giving back the 400 pounds," said the old woman with a laugh.

Whereupon Patosh also had to laugh.

"Let's go straight there and get it done Pat."

Without asking any further questions, Patosh just nodded and thanked the old lady for her hospitality.

"We'll see each other again soon. Hurry up. I'm going to prepare a leg of lamb, so don't keep me waiting too long." she said kindly and also happy to see her Roselyn smiling again. Roselyn was driving an old Mercedes G model that must have once done military service for some army, for the green paint was dull and the spartan interior bore witness to that very service. A CB radio holder and radio set hung in the middle, giving the whole thing a somewhat exciting atmosphere.

"Interesting car."

"Daddy loved this car. He always drove it to the hunt...."

"That's what I don't quite understand. What should I call you anyway? Roselyn or still Mary?"

"Just call me Rose and yes. It's a very long story, but it will have to wait. The best time to tell you is after dinner when MUM retires. She can't know anything or her heart will break. Anyway, you are here and that makes me so happy. You hardly changed after these three years."

"You have. You've become prettier and not so punky," Patosh said with a laugh.

Patosh paid William his bill and thanked him for his kind welcome and for the ride to Connington on the Shyre. He tried not to show the bitter aftertaste that arose in him as he shook William's hand in farewell.

"Always glad to see you again, sir." He only said. Then the journey went back to the residence that once belonged to the Wellington clan and the promised thunderstorm that old Mary had spoken of when she was not so hospitable to Patosh.

Thunder and lightning accompanied them on the way and the rain pattered heavily on the tin roof of the old SUV and despite its age, overcame the difficult terrain with ease. The farm appeared on the dark horizon and as the car parked outside the front door, the pair ran to the door seeking shelter as the rainfall increased rapidly. The timing couldn't have been better, because five seconds later, they would have entered the house soaking wet, which old Mary would not have liked. The delicious smell of roast meat wafted towards them.

"There you are. Roselyn, set the table and you, young man, help. The plates and glasses are there and you know where the cutlery is, Rose."

Mary opened the oven and basted the roast with ale and it sizzled as it roasted to a crisp. Two hours later, everyone sat at the table and enjoyed the divine meal. The meat was so tender that it fell off the bone just by looking at it and the roast potatoes and mint sauce enhanced the aromatic decadence on the tongue. A red Burgundy was served after the sherry, and the meal was rounded off with port, cognac, Stinton cheese and custard pudding.

"I still have a few Havana cigars in Daddy's humidor. Would you like one?"

"You may call me Patrick, Patosh or Pat, madam. I wouldn't say no, but I don't want to overstretch your hospitality. Are you sure I won't seem impertinent if I take a cigar from your late father?"

"Before they dry out, I'd rather see them smoked up and you, Patrick, are a welcome guest now. Don't worry. I don't think Archie will hold it against me. Go ahead and help yourself."

Patosh took a Monte Christo from the box, smelled it and skillfully lit it. What a pleasure and yes, that's the way to live.

"Archie really liked smoking these. At last the room is filled with this exotic aroma again, because I never minded this smoke. How long are you planning to stay here Patrick? I'm only asking so that I can arrange the guest room accordingly."

„Three to four days ma'am. That`s the plan."

"You may call me Mary."

"All right, then. Mary." Patosh said with a smile and he found it just as pleasant to be called Patrick. He hadn't heard his real first name since he was a child and so his parents only called him Patrick when he had done something bad. Mary took her time clearing the table and looked towards Roselyn, as she was plagued by a question she didn't want to wait any longer to answer.

"Tell me dear, did you use my first name when you met this gentleman, because he was looking for a Mary Mitchell and I'm sure it wasn't me."

"Yes MUM. I used my middle name because I wanted to be safe with strangers and couldn't give away my identity like that. But I got used to being called Mary as Pat rendered it so sweetly. I hope you're not too angry about it."

"No, no, my child. But you should have seen his face when he saw me instead of you. I still have to laugh inside. You two are strange jokers. Now help me clear up and then I'm going to bed. It's been a long day and I'm sure you have a lot to tell that's none of my business."

An hour later, everything was cleared away and washed up and the old lady excused herself because it was time to stretch her old bones.

"Good night, my dears."

Mary Mitchell left the room and it was some time before the silence was abruptly interrupted by Patosh.

"I don't want to lie to you Rose. I still have trouble calling you Rose. It's all very confusing for me. It was already confusing when you lived with me as Mary and told me your story. But now I don't understand anything anymore. I've been living in a very bizarre world ever since I met you. Nothing makes sense anymore, but at the same time I have learned a lot. I'm not here by choice Mary, forgive me, Rose. Three Venusians came into my pub in Lontzen and I knew immediately that they were not human. Their demeanor and their Vybe scanner had given them away. They told me clearly and unambiguously of the need for your return to Venus. I was to search for you, find you and convince you. They also gave me this address here and I think it has something to do with interfering with your free will regarding some law that allows this action in special cases. Your father had to give up his position at the High Council and you should, no, you must return to take his place. They also said that from Venus you would be more successful in your mission to make a positive difference on this planet. They clearly described the consequences. I didn't know where you were or what you were doing all this time and I had my doubts about accepting their assignment because you have to understand Rose, I thought about you every day and no matter how much I wanted to push you out of my life,

I couldn't. I only accepted the assignment to see you again, no matter what you decide."

"Do you want me to leave the earth forever Pat?" she asked sadly and with a serious look.

"No, of course not. What I want most is for you to come to Lontzen and live with me...."

"I can't leave here. My mother won't make it much longer because she's been diagnosed with a rare disease that can't be treated. I know her illness all too well and I owe you an explanation because I know that nothing makes sense to you as you sit here. My father is not Archibald Basil Wellington, nor the man who supposedly ran off to Aberdeen, but KLTXG. This is at least part of the truth. I know you must have wondered how one can have two fathers, but this part of the story is one that I am not at all proud of, if I ever had any pride. You have to believe my story, the one I'm going to tell you now and let me finish. You can ask questions afterwards. OK? Archie is my grandfather, even though I called him Daddy. He's my mom's illegitimate father."

Patosh just nodded and his stomach told him that the horror was just beginning.

"My mother was abducted by a UFO when she was young. I'm sure you've heard stories of people suddenly disappearing and then reappearing. Some still had a memory, others only a fragmentary idea of what happened to them.

Then there were those who couldn't remember anything and these abductees were still used for experimental purposes because they had a higher DNA compatibility. They were used as agents on earth, so to speak, without knowing it. My mother was such an experimental subject. She was mentally manipulated into thinking she had been impregnated by someone else, but that was not the case. On the same day of the abduction, KLTXG mated with mom and I was created and right after the mating my mom was molecularly returned to her bed. How do I know that? Right after I was born here on this earth, I was also "abducted". Stolen from my mother, so to speak, and she got a replacement of me in hologram version. My mother lived with a simulacrum of me and during that time, I got my training on Venus for later assignments on Earth. You have to understand that KLTXG, my Venusian father, mated with thousands of beings to spread his agents throughout the universe. This is nothing unusual in itself, because other planetarians do this too, with the difference that they don't need abductions, because they get plenty of volunteers for this project. Only you humans are not ready for this, because you are so mentally retarded that I almost feel sorry for you. Especially as my mother is a human being herself and still has no idea exactly what happened to her. Archibald only believed that a stranger had been my father, because he had actually believed that he had impregnated my mother. But the fact is that there never was one from Aberdeen. Jane, Archie's real wife, could never have children because she was barren herself, but Archie liked to do it with Grandmother and mostly in the stable.

She was a maid and had a child with Archie, my mother Mary. KLTXG took advantage of this situation and when mother, Mary, came of age, KLTXG kidnapped her and mated with her. Here I am. But he must have noticed something about me. Some gift, some ability that I didn't even know I had, because he kept me on Venus after I was born and developed a very strong compatibility with me. Mother, Mary, received a hologram of me and yes, I was to become KLTXG's successor one day, but I also have a deficiency that he had taken into account, but was willing to take the risk. I am half human. A true Venusian would not take such independent actions, like my escape from Venus, because it would contradict the principles, since everyone has the same polarity and exists in the same density, or layer of development. I thought the same of myself, until one day, purely by mistake, I got a glimpse into the secret soul archive. I had been commissioned in a completely different matter, where I was supposed to obtain knowledge about the sensitivity of the assignment, and that's when it happened. Normally, only the elders of the High Council are allowed to look into this secret archive, but for some reason I couldn't explain, I got in. I found my synopsis, you would call it a matrix or a file. A microsecond later I knew who I actually was. Everything inside me collapsed and mentally nothing worked anymore. My Venusian principles disappeared. All those good and unprecedented qualities of unconditional love, free will, the right to the sanctity of every being, service to others, etc., disappeared.

One contradiction followed another and this had been going on for thousands of years with planets that were not on the level of the Venusians or higher. Yes, they wanted to help, but they used the very methods that we had been forbidden to use. Among other things, the LIE. It didn't take long for my human characteristics to suddenly make themselves known and for emotions to develop within me, because the truth had not only set me free, it had made me look very miserable. I couldn't confront KLTXG and I managed to isolate myself telepathically so that no one could spy on my thoughts. But how long would I have been able to do that? More and more human characteristics developed in me, which I recognized as weaknesses. I became insecure despite all my Venusian possibilities and I still had the privileges of the High Council within me. Not those of the elders, but more than I was entitled to. I said earlier that abductions for knowledge purposes only occurred on planets with a low density of development and Earth is one of them. Had we landed and asked you nicely if you would volunteer to mate with our gender for experimental purposes, one of your ridiculous panics would have erupted, but we had to continue our research to develop improvements in the universal balance. These abductions were never malicious, but in my case I saw this lie that was forced upon my mother and also my earthly, chosen grandfather all these years. After that, I escaped and you know the rest."

"So you didn't escape to save this earth." Patosh asked, almost disappointed.

"No. Earth is very capable of coping with many things and our resources are limited in order to be able to exert an influence should this planet actually become cold. We can only do something in an advisory capacity, but it is up to you to take the advice."

"What will actually happen if you return to Venus?"

"I would be deactivated, which would be tantamount to execution. My father, KLTXG, would also have no influence. They already have a successor for him and those three strangers in Lontzen only manipulated you."

"I thought Venusians wouldn't do that. The Orion group is known to use negative manipulation...."

"When the balance on Venus is at stake, extraordinary measures are taken."

"So this measure only applies to the balance on Venus and not to the entire universe?" Patosh shot back almost angrily.

"We are a speck of dust in the whole, just like this planet is. Do you think we Venusians would be enough to influence the entire balance of the universe? Another lie of special measures. The Orion Group now knows the situation and is shamelessly exploiting it. They know that we Venusians have a problem now, because of me, and they will do anything to keep me alive.

I am a pawn, because as long as I am alive, I am a danger to Venus, although I would never do anything to harm this planet. Venus is a Garden of Eden. The knowledge and vibration from her energy source is unique. Venusians are friendly, peaceful beings and I have a heavy burden to bear because I have harmed them without meaning to."

"Your cosmic father likes to play God...."

"Don't put that word in your mouth. You and your god. A superstition that only increases your stupidity, as the entire Orion group already does. Your delusion of a being that has human features and decides over death and life, heaven and hell, war and peace is just another tyrant in the circle of your superstition. Yes, you feel drawn to something higher. What you call God is a perception of vibrations, energies, exchanges of cosmic influences. To explain it to you would be impossible, because you do not have the understanding to do so and it would only overwhelm you. To get there, you need maturity and evolutionary development."

"Yes, yes. We humans are all stupid..." protested Patosh.

"The best example of this is your reaction, my love. Please don't get angry, because I'm trying to bring you closer to the real truth."

"What about the other three? Jonathan, Martha and Fred? Where are they?"

"Jonathan, Martha and Fred live in Bedford. They opened a grocery store two years ago after selling the finca in Spain and we moved here together. I've managed to persuade them to stay close to me in case things get out of hand with the search operation we've been put on. They have been taken in at Bedford and business is going very well. Jonathan has bought an old house for himself and his family, well, more like a cottage, but they are happy and have forgotten about the whole thing. I can't imagine what the consequences would be if I told them about your mission. They would never agree to go back to Venus because their lives would be ruined. You should see how passionate they are about it, and Fred is also very popular at school, not to mention his school results, where everyone is already talking about Fred becoming a second Stephen Hawking."

"God forbid. I would never wish to see our Fred in a wheelchair. But yes, you're right. So what should we do?"

"I don't know. The only reason we're still here is because the Venusians can't just force us to return. That would further destabilize the laws of our principles, and the particular measure of interfering with the free will of others has already led to dire consequences. The High Council is aware that the Orion group is just waiting to throw us completely off balance, because if our own kin were to expel us from Earth, it would be the end of our way of life. We would have completely broken our own law and the Orion group would have free rein to exploit the entire universe to their advantage.

Everyone would become their slave."

"I see. That's quite a dilemma we're in. I wonder why you are here on this planet at all? Isn't it true that this whole problem was caused by your interference thousands of years ago? Even if you came here to help us, the Venusians were already interfering with the free will of humans back then with your appearance," Patosh dared to criticize Roselyn.

"The real problem is that the humans are not from Earth itself, but were genetically reproduced elsewhere. You are here because you would not have been viable elsewhere."

"Wait a minute. Are you saying that we were artificially created?"

"Yes Pat, exactly that. You were created on Venus, and to be honest, the basic idea wasn't honorable. Exactly eighty million years ago a plague broke out on Venus that wiped out more than half of our species. You have to understand, Pat, that we were not as advanced as we are today and that we were not suited to physical labor simply because of our physique. When there were still many of us, we could accomplish a lot together, but when we were almost decimated, a solution had to be found.

"I suspect something terrible," Patosh cried in horror.

"I should have told you when we were still living in Spain, but I was afraid you wouldn't believe my story and would think I was crazy. I'm telling you everything now because I don't want to lose you again and I want you to understand why I can't return to Venus. My Cosmic Father has already carried out his last official act and has thus thrown himself out of office, to use your words. If he had just left me alone, it wouldn't have come to this. I would simply have been condemned for life, deleted from the system like a digital virus and life would simply have gone on as before. We both, my cosmic father and I, brought all this on ourselves. I through my escape and he through his irrational actions. Something that you wouldn't have thought possible had happened, because other unwanted species became aware of it. I don't have to repeat myself about what will happen to me if I return. The same goes for Jonathan, Martha and Fred. So the whole thing has become a lottery. If I stay here, two things can happen. Either nothing, because they don't want to upset the balance any further, or we will be abducted by force and that would trigger a hellish spectacle in the universe. A council would be called where all the heads of our solar system would meet and then it would be decided what would happen to us all. With Earth and Venus, and believe me, the bad guys will be among them too."

"You've opened a Pandora's box with this. But that doesn't get us any further in finding a solution.

But what I don't quite understand is that you're on 'vacation' on this planet just like we are on the Canary Islands. Do the people from Orion do the same?"

"No. They come here to infiltrate and manipulate people, as I mentioned earlier. Their technique is to telepathically manipulate the consciences of desperate, suffering people with low self-esteem. This is what makes it so dangerous, because these weak people are very susceptible to such negative therapies in order to shift the blame for their misery, incompetence or failure onto others, namely those who are deservedly better off. I am not talking about those who have acquired their wealth by criminal means, but about those who have worked really hard for it and let others share in their success. These people are the target for envy, jealousy and resentment. The world is full of losers and do-nothings and everyone is responsible for their own fate. At least for most people. You are given a mission at birth and this is to love, to be happy and to share this happiness with others. Of course, others have to do the same, otherwise the cycle is never complete. 75,000 years ago, this was still the case on Earth, but then the Orion clan succeeded with their goal when we were removed from Earth for the war. An incorrigible mistake and we fell for the ruse. But to get to the point Pat, the only solution to this problem would be to give up everything I've lived for and let myself be taken to Venus. Peace would be restored, but a lie would be covered up and I and the other three would be deactivated."

"We certainly don't want that, Roselyn," Patosh said thoughtfully.

"Then I'll go to Venus for you!" came suddenly from a dark, obscure corner.

"MOTHER!" Roselyn screamed in horror. "Did you hear everything?"

"Yes, my child. I knew from the beginning what was happening to me, because I had regular nightmares about it, but I never told anyone. No one would have believed me. I remember very clearly how and what had been done to me, even if your cosmic father assumed that I had forgotten everything, he had not considered one thing. I had no fear and therefore my memory field in my brain could not be manipulated.

The Venusians still don't know that today. They only had to deal with panic-stricken individuals and therefore had an easy game with them. However, I have to say one thing, because it would not be fair to just leave this matter out in the open without mentioning the wonderful experiences that came about as a result. I was never hurt and your conception, my child, happened through a DNA infusion, if you want to call it that. It could not have happened telepathically, because this is only possible from Venusian to Venusian, but not when another species is "fertilized". Fascinating, isn't it?

"Indeed it is. This is fascinating Mary. But didn't Archibald, your father, know anything about it?" Patosh asked, overwhelmed by the old woman's confession.

"He knew only too well, for I told him everything. Archie was a wonderful man, despite his passion for gambling and everything else that is so frowned upon by society now and then. He was an honest man and he loved me very much. So much so that he didn't mind knowing Roselyn wasn't his earthly granddaughter. I told him everything and he believed me without doubting it for a moment, because you couldn't make up something like what happened to me, also because he had experienced sightings in Connington on the Shyre several times and I wasn't the first to suddenly disappear. These incidents happened at regular intervals. It used to be every three years, then every five years and finally every ten years. The "abductees", if you want to call them that, all reappeared and all of them, apart from me, could no longer remember anything. Many of them still live in Bedford and the surrounding area, but there's no point in talking to them about it. You should convince KLTXG to take me with you, since I can still remember everything, and then you will have to undergo a complete memory treatment. In other words, you Roselyn, as well as Martha, Jonathan, Fred and also you Patrick, agree to a complete erasure of your memories as far as all this is concerned. You must also realize that all your privileges will be withdrawn, Roselyn, but I think you would be only too happy to do without that."

"Not quite mother. Such treatment also means that I will no longer remember Pat, because the clock will be set to zero from that point on. But I love him and always want to remember him.

I also don't like the "privileges" thing. Who is supposed to draw attention to these abuses that happened if I no longer have a say?"

"Don't forget one thing, my angel, the Orion clan is not sleeping and is just waiting to report a dubious change in the High Council. Your appointment will be scrutinized and scrutinized to the smallest detail, and worst of all, a council of independents will be formed, and they will leave no stone unturned until they find something. Especially not those who belong to the Orion clan. Your escape has made you a target for others, and your cosmic father is done for if you don't return. He will be deactivated. But I could negotiate and offer myself in your place. I don't have long to live Roselyn and the pain is getting worse, so please let me decide for myself how I leave Earth. Your death would make no sense, and don't worry. If you two are meant to be together, then erasing the memory can't change your love. Fear wouldn't be appropriate right now, so let me do it."

"I don't want to know about it, Mom. It does shock me that you've been hiding your knowledge all these years, because after what you've put on here, you're very familiar with the High Council's machinations. I wonder to what extent your knowledge of the Venusians is sufficient, because you have obviously become an expert without ever telling me.

'What was I supposed to tell you? It was selfishly not just for your protection, but for mine as well.

The Venusians should believe that I don't remember anything, otherwise we would have all been eliminated long ago. KLTXG had made the mistake of seeing something special in you and kept you on Venus. He had developed feelings for you, even though that should never have happened because there are no feelings there. That was a big mistake. He should have let you go to Earth as soon as you were born and controlled you telepathically from Venus in order to achieve his research goals, which in themselves had only good things in mind. You yourself know that Venus knows no evil and that its inhabitants have only one thing in mind. Unconditional love. You both, KTLXK and KLTXG, have caused this imbalance and in order to correct it you must now compromise, my dear daughter. Your deactivation and that of the other three only makes the loss greater, but I have lived my life and I have had a very good life. Don't be silly."

Roselyn sat looking into her mother's empty eyes, which looked soulless and exhausted. Exhausted from the years of keeping her knowledge secret and yet there was also a redemption to be found, for she had finally broken free of that burden and shared with her daughter, her crushing secret.

 "You said that feelings are unknown on Venus and yet you speak of the unconditional love that prevails there. How is that possible? Is that possible?" Patosh asked doubtfully, for he too had learned a lot in recent years from his relationship with Roselyn, then Mary, in Spain and during their travels through Europe.

He hadn't questioned so much back then, out of consideration for her, Roselyn. Also because he couldn't believe everything he heard. Here, however, at Connington on the Shyre, he was three years older and now, when he found his great love again, he was very anxious to understand everything thoroughly and not to repeat the omissions of that time.

"What is meant by love here is not the same Patrick. On earth, love usually also means suffering, but love is the absolute opposite and my father Archibald understood this very well. Love is the elixir of life in the universe and suffering is a product of human emotions. ERGO, feelings have no existence and no place in the universe. In the universe, you serve others to keep the cycle going and to evolve in spirit. Universal love is given as a matter of course, without expecting anything in return, which is no longer the case here on earth. Sexual love also exists in the universe and serves the exchange and regeneration of energy. Feelings interfere with love, because feelings bring jealousy, conflict and possessiveness into play. You have to prove your love for someone every day on this earth, which in the end is no longer love. Mercy and compassion, as rare as these qualities have become, should exist unconditionally, and automatically in our daily lives. However, these qualities are becoming increasingly rare in our lives. Feelings and love have nothing to do with each other in the universe and there is no need to prove it. You may ask how I know all this. My abduction was, in many ways, a blessing because it opens your eyes and if you can resist the temptation of the

Orion Group, this blessing is indelible in you. If one experiences such an "abduction", he or she comes back changed. Cleansed and reset, if you like. Many of the "abductees" have unfortunately relapsed, but the few who were able to resist also bring hope. Therefore, for me, there is no going back in my decision. Patrick, take my suggestion to those who have visited you and convince them that it is a good option, because you still have your whole life ahead of you."

Patosh listened to old Mary to the end and didn't say a word for minutes and Roselyn, who by now was in tears, not quite sure whether from anger or regret, couldn't get a sentence out either. Twice she blew her nose into a handkerchief and finally said.

"You're right mother. I will accept your offer, even though I'm sure it will mean your death."

"There's no way of knowing that for sure Roselyn, because the Venusians aren't murderers. They are only responsible for balance and deactivating does not mean killing anyone for a long time, only immobilizing and who knows, maybe my body can regenerate. But I can't go on living like this."

"Do you believe in an incarnation Mary?" Patosh asked uncertainly.

"Yes, but it doesn't happen the way the world imagines. You can come back, but only on a voluntary basis and if you are willing to do service for others.

That means returning to help. Others are sent as travelers to other solar systems and then return belonging to a different density. However, caution is advised, for the same applies to the Orion clan. Every twenty-five thousand years the "harvest" happens. Souls are promoted or not, if you can interpret it that way...."

"Mother, don't tell so much. It's too dangerous. You don't know if they're listening. " Roselyn interrupted her.

"You're right, my child. I'm glad you've come to your senses and I hope that you, Patrick, understand all this, because I know how it must sound to someone who isn't privy to it. But the worst thing is that I have kept silent all these years and left my daughter in the dark. There is no more time to lose Patrick, because I sense that an answer is expected soon. So when do you plan to return to Belgium?"

"On the next flight Mary. I think tomorrow evening." Patosh said sadly, looking at Roselyn, who sat there wiping the tears from her eyes.

"I'm afraid I can't come with you Pat. I`ll be noticed right away." she said, keeping her composure. Patosh just nodded.

"I have one more question. What about the Orion clan? Don't you think they'll do anything to kidnap you Roselyn and maybe you too, Mary? You two are a valuable pawn to them."

"I don't think that's possible, as they can only work telepathically and not physically. Besides, the Venusians would know about it and they are more advanced in that respect.

But I'm not omniscient and shouldn't rule out this possibility," said Mary, a little uncertain. They hugged again and Patosh thanked them for their hospitality before they all went to bed.

Roselyn took the other guest room, for the wounds of the past had not healed and she needed time. She was no longer the Mary she once was and Patosh knew this only too well as he too was troubled inside and so he could not organize his thoughts as he usually did so confidently.

Back to Lontzen

Patrick was smarter this time and rebooked his flight because Heathrow was far away and Luton was practically round the corner. Roselyn drove him to the bus stop in Bedford as they both didn't want to take any risks as they felt they´re being watched, and most probably were. Patosh only knew one thing. He had to be strong and suppress any weird thoughts, because the Orion-Clan was certainly already at work trying to manipulate his thoughts. In Bedford, Roselyn and Patosh kissed passionately once more and neither could make any promises to the other as to when and where they would meet again. Now it was time to negotiate and hope that the Venusians would accept the offer. When he finally arrived at Luton, Patosh checked in at the BA counter and collected his boarding pass from a machine. No one was sitting or standing behind the counter to greet the passenger personally anymore. The passport was placed on a scanner and the boarding pass was printed out. People slowly but surely became superfluous, except at the security checkpoint. Belts, jackets, shoes and all other small items such as coins, keys and mobile phones were placed in a plastic container before going through the X-ray scanner. He was lucky because he wasn't called back and Patosh hurriedly put his belt, shoes and jacket back on. His flight wouldn't take off for another 75 minutes.

Enough time to have a caffè, which was then swapped for a beer, as the beer was almost a pound cheaper. Nothing made more sense it seemed. But the most expensive item on the Menu was the mineral water, and Patosh thought about his prices in the pub.

How cheap his prices were compared to this usury. He was able to detach himself mentally and thought of Georgette, hoping that she had been on top of things during his brief absence and yes, it had just been 48 hours but they seemed like seconds.

'Excuse me, are you travelling to Brussels?' a gentleman in his fifties asked him kindly, suddenly taking a seat at the bar stool next to him.

'I caught the train from Bristol and it was already thirty minutes late. I hope I'm at the right gate?'

'You are sir, you've got over an hour,' Patosh reassured him.

'A beer for me too, please,' the stranger ordered from the barman, still sweating from running.

'Travelling is no fun any more and this stupid security check is probably the last straw. You're just treated like a criminal if you ask me.'

'That's true. I'll be glad when I'm back home,' said Patosh in agreement.

'Are you from Brussels?' asked the stranger.

'Not quite.'

'I have to take the train from Brussels. I'm going to Lontzen to visit my sister,' he said excitedly. Patosh realised at once that this could not be a coincidence, for how likely it was that anyone should want to go there, especially after all the fuss at Connington on the Shyre. Patosh stood firm and said nothing more, nor did he feel like making small talk with the stranger, but what to do if the person next to him wouldn't stop talking? Just get up and leave? That would have been unfriendly and, as a pub owner, he was not. Instead, he let his ears be filled with chatter and just nodded in agreement every time he thought he had hit the right moment.

'...You should know that although I'm Belgian, I've been married to an Englishwoman for 23 years. I work at the road traffic office in Bristol. My Lucy wouldn't normally let me leave so quickly, but this time she couldn't hold me back because I have a strange hobby. UFOs...Yes, I know, you're probably thinking '...What a weirdo...', but supposedly six of them were spotted in Lontzen last night and suddenly disappeared into a lake or a river. '

'I see. And what are you going to do there in Lontzen? Dive for them? I thought you visit your sister.' Patosh asked, annoyed.

'Who me? No, not me. Do I look like an athlete? My mates do that. Two are already travelling from America and three others are coming from Spain, Germany and Norway. Experts with years of experience.'

'Experience in diving?'

'Not only. Ufologists, like me. Sure. Sounds pompous, we don't have any training or a diploma for it, because let's be honest, it's more of a passion and a hobby. But what else can we call ourselves other than Ufologists?'

'I see. What do you do after that? After you've found the spaceships?'

'Well, hang a big bell. People have a right to know that we've been lied to for years and that they live among us. Our lobby is getting bigger and bigger and....'

'Do you have any proof? Blurred photos are not enough and there's a lot of fraud going on. You can't believe much of what you're served these days and don't you think the aliens would show themselves if they wanted to be seen? Well, but what do I know. Everyone has a right to a hobby.'

'Don't you want to know if they do exsist? Wouldn't you be interested?'

'I just don't think people are ready for such a shock.'

'PASSENGERS TO BRUSSELS ON BA 433 ARE ASKED TO GO TO GATE 35A. THE ENTRY.....'

'That's for us!' Patosh shouted gratefully, because he couldn't listen to any more chatter. If only this guy knew what was really going on, he'd find a different hobby. The bill was quickly paid and they made their way to the gate, but instead of the stranger detaching himself from Patosh, he clung to him. Patosh only hoped that they wouldn't be sitting together and his prayer was answered. Again, Patosh got an aisle seat, this time near the front, and the stranger went to a window seat at the back. In Brussels at the latest, Patosh could quickly break away from this parasite and run off, as he was only carrying hand luggage and didn't have to go to the baggage carousel. Less than an hour later, the Airbus A 320 landed in Brussels and as soon as the front door was opened, Patosh took his legs under his arms and ran off. But that didn't solve the problem, because he also had to take the train to Lontzen and who knows, maybe they would meet again there, but he was lucky here too, because there was nothing to be seen of this hobby UFO expert for miles around. Exhausted, he arrived in Lontzen shortly before 11 p.m. and Georgette picked him up by car. They hugged and drove off. Patosh could dimly recognise the stranger as he took a taxi and drove off and, relieved, Patosh was able to concentrate fully on what Georgette was saying.

'So boss. There's nothing to tell,' she said with a smile.

'What about alleged sightings? Have there been no UFO sightings?' he asked curiously, but Georgette just gave him a puzzled look and laughed.

'No, boss. Everything's quiet here and believe me. No UFOs have been sighted. Nothing in the press or on TV and the guests haven't seen anything either.'

So who was this stranger to start such a rumour? The Lontzeners were already experienced and had probably experienced more sightings and verifiable situations than any of these ufologists and if Georgette says that no sightings have taken place, then none have appeared. This stranger was something quite different from what he was saying and Patosh became uneasy. Was he one of the Orion clan?'

The days passed and the pub, called the 'Golden Mug', was fully booked to the last table every day. Georgette was overwhelmed with work and Patosh had to hire a cook and an additional waitress. They were paid on commission and were allowed to keep the tips, except for the cook, who wanted a fixed salary. Patosh was also overwhelmed with everything by now, as he hardly had any time to do anything for himself and the three strangers he absolutely had to meet didn't turn up, which worried him. He tried telepathically several times, but to no avail. In the end, all that remained was the Vybe Scanner, which could not only produce money, navigate and create hollograms, but was also suitable for communication if you knew your way around it. But Patosh had to struggle with difficulties, because supposedly you had to enter a decrypted code that was only assigned to Venusians. Of course, Patosh didn't have it.

His thoughts about Roselyn were only distracted by work, but as soon as he had nothing to do for a second, he thought about her. He pined for her and wanted to disappear far away with her, this time to a place where no one could be found. To Patagonia, perhaps. If the Nazis could do it, why couldn't he? The social media reported weekly on television, mostly via MyTube, about all sorts of things. UFOS were of course a main topic, but Patosh was often bored and annoyed by the mostly dubious blogs and so he also liked to look at other topics. For example, he noticed a blog with the title 'Grey Wolf' the escape of Adolf Hitler. It reported on the possible escape of this monster to Patagonia in Argentina. He allegedly did not take his own life, but ran off there with other of his henchmen and the bodies found at the Wolf's Lair did not belong to him and Eva Braun. She had also disappeared and they had allegedly fathered a daughter together. Patosh was struck by the beauty of this Patagonia, but also by its remoteness from the rest of the world. You could hide there and you would be untraceable, at least for a long time. He would disappear there with Roselyn and say goodbye to the civilised world forever. Why not run a pub in Patagonia? As a Belgian, he would certainly be welcome.

'Patosh, two Stella, two Orval, a pastis, two half chickens, two onion soups and three portions of chips.' Georgette shouted over the counter.

'Coming right up.' confirmed Patosh, who tapped the beers, prepared the pastis and passed the food order on to the chef.'

In all the chaos, Patosh didn't realise that there was someone among the guests that he would have preferred not to see again, but distracted by all the orders, his eyes were only on the till and the taps. By now Patosh wasn't even sure how many of the guests were possible holidaymakers from outer space. Most of them were UFO freaks who had created a second Rosewell out of Lontzen. It was always lucrative for business, but the peace and quiet was gone. This all happened overnight, the very next day after his arrival from Luton, but according to Georgette no sightings were made in his absence. There was no mention in any newspaper of multiple UFOs playing tricks over Lontzen and yet, out of nowhere, scores of coaches were now travelling in daily with sensation-seeking fans. They travelled in groups with exotic names like UFOMANIA, ET-DILIRIUM and HOPE OUT OF SPACE and if you thought they were hippies from the sixties, you were very much mistaken. There were professors, actors, authors, rich entrepreneurs, retired politicians and others. But who had caused this chaos overnight? The person responsible was sitting in Patosh's pub. It was none other than the man who had harassed him at Luton airport and who, purely by chance, had come to visit his sister in Lontzen. He wasn't a spy for the Orion clan, but an ordinary lunatic who was getting rich at the expense of others. He sold fantasies and tried to present himself as a cosmic prophet, as several had already tried to do and got rich as a result, like that RAFEL guy.

He was also the organiser of these UFOMANIA trip. Not Rafel, but the man from Bristol. At his table, there were also several gentlemen who looked like sort of Rambo characters. Men who could just as easily have been mercenaries and who, despite their physical swagger, didn't stand out at first. Compared to Patosh, however, this organiser knew who Patosh was and the visit to the pub was no coincidence. The whole chaos unfolded when Robert, the farmer who found the metal plate, put it up for sale on the internet and the buyer was none other than the man from Bristol. He was neither married nor did he work in the road traffic department as stated, Patosh later realised. He was nothing more than a homosexual pensioner who, after working for the post office as a postman, had turned his passion into a profession and, as one could see, with success. Neither had he a sister in Lontzen. Robert, the farmer, had ended up selling the board to the man for 800 euros, but what Robert didn't realise was the real value of this tinny nuisance.

The next morning, Patosh went shopping and travelled the country road that ran alongside the river and eventually led to the lake. He noticed several vehicles and two patrol cars and initially thought it was a tragic swimming accident, until he recognised the man who was supposedly visiting the sister in Lontzen. Patosh braked and parked the car at the side of the road and, guided by his sudden curiosity, crossed the road. Several divers were on motorised inflatable boats, scouring what appeared to be a section of the lake.

'What's going on?' he asked the first police officer he met, who happened to be a regular visitor to the pub.

'Ah Patosh. What are you doing here?' he asked in surprise.

'I was on my way to the shops and recognised the fat man down there. I wanted to know what he was doing here and what this was all about.'

'He's an Englishman. President of some UFO organisation and he's exercising his right to dive in the lake. Everything is authorised and registered with the police.'

'What's he looking for?'

'Well, what is he looking for? Spaceships. What else. As if we had nothing better to do. Look at the mess. All those onlookers littering the shore with their Coke cans and whatnot. This Europe has become nothing but a madhouse.'

'Tell me about it Hans. What's that git's name?'

'But only because it's you. A certain Malcolm Jenkins or something like that.'

'I see.'

'Do you know him?'

'No. We crossed paths at Luton Airport and he told me he was Belgian and was visiting his sister in Lontzen. Strange person.'

'His passport says he's English. He lives in the White Crane. The guesthouse is fully booked for weeks and more visitors are expected.'

'Thanks for the info Hans. I owe you a beer.'

'I'll get back to you on that.'

Patosh walked down the slope and tapped the stranger on the shoulder, who was busy shouting out instructions.

'Hello, do you recognise me?' Patosh said with a serious expression.

'Yes, of course. How pleased I am to see you. I've been a guest at your establishment several times and have tried to make myself known, but you were swamped with work and I didn't want to disturb you. I hope business is going well?' said the plump gentleman with a smile.

'Yes, thanks to you I suppose. But what are you really looking for here? You don't have a sister in Lontzen, do you?'

'I'm looking for the truth, Mr Van de Brog, even if I have to use the opposite to get it. I had to lie to you. I'm sorry. Trust is something I don't have, so many times I have been deceived in life and so I became cautious.

I hope you forgive me. One of your residents had sold me a metal plate over the internet because I found the symbols on it very interesting. According to his story, the thing fell from the sky and almost killed him. I had to have it and luckily I was able to buy it for a good price.'

'But this whole theatre here must cost a fortune...'

'It does indeed. I sold the tin to a Russian for a fortune and, as you can see, I'm investing that money in this operation. I don't actually earn anything from it.'

Patosh was not convinced by the explanation, because the meeting in the airport bar in Luton could not have been a coincidence and how did this man know Patosh's name? He had never been addressed by his surname.
The tin brought Robert to the pub only recently, not eight days ago and during those eight days Patosh met the three alien 'holidaymakers', travelled to Connington on the Shyre and found his Mary again who was actually called 'Roselyn', learnt a whole new story about her, met this guy in a bar who supposedly bought this tin from Robert in no time at all and apparently didn't need a week to get all the official permissions, as an Englishman, in Belgium, to undertake such ventures that would not be taken seriously in an otherwise prevailing reality. Just to be allowed to cut down a tree in one´s own garden, a permit for a Belgian would take almost a month to be issued and here, he got it in no time for something that would normally have taken years.

The official mills in Belgium grind slowly, but apparently only for Belgians. Something was wrong here. Patosh said goodbye to Mr Jenkins and drove on to do his shopping, but the gears in his head were spinning hotly, because 1 plus 1 suddenly equalled 3 and not 2. He couldn't get Roeselyn out of his head and now this Malcolm Jenkins was also interfering with his mind. He mustn't forget to buy some aspirin, because it wasn't on the shopping list, his head was buzzing so much. After three hours, he returned and unloaded the small van, along with Georgette, Silvie, the new waitress and the new chef, Roland. Fortunately, the pub was only busy with the usual regulars, so there was plenty of time to make preparations for the evening ahead. There was no doubt about finding out more from this man from Bristol, as he could disrupt the negotiations with the three aliens should they arrive unannounced one day. Patosh had to win his confidence and if Mr Jenkins appeared that evening, he would sit at his table and provoke an informative conversation. But first the menu had to be updated, as the prices had now been raised. Patosh could no longer see the point of making peanuts and he didn't believe a word Jenkins said when he said that he wouldn't earn anything from his endeavours. Nobody does this sort of thing for free and he, Patosh, was sure that Jenkins would collect a good commission from the travel companies. All these UFO freaks were being ripped off by Jenkins and most of them were well off. He warned the regulars about the new price changes and assured them that it didn't apply to them. They would continue to pay the old price, which reassured them.

Evening came and so did Mr Jenkins and his crew and they were greeted with an exaggerated friendliness by Patosh. Jenkins was pleasantly surprised at such a welcome, especially at the newly allocated table, which remained reserved for the duration of their Lontzen presence. Patosh personally took the orders at this table and directed Georgette and Silvie to the other tables, which they didn't like as they were worried about their tips, but the boss assured them that he wouldn't keep any of it and would send it to them after closing time. The beer, spirits and wine flowed freely and after Patosh had convinced himself that he had raised the spirits at the table by several per cent, he sat down. His opinion of Mr Jenkins hardly changed, despite the feigned friendliness, but the crew turned out to be a group of friendly and fun-loving individuals who were on this quest purely out of a sense of adventure and personal interest.

'Now tell me Malcolm, how did you get my surname? Hardly anyone knows it,' Patosh asked in passing.

'Robert, the farmer, had told me about you and that's how I got your name. I wanted to pick up the disc in person and Robert had given me the address of the 'Golden Jug' to pick it up. But as I still had a lot to do, we decided to organise it by express mail. You should know, dear Patosh, that I know all about postal matters because I was once a postman. Now retired. Live in Bristol with my friend who has nothing to do with UFOs and thinks the whole thing is a pipe dream. I should break up with him, but it's not easy after ten years.

He owns half of the house we bought together.' Mr Jenkins didn't seem to mind talking openly about his homosexuality, because yes, everyone was living in the 21st century, except Patosh apparently. He remembered Roselyn telling him back in Spain that on Venus it didn't matter who was compatible with whom and that this reservation only existed in the backward planets.

'And you really think you're going to find spaceships here in Lontzen?' Patosh asked, now a little tipsy himself.

'Faith moves mountains, my dear Patosh, and yes, I firmly believe it. The world must know the truth, because we know nothing. Absolutely nothing. We have been misled for millennia and remained stuck in this darkness, also caused by our own ignorance and comfort. Thousands have reported sightings all over this earth and thousands cannot be wrong. In a universe like this, it would be presumptuous to think that we are the only ones. There wouldn't be an Area 51 unless there was something to be vehemently concealed and this sudden progress we are experiencing in a very short space of time cannot have been brought about by human intelligence alone. Humanity is being kept stupid because only a few people ask questions. Most are happy to go to work, submit to a manipulative system, pay bills, satisfy banks and be lied to by the same system, instead of getting their arse off the sofa, exploring the world, discovering the purpose of being and experiencing the freedom we all talk about.

All these wars, these sudden viruses, these foreclosures, these social divisions, this tyrannical subordination of a system that calls itself democratic is evidence of a development that no longer fits in these times. I pray every day that we can free ourselves from this crisis and be human again. But for this we need the help of others and this help can only come from the universe. I have spent years researching aliens and the universe and even if all this is not true and everything turns out to be a figment of my imagination, I would rather submit to such a delusion than the one presented to us by the media and governments. Do you understand me Patosh? I am 56 years old and have only carried letters back and forth, but at least I had contact with people. I could just about live on it, but everything was more human than it is today. The digital future also means using people less and less, see emails, FAT Book and others. You don't go out anymore and you don't meet up like you used to. I very much hope that we will experience visitors from outer space, but most of all I hope that they will recognise themselves and be friendly to us. We need humanity again, because it will soon be gone if things go on like this. That's why I'm looking for the spaceships. I would like to make contact with them.'

Trouble in the Universe

Days, even weeks, passed since the meeting in the pub and Mr Jenkins' diving work continued, but without success. Patosh could have told him straight away that they would never find the spaceships because they were invisible and undetectable. That's how the spaceships are set up when they visit alien planets that don't belong to the Confederation of Space, but Patosh would have given himself away and the chaos would have been overwhelming. He now regretted the Englishman's wasted efforts, but at the same time these futile endeavours were very good for business and not only he, Patosh, benefited from them, but the whole of Lontzen. However, Mr Jenkins' moods changed daily as his nerves were frayed and his funds were running low. All his sponsors asked him daily how the search was progressing, but he could only put them off, which naturally annoyed them. His own funds were long gone and so were his hopes. But Patosh kept building him up, as Mr Jenkins was becoming a welcome guest and, as said previously, his presence was good for business.

Patosh received a phone call on a Sunday morning. It was Roselyn. 'Mother is very unwell,' she sobbed on the phone, which worried Patosh considerably.

'I try to contact the Venusians every day, but I can't manage it Roselyn. I also don't have the code for the Vybe scanner.'

'It's no use to you Pat, otherwise I would have given it to you long ago. With the code you also have to undergo a telepathic scan, because the DNA of every Venusian is registered and you don't have this authorisation. What you can do is just wait.'

'But what if Mary's condition gets worse and she, God forbid, dies?'

'Then it will be too late anyway and me and the other three will be finished. Or not, if the Venusians simply ignore us because of the council they fear afterwards.'

Just as Patosh was about to reply, three people suddenly entered the pub and Patosh couldn't immediately recognise them. He felt a shiver of relief when he recognised the Venusians.

'They're here.'

'Who?'

'The Venusians. They have just entered the pub as we speak. I'll call you back, dearest.'

'Don't do that. We're probably being bugged and I'm calling from a phone box. I have to tell you something else Pat. The Orion Clan is already in Bedford and we're being watched every day. Mum is being telepathically 'greeted' by them all the time.'

'Greeted?' Patosh asked, confused.

,,Yes. That's what they call their manipulation attack.' I'll call you again tomorrow. I miss you Pat.'

She hung up and Patosh didn't even have a chance to say goodbye to her, which put a knot in his heart. He hung up as well and immediately strode over to the aliens, who retained the same molecularly human appearance as the first time.

'About time,' Patosh grumbled, visibly annoyed.

'We've been busy.' apologised the elder.

'What's this rubbish? First you push one and then you take your time with it. Are you taking the piss?

'We don't use such vocabulary, but we understand your annoyance. But rest assured that we're not taking the piss, because things are going haywire in the universe at the moment and we're also on fire, to use your words. On the one hand, the situation is very, how shall I put it, critical, because now not only the Orion clan wants to push ahead with the Council, but also three other planetary members of two solar systems. We have not seen such chaos for millions of years. The High Council on Venus is leaderless and so we have become the target of others.'

'That's to bad. Follow me, since we can't talk here.'

Patosh led them to a private room and had Georgette bring them drinks, and when she left, he started talking.

'The following situation......'

Two hours and several drinks later, no compromises or solutions had been reached because the Venusians were stubborn.

'What should we do with the mother? We need KTLXK!' said the younger of the three.

'Are you guys slow on the uptake? How many times do you want me to repeat myself? She doesn't want to go back and the fact that KTLXG got involved with an Earthling makes her a citizen of this planet, even if she was born somewhere else.

She has human DNA as well as your own, which supposedly is hardly different. She and the other three want to undergo this remembrance procedure so that they can stay. Since when do you interfere with someone else's free will in this way? I thought that was a taboo with you!' Patosh shouted at him.

'Not in this case. This is about preventing a catastrophic imbalance. If the Council is convened, the Orion Clan will maltreat us to such an extent that our position in the Confederation will be jeopardised.'

'And whose fault is that?' Patosh complained and continued:

'That's what happens when you sexually harass other planets. You really are a perverted bunch. What do you think Earth is? Bangkok? See to it that you get your shit under control and settle for the mother who at least has the balls to sacrifice herself for your misdemeanours, otherwise I'll also plead for the council, understand? Now put your Martian arses back in your flying saucers and get out. Here's your Vybe scanner back. Now get out and don't come back to me with a negative answer or I'll go to the press.'

'The press?' laughed the youngest, but the eldest gave him a warning look.

'We'll make your suggestion and hopefully we'll come back with a positive result. Please keep the Vybe Scanner. Here's your code for communication, by the way. You are now registered and can contact us directly at any time. Thank you again for your commitment and efforts. The love of the Creator be with you.'

'Just a moment. There's something else. I've got a weirdo here who's looking for the spaceships. He's hoping for a lot from you and wants nothing more than for aliens to come to the aid of this planet. Can you support him? I feel sorry for him, because he's a bit overwhelmed by his hopes.'

'You mean Mr Jenkins?' asked the elder.

'Yes. How do you know that?'

'We've had our eye on him for a long time. I think he has proved himself worthy. We'll think about it.'

They disappeared as inconspicuously as they had come and Patosh went back to his work, not without passing the Englishman, who had just finished his sixth beer and was wallowing in despair, and giving him a friendly pat on the shoulder, he said:

'Everything will be all right, Mr Jenkins. Everything will be fine.'

'Your word in God's ear Patosh.'

The day came when dozens of people excitedly entered the 'Golden Mug' and a loud, incomprehensible gibberish developed. Patosh hardly noticed anything, but Silvie, the new waitress, told him that Mr Jenkins had found what he was looking for and that he and his crew were very happy about it. However, the people who entered the pub were not Mr Jenkins and his crew, but the UFO freaks, because they were there live when two divers shouted out the HAPPY MESSAGE from their inflatable boats. With a probe equipped with underwater cameras, they had actually found something that had the structure of a wreck. It was definitely not a boat, but something that could not have come from 'this world'. These were Jenkins' words during the interview, hours later. Without knowing it, they discovered the wreck of the holidaymakers named Jonathan, Martha and Fred, or KTKGH, KTUIT and KTOPK in Venusian.

But how could it be possible, Patosh wondered. The answer came quickly via telepathy. The Elder had kept his promise and allowed the invisibility to be cancelled, at least for the wreck of the holidaymakers. The others remained invisible, because there was no doubt that the search party for Roselyn was still on Earth. They had found her, but they were waiting for further orders should the state of emergency occur. Despite all this, it was the beginning of irrevocable confirmation of the evidence of an extraterrestrial presence on Earth. Now there was no longer any need to believe flimsy excuses from the government, because the lies had finally stopped. At least that's what people believed at first. In the evening, Malcom Jenkins and his crew arrived at the pub and celebrated their victory like Romans after a successful campaign. Jenkins' mobile phone never stopped ringing and the sponsors promised him further support. Lifting the wreck out of the water costs money. A lot of money, but the biggest problem would be keeping the onlookers under control. But first there was the find to celebrate. Patosh had his hands full that evening and Jenkins was interviewed on television. He became a star overnight and turned Lontzen into a place of pilgrimage for UFO enthusiasts from all over the world. On the internet, hundreds of blogs suddenly appeared on My Tube and other social media, caused by these UFO worshippers who were now overrunning Lontzen on a daily basis. However, the discovery attracted not just cranks, but very serious individuals and Patosh felt a sense of déjà vu like when Camille was still in his life and the first sighting, including the Belgian Air Force chase, happened.

The men in black appeared again. Jenkins and his crew disappeared from the scene at the drop of a hat. The lake was cordoned off by military units and at night, excavators and extra-long trailers appeared to salvage the wreckage. However, this was not without incident. Hundreds of protesters obstructed the work and turned Malcolm Jenkins into a whistleblower like Jullian Assange. Slogans such as 'Set Jenkins free' and 'Where is Jenkins' were shouted at the top of their voices and if you thought the military had an easy time with the protesters, think again. There was no shortage of violence and the people of Lontzen were literally fed up with the military's intervention. It was clear that freedom and the right to seek the truth were not only being suppressed by their own government, but also by the typical arrogance of America. The Belgians, as well as the rest of Europe, were simply fed up with being lied to and the inevitable happened. Civil war-like riots. In the end, there was nothing left to do but to salvage the wreckage as quickly as possible, get out of Lontzen and release Jenkins, which is what happened. A heavy CH-53 helicopter hovered in and dragged the covered wreckage away underneath it, which turned into a near suicide mission for the pilots, as the operation took place at night, under heavy wind conditions and under the spotlight of the press and an agitated populace. Jenkins was released the next morning. Changed and intimidated, he did not want to give any interviews and simply wanted to be left alone. The crew was sent home and the freaks left Lontzen as they came. By bus. The rubbish and the peace and quiet were the only things left behind in what had become a ghost town overnight.

Malcolm Jenkins entered the pub one last time to say goodbye to Patosh, but Patosh asked him to stay. He wanted to give him a present, because his efforts would not have been in vain.

'A gift?' asked Jenkins, still shaken by the incident.

'Yes, but first I need to know how secretive you are Malcolm. I need to know if you're doing what you're doing purely for financial gain, or if you're really doing it out of conviction, a scientific thirst for knowledge and a willingness to have an open mind about this whole story that I'm about to initiate you into.'

'I don't know what you're getting at Patosh. You've seen for yourself how I've invested every last penny of my own money in this venture and how I haven't kept a penny of the sponsorship money either. I am poor as a church mouse. I have nothing left, so that should be proof enough for you,' said Jenkins, annoyed and almost offended.

'Good, I need someone I can trust unconditionally. What I'm going to tell and show you is for your eyes and ears alone, because a lot depends on it. I'll start with the simplest. Yes, the spaceships you are looking for do exist. You could not find them because they are invisible to the public. They only become visible when the aliens want to make them visible. You found the wreckage because they made it visible to you in order to help you, but also because they believe in you and have gained your trust.

They need someone in their earthly guard, if you want to call it that, to act as an ambassador for them. I am one too. It could be you if you want it to be. However, others must not know about this privilege given to you, because your life depends on it. Do you understand me?' Patosh asked the now very curious Jenkins.

'You can count on me Patosh. It's no coincidence that our paths crossed because there are no such coincidences.'

'You've seen what happens to those who seek the truth and find it. They are silenced. You became very dangerous for a few in the upper floors and you are certainly not the only one who had to go through such treatment. Wait, I'll bring us a bottle of Chateau Lafitte, because one can't talk about it sober.'

Hours passed and Patosh asked Georgette to take over the bar and Silvie to serve the guests. The pub was also only half full after all the UFO freaks had left disappointed, reducing the workload. Jenkins couldn't stop being amazed and listened with rapt attention, because what he was hearing surpassed anything he had learnt in all those years. Patosh also made it clear to him that his task was different from the one Jenkins was supposed to do. He wanted to save the story about Roselyn and Mary for the very end, as he wanted to be sure that Jenkins would accept his offer.

'And what do you want me to do, Patosh? I'll do anything, because I have no one waiting for me.

My purpose in life has been trampled underfoot and I've been made a laughing stock.'

'Not quite true. You've got your mate in Bristol and you've also opened a big can of worms with the work you've done here. The world isn't so blue-eyed any more. Be proud, because your name is now known and famous worldwide.' Patosh tried to comfort him.

'My partner left me while I was working here. He found someone else and voluntarily offered me his half of the house to buy. But I'm broke, so we have to sell the place. You don't know the English, Patosh. You're only a hero if you're successful, but a zero if you fall flat on your face, as in my case. So? Give me a reason to go on living Patosh. I need a task'

'As luck would have it, you will be working for me from England. Near Bedford is a somewhat impoverished county called Connington on the Shyre. Two women live there. An elderly lady, Mary Mitchell, and her daughter Roselyn, who is my life- partner. They are, how can I explain it to you, not from this world, at least not Roselyn. She is a Venusian. Your job will be to stay with them and report to me on everything and everyone. They are being watched and their safety is at stake, as not only earthly agents are looking for them, but also not so friendly ones from outer space. Your mode of communication will be a phone box, as this will not be intercepted, at least I hope so.

We also have to come up with coded procedures, such as 'The aunt is well or not well ect...' Come up with something. I'll pay you well for it and cover all expenses.'

'I'll do it Patosh. I can't believe what you're telling me, but I need to know a bit more about these two ladies. How do you think they will receive me, since they don't know me?'

'I'll give you a letter and it will explain everything to them.'

Patosh told Jenkins the story he had saved for last and Jenkins took notes. What he heard was hard for him to believe, but he had to, because he really should use an open mind here.

He found himself in a mysterious world again and he felt at home in it. After the bottle of Chateau Lafitte had been emptied, the Englishman asked when it was to start and Patosh shocked him with the answer.

'Tonight. I'll drive you to Amsterdam, where we'll buy you a ticket to Luton and you'll go straight to Connington on the Shyre from there.'

'But why Amsterdam and not Brussels Patosh?'

'I think I'm also under surveillance and we shouldn't leave any traces. Brussels is too risky for me, especially after your performance here.

You were my best guest when you dragged me into the limelight.'

'I'm sorry about that,' said Jenkins, somewhat intimidated.

No sooner said than done. Patosh left Georgette in charge of the pub and they left Lontzen in Gerorgette's Peugeot with destination Amsterdam. The journey went smoothly and they arrived at Schiphol Airport at four o'clock in the morning. Everything was still closed at this time of day, but they found a café that was open 24 hours and ordered coffee and croissants. Time dragged on like chewing gum and it didn't want to get any later. Finally, around eight o'clock, the first ticket counters opened. Patosh quickly bought a one-way ticket to Luton and Jenkins took the first KLM flight. The Englishman was able to find instructions in an envelope he had taken with him, which told him the best way to get to Connington on the Shyre, and as chance had been kind to Patosh and Jenkins again, Jenkins was able to ask his cousin in Luton if he could lend him a car, as his cousin was a used car dealer. Patosh, however, made his way home as soon as Jenkins walked through security to catch his flight. Arriving at Lontzen exhausted, Patosh was in for an exciting surprise. The three 'strangers' were sitting at the usual table drinking beer.

'Welcome back,' Patosh greeted them with a friendly face and sat down with them.

'First of all, thank you for your kind gesture to Mr Jenkins.'

'You're welcome. It's just unfortunate that the truth, as usual, is not welcome on this earth,' replied the elder.

"I hear you. " Do you have an answer to Mary's offer?'

'I have one. But there are a few points to consider that the Mitchells won't like. The remembrance procedure can only take place on Venus and so all five, that is Roselyn, Mary, Jonathan, Martha and Fred, would have to be brought there. Mary would then remain on Venus and the others would return with no memory of their Venusian past. We can't carry out the procedure on Earth. '

'Would Roselyn forget me after this procedure?' Patosh asked anxiously.

'Yes.' said the elder without batting an eyelid.

For Patosh, this 'yes' couldn't be a more painful stab to the heart, but there was no other solution. It was just a pity that Jenkins had already flown off, but this milk had already been spilt.

'How much time do we have?'

'Exactly seven of your days. After that, a spaceship will come and pick them up one way or another. If they accept the offer, they will receive the seal of the High Council, which is equivalent to a binding contract on your Earth. This agreement will not and must not be broken, neither by us nor by you.

Roselyn knows this seal. She used it often enough when she was still one of us. Seven days Patosh, after that I will see you in Connington on the Shyre. Give our regards to Jenkins. He should have arrived there by now.'

Escape

Patosh was under a lot of pressure, because seven days passed quickly, and he couldn't just turn his back on Lontzen. Yes, he loved Roselyn very much, but how often he had to fight his thoughts when his inner voice tempted him with words like: 'I wish I had never met her and our paths had never crossed.' If he had been a good Christian, he would have immediately crossed himself and asked God for forgiveness for such thoughts, but since he was becoming more and more of an atheist after all the incidents, he simply erased them through inner suppression. Of course, he did not regret that Roselyn had appeared in his life. Was it maybe the Orion Clan who had been lingering over these bad insights and 'greeted' him?

'Bullshit!' he shouted to himself as he realised he was slowly going insane. The mobile phone rang and he thanked someone up there he wanted to call God, because the display showed 'Jenkins'.

'Malcolm. Thank the heavens. Tell me how everything went.'

'Good morning Patosh. Well, I arrived last night and had to spend the night in the car because there were a lot of black vehicles around the farm. It turned out to be some police officers, maybe even MI 6, I can't say for sure.'

'Men in Black I can imagine,' said Patosh angrily.

'That may well be. I didn't have the chance to approach Roselyn and Mary since I didn't want to end up in prison again, but I'm not giving up. Do you have any idea how I can reach them?'

Patosh thought about it, but he couldn't come up with an idea easily. He couldn't call them either, as they were certainly being tapped and he didn't want to take any risks.

'Have you got a torch with you?' he asked Malcolm

'Yes. Why?'

'Can you use Morse code?'

'No, I can't. I know what you're getting at, but it would attract attention. They would notice.'

'Is the press working there too, by any chance? If so, get yourself a press pass somehow and mingle with them.....'

'There's no press here and it looks like none can get here either, the whole area is so secure.'

'Merde!' Patosh shouted, beside himself. He thought about using the Vybe scanner to ask for help, but he wanted to keep the Venusians out until the end, for fear of betraying Roselyn. But if nothing else helped, there was nothing else to do but use the Vybe Scanner.

'OK. Do me a favour and drive to Bedford. Sign in at 'The Red Lion Hotel' and ask for the boss. His name is William.'

'William and go on. His surname would help Patosh.'

'I don't know the surname Malcolm. Just tell him you're a friend of the Belgian who owns the pub and has stayed in his hotel before. He's sure to remember. Ask him if I can call, because it would be important.'

'OK. Give me two to three hours. I have to leave here first and get myself together. I'll call you.'

Jenkins hung up and Patosh's head ached. Roselyn and Mary couldn't stay there any longer and an escape plan had to be made, but easier said than done and as he turned around to turn his attention back to the guests, he noticed a commotion outside his inn. Several blue lights appeared from a distance and this did not bode well for him.

'Georgette. I have to go. Whatever happens, I will explain it to you one day. But I have to leave, do you understand?'

'Yes, boss. What should I say if someone asks me?'

'I'd go to Toulouse or Berlin, I don't know. Think of something, my darling. Run the shop as before.'

Georgette just nodded and suspected something terrible, because she also saw a police motorcade approaching the pub from the window. When she turned around, Patosh had already disappeared with what he had on him. It was fortunate that he grabbed the Vybe scanner in time before he left, otherwise he would have had nothing to help him escape. In the old Peugeot, which didn't even belong to him, he sped along the main road towards Calais. After just under two hours he reached Dunkirk and a short time later the canal railway station in Calais. He was supposed to pay eighty-four pounds for the ticket, but could only do so in euros.

He gave the man at the counter one hundred euros, who changed it into pounds and demanded another ten euros for the exchange fee, which drove Patosh mad. But it would have been stupid to argue here.

'I'd still like to see your passport, please.' asked the man at the counter and handed it back to him with the train ticket.

'Have you ever travelled on this train before? Do you know the procedure?'

'Not really,' Patosh replied.

'Good. You follow the sign that says 'Train to Dover. An attendant will direct you to the carriage and you will remain seated in your car for the entire journey under the English Channel. The journey takes about half an hour.

Smoking is absolutely forbidden during the whole journey. Have you understood everything?'

'Yes, I did.'

,, I wish you a good journey then,' said the man behind the counter in conclusion.

Patosh did everything as instructed and a man in a yellow vest showed him the way. The Peugeot had to be driven into the wagon sideways, which was very unusual for someone travelling to England in this manner for the first time. It was rather interesting. Patosch remained seated in his vehicle, which actually belonged to Georgette, and he was lucky that nobody asked for the vehicle documents. But what it will look like in England remains to be seen. The side door of the wagon closed hydraulically and a short time later the train started moving. It was fascinating and scary at the same time, as you were disorientated and there were no windows looking out, just an aluminium wall to the left, right, front and back. Suddenly Patosh was pressed into his driver's seat as the train picked up speed while crossing the channel and seemed to be going faster and faster. The ticket seller was right because after 28 minutes the train slowed down and two minutes later it stopped. Now the other side door of the carriage opened hydraulically and another attendant hastily waved the Peugeot out with trowels. Patosh needed to concentrate, because in England the English drive on the wrong side, but the English saw it differently and so did the whole Commonwealth. At the station exit, a customs officer asked for the passport and Patosh drove on relieved when they didn't ask for the vehicle documents. The difficulties would have been unimaginable if he had crossed the border in a car that did not belong to him, but to a Georgette Gautier. He was also surprised that no one had spotted him after all the excitement in Lontzen. Had he reacted in panic? Was he even becoming paranoid? He switched on his navigation aid on his mobile phone and entered Bedford as destination and two minutes later the system received the desired signal. Patosh stepped on the gas and looked for the quickest route to his destination. The M20 would be the best connection and three hours later he parked outside the Red Lion Hotel. He quickly produced a thousand pounds over the Vybe scanner so that he could use cash instead of a credit card to avoid leaving a trace and when he checked in, Malcolm Jenkins was in for a big surprise.

'What the hell are you doing here?' he asked him

'Long story. Let me have a hot shower first and I'll meet you at the pub in, say, an hour.'

'Agreed Patosh. You haven't missed much as William won't be back for another two hours. Some event he had to attend, the baman said.'

'Good, brace yourself my friend. It's going to be exciting.'

Jenkins was on his third pint and at last Patosh appeared in the pub looking for him. He took a seat at the same table and ordered a scotch with ice, because he needed something harder.

'Tell me. What's so exciting?' asked Jenkins.

'When you hung up this morning, I saw a police motorcade approaching my pub and after what you told me about Mary's Farm being surrounded by officers, I was so scared that I probably acted irrationally and just put my feet under my arms and left. Maybe they're looking for me for some reason, even though I haven't done anything wrong.'

'You don't have to do anything to suddenly be harassed by the authorities. You did the right thing, because I tried to reach you. But you were probably already travelling and so I called the Golden Jug. Georgette was on the line. She was upset and just said that she couldn't talk because the pub had been raided by the police. They weren't looking for you, they were looking for me again. But I am glad that you are here.'

'Why are they still looking for you? You've already paid for your actions, why don't they leave you alone?'

'I don't know. Supposedly they found provocative papers at my house and my ex, that bastard, turned me in to the cops so he could move into my house with his new lover.

Anyway, they're after my arse. Two old sponsors also want their money back, which I can't refund under any circumstances. How could I? Legally, they can't do me any harm because I had secured myself contractually.'

'What kind of papers were those?' Patosh asked him with relief, knowing full well that he had acted too hastily but yet was in the immediate vicinity of a person wanted by the police. There was no question in Patosh's mind, however, that Jenkins was being terrorised here for some other reason, and Patosh wanted to know the truth.

'There's something you're not telling me Malcolm. Tell me the truth or I'll relieve you of the assignment.'

'Don't you start now Patrick. I haven't done anything wrong and people are trying to smear me. They've found a scapegoat for something I can't explain either. I've only heard the beginnings of a rumour. Allegedly the spaceship they took from me was suddenly stolen. But I rather think that your friends have something to do with it. Your Venusians. Anyway, I had a fit of laughter when I heard that.'

'Stolen?' Now Patosh had to laugh too.

'Like I said. It's just a rumour, but where there's smoke, there's fire, as they say.

'Who started such a rumour, I wonder?' Patosh asked, still amused.

'I still have friends and you'll be surprised how many I still have even in the police force.

They also have witnesses to sightings who can't be lied to and yes, one from Scotland Yard, a long-time friend of mine who is now retired, let something like that leak out but couldn't confirm it. What do we do now? The question is, what do the cops want from the two women in Connington on the Shyre? Have they got onto their trail?'

'No idea. But shortly after you left, I got a visit from the three Venusians I told you about. They set conditions and we only have six days left as we've already wasted this day. We have to get to the women and now that I'm here, the plan has changed. At first I thought about escaping, but now I think it's better if that doesn't happen. But we need to get into the farm undetected and for that we need William, the landlord of this hotel.'

'Are you saying that the Venusians have agreed to Mary's offer?'

'Yes and no. The procedure for the negotiation has to take place on Venus and they have to go back. Allegedly they have confirmed this 'agreement' with some kind of an official seal and assured the return of Roseyn and the other three. But Mary has to stay there. The ultimatum was seven days and now there are only six. Roselyn and Mary must be informed and agree,' said Patosh, inwardly shattered.

'And what if they don't?' asked Jenkins.

'The spaceship will appear one way or another and depending on the decision, things will go peacefully or less peacefully.

In other words, if Roselyn and Mary agree, Roselyn and the other three will be allowed to come back, but if they are forced to come to Venus, they won't have the slightest hope of returning. Worst of all. They won't remember anything and Roselyn will forget me.'

'That's bitter, of course, my friend,' Jenkins said quietly.

'You were looking for me?' William suddenly called through the pub's front door.

'What a pleasure to see you again, my Belgian friend. And who else do I have the pleasure of seeing?'

'Jenkins. Malcolm Jenkins....'

'But not the Jenkins....'

'Forgive me, sir, but I'd be grateful if you wouldn't shout my name out. I'm here incognito, if you understand.'

'Of course. Forgive me. Well, it's still a pleasure. Will you be looked after?' asked William.

'Yes, yes. Don't worry William.' replied Patosh.

'How can I help you?' William asked without wasting time.

'Can you sneak us into the Mitchells' farm?' Patosh asked quietly.

William couldn't hold back a mischievous grin but replied with a 'Yes, I can.'

'It's pretty busy up there. Lots of police and other authorities. Do you know anything more?'

'No, William. All I know is that they need our help. I also know that you're not on good terms with each other...'

'No shit. Archie was my best friend. I know they blame me for his ruin, but that's not true.

Quite the opposite. How many times did I warn him to quitting gambling and how many times did I drive him home as drunk as he was. We grew up together and my father was a chauffeur and gardener at the Wellingtons. He also got Margareth the job as housekeeper, who had nothing better to do than spread her legs for Archie. My father was rewarded with the sack when Jane found out, as it was his fault for bringing her into the house. Archie couldn't do anything about the sacking as he had been caught in the act. He kept coming to the Red Lion anyway and continued to get drunk. My father didn't live long after he was kicked out and yes, I hate Margareth and her daughter Mary for that because she didn't even turn up to my father's funeral. Young and beautiful as she was then, she only had the Baron on her mind and Jane, who remained childless, took revenge on the wrong people. Nevertheless, I always paid my respects to the family because I miss Archie. At least he had the balls to admit that he seduced Marga and that my father had nothing to do with it. But women are like that. Scorpions in human form is all I can say."

'I'm sorry to hear that William. But I can't quite share your opinion. People are what they are and resisting temptation is a difficult situation for both men and women. I am very sorry about your father and I can understand why you are so disappointed in women, but I have learnt from my experience with Roselyn. Aren't you married, William?' Patosh asked.

'No. Let's continue with the text. So you want to get into the farm unmolested and I know a way. Archie showed me when he had to go home drunk and didn't want to wake up Jane. I'll help you.'

'That's great William. I'll show my appreciation.'

'It's all right Patosh. I'll do it for Archie because I know how much he loved his Mary. He had liked Jane, but never loved her. She was just too cold. When do you want to start?'

'Tonight!' Jenkins exclaimed enthusiastically this time. 'There's no more time to lose.'

'I don't need to ask what it's about, do I?' William asked, already knowing the answer.

'If everything gets done, then maybe. Depends on many things. But be sure of our gratitude,' said Jenkins, looking suspiciously long into William's eyes.

'Tell us about your plan, William.' Patosh said as he began to find the situation between Jenkins and the innkeeper creepy. Was this why William wasn't on good terms with women? Did he, like Jenkins, have homosexual tendencies? William took a piece of paper from behind the bar, pulled his Parker pen from his breast pocket and drew what appeared to be a secret route leading to the basement of the main building.

'As you've already realised, it's a tunnel, the entrance to which is in this part of the forest and which nobody knows except me and the late Archie. Probably most of his male ancestors, who were also drunkards and not on good terms with their wives. Anyway, you have to go through this tunnel. Don't worry. I will accompany you. There is a light switch here....' William pointed to the right of the drawing. It's a four hundred metre walkway and the path is narrow and deep, so it's not for those with back or foot problems. The door to the cellar vault is heavy and Archie had installed an electric switch so that it could be opened and closed electrically. I just hope it works, because sometimes the system goes haywire and it takes a lot of force to push the door open. In the cellar vault itself, the door is disguised as a wall. From there, a staircase leads to an abandoned corridor that even the maids didn't like to use. They thought it was spooky and dark. I suggest we go there at a time when these policemen and who knows who else are tired and lethargic. I think two o'clock in the morning is a good time. What do you think?'

'Good plan William. Let's do it like this. I don't have to mention...'

'Come on Patosh. We're colleagues and I'll keep my mouth shut. Like I said, I'm doing it for Archie. You look hungry and tired, so have something to eat and then off to your bunk.'

'Eye eyey captain!' shouted Jenkins in amusement.

William got up to go to the kitchen and Jenkins and Patosh murmured amongst themselves in low whispers.

'Can we trust him?' asked Jenkins.

'What else can we do Malcolm? We have to get into the farm and warn and prepare the women. You must realise that we have to stay there until the end.'

'And your pub in Lontzen?'

'Don't worry. Georgette will take care of it and when it's all over, I'll go back.'

'Who knows what will happen to us, Patosh.

Have you ever wondered if they'll let us go again, your Venusians? And what about the cops and the Men in Black? If they catch us, we'll end up in some basement in Area 51 with all the Martians they're holding there.'

'Oh stop being crazy Jenkins. This isn't a fantasy world you've been living in for years, it's bitter reality. You only know the theories that others have speculated about, but here you will experience the truth before your eyes and most likely revise everything you have learnt over the years. What they will do to us is written in the stars. We must see to it that we get away as quickly as possible and unrecognised.'

"All right, allright. No need to be snippy my friend. I have a right to be worried, because to be honest, I'm a little scared. My curiosity will drive me to my death one day.'

'I'm sorry. We mustn't make any more mistakes and be strong. Above all, we have to stick together.'

'So, dear ones. Mash and Bangers, just like my dear mum made it. Enjoy. I'll bring you two Guinnesses to go with it.' Said William, who appeared from the kitchen unnoticed.

The fat sausages, laid on a bed of mashed potato and thick brown gravy, looked delicious and Patosh and Jenkins gorged themselves greedily on the meal

'The last supper,' Jenkins joked, and all three of them laughed.

At two o'clock on the dot, an old Land Rover with three men in their prime set off. Destination; the forest of Connington on the Shyre.

Not a word was spoken during the whole journey. They seemed to be meditating, so deeply absorbed were all three of them and not even the thunderstorm, which made itself felt on the black horizon with the occasional flash of lightning, could distract them from their concentration. It was as if they belonged to an elite unit, such as the SAS, and there was no turning back from this mission. After what seemed like an eternity, William reached a dirt track leading to a forest and drove along the difficult path with the gear reduction engaged.

'God bless the Queen and our Land Rover,' he muttered with a smile.

'The Queen is no longer with us, if you don't know.' protested Jenkins, who didn't like such jokes about his beloved Queen.

'We all love our Queen, even beyond death old chap. She's still alive as far as I'm concerned,' countered William.

'So, we're here. I just have to park the car and hide it with leaves and twigs.'

Patosh and Jenkins looked at each other, shaking their heads, but refrained from commenting. The main thing was to get them into the main building. After a short climb, William pushed leaves and branches aside and a hatch, concealed by a wooden door, appeared on the ground. Jenkins held a powerful torch on it and quelled the fear that seemed to take control of him as his hands began to tremble. William grabbed his hands and steadied him.

'Breathe in and out slowly old chap. It'll be all right. Patosh, you last. First me, so I can find the light switch, then Malcolm so he can calm down, then you, so you can close the hatch from the inside, understand?'

When Patosh finally stepped through the hatch and closed it from the inside, a light bulb burned dimly, illuminating a few steps and a narrow corridor behind them. Then the torch had to do the job, because the electric light didn't reach any further.

'Watch comparison!' William growled.

'What, really?' Laughed Patosh, who thought this was a little exaggerated.

'Yes, really. We have a maximum of 25 minutes for these four hundred metres, after which we'll run out of oxygen in this damp, muddy hole, cappish? So, watch comparison. It's twenty to three. We must have reached the door by five past three."

'Why haven't you left any oxygen cylinders here?' asked Jenkins.

'Good idea, complain to Archie and now shut up or we'll run out of air. I'll go first,' ordered William.

At exactly three o'clock, they reached what was supposed to be the door to the cellar vault. William took another deep breath before pressing the electric door opener.

You could hear small electric motors rattling and yes, the door moved slowly and squeakily, like in a horror film, but you could also hear the electric motors apparently running out of juice and, as the devil would have it, the door got stuck halfway. Patosh and William could just about slip through, but good Jenkins, who has always been a foodie in his life, would have his problems.

'I should have given you salad instead of sausages my dear,' mocked William.

'Ok, let's do the rest with our hands, so push.' and with all their might they pushed the heavy door open. They were inside. Mission accomplished. .

'Follow me.' William whispered and strode forward with his torch held out. They reached the kitchen and climbed the stairs that led to the living room where they, Roselyn, Mary and Patosh had sat together not so long ago.

'Don't switch on the light or the cops will see.' Jenkins remarked, but then fell to the floor in the darkness, hit by something hard, leaving a dull thud. Mary was suddenly standing in front of them with a pump-action shotgun and Roselyn behind her.

'PAT!' Roselyn screamed with joy and ran to him. They hugged and kissed while William tended to poor Jenkins, who felt a bump on his forehead.

'What are you doing here and why is this traitor of a William in my parlour?' asked old Mary angrily.

'We couldn't help ourselves to get to you. I have very important news and time is running out, Mary.' Patosh placated. 'Without William, we wouldn't have managed to get in here.

'You cutthroat know the tunnel?' Mary shouted at William, her shotgun still pointed at him.

'Calm down Mary. How else could I have got good old Archie home without Jane noticing?'

'You men are all the same and dangerously stupid. Don't you think Jane knew about the tunnel? I knew it too, because when Archie staggered drunk through the corridors, it wasn't exactly quiet.'

'And why didn't you use the tunnel to escape?' asked Jenkins, holding his hand over the sore spot.

'And who are you, you troll?'

'His name is Malcolm Jenkins....' Patosh tried to introduce him.

'Oh. The UFO freak from the telly. Now I recognise him too. I've always watched your programmes with a laugh, what a terribly good comedy And what do we have the honour of welcoming you here with?'

'Patosh will explain everything. I need something hard to drink.'

'You know where the whisky is William. Best pour a glass for everyone.'

'Yes, Mary. Gladly.' said William, who couldn't believe he was allowed to stay.

Patosh, still holding his Roselyn, took a seat on a leather armchair and began to explain the terms the Venusians were offering and Roselyn and Mary listened. After an hour, silence fell as the women pondered and didn't say a word.

'So we just have six days.'

'Five and a half to be exact.' Patosh corrected.

'What do you think Roselyn?' Mary asked her daughter.

'The seal is binding, but one thing is clear. We won't be able to remember anything afterwards. I will forget you, dearest, and I don't want that.'

'I'll be here to try again with you, my darling. But then you can live here as you always wanted. Jonathan, Martha and Fred too. They need to know. '

'They're already here. They're sleeping in the guest room upstairs. I asked them to take a holiday and close their shop for a while, but they didn't want to, so they left the management to a good customer for the time being in the hope that they would return and remember their shop.

I gave them some idea of what to expect. That convinced them, but I didn't think the Venusians would take me up on Mother's offer.'

'Well, they did, but with crushing compromises. We must not lose another minute. What should I tell them, because I have now received a communication code?'

'Give us some time...'

'Roselyn. We don't have time. Every minute that passes could be our last in freedom. Those monsters out there could launch a surprise attack at any moment and invade here with tear gas and whatnot. I don't really know what else they're waiting for,' Mary interrupted.

'May I suggest something?' interrupted William, who seemed unsure and didn't really want to get involved in all this charade that seemed very suspicious to him.

'How much do you old rogue know about everything that concerns us?' asked Mary, unfriendly and visibly nervous.

'Nothing, I know nothing Mary. I guarantee you that. But I do recognise when someone I hold in high esteem, and yes I do, is in distress. Please don't forget that Archie and I were best friends, even though he was a few years older. I feel somehow responsible for your safety, even though you didn't feel it necessary to attend Dad's funeral. But that's water under the bridge....'

'I was there and so was Margareth when they buried your father, or do you think I'm a heartless witch?

I still hate Jane for what she did to him and us and yes, I wanted to run away then, but for reasons unknown to you, I couldn't.'

'You were there? But I didn't see you,' stuttered William, ashamed.

'No, you couldn't see us William. I watched everything from the background and cried like a daughter who has lost her father. Your father had always helped me and I will never forget that. When you hear the whole story one day, you'll also see that my mother didn't spread her legs for anyone, besides Archie`s and it wasn't until Jane filed for divorce and Margareth officially became Archie's wife that I gave myself to him as his legit daughter.'

'Yes, but you were born before the divorce...' William intervened.

'You're a clever chap Will and we'll leave it at that. Firstly. So? What did you want to suggest?

All eyes now turned to William, who poured himself another glass of Scottish single malt and finished it all in one gulp.

'We all leave through the tunnel tonight. Twenty miles from here I have a small hunting lodge that should suffice as accommodation for the next five and a half days. We'll leave them out there languish in the dark. We want them all to think you're still here, but by then you'll all be in the hunting lodge.

This will at least buy you all some time. I have no idea what will happen in five and a half days, but I think I'd better not know everything.'

'And we're supposed to trust you?'

'Yes, Mary. You should.'

'We accept,' said Mary with a quick decision.

'But Mum....'

'No buts. Go upstairs and wake the three of them up. We're getting out of here.'

'And what should I tell the Venusians?' asked Patosh, impressed by Mary's decisiveness.

'First of all, nothing Patrick. Let them rack their brains.' said the old lady, unimpressed.

'If they want to know where we are, they will, or do you think they're not watching us right now?

'And the Orion clan?' asked Patosh.

'They're watching us too. Let's give them a show they'll never forget and the pump gun will come with us.

Vacation Block

In the meantime, other scenes were unfolding on Venus, as KLTXG, Roselyn's cosmic father, was removed from his position as head of the High Council and a successor had been appointed, but as this post once belonged to Roselyn, the Venusians had a problem making a logical decision to allow the intended successor to take office immediately. Should Roselyn come to her senses, which everyone now doubted, her chair could not have been occupied by someone else, as this had been the rule since the beginning of the All. Roselyn, KTLXK, was given the promised days, but after that the chair was immediately handed over to KTKFK, the intended successor.

Who was this KTKFK? Was he any different from KLTXG? Basically, he wasn't, because on Venus there were no differences, no feelings, no emotions, no compromises and everything ran according to a fixed and well-organised pattern. However, and how could it be otherwise on a planet with a High Council, there was also a court. According to the human calendar, KLTXG, Roselyn's cosmic father, had to appear there every day and if you thought it was friendly and gentle, you should think again, because here an ex-chief had broken every law since taking office, unnoticed by others, which had applied to everyone on Venus for thousands of years, regardless of whether they were chiefs or not. So how was it that someone like KLTXG could break such laws and how was it possible to overlook these offences?

'KLTXG. You are on trial here for abuse and for violating our way of life and tradition. Several times you have interfered in the free will of other planetarians and several times you have allowed compatible mating with other planetarians without prior conviction of their suitability and actual compatibility. See the case of Poratio on Astranoma, Ambrosia on Kunaptia and now the most recent case, Mary Mitchell on Terrarion, AKA Earth. In the latter, KTLXK was conceived here on Venus, who remained here on Venus after birth against our traditions and rules, was instructed and promoted in our knowledge and secrets as well as our density, although she had human molecular structures in her DNA and was finally admitted as a member of the High Council through error, which we have since also admitted, and was honoured with the seal of succession for the presidency of the High Council. What do you have to counter these accusations?'

'I plead guilty to all the charges brought against me,' KLTXG replied emotionlessly.

'Can you at least explain to us why you let it come to this, my dear and valued friend?'

'Our progress for the enlightenment on some planets, in different solar systems, was too slow and I wanted to speed it up by instructing the created beings in our secrets so that they can transfer them further to their planet. However, this should be done from Venus and not, as unfortunately in the case of Mary Mitchell, or should I say Roselyn Mitchell, because she is the begotten result of my intervention, on Terrarion. I did not take this error into account, although I was well aware of the risk.'

'So with your statement here you are admitting that, firstly, you consciously and deliberately interfered with the free will of others, secondly, you betrayed our secrets and thirdly, you knew the risks and yet did not take them into account. I now ask you KLTXG, was this done out of pure stupidity or for other reasons that do not seem logical to us, because what you have committed is high treason.'

'The planets you speak of are on the verge of disintegration and if we just sit around and watch and hope that these far undereducated beings who still wage wars and lust over greed and power would do even the slightest thing to help their planets, you are accused for complicity of having done nothing about it and belong, like me, in this dock. How are they supposed to develop at this stage if there is no free will intervention, because apparently the Orion Clan has already taken full control, at least on Terrarion. Look at the mess on Earth. Nothing is going according to universal order and nothing makes sense down there anymore. Is that what we stand for?

Service to others also means, if necessary and in extreme cases, interfering with free will. I have tried to avoid it and in most cases I have succeeded, but not on Terrarion. Yes, I made the mistake of keeping Roselyn, or KTLXK, here on Venus and sending Mary, the earthly mother, back with a hologram of her daughter. That hologram disappeared the moment KTLXK grabbed a spaceship and decided to leave Venus for good. Her human genes had taken control of her, primitive as they are, imbued with the emotional and earthly soul power that apparently surpasses ours. Yes, KTLXK also has our DNA, but the small percentage of the earthly one had won out and we are experiencing the result of this here and now. Do I call it good? I have no answer to that, but I must admit that I love my daughter dearly and I will support her with all my strength to help her and I ask you, my brothers, to keep your word, keep Mary here, do the memory procedure without reservation and let her back on earth. They will have no meaning for us afterwards and therefore fulfil no purpose....'

'Exactly, my brother. You say it in your own words.' KTKFK, the intended successor, suddenly intervened.

'So what difference would it make? They could no longer serve our purposes after the procedure, not as ambassadors, agents or as an earthly base. So why bother to bring them back at all? You know the answer brother. They must not reveal our secrets to anyone, that's why.

But what happens if others who knew them on Earth suddenly can't talk to them because they no longer exist for Roselyn and the other three? Wouldn't these old friends wonder what had happened to them? Why they no longer remember the customers in the shop or why the old Mary has suddenly disappeared from the scene forever? I am against a complete elimination of memory. What real and useful purpose would such a thing serve? We would also be letting the Orion clan look into our cards if we were to carry out such an intervention. An intervention in free will. It is not the memory that should be eliminated, but that of the police and the other forces that have now suddenly woken up. They should be cleared of any suspicion and Roselyn and the other three left alone. Old Mary can then breathe her last in peace on her country estate, but there is a price to pay and yes, they would have to appear before us on Venus and I mean the other characters who have now suddenly become involved. What a contradiction to the previous said you think? Let me tell you what we do. Here on Venus, Roselyn, Jonathan, Martha and Fred, as well as Mary, this Patosh, Malcolm and William, will undergo a procedure whereupon they will keep their memory, but their polarity will be so customized to serve us, on the basis of unconditional love of course, and be prepared before entering the fourth density after death. They will not have to undergo anything shameful or disgusting, only their vibrations could be continuously read and defined by us through this suggested frequency modification. Wouldn't that be a better solution?' KTKFK concluded questioningly.

'In what way is this not an interference with free will, brother?' KLTXG asked

'To the extent that any damage you have caused will be equalized and the lives of these souls will be allowed to continue without torment and mental pain, and the Orion clan will have the wind taken out of their sails as they will remain unreachable for the Orion clan. But you, my brother, must pay for your negligence and be disciplined, and for that I demand the ultimate punishment. Deactivation on Venus and transfer to Terrarion, in addition to the complete elimination of memory of everything you have acquired here on Venus and given to you by us through entrusted love. You are not worthy to continue to carry such privileges with you and will be cast out to third density with immediate effect. At least your victims have nothing more to fear and should not be further punished for your misdemeanours. I ask the High Court to put this plea of mine into effect immediately and to finally confirm me in my office without further delay. We have had to watch this Soap Opera long enough and we can gladly do without an extraordinary council."

The judge looked round at the panel and spoke.

'Who is in favour of the plea of our esteemed KTKFK?'

All hands went up and thus the case on Venus was closed.

All rise for judgement.'

'The plea of brother KTKFK is accepted and the defendant is found guilty on all counts. Furthermore, after this verdict, KLTXG will undergo the memory elimination procedure and will be transferred to Terrarion on the next spaceship and banished forever. All privileges he received on Venus will be revoked and he will be transferred back to third density.

Furthermore, KTKFK will become the new head of the High Council with immediate effect in order to ensure stability on Venus and to forfeit the need for an off-duty council. The judgement is pronounced and the court withdraws.

KLTXG disappears from the scene and reappears as an ordinary human somewhere in Mongolia. Nothing more was ever seen or heard of him.

KTKFK took his duty very seriously and acted immediately, banning all holiday flights to planets not belonging to the Confederation, which naturally led to disagreements among the Venusian holidaymakers, as their favourite planet, Terrarion, was now blacklisted. Hundreds of spaceship reservations were cancelled, which was a real nuisance for the holidaymakers and the spaceship rentals. All the other planets were fully booked or didn't have the charm and beauty of Terrarion.

But time was ticking and KTKFK was already preparing the pick-up committee for the five on Earth. To avoid major chaos and unnecessary disruption to the retrieval operation, KTKFK, the new leader, sent an order to all holidaymakers who were on planets outside the Confederation. They were to return immediately to their spaceships and return to Venus, and his fears were justified, as all terrestrial secret services and military forces had been ordered by their governments to search all lakes, rivers, mountains and other terrain for damaged spaceships. The wreck, which was stolen from Lake Lontzen as soon as it was removed, had caused a scandal within the relevant agencies and made the secret services and politicians the laughing stock of the press and media. The greatest fear, however, was that some crank, be it Malcolm Jenkins or the thief of said wreckage, would use the stolen spaceship to make himself important through the media and publicise the truth, which under no circumstances should be shared with the civilian population. Of course, the Earthlings were working on building mysterious spaceship locators and also spaceships 'Made on Earth', but they were still a long way from achieving anything through 'reverse engineering', as the Americans call it. The stolen wreck was not stolen, but was retrieved by the Venusians. How they did that is anyone's guess, but the CIA, MI 6, KGB, Mossad and the rest of them are still beating their heads on the wall of shame.

For them, the wreck was still on Earth and KTKFK did not want to risk his Venusians being unnecessarily hindered on their return. The High Council had indeed chosen a good and dutiful successor to the Chief. The EXODUS happened by day and by night and nobody noticed the departure of hundreds of returning starships. Not only Venusians were there, but also aliens from other planets, because Terrarion was and is to them as Ibiza or Las Vegas is to us.

A Land Rover drives through night and fog.

William, Patosh, Malcolm and the other five managed to escape through the tunnel unnoticed. Mary had great difficulty breathing, as the narrow passageway and the higher oxygen consumption due to the additional people also sucked the remaining energy out of the old lady's lungs. Patosh carried her the remaining hundred metres and when they reached the hatch, it couldn't be opened quickly enough. Everyone threw themselves exhausted to the ground. Even Roselyn, who, as an alien, should have been fitter, but she had been on this planet for too long by now and was increasingly taking on the characteristics that were native to this planet. Wisps of fog billowing out through the exhalation of their exhausted lungs gave away their location if they didn't make their way to the Land Rover as quickly as possible, which they did at William's insistence. The car was stripped of its camouflage and there was barely enough room inside, as there were now eight of them. William started his car, which took a few tries at first, but then the engine rattled and they drove off. It was a humid summer and a fog was developing, which made it difficult to move forward and the windows were constantly fogging up. You could barely see your hand in front of your eyes.

The thunderstorm had been moving southwards for hours, but what remained was the cool precipitation on warm ground. The path became stickier and the Land Rover sank deeper into the mud due to the extra weight, struggling even with the gear reduction engaged. But a cry of relief came from William as he felt firmer ground beneath the wheels and without further hesitation, headed north towards the aforementioned hunting lodge. Despite the warm night, Mary was freezing and Martha and Fred weren't feeling well either. Jonathan, however, couldn't stop talking because he was so happy to see his old Belgian friend again. They swapped old stories about how it all began and now they were sitting here together again. Yes, fate is a strange thing, even for aliens.

"I have a thermos flask of tea somewhere in the back. Please give it to them Patosh, maybe it will warm up their bones again,' Said William when he saw how bad Mary was feeling.

'How long is the journey Will?' asked Roselyn.

'At this rate, about an hour, but I'll do my best.'

It was now five o'clock in the morning. Had the officers noticed anything yet? No, they hadn't and finally William reached the hut, which was in a remote forest area. The fireplace was filled with wood and put into operation immediately and Mary was placed on one of the plank beds and covered up.

Roselyn and Patosh looked after her and Martha was also there to comfort her. Jenkins, William, Jonathan and Fred tidied up inside and outside, as William had not used the hut for two years. Empty beer cans and bottles, as well as scraps of paper and tins of chocolate and pea soup, were collected and disposed of. Three hours later they were living in a clean and warm hut and lo and behold, they found tinned food with an expiry date that was still acceptable. Mary recovered quickly and the warm soup cheered her up. The others also regained their strength and thanked William profusely, for without him they, Patosh and Jenkins, would never have got into the farm and would never have got out again.

'I must get back to Bedford or my absence will be noticed. I'll be back the day after tomorrow with fresh provisions. It's best not to use your mobile phones and watch out for chimney smoke. It could attract the curious.'

'Let's do it William. Drive carefully and thank you again my friend,' Patosh thanked him.

Jenkins hugged him and Mary did so too and they watched him drive off in his Land Rover, which became a symbol of liberation for everyone.

Day zero has arrived

William came back to the hut as he had promised, bringing provisions, clean clothes and also disturbing news for Patosh that would cause quite a mess. But William took his time and distributed the things, which the others gratefully accepted like Christmas presents. These days, they were happy about every little thing that brought colour in this impending darkness and they fried eggs, bacon and sausages and drank coffee and tea. The image of a cheerful and carefree Sunday picnic emerged and as soon as there was some peace and quiet, William grabbed Patosh and whispered something in his ear. They went outside, which the others didn't notice in their conversation.

'Shoot William. What's on your mind.' Patosh asked a little more curiously.

'I had a call from Belgium. It was your Georgette from the Golden Jug and she sounded pretty excited. The police are also looking for you now and you're accused of stealing the wreck as an accomplice. They've always kept an eye on Jenkins but now they're also looking for you and the bad thing is, Interpol has been called in. But I got this news from a different source. One of my lodge brothers is with Scotland Yard and after a few beers in my pub, he told me a lot of things. I asked him what was new at his place of work and he told me that an international search had been launched for you. Your pub in Belgium was closed at first and Georgette had kept tight despite all the threats.

I should get to know her. She seems like a good girl.'

'Blimey. That's very worrying, of course. The ultimatum expires tomorrow and I still haven't made contact with the Venusians. Your brothers? You mentioned a lodge. Are you a freemason?'

'I thought you already knew that. My whole pub is full of their symbols and decorations. Yes, I am a member of a lodge, like many Englishmen, but I see nothing wrong with it. You can also turn a nunnery into a brothel. All you need are envious people and people who declare us to be monsters and say bad things about us. I'm proud to be one and believe me, you're glad you met one, because someone else wouldn't have had so much sympathy for this hocus pocus.'

'Hocus pocus? You can't be serious. Stay here and I'll prove it to you tomorrow. ' Patosh replied angrily.

'Oh, don't you worry. I'll stay here my friend, because I won't let you take that away from me. If I were you, I'd let whoever's up there know where you are, because there were already the first roadblocks on the way here.'

Patosh turned pale in the face and hurried back to the hut. He took Roselyn and Mary aside and told them what William had already said.

'I'll contact them now via the Vybe scanner. You Roselyn must show me how to enter this code. It's time for you to leave this planet, because the police are not far away.'

Roselyn and Mary went outside with Patosh and ordered the others to stay in the hut.

Roselyn switched on the Vyber scanner, which she was able to do telepathically, and immediately a field appeared where they could choose what they wanted to do, just like an ordinary earthly link. But Patosh realised that nothing that had been developed and built on this earth in such a fantastic and modern way and in such a short time had originated from human brains, but had been helped along from the cosmos. The display made it clear.

Roselyn found the 'menu' where the code was to be entered and this was switched in such a way that one was connected directly to the head of the High Council. Roselyn entered the code and a hologram immediately appeared before her eyes. However, it was not KXTLG who stood before them, but a stranger, and Roselyn and Mary were particularly surprised.

'Who are you?' asked Roselyn.

'I am KTKFK, the new head and you must be KTXLK.'

'What happened to KXTLG?' asked Mary.

'He was deactivated and banned from Venus for life. I am now solely responsible for the retrieval operation, but it shall not be to your detriment. You will all be taken to Venus and will return in the same way. I will not take away your memories, but I will soften them a little and you, my dear sister, can return without giving up Patosh. But in return you must continue to serve us on earth. Mary can also spend her last days on this planet if she wants to. That is my promise.'

'What do you mean by serve? What do I have to do? Am I no longer entitled to a seat on the High Council?'

'No, you no longer have that. Only pure Venusians are allowed on the High Council and what KLTXG did to you broke all the laws and rules of the universe. Your rights have been forfeited, but you can travel back and forth at any time and report back to us in this way. You are to become our ambassador here and set up a safe house for our travellers in the future. This will allow us to combine the pleasant with the sensible and also keep the Orion Clan at bay. They have become too powerful on Terrarion and we need your help to at least balance things out,' said KTKFK.

'We are no longer on the farm.' Patosh called from the background.

'I already know that. You have behaved in an exemplary manner in this matter Patrick van de Brog and the universe thanks you.

We will have to pick you all up today, because you are in danger. Get ready.'

'When exactly was it supposed to happen?' Mary asked.

'You decide. Immediately, too if you so desire. What else do you have here that's holding you back? Your farm, dear Mary, has already been taken by the security forces and I'm afraid this hut won't give you protection for long.'

'And where exactly is this supposed to happen?' asked Roselyn.

'There is a clearing less than three miles from here. We will land there and wait for you. But be quick.'

'We'll do it now and immediately. We'll just get the others. Where exactly is the clearing? Asked Mary anxiously.

'William knows it. Be there.' and the hologram disappeared.

Yes, William knew the clearing and Patosh and Jenkins helped Mary and the aliens pack up. Martha was the most excited and Fred didn't know exactly what was going on as he became more and more human.

'I don't want to go back. What about all my friends and my rugby club?' he protested.

'Relax, my darling. We'll be back and everything will stay the way it was.' Jonathan reassured him.

'And you believe that Dad?'

'Yes, I do and I forbid you to give up your Venusian heritage completely. You are what you are here thanks to your roots, never forget that. Now shut up, pack up and don't talk back. Understood?' Jonathan ordered in a way he didn't recognise.

'What do we do after they all disappear?' asked Jenkins, a little uncertain.

'Put our legs under our arms and get out!' replied Patosh.

'You can stay with me...'

'No, William. You've helped enough and we don't want to drag you into this. You won't know us after this spectacle. It's better this way, believe me.'

'OK. Suit yourself.'

'I'm going to miss you, my sweet little sparrow,' said Jenkins, but William only understood this approach jokingly. Jenkins, however, took a liking to William, though no one was sure what his disposition was.

'So go and see how far they are and I'll drive the Land Rover around.'

'All right, Will.'

They all got into the Land Rover and it shouldn't have been a minute later. Fred pointed to the back and you could see tiny blue dots flashing, which were no doubt blue lights from a police patrol. William stepped on the gas, regretfully it would have been just as good to win a derby with a donkey. The lights came closer and closer and suddenly an oversized, shiny silver disc shot silently above them. William, Jenkins and Patosh were left speechlessly flabbergasted because yes, here they were, experiencing it in the flesh. A flying saucer, a UFO, a spaceship or whatever you wanted to call it overtook the Land Rover and hovered a few metres in front of them.

'What the...' William didn't get any further. The Land Rover hovered bag and baggage above the ground and was literally sucked vertically upwards, like an ant being eaten by an anteater

'Impressive. A 'GALAXIA TITANICA' was all Roselyn said as she recognised the High Council's flagship. But William, Patosh and especially Jenkins, who was about to wet his trousers, didn't think so.

'That wasn't the deal Roselyn,' protested Patosh.

'I know, but look down. Do you want to go to prison? We're being rescued right now.'

The police came for them, but they had no power over such a sighting, for they too were overcome with fear.

Police officers had never seen anything like this in the past and a Land Rover floating in the air and being sucked upwards had never even been seen on film before. It was tragic in itself but also hilarious at the same time.

A hatch that opened like the aperture of a camera lens became visible and closed again silently when everyone was on board. The Land Rover, however, much to William's displeasure, was spat out like a cherry pit and landed less than two metres away from the police convoy.

'NOOOOOO!!!' screamed William as he saw his beloved vehicle break into thousands of pieces. 'You bloody bastards!' but no-one but them was in the spaceship and all the earthly hunters saw was a flash of light that silently and instantly evaporated into nothingness.

'You owe us an explanation Roselyn!' shouted Jenkins, visibly beside himself, and William was also stinking mad, but before Roselyn could say anything, the hologram appeared again. It was KTKFK.

'Welcome aboard. That was close, wasn't it?

'Listen, you Martian. That went absolutely too far, the thing with my car. It belonged to my father and was priceless to me.'

'Oh you humans and your sense of material things. That's what's holding you back in your development. A piece of worthless iron that can upset you so much, my dear William. But don't worry.

When you return, your 'tin favourite' will be standing in front of the 'Red Lion' again. My word of honour.'

'Aluminium. My Land Rover was eighty percent aluminium.' William replied a little more calmly when KTKFK assured him that he would get his car back.

'Yes, aluminium, who cares.' laughed KTKFK.

'Something different. What's going to happen to us?' Patosh asked legitimately.

'Everything in its own time. Get some rest and enjoy this short flight, because you'll be tired when you arrive.'

'Don't we need spacesuits or anything else? We're humanoids and we're used to the gravity.....' asked Jenkins when he was rudely interrupted.

'You don't need anything with us. We'll take care of everything. Like this. I'll switch off now and you'll be put into sleep mode. See you soon.'

Between heaven and earth

Patosh was missed in Lontzen and not only by the police, but also by his regular customers. For them, the Golden Jug had become a popular centre where people met and chatted. There wasn't much else going on in this town and now this social centre had been removed. It really was as if they didn't want to see people happy any more and whoever was working on something so diabolical had succeeded. The Ipad and the mobile phone became more of a curse than a blessing, because nobody out there could be talked to, they were so engrossed in the display of these infernal devices. With the closure of the pub, the hearts of the people who lived and grew up there were also closed and the mood and lust for life were driven out. Georgette and Silvie, who were now unemployed, also despaired and Georgette in particular went to the mayor's office every day to fight for the reopening of the pub. But without success.

"I don't understand you Pierre. We all grew up together in the same school and co-founded this town. You played in the same football club as Patosh and you used to be good friends...' she shouted at the mayor.

"We still are Georgette, or do you think I like how I can't do anything about it? But if Interpol gets involved, I'm powerless.

315

I've even expressed my displeasure to the chief of police in Brussels, but I'm talking to a wall."

'Silvie, the new chef and I are for weeks unemployed for something Patosh didn't do and I'm being accosted by the others on the street every day....'

"Then let them choose another pub, what the hell. Life must go on for everyone Georgette."

'"Merde, to hear this from your mouth Pierre, breaks my heart. I'll tell Patosh so when he comes back and he will come back. I'll make sure you don't set foot in the Golden Jug again!" Georgette ran out of his office and slammed the door loudly.

'Georgette, wait...' the mayor called after him, but if you mess with Georgette, that's it.

When they arrived on Venus, the passengers of the GALAXIA TITANICA were met by some aliens and Patosh, as well as Malcolm and William, were quite astonished, because these figures didn't look very pretty. Long, slender figures with long arms and long legs and a face shape that was oval from top to bottom, but the upper part was suddenly straight and horizontal, like a table top. This reception committee were not Venusians, explained Roselyn, who was beginning to change into something else herself. She shed her human appearance, which happened automatically on Venus, one returned.

"They are Paraeans from the planet called Paraeon. They've been sent to Venus as exchange personnel,' she said, smiling and visibly happy to be back, which Patosh noted with mixed feelings. Mary remained human in appearance, as she belonged to the human species, but Jonathan, Martha and Fred also transformed into what they had always been in reality. They also strolled along the corridor with long arms and legs, but their heads were oval-shaped.

But who was Jonathan and who was Martha or Roselyn? They all looked the same and you couldn't tell male from female. But Jenkins, who had spent years studying aliens, immediately recognised the difference. It was the gait. The male walked with an angular, dragging gait, while the female showed a certain grace. Yes, the gait could even be described as sexy and similar to that of human women. You could see it in the swaying of the hips, which swung back and forth like a little bell.

"Oh Jenkins. The things you notice,' William said with a smile. 'I thought you didn't like women.'

'Don`t tell me you`re jealous, Will,' Malcolm countered.

'I hope you don't find my looks repulsive.' Patosh suddenly heard someone say in his mind. It was Roselyn, who would only speak telepathically from now on, because that was how all communication worked on Venus. Something Jenkins and William also had to get used to.

Patosh didn't know how to respond and just shook his head in the negative. He didn't find her repulsive, just different. They continued walking until they were suddenly standing in front of a plasma wall, because there was no other way to call this liquid gelatinous wall, as then one of these Paraeans held his right hand on it and an opening appeared, reminiscent of a gateway from a science fiction film. Behind it was the universe. No floor, no walls, no rooms, just the emptiness of space and beings moving back and forth and from top to bottom.

The Paraean asked, telepathically of course, to step through this opening, but the three men refused, understandably having to endure a horror show in their minds.

"Nothing will happen to you. You will float like we do. Just follow us,' Roselyn assured them.

"Don't worry men. I had to go through that too back then. It's just as she says.' Mary also reassured them, but it wasn't reassuring at all. Patosh was the first to step into this void, followed by William and finally Jenkins, who covered his eyes and lo and behold. Like the others, they were floating in empty space, surrounded by stars and darkness. Jenkins remembered that as a child he had a wallpaper on the wall of his room that depicted such a scenario and now it has manifested itself into reality for him. He became religious at that moment and thanked God for this marvellous gift.

Three figures came towards them. They were KTKFK and two others from the High Council.

"We are pleased to welcome you here. We are especially grateful to you, KTXLK, for the trust you have placed in us. I'm sure you know KTZOP and KTKRE to my left and right."

"Yes, I know them. Greetings, brothers.' said Roselyn, unaffected and emotionless. Everything human seemed to have been deactivated in her.

"Before we subject you to the procedures, let's talk about the duties of your position when you return back to earth, my sister. To do so, you would have to separate from your group and follow these two brothers, who will then instruct and prepare you. The others, apart from Jonathan, Martha and Fred, who are now called KTZRE, KTMTH and KTWFR here, will have to wait in a so-called waiting room. Jonathan, Martha and Fred will also follow the two brothers, because we will start the process with them immediately.   As soon as the Head had said this, Patosh, Jenkins and William were the only ones standing in this void, with only the Head to keep them company. A room appeared, it was a hologram and since you could float, you didn't need chairs or armchairs. You didn't feel hungry or thirsty either, although Venusians fed in the same way.

'Do you have an appetite for a Mangaria salad or a Milky Way bar?' the Head asked kindly, knowing full well that these men would not eat anything they did not know. But he was wrong, because Jenkins was always hungry and even if he didn't know these cosmic foods, he wanted to try a scientific experiment.

"Why not? I'll have both. Let's see how the food tastes on Venus!"

"Taste? We don't have a sense of taste like you do. An energy exchange takes place telepathically when we eat and our free will decides whether the meal is compatible or not,' KTKFK explained.

'Sounds exciting anyway.' Jenkins assured him and then the other two ordered the same. Even KTKFK was surprised and praised the adventurous spirit of the men.

Of course, the Milky Way bar on Venus had nothing to do with the one we know on Earth. There was no chocolate with a white cream filling to tantalise the tongue, no, it tasted of nothing and looked so unappetising that even Jenkins lost his appetite.

Even telepathically, nothing seemed to be stirring in the human brain, because the only thing that seemed compatible was disappointment for the three of them.

'Interesting,' William said and placed the bar, which looked like a small sea cucumber, back on a holographic plate.

'Mangaria salad is a delicacy here on Venus.' KTKFK assured him, but his words were not convincing. Jenkins, however, was not a spoilsport and took a leaf that looked bluish purple and had a triangular shape. He chewed and chewed and suddenly stopped chewing. A feeling of happiness came over him and he smiled as if he had seen unicorns. He also looked down at his genital area, which was fortunatelly covered by his trousers, and noticed a bulgy swelling, which made him glow even more. His whole hormone balance began to fluctuate and it seemed that his testosterone balance did too. He touched himself there and a 'WOW' shot across his lips.

"With this salad, we men wouldn't need VIAGRA any more. Guys you have to try it!" he shouted with a laugh and neither of them had to be told twice. Not only did their sex drive increase when they ate this tasteless vegetable, but their general well-being increased many times over. Pain in the back, knees or hips vanished into thin air. Patosh suffered from this on earth, as did William, and it felt like a liberation to be rid of after years of torment.

"I can see that the Mangaria salad has a different effect on you than it does on us. Very interesting.' KTKFK realised.

'So we should take some of that back with us.' Jenkins insisted, causing even the head of the High Council to make a clacking noise that sounded amused. Was he laughing telepathically?

'I see you like it here.'

"Well, you can't say that just yet. It's fascinating and breathtaking, but scary at the same time, please don't misunderstand. I mean, we could have never imagined such sensations. Nothing is missing and you don't long for any desires. This is how I imagine perfection. Why doesn't this also exist on our earth, I wonder?' said Jenkins, overwhelmed.

"You have to learn to recognise yourselves. You humans have forgotten how to do that and only very few are still able to do it. You have become impure, and not even through your own fault. You have been blinded and we once let you down. I have to admit that. We too once had to learn a lot and work on ourselves, but now we have moved on because we have recognised ourselves. You still have a long way to go, but it will happen."

'Show us how we can do it again.' Patosh said.

'We offered it to you, but you refused.'

"I don't know who you offered it to, certainly not me. Show us the way and maybe we can at least make a small contribution after we return."

"I praise the honesty in your words Patosh, you who have already contributed a lot by not giving up on Roselyn. I will consider it. But now come to rest, for you will stay here for a while."

There is no time calculation on Venus, but one year on Earth corresponds to only one day on Venus. In other words, Patosh and his people stayed on Venus for three days according to their calendar, which corresponded to three years on Earth, but KTKFK found it superfluous to explain or inform them of this fact and why explain something if you are not asked about it. From this point of view, all Venusians were between three hundred and one thousand five hundred years older than the terrestrial species on Terrarion, which would naturally lead to consequences when they returned. Roselyn agreed to the duties imposed on her and Mary decided to stay on Venus, as she could no longer be of use to anyone on Earth and her death should not be an emotional burden on others. Better to say goodbye here than on a planet where people feel sorry for themselves and spend more time living in self-induced darkness. Roselyn, Patosh and the others should get a fresh start without having to face obstacles on their way, and that would make Mary feel more comfortable. The memory procedure was not eliminated, as its predecessor KXTLG had intended, but modified. The experience learnt and acquired was to be retained so that the mistakes made were not repeated, but logical and clearer thinking was improved and promoted. Roselyn decided to build a kind of bed and breakfast for aliens from the estate that Archie had already bequeathed to her. A landing site for spaceships would be constructed in such a way that it would be impossible to locate them and why constantly hide in a lake, scare the fish and get out of UFOs soaking wet? A dry variant should be possible and a plan drawn up for it on Venus. Jenkins wanted to grow Mangaria, but a Venusian made it clear to him that this 'vegetable' could only grow on Venus and that he, Jenkins, should rather try magic mushrooms, which are already native to Earth and are easy to plant. The effects are similar to those of Mangaria lettuce, with the exception of a few symptoms. So they came to an agreement. Roselyn would convert the Wellington Estate into a refuge for incoming 'holidaymakers from outer space', Jenkins could continue his research on the estate unmolested and work with the aliens to build a better world and gain a better understanding of the whole, Patosh would turn his back on Lontzen and leave the pub to Georgette and move in with Roselyn, and William would carry on doing what he always did. Running the Red Lion Hotel. Jonathan, Martha and Fred hoped to continue running their grocery shop and leave everything else behind, but they too would be of service to the new arrivals and hold seminars once a week, as they did in Spain, but this time for the 'holidaymakers'.

KTKFK was not allowed to interfere any further in their lives, otherwise he would be no better than his predecessor, and when the day came to say goodbye, they all met at the same place where the GALAXIA TITANICA had once brought them.

"I thank you for everything, my Chief. Your grace will not be forgotten and your wisdom shall be blessed.' Roselyn said telepathically and KTKFK thanked her with a touch on her forehead.

"Take care of them my sister, but also of you. The blessing of the Creator shall accompany you. You will meet another world down there, because I didn't mention anything about time. That shall be your task. We will help you with everything you need, but you should demand our help, because we must not interfere. This error shall be over once and for all. Don't worry about Mary."

They all said goodbye and as sad as they should have been to leave Mary behind, they felt nothing, because feelings did not exist on Venus. They boarded a smaller spaceship with the name. 'Stupor Mundi'. A joke that KTKFK allowed himself to make to suggest to them that the world would indeed be amazed one day, as a long time ago, an emperor named Frederick the Second from the Hohenstaufen dynasty was called by his supporters, because he understood and used the universal power as early as the Middle Ages.

Jenkins found this interlude very amusing and fitting at the same time. They didn't turn round to say goodbye and got in.

Nothing seems as it is

Roselyn skilfully landed the ship on the Connington on the Shyre estate and switched on stealth mode, which made the vehicle invisible. On the way back to Earth, Roselyn made it clear to the Earthlings, Patosh, Malcolm and William, that they were now three years older and should not be surprised at how Earth and their loved ones would receive them. But Roselyn would also be surprised, because KTKFK had really taken care of everything. A Land Rover stood outside the front door of the farm and William wept with joy, for it was the same one that had been destroyed before his eyes. Roselyn opened the letterbox, but it was empty and the garden was well kept, as if she had never left Connington on the Shyre. The police and security who had driven her to flee were gone and the only one missing was Mary.

It turned out that KTKFK had created holograms of them when they left Earth and he had also used Venusians as lawyers in human form and the case regarding the wreck theft vanished into thin air so that peace and quiet could be restored. They entered the old villa and saw their holograms, at least those of Roselyn, Jenkins and Patosh. These deactivated the moment the originals entered the house.

"William, Jonathan, Martha and Fred. Your holograms will also say goodbye when you return home. Behave as if nothing has happened and return to normality,' Roselyn asked with a smile.

"I wasn't wrong about the Venusians. Their love is unconditional.' And with moist eyes, she telepathically thanked KTKFK one last time, but he didn't answer back.

'I think I have to go back to Lontzen to see what's going on,' said Patosh.

'OH yes, and I'll go with you.' Jenkins said, but Roselyn asked Patosh to get his things in order alone, because he wouldn't be seeing Lontzen again. Jenkins understood and nodded in the affirmative.

'I'll be on my way tomorrow.'

'What about us?' asked Jonathan. 'How do we get to Bedford?'

'With me, of course!' offered William. 'Now that I've got my Landy back.'

"Then let's get to work. I'll go and do the post. I'm sure there's a lot to catch up on after three years." But she was wrong. Her hologram took care of everything and she found an empty desk in front of her.

In Bedford, William unloaded the little family in front of their grocery shop and the holograms detached themselves. However, the cashier looked at them a little puzzled when she noticed the three of them outside and not inside the shop.

'I should try a different gin,' she said to herself.

"William's hologram dissolved the moment he walked through the door of The Red Lion and found everything as it was on the day he left. His mail was done and he was greeted as he always was.

"How do you do it old house. You always look so young,' said one of the guests in the bar. William just smiled and thought: 'Mangaria salad makes it possible." and most of all he was pleased that he hadn't dreamt it, but had experienced it in the flesh. Would he tell his lodge brothers? Better not.

'The Easy- Jet flight to Brussels with flight number 476 is ready for boarding...' shouted the loudspeaker in the Luton terminal. Patosh, who was sitting at the same counter where he once met Malcolm Jenkins and found him annoying, paid the bill and headed for the gate. How everything in life develops and how nothing is as it seems, he thought to himself, looking at the people who had no idea, what was actually really happenjng around them while wandering around like lost ducks. How bizarre reality really is and how unpredictable at the same time. He realised that Jenkins was right when he said '...there are no such coincidences...' back when they met. How often had he, Patosh, turned away annoying people who happened to meet him and how often might they have changed his life if he hadn't been so dismissive. But in the case of Jenkins, fate decided and people always meet twice in life.

The flight passed quickly and without complications. At the car hire agency, he showed the printed reservation certificate and thirty minutes later picked up the hire car from the garage. He would reach Lontzen in the evening, but what would he find and what would his friends say when he 'gives away' the Golden Jug to Georgette and, above all, what would she say?

A thousand thoughts buzzed in his head, but he managed to suppress them, because he knew that new doors were opening for him and the past no longer had a place in his life.

The time with his EX wife Camille had been wasted years of apprenticeship, but that was over now. He didn't realise how quickly time had flown by as he arrived. He entered his pub unsteadily, where he was greeted by his friends, as always. Gouillomme, Francine, Robert, Jaques and everyone else just said 'Salut Patosh' and that was that. His hologram disappeared and Georgette kissed him left and right on the cheeks, as she always did.

'How's it going Georgette?'

'Same as always, boss.'

'By the way, I think you should buy a new car, your old Peugeot won't last much longer.' Patosh tried to find out a bit more.

"Are you joking? You bought me a new one three years ago and it's still going strong.

But thank you, boss. You're lovely." she replied, laughing and shaking her head. He was not mistaken. It was just as he had hoped and all the problems had disappeared from the face of the earth. A weight fell from his shoulders and he hugged Georgette like never before. But she only looked at him with even more astonishment.

"We need to talk. Tell Silvie to cover for you for 20 minutes."

He found everything in his office tidy and clean. Not a speck of dust, not a cobweb and not a cigarette ash that an ex had left behind without ever lifting a finger to clear it away.

"Shoot, boss. Don't keep me in suspense, because I'm rarely called into the office and usually only when I've done something wrong."

'So sit down...who's barking all the time? ....' and when he turned round, he couldn't believe his eyes. Mr Gonzales was standing in front of him, happily wagging his tail as if nothing had happened. What a film was going on and yes, Mr Gonzales was made of flesh and blood and was not a hologram. Patosh picked up the dog and hugged him tightly. Tears ran down his cheeks and Gonzi licked them away as if to say. 'Don't cry, it's all right.' A long-forgotten pain resurfaced when he saw the images of his dead dog and now the pain that had haunted him like a shadow all those years was gone. Now, that he had his GONZI back.

"Should I be worried, boss? You're behaving strangely. Just an hour ago you were snapping at the mutt because he always runs between one`s legs and now this. Let me bring us two cognacs, because you need it."

"Don't bother Georgette. I should still have a bottle of Hennessy in the drawer. Here it is and it's still full, well what do you know." Patosh opened the bottle and poured two glasses of the liquid gold.

It was obvious to Patosh that KTKFK had something to do with Mr. Gonzales`s resurrection. His gratitude could also be shown in this manner for the involuntary service to others.

In this case, the service to Roselyn and Mary. But what happened to the memory of the incident in the parking lot at the supermarket where Mr. Gonzales was stabbed? Was that the modification of polarity in the memory field?   A legitimate intervention in free will? No matter. Gonzi had risen again and too many questions could spoil the day

'Cheers... Georgette, I'll leave you the Golden Jug. I've found someone and I'm going to move in with her. I'm also no longer the fittest to continue running the shop and since you've always served me faithfully and loyally and marched with me through thick and thin, I think it's only right to thank you by handing it over."

'But...'

"I don't want to hear any buts. Tomorrow we'll go to the notary and arrange it. Everything should be in order, shouldn't it? I'm convinced, my darling, that you'll run the business without any problems, right? What do you say?"

Georgette didn't say anything because she didn't understand anything. Did she hear correctly?

"But boss, where do you want to go then? How am I….how are we supposed to manage without you? You are our pillar, our rock... What will the others say when you're no longer here? It will never be the same again if you go....No, no, that's not possible.' Georgette started to cry.

"There, There, my little girl. You can do it. Silvie will certainly support you and the regulars have mostly turned to you. Please accept it, otherwise I'll close the shop for good and I don't want that. With you, I know it's in good hands. I'm getting married and moving to England Georgette."

"TO ENGLAND? Oh my God, even that!' she sobbed uncontrollably, but Patosh soothed and hugged her and he too felt the coming separation from everything he had once built and the people who had always stood by his side. How his life would have ended if these aliens had never come to Lontzen and for a moment he even wished they hadn`t. In the end it was they who brought all this confusion that had thrown his life so out of joint. As far as he knew, UFOs could only be seen in the USA. What gave them the idea to come to Belgium and even to Lontzen?

"All right, boss, I'll take over the shop and have it transferred to my name. But if you come to your senses and want it back, the Golden Jug will be yours again without further ado. That's the only way I'll accept it."

"It's a deal, my angel. Now go back to work. I'm still the boss here!"

It took four days for the Golden Jug to be signed over to Georgette, because the mills were grinding slowly in Belgium too and Roselyn was calling every day. She needed Patosh at her side more than ever and Jenkins, who had a big task ahead of him, was now also swamped with work. A landing pad had to be built with a hall that resembled an aeroplane hangar, but had to be built underground to keep prying eyes away and that was the problem, as such a project would raise eyebrows and, of course, curiosity. This is where William would come in.

He knew people in the lodge who had been out of work for months and desperately needed the money and these brethren had to be well chosen, for if anyone could keep a secret it was, one would think, a Freemason. The site at Connington on the Shyre was also difficult to access and off-limits to private individuals. So security forces were also needed, and who better than the brothers who had served in the Royal Army and now had nothing more to do when they were no longer needed in Afghanistan and Iraq. William had also been given a rather piquant task, but he couldn't say no to it. Now that he had had all these experiences and realized how much his life had changed. There was no going back for him. Like the other friends, he had changed as a person. His guests at the Red Lion and his brethren from the lodge noticed this too.

Then, on the third day of his stay in Lontzen, old Mary suddenly appeared in the Golden Jug and Patosh lost his tongue. She appeared like a ghost out of nowhere. Was she a hologram? He didn't dare go up to her and so she walked up to him. She looked at him and had tears in her eyes, but a smile of joy lit up her face, making her look younger.

"I'm cured, Patrick," she whispered, "a miracle has happened. My illness was cured and so I decided to return. KTKFK, however, sent me here instead of to Roselyn. I am to tell you that a greater task will come your way and you are to face it, no matter how difficult."

"Mary. I still can't believe you're here. Roselyn will be beside herself with happiness. I have the news and I thank you. Will you stay here until I've finished my business?

"No, Patrick. I'm on the next flight to Luton this afternoon. I want to see Roselyn."

"Can you please take Gonzi with you? He'll get on wonderfully with Harry."

"Well, I don't know. Two males. But I'll take him with me, because Roselyn will be just as happy to have him. I'll take him with me straight away. Then I can prepare myself better for the flight..."

"Stay here and rest. It's still a long way to the flight Mary..."

"No, Patrick. I want to go now. Don't worry about it. You'll be joining us soon."

"Yes, I will Mary. Please promise Roselyn that as soon as the pub is signed over, I'll be on the next flight."

"I will Patrick."

She took Mr. Gonzales by the leash, who voluntarily left the pub with her without protest.

But what Patosh didn't realize all this time was that he was under constant surveillance. Not by the Venusians, not by the Orion group, since they knew what a tough nut he was to crack and had almost given up on him, but by a secret special organization of earthly origin, where nobody knew exactly who they belonged to.

Patosh and Georgette left the notary's office on Waterloo

Boulevard in Brussels to have a drink in the bar of the Hilton's Hotel that specific day. Georgette chose her cousin as a notary in Brussels to save money, as the notary in Lontzen would have been overworked and overpriced. In her opinion, the journey to Brussels would have been more worthwhile, also because she didn't want to be immediately attacked by her colleagues and friends, who were more envious and resentful than happy.

"I'll just go round the car and get the mobile phone. I left it there, I'm an idiot,' said Patosh and hurried to the hotel car park. He reached Georgette's Peugeot and before he could put the key in the door lock, he was overpowered by several men and thrown into a waiting van. He felt a sting in his neck and then the lights went out. Meanwhile, Georgette was waiting in the hotel bar and had ordered two glasses of champagne to celebrate. She was now the boss of the Golden Jug, but Patosh was nowhere to be seen. After an hour, she paid for the drinks and left them untouched on the table. She was told at reception that the hotel bill had been paid by a Mr John Miller rather than a Patrick van de Brog, but she didn't know a John Miller and she and Patosh had no plans to check out of the hotel as they were invited to dinner that evening at her cousin's, the notary, and it wasn't until the next morning, after breakfast, that Georgette wanted to drive back to Lontzen and Patosh fly back directly from Brussels to Luton.

Georgette suspected that something bad must have happened, because Patosh wouldn't leave her so easily without saying goodbye. She ran to the car park and found the car there, the keys lying on the ground, a pair of broken sunglasses and bloodstains on the door handle.

'Mon Dieu, mon dieu...' she stuttered and ran back to the hotel reception.

"The police. Call the police now!' she shouted. The police arrived one hour later, took the forensics and asked Georgette hundreds of questions, which she answered as best she could, crying and sobbing.

"There are indeed traces of violence. Did he have enemies?' the inspector asked, but Georgette answered in the negative. However, she told him about Patosh`s partner in England and passed the details on to him.

'I advise you to go home and be available for any questions you may have,' he said to her gently and Georgette just nodded in the affirmative, cancelled dinner at the cousin's and drove back to Lontzen. But there was nothing to celebrate in Lontzen when she told the others what had happened and that there was no sign of Patosh.

Where the hell was Patosh?

High above the Atlantic, at an altitude of 12,000 metres, a Gulfstream 550 was flying towards Langley, Virginia in the USA. In the private jet, Patosh was awakened from his anaesthetic and a hot coffee infused life back into his veins.

'Where am I and who are you?' was the first thing he asked.

"You are on your way to Langley Virginia, Mr van de Brog. We are sorry to have to take such measures, but you would not have come voluntarily if we had asked nicely. We are from the CIA and belong to a special department that deals with cases that cannot be explained by physical and logical means. This is where you come in, because we have been observing all of you for a very long time. You, the two Mitchells ladies, Malcolm Jenkins and this character, the landlord of the Red Lion in Bedford, have secretly disappeared from the villa in Connington on the Shyre. These Brits and their names huh…. Strange things happened after that. Among other things, people don`t want to remember such incidents anymore and our British colleagues from MI 6 and Scotland Yard think we are fantasists. Suddenly files disappear, videos and other evidence as well and the case is put on AD AKTA after three years and declared to be a bad joke. Well, Mr van de Brog, we don't do that. We don't AD AKTA anything, because we have evidence of your complicity......"

'Complicity in what?' Patosh asked with a laugh.

"Complicity in alien matters. A spaceship appears and disappears in front of the police eyes, a Land Rover falls out of the sky, people are abducted by aliens and disappear for three years and then the case is forgotten and the interest is shut down? Our British colleagues behave like hypnotised robots and laugh at us...."

"So you admit to extraterrestrial life? Interesting after all these years of lies and denial.

"Of course we admit it, but we can't just blurt it out. Think of the Russians, the Chinese and the power games that could result."

"I just see how you don't want to share this knowledge for the good of humanity, but only use it for your perverse power purposes. What opportunities we have missed in all these years because of morons like you. Energy crises and wars would have been eliminated from the world once and for all..."

"BLA, BLA, BLA, Mr van de Brog. You only see everything in black and white. Do you really think we're not interested in world peace? The problem lies deeper, what shall I call it... cosmic. Do you know how many species there are up there, and among them not necessarily friendly ones? We have the whole basement full of them, but not in Area 51. We use this area to deceive the others. Let them believe that we are playing our games there, but the whole thing is taking place somewhere else. We can't trust anyone, because people aren't able to keep secrets to themselves.

After ten years at the latest, people will start talking. Conflicts of conscience, sensationalism, delusions of grandeur, what do I know, we humans have faults and as you can already see for yourself, I have said too much. Your Venusians haven't told you everything, have they?"

"I'm not saying anything. I'm simply kidnapped and flown to the USA against my will. There's no bigger bunch of hypocrites than you are in this world with all your slogans of freedom and democracy, wars, wars and more wars, that's all you know. Ah, not to forget printing money. Once trillions that you invent out of nothing have been spent, you print more trillions. Then there's the whole scam with viruses and vaccinations. I ask myself, how can you have such hatred for the people who still vote for you? All the governments are globally corrupt in this world and then you come and tell me how angelic you are and I only see everything in black and white? Fly me back immediately, otherwise I'll cause a scandal that's got a lot to do with it? I'm just an innkeeper, not a spy, an agent or any other kind of wanker like you are and you can threaten me as much as you like, you won't impress me.

It's probably a bad film what's going on here. I think Hollywood is to blame for everything. I don't know anything about aliens and UFOs. Whatever you're smoking, stay away from it."

'So you refuse to work with us?'

"I don't know you. You didn't even have the decency to introduce yourself and I don't do anything for nothing and as long as you treat me like I'm a piece of cattle, I won't say a word. I have nothing to interest you either. Yes, Jenkins lived in Lontzen for quite some time and found a wreck in the lake where nobody knew exactly what it was until you turned up with your helicopters and all that Rambo posturing. That's what really created the hype, because it proved that you had something to hide. Jenkins and his crew came to my place for beer and dinner. That's all there was to it."

"Was there? You were always together after that." Mr Miller, let's call him that, slammed photos on the table. They showed Jenkins, William, Roselyn, Mary and Patosh together at the villa. At some point, cameras were apparently installed inside the building without their knowledge and conversations were also recorded, because the tape recorder followed seconds later.

"Don't deny it Pat. I'll just call you that, because this is getting too personal. I'm not going to fly you back, I'm going to show you a few things so that you don't walk around with those rose-tinted spectacles that make you think you're in a perfect world. The situation is very serious and yes, what is happening here at the moment is becoming too much for us too. You will be amazed why things are happening the way they are in this world, because things have not been human for a long time.

Are you familiar with the Orion Clan or have you at least heard something about them?"

Patosh looked at the photos in horror and stopped the tape recorder, now realising how hopeless his situation was.

'What exactly do you want and what should I call you?'

"Call me John. Just John and what I want is for you to work with us. It's been years of silence to avoid a monstrous panic Pat, because nothing is as it seems. Do you understand me?"

Earth is not a holiday destination

The jet landed at Langley Virginia and, as seen in Hollywood films, a convoy of black GMC Yukon SUVs drove up. Agents with dark sunglasses, bodies that proved a daily visit to the GYM, earplugs stuck in their ears and always ready to hand, the Beretta, Glock or Heckler and Koch hidden behind their black blazers, surrounded the aircraft. 'John Miller', Patosh and other officers got into the vehicles and left the airfield at high speed. Patosh sat in the back, along with two of those extra-wide goons who threatened to squash him, and not a word was spoken on the journey. He realised that Roselyn and Georgette would be wondering where he was and that a phone call was probably out of the question. After two hours of driving, a gate, which was wrapped in barbed wire, opened electrically and a sentry saluted the convoy in military fashion. Suddenly it stopped in front of another aeroplane. The civilian version of a Boeing 737 painted white and red and without further delay, Mr John Miller pushed to board. Less than fifteen minutes later, the 737 took off. Destination unknown. There were other people on board the aircraft who gave the impression of scientists and professors based on their clothing. Old jackets and bow ties instead of ties and hairstyles that had not seen a hairdresser for years expressed an intellectual character.

Patosh was greeted in a friendly and euphoric manner, as if they had been waiting for this Messiah.

'Would you like a coffee or tea?' asked the flight attendant, who was now wearing a US Air Force uniform.

"Can I have something stronger? A Jack Daniels perhaps?' Patosh asked her almost pleadingly.

"But of course. With ice?"

'Yes, please.'

'Oh Sharon, bring the whole bottle and three more glasses.' one of the gentlemen called after her.

"Mr van de Brog. May we introduce ourselves before we open up to you? My name is Professor Alfred Farnham, to my left is Professor Richard Curtiss and you already know Michael Robertson."

'How do you do, gentlemen, but Mr Robertson introduced himself as John Miller...' replied Patosh with a grin.

"Oh, Mike. You and your common names. Forgive him Mr van de Brog, I hope you understand this secrecy. May I call you Patrick?"

Patosh was pleasantly surprised by this gentleman, who had something fatherly about him, and he agreed.

'You may...Alfred.'

"Very nice...ah here comes the bourbon. Thank you Sharon."

The flight attendant smiled briefly and disappeared again.

"Before we can talk any more, Patrick, you have to sign a confidentiality agreement. Would that be all right with you?"

"Yes, that's fine, but it's mutual, of course. I'll only talk if I can recognise the seriousness of the situation, not before,' Patosh replied unequivocally, which impressed the men.

"But of course. Richard, be a dear and give me the documents to sign,' Professor Farnham asked his colleague, who took the documents out of a leather briefcase that looked more like an old school satchel. Farnham showed Patosh where to sign and Patosh read the pages carefully. The contract was very simple in its form. Not a word was allowed to be spoken outside the time Patosh was in their company and so he had no problem signing in the appropriate places.

"Very good. Thank you Pat, I'll get straight to the point. We're flying to Area 51, but we'll only be there for two days so that you can get a quick idea of how unimportant this place actually is. At least for our business. From there we'll continue by helicopter to our actual destination. Don't worry. It'll be a short flight, but as I said, only in two days so that you can recover a little."

"So Area 51 is unimportant? What a pity....." Patosh said with disappointment.

"It used to be, but in the eighties this place got too busy with weirdos and freaks, so we had to relocate. We're working on other projects here that aren't our thing. To what extent can you tell us something? They say you and your friends were abducted by the aliens and taken somewhere?' Farnham asked cautiously.

"We were not abducted. We came along voluntarily, but as I said, I'll tell you more when I realise what this is all about. Please remember that you abducted me and not the aliens."

"How true, how true, and of course we apologise for that. I'm afraid you'll see how serious the situation is with your own eyes soon. Prepare yourselves for something you didn't expect in your wildest dreams Pat. I'm sure you'll have no doubts about having to work with us afterwards." Professor Farnham said seriously.

'How are Roselyn and the others?' asked Richard Curtiss, who remained silent the whole time.

'You know Roselyn?' Patosh asked with a smile.

'Yes, I know her very well,' which really made Patosh's attention explode.

'How so?' he asked him curiously.

"She came to see us years ago. Telepathically, of course. I had been working in this field for years and suddenly made contact with her. It was such a shock for me at first, but over the years a friendship developed between us. After that, however, all contact broke off and I still don't know why."

'You're telling me an old wives' tale, Professor Curtiss."

"No Patrick, I'm not. She provided us with important information and warned us about some of the species from outer space that are already here on this planet. We want and need to make contact with her again...."

"Apparently everyone wants that. I can't say anything until I've convinced myself that you're not some sort of wind eggs.

I don't care what you do to me, but I care about my friends' lives, especially now that they....' Patosh bit his lip.

"Give me time gentlemen. I need to process all of this first."

It was already evening when the 737 landed on the long tarmac runway in the state of Nevada and they had a Hummer jeep drive them into the main terminal. Patosh was given a visitor's pass, which had already been produced on the flight there, and was accommodated in one of the guest rooms available for special visitors.

'I'll pick you up in an hour,' said Mr John Miller, whose real name was Michael Robertson, if that was indeed his final name.

Patosh took a hot shower and then found everything he needed, as he had no luggage with him. A black overall, a T-shirt, a pair of socks and pants, as well as toiletries such as toothpaste and shaving kit were waiting for him on his bed. An hour later, he was picked up by a sergeant and a lieutenant and taken to a sort of canteen where the others were also sitting at a table waiting for him.

"Ah Pat, it's a good thing you're here, because we're starving. Come on.' Farnham said with a friendly smile and led Patosh to the narrow aisle where they could grab a tray and cutlery and take various salads and sandwiches from the display cabinets. Patosh took a Caesar salad and an original cheeseburger with fries from the food counter. There were no alcoholic drinks here, so he took a Coke Zero. Back at the table, they ate and didn't say another word about aliens or Roselyn or anything else that could have spoilt the evening. There was time for that the next day.

The next morning, Patosh was picked up by the same staff as the day before. This time he was taken to a kind of lounge for VIPs, where the atmosphere was a little more upmarket. Bookshelves, leather armchairs and an oversized old globe gave the impression of a rather British affair, but this was not the case and Patosh realised this immediately when an American general suddenly stood next to him and greeted him loudly in Texan. Patosh had difficulty understanding him at first, but fortunately Professor Farnham, Professor Curtiss and Mike Robertson entered the room and interrupted the very enthusiastic general in a friendly manner.

"General Cooper, I see you have already made the acquaintance of Mr Patrick van de Brog. After breakfast we will go to the briefing room together and discuss our conversation in more detail."

'Pleased to meet you General Cooper.' Patosh said with amusement at the cowboy in US Air Fore uniform.

There was coffee, scrambled or fried eggs, as desired, and plenty of bacon, beans, toast and orange juice. Nothing was lacking, so to speak, and they tried to make Patosh's stay as comfortable and friendly as possible so that he could gain trust, because they needed him. The sun must have been shining hot out there that day, because the light shining through the windows was bright and dazzling. There wasn't a cloud in the sky and only the typical American habit of running the air conditioning on full blast kept the temperature pleasant and cool in the room.

After breakfast, however, no more time was wasted and a dark blue bus drove them to a hangar-like building where tens of security guards armed with MP5 submachine guns kept watch. Several F 15 fighters stood around in the hangar and Patosh realised that these were no ordinary fighters, but modified ones. They had strange probes on their tails and their noses were longer than the conventional ones. Patosh knew his way around aeroplanes as he had served two years in the Belgian Air Force, but they had the Mirage 5 and he was just 19 years old. He had always been interested in aeroplanes, but due to his asthma attacks, which were still prevalent at the time, he was unable to become a pilot himself. Now he was too old for it and he dreamed of what it would have been like if he had made it back then. But General Cooper drew his attention to the lift that took them all down ten floors. Patosh noticed the difference in pressure, held his nose and pressed lightly through it and his ears popped open again. It was like being in a spy film and he had only experienced something like this in the cinema or on television. The lift came to a halt and through a grey corridor made of reinforced concrete, which looked more like a bunker, they passed through a steel door where Professor Farnham first had to enter a code and his thumbprint was read by a scanner. What surprises would Patosh's life have in store for him, for he had already received more of life's privileges as a pub owner through his acquaintance with the aliens and now all of this. Why him? He asked himself, but fate sometimes reaches for a ball like in a lottery drum and fate doesn't care what number is on it. A large steel table, several chairs, a light projector and a blackboard were the only utensils that filled the room and after they took their seats at random, General Cooper immediately began his lecture.

"Mr van de Brog, let's get straight to the point, because we don't want to waste each other's time. Everything that is said and discussed here is subject to the strictest secrecy. I don't even want to talk about the punishment for non-compliance because, Mr van de Brog, I want to gain your trust. We are here to show you that you have put yourself in grave danger, not only on your own behalf, but on behalf of the global community. What you will see here today will convince you that we are not just dealing with friendly aliens. Unfortunately this is the case, but fortunately those who are friendly to us are advising and helping us, and that is NOT, and I emphasise it again, not the Venusians. At least that is the current state of affairs. We know that you were on Venus, because where else did the spaceship fly when you disappeared from Connington on the Shyre? We can no longer hide the existence of the aliens, as thousands have already seen it and we are running out of steam, but we have a huge problem. The Venusians will take over on Earth and make us submissive. Roselyn, who worked for us at the time, or let's put it another way, worked with us, proved this clearly and warned us about it. She was on the High Council and had overheard a lot and yes, she had spied for us, because let's not forget, she's half human. You wonder how she came to us in the first place. Well, Mr van de Brog, sometimes Hollywood films don't seem that far removed from reality. She applied to the Air Force as an analyst and passed all her exams with top marks.

That caught our attention and we slowly but steadily promoted her to higher departments. But what we didn't know was that she was also spying for the Venusians. We caught her in the act. I've worked in this field of extraterrestrial phenomena since the seventies, and believe me when I say that this department still doesn't have a name, that's how top secret we are. When KTXLK got tired of being interrogated, we finally got closer to the truth. She also opened up because no one came from Venus to help her and she felt betrayed by them and no, we don't use torture if you harbour such thoughts here now. I am totally against it as I already was in the Vietnam War. She was commissioned by her cosmic father, KTXLG, to spy on us and tell him all about Area 51. This is the reason why nothing will be found here, but the appearance of a dubious base must remain. Before we take the helicopter to the actual location, where your eyes will be opened, Mr van de Brog, we had to fill you in on the matter. Roselyn disappeared and never came back and we still feel betrayed by her today. What is she up to? Has she switched sides? When will they launch the invasion and enslave us like they did before?"

'You scare me General and yet I can assure you that Roselyn would never harm this planet...'

"She might not, but we are in the dark because of her. There is a power struggle between Venusians and other confederations, that much we know. The Orion Clan has already made itself comfortable in the highest echelons of all areas of our country. In industry, in education, in the media and much to our concern, in politics or do they think we want all that is happening? Nothing makes sense anymore. What was bad is now good and what was wrong is now right. Our civilisation is being destroyed by these circumstances and everything our ancestors fought and died for would have been for nothing. If the Venusians are as good as you think they are, where does that leave them? Roselyn promised to help us, but apparently something has happened up there and unfortunately the US Air Force doesn't have the technology to take a look."

'What exactly did Roselyn warn you about, General Cooper?' asked Patosh, visibly shocked.

"Ah. Excellent question Patrick. I'll call you that now and you can call me Freddy. My first name is Fredrick, but nobody calls me that. Roselyn warned us after realising for herself what the High Council's intentions were under KXTLG. I'll list the threats. Destruction of all capitals, chaos and famine due to the collapse of the financial system, artificially created anarchy according to the motto, only the strongest survive and the rest are enslaved, but that's not all. Man as such is to be abolished. Have you not wondered what is happening around you Patrick? In Belgium, Spain, Germany, England and the rest of the world? Not to mention the USA.

Do you know what makes us different from animals Patrick? Animals would never hand over the leadership of the herd or the pack to an idiot, but what's going on here is beyond comprehension. Look at the current government leadership. Scary, isn't it Patrick?"

Patosh no longer knew what to think.

Was this all just a set up so that he would betray the Venusians and thus Roselyn? KTKLK, the new head of the High Council on Venus, was anything but a power-hungry monster and the question arose in his mind: what motives did his predecessor, KXTLG, have for committing such breaches of the law and rules on Venus?

They had the same DNA and were compatible in terms of density. None of this made any sense. Interfering with the free will of all beings was a taboo and yet KXTLG had violated it, at least a few times, to get Roselyn back. What was the real reason that started the ball rolling back then, when Mary, who he had met on holiday, fled Venus? Was it perhaps not an escape but was she following an order given by KXTLG? Was he, Patosh, just being used and taken for a ride, which in itself was nothing difficult, as he still believed in the good in people? No, no, that was not his Roselyn. She would never be so cold as to break his heart again to such an extent. But back then, in Spain, he had left her and not the other way round, so he had broken himself and probably her heart too. The old memories came flooding back and doubt after doubt clouded his mind.

"All right, then. Show me what you've got to show Freddy. I want to see proof of your assumptions and not rely on words that could manipulate me."

"Rest assured, my dearest, that I am not trying to manipulate you. But after that I expect your co-operation, unconditionally, otherwise you will be allowed to enjoy this 'LUXURY' for an indefinite period here on Area 51. I have no more time for these children's games!' the general shouted clearly.

A Black Hawk helicopter was ready for them. They flew to Edward's Air Force Base, but only to refuel and then headed along the Mojave Desert, where they approached a mountain that was impossible to land on. Patosh was about to scream when the rotor blades came menacingly close to the rock wall and General Cooper grinned with amusement at the panicky look on Patosh's face. The wall suddenly opened and an illuminated hall was revealed. Shortly afterwards, the pilot masterfully placed the helicopter on the narrow platform and switched off the engines. There were guards everywhere you looked and dozens of procedures to follow before you reached a lift again, this time going up. The air was stuffy and the ventilation system seemed unable to cope with its task, as Patosh felt sick and began to gasp for breath.

'We're almost there Pat.' General Cooper reassured him, who seemed to be coping well with this condition.

After several metres they came to a barrier and a road opened up in front of them. A bus drove them to an entrance and Patosh was fascinated. He had never seen a motorway cut through the side of a mountain and it was highly likely that only 0.5% of the American population had ever seen one. The chosen elite of men and women who have dedicated themselves to this task. It must have cost billions and this structure alone suggested much. Americans took the alien thing pretty seriously. Patosh wanted to make a joke about the moon landing and ask if it had actually happened, but he didn't want to overstep the mark because Freddy, as he now called the general, only had a small arsenal of humour.

"OK boys. We're here. Masks and protective suits are ready in the cabins. Please get dressed and go through the other door,' he said as the bus stopped in front of a door. Twenty minutes later, they met up again in a lounge. Patosh, the two professors and Mike Robertson followed the general and the plastic visor fogged up a little as they exhaled, but this soon cleared completely.

"Here we are in front of the first cell. Inside is a friendly species from the Centaurus solar system."

'Centaurus?' Patosh asked. 'Never heard of it.'

"Because nobody knows it. The universe doesn't show its cards everywhere, Patrick, and this species is called Ketone. We call him Bill and Bill has become a good friend. Here, let me demonstrate."

The general opened the cell door and they entered the cell. Patosh's heart skipped a beat when he came face to face with this being, who had humanoid features and only differed slightly from the earthly ones in appearance. Freddy shook his hand and so did the professors.

"Come on Pat, don't worry. Say hello to Bill,' said Professor Farnham reassuringly and Patosh did so hesitantly. As soon as he touched the hand, however, he felt an unusual energy. Data-like, he took in information that told him all about Bill's origins and home and a soothing love that made him smile with warmth and happiness. Bill also conversed with Patosh telepathically and assured him how pleased he was to have made his acquaintance. He should not worry, he said, because he had no negative intentions. This went on for half an hour, but then the general pushed on to the next cell.

They left Billy's cell and walked to the next one. A sergeant major opened the green iron door, but before stepping inside, Professor Farnham warned Patosh that with each successive cell, the species and behaviour of those inside would change. Cells 1 to 4 are occupied by the friendlier species, but this friendliness diminishes as the cell number increases. From cell 5, the colour of the iron door changes to yellow, this colour being an indicator of the aggression rate of the species concerned. Patosh nodded in understanding and followed the others into cell number 2.

"Hello Charlie, how are we doing today?" Professor Farnham asked the short, chubby Allien, who was small in stature and reminded Patosh a little of Jaques, a regular visitor to his former pub. However, his eyelids closed and opened like a reptile. He also had an extremely small nose compared to Billy from cell number 1. Charlie didn't make a sound, but talked to Farnham telepathically.

"Of course Charlie. I'll get you the books. Also the wool for your crochet. My goodness, you've knitted something very pretty. For me? Seriously? That's very sweet of you Charlie. Thank you."

The alien handed Professor Farnham a home-knitted scarf and turned his gaze in a flash to Patosh, who was startled by the speed with which he turned his gaze, which apparently made the alien laugh. He made strange noises and held his stomach.

"May I introduce you to Patrick van de Brog, Charlie? Shake his hand. He's a friend and wants to help us," said Professor Curtiss this time.

Patosh reached out his right hand to the alien, but he extended his own in the telepathic way that had already become familiar. Patosh felt a handshake that felt dry and warm. Suddenly Charlie began to talk to him and Patosh heard clear words, as if they were talking to each other loud and clear as usual.

"The blessing of the Creator be with you, Patrick, who is also called Patosh," the alien said, which put Patosh in amazement, wondering how he could know that he was usually called that. He was never called Patosh here on the base, but the answer was not long in coming.

"I know all about you. Don't you worry, the others can't hear us because I have the ability to distort our conversation. They telepathically hear something completely different from what we're talking about. However, I trust you because you possess very good vibrations and I can tell that you are a discreet person. Don't believe them. They are holding us here and I'm sure you can see that already. We are not free and cannot move as we would like to, even though we have come with peaceful intentions. You, Roselyn and the others are in great danger, but play their game for now. What is happening between us right now, my friend, is happening within microseconds and I will transmit the relevant data to you in this way which are meant only for Roselyn. You will have no insight into it. Tell her you have met with someone from the planet Corantio. She will know about it. All you have to do, Patosh, is play this game.

Give them the feeling that you are willing to work with them, sign a contract with these beasts if you have to. The next cells with the green door are occupied by other species of a friendlier nature, but don't be fooled. They are suspicious of humans and rightly so.

We are not inherently bad beings, nor are you, but we are not without our faults. The species behind the yellow door will prove it to you, but they have only become what they are because they have been experimented on. They were once housed behind a cell with the green door, but after several unsuccessful experiments, they are now categorised as defective by these "researchers". Genetic manipulation of different species to see if we can be mixed. But the real main goal of these criminals will you experience behind the red door. There you will find the most dangerous creatures imaginable. A product of your science. Killer machines assembled from all kinds of genetic experiments. Your military will stop at nothing and what they call artificial intelligence does not only refer to computer-controlled machines, no, it also refers to genetically manipulated living beings, mixed from all possible solar systems, who have settled on this planet to advise and help. Unfortunately, you humans are also a product of our own experiments, which, it seems, are also proving to be flawed. However, I do not wish to apportion blame here, but to warn you and yours. Hand Roslyn the data. She will understand when you tell her that you have met someone from Corantio. Make sure you get out of here alive, but you will only succeed if you play along. They will insert a chip into you so that you can be watched, tracked and controlled at all times. Roselyn knows how to switch it off. These idiots really think they're on to us technically. This conversation is now over."

"Well, Charlie, we're glad you like Mr van de Brog. I will immediately arrange for you to be supplied with Dan Brown's and Hemingway's books. What? Tom Clancy as well? You don't want to become a conspiracy theorist, you old fox. Yes, even the coarse wool. Purple, green and azure. You'll get it today, my friend. I'm afraid we have to move on Charlie. Now say goodbye to Patrick."

Dazed by the conversation with "Charlie", Patosh followed the others to the door. He turned to Charlie once more and nodded to him before leaving the cell completely. Without another word, they walked down the corridor, but much to Patosh's surprise, a lift was used to take them directly to the cells with the yellow door, which appeared to be one floor below.

"What about the other cells up there? There were three green doors left," Patosh asked curiously.

"They're asleep now. These are species with a very peculiar internal clock, if you know what I mean. You can't wake them up, otherwise it could have fatal consequences for them. Strange creatures. One of them is a Venusian. Unfortunately, I don't think he'll be around much longer. He's infected with something, a virus we don't know yet. Professor Curtiss is still dealing with this problem, but is getting nowhere. At least not at this point. This virus doesn't come from this earth Patrick and that's why we have to be very careful with everything." Professor Farnham assured him.

"I see." Patosh replied dryly.

"The creatures behind the yellow door are chained up. They show depressive and sometimes aggressive characteristics, which I think are psychosomatic in origin. Post-traumatic disorders, similar to those suffered by our soldiers when they return from war. We suspect that these species are not naturally evolved this way, but are extremely sensitive to changes in their environment and others. A conversation with this species, I consider inappropriate at this time, as you will most likely not be able to do anything with it...."

"I still want to go in there and at least try, otherwise it goes against our agreement Professor. Friendly species don't give me any idea of the real danger you were talking about before. So let me in and let me decide whether I want to work with you or not. So far, I've only been able to see friendly creatures in captivity, which surprises me a little."

"Yes, of course. You're right Patrick!" shouted Professor Curtiss soothingly, trying to avoid an unnecessary discussion. Professor Farnham was horrified, however, because no one had ever dared to speak to him like that before. Caught off guard and not quite as enthusiastic as before, Farnham signalled the Sergeant Major to open the door. Mike Robertson, however, was amused by the previously underestimated Patrick van de Brog. He liked the somewhat rough, Belgian manner. Patosh was undeterred and wanted to know exactly what was going on, especially after the conversation with "Charlie", whose name was definitely not Charlie.

The yellow door opened and the whole thing took on a sad and unpleasant air. It reminded Patosh more of a mental asylum cell when he saw a creature sitting in a corner on the floor in an embryonic position. Yes, it was more like an alien, because that's what they looked like on Me-Tube and other social media. Oversized, grey head, oval black eyes without the whites or pupils and a skinny, bony figure. The comic books and the conspiracy press made you believe you were looking at one of these every day, but was this one real or just a dummy made by those Frankensteins in the Nevada desert? This creature just rocked back and forth and its eyes stared into space. Patosh tried to make contact with it, even spoke to it, but there was no response. At one point, the creature turned its head towards him and Patosh thought he could recognise tears, but how could this be? Hadn't Roselyn said that most beings in the universe who belonged to a higher density felt no emotions and lived out their existence emotionlessly? Patosh suddenly felt a very deep melancholy and he himself fell into a deep depression. The energy was definitely negative and the more negative it became, the more he, the alien, seemed to grin. Patosh now understood that this little arsehole was playing a game with him and the more Patosh tried to escape from this state, the more he felt this paralysis that was holding him back.

He was trapped in his own senses and felt chained from which there was no escape, just as he had sometimes experienced in a dream, when he dreamt of sitting in a car that was sinking deep into a lake and he was slowly drowning and the more he struggled against it, the more he could not move. He always woke up sweating and screaming.

Farnham, Curtiss, as well as Robertson, watched tensely and let it happen. He didn't want to listen, this arrogant, Belgian idiot. That must have been the thoughts in Professor Farnham's brain at the time. However, the creature let go of Patosh and released him from this torment.

"Now you can see for yourself how I feel." Patosh suddenly heard inside himself. A telepathic signal that was apparently meant only for him, because the others did not react. Could this creature, like Charlie, make contact unnoticed with those it considered trustworthy? Who knew for sure. Patosh knelt up again and stood right next to Professor Farnham.

"Where did he come from?" Patosh asked sternly.

"We don't really know. We don't know most of the planetary systems where some of these beings came from, because not even our most modern telescopes reach that far. They often don't have names that would assign them to their 'home'. They are mostly symbols, with which we can do very little. Perhaps the next door will shed more light on the matter, because this species is the same as the one here, but more talkative."

"Then there must have already been an idea of where they came from."

"Shadowy. We can't do anything with the information. But maybe it will want to talk to you. They know us, but they refuse to confide in us," Curtiss said with a shrug.

"I wonder why. Well then, off to the next cell. Maybe we'll find out more there."

"Wait a minute. This isn't some kind of detective story." protested General Cooper. "You're acting like a... like a... Inspector from Hawaii Five Zero or Miami Vice. That's not how it works. You haven't signed a contract yet and I can't allow you to be so flippant about this...."

"I've already signed a non-discloser agreement...." Patosh now shouted rather irritably.

"Yes, a non-discloser agreement is not a contract my best man....."

"If you want me to work for you, I need to go to the next cell and then visit the ones with the red door, otherwise this won't work."

"All right, to hell with it. Let him into the next cell Sergeant Major." came out almost spitting from the General, who was blushing with rage.

The next cell showed the same creature, but more relaxed and standing rather than crouching. Only now was it possible to recognise the actual posture of this creature, which, leaning slightly forwards, gave the impression of a hunchback.

"Tom. How are we doing today?" Professor Farnham asked in a friendly but serious manner.

"Alfred. Old house. I'm fine and apparently so are you. You've put on weight," everyone was told telepathically.

"It just seems that way. These new white coats make you look fat. May I introduce you to Mr Patrick van de Brog? He's a new employee who's doing a tour here to get a feel for the place."

"Ah yes. Pleased to meet you Patrick. I hope you'll like it here." came sarcastically from the alien.

"Thank you Tom. May I know where you're from?"

"Why?"

"Well, just out of curiosity. It's not every day we get a visit from an alien on this planet..."

"Oh no? And you want to hire him here?" Tom asked, ironically and with a demonic laugh, turning to the others.

"My young friend. I don't know what these gentlemen have told you, but believe me when I say that aliens visit this planet every day.

We are only the ones who have been caught, but there are others who have volunteered to work with these criminals."

"Well, well Tom. No need to be so unkind. We want to learn from you, but we can't do that if you don't want to behave like a guest here. We're not criminals, just concerned citizens of this planet."

"Forgive me Alfred, of course. Now back to you Patrick. Our planet has no name as such. It is characterised by symbols that are as old as the universe itself. You will never understand it, because they would make no sense to you. But to simplify it for you, we can call it the Second Earth. Our Planet is very similar to yours. The molecular structure is identical. We have an atmosphere, air, water and the soil is almost identical to that of Earth. However, the temperatures and gravity are different. Much colder and you would weigh a hundred times as much there. If you were to enter our atmospheric layer, you would not survive.

Your spaceship would fall to the ground from the greatest height and shatter into tiny pieces because the gravity is so strong. You have nothing comparable, technically speaking, to deal with such a force. Will that do for now, Mr van den Brog?"

"Why does he get such information and we don't Tom?" asked General Cooper, sounding like an offended child.

"I don't know. He looks so innocent and not like you guys, who torture us with samples and sensors and if that's not enough, cut you up alive...."

"Enough Tom!" shouted Professor Curtiss, beside himself. "This conversation stops now."

General Cooper and Professor Farnham thought so too, but apparently not Mike Robertson, who wasn't smiling this time around. Did he feel sorry for the creature and even sympathise with the Belgian's behaviour?

The red door

General Cooper was in a hurry and didn't want to spend any more time with the aliens behind the Yellow Door. He urged everyone to go to another elevator that held the sign "Red Zone". They went down a few floors but there must have been a lot more, because the ride wouldn't stop and only when the elevator slowed down did they know they were approaching the doors of hell. The professors, Mr. Robertson and the General all radiated an uneasy and very nervous tension, but Patosh was excited to see what was in store for him. He remembered with amusement about the prize draw show, "Which door will you choose, 1 or 2?" Usually the candidates were unlucky and instead of the sports car, they only got the lawnmower and a year's subscription of fertilizer. But this was different, because asking for door number three could cost you your life, or mean you would never be able to enjoy life as you knew it again. The elevator came to a stop and a long, dark concrete corridor led straight ahead as the door opened. Sensor-operated lights lit up, illuminating the path ahead of them. Guards everywhere they looked and scientists in security suits hurriedly greeted the professors and the general with a nod.

"In here, please." Cooper said as he opened a door that led to a room with hundreds of screens.

Men and women worked behind the screens and the whole thing had a somewhat surrealistic ambience, as if you were at the NASA center just before the launch of a Saturn 5 rocket. Equipped with headphones, they were monitoring something, but what?

"General! I haven't seen you here for a long time!" a man in his mid-fifties called out, holding out his right hand to the general.

"Dr. Friegstaad. I thought you were in Oslo, enjoying a well-deserved vacation. You don't have a home either, do you?" replied General Cooper, visibly pleased.

"What wife would put up with me at home for more than a week? No, no. The six months of vacation just turned into fourteen very long days for both of us until my wife got fed up with me for good and asked me to just go back to work and here I am. "

"I hope she still believes that you, dear Dr. Friegstaad, work at the University of Alberquerques." the general asked him anxiously.

"Yes, yes. Don't worry. She firmly believes in it and we want to keep it that way. But what brings you here and with such distinguished guests as Professor Farnham and Professor Curtiss? Michael, are you here too?" The men greeted each other hastily.

"You already know these gentlemen, I see. May I introduce Mr. Patrick van de Brog from Belgium?"

"How do you do, Mr. Van de Brog?" They shook hands and looked at each other in a friendly but suspicious manner.

"You know that you must have been given a special security clearance for this area?"

"He has, Doctor. He's with me. Mr. van de Brog is an important link in the chain of communication with the Venusians and that's why he's here. I want him to gain an insight into the diversity of various aliens and get an idea before we send him on his first mission."

"I see. Then please come in and you, Mr. van de Brog, follow me. Luisa... please prepare screen for cell 34. Activate cameras 1, 3 and 5...come on, come on. May I call you by your first name? It would be easier for me. My name is Claas, by the way."

"Of course Claas. You can call me by my first name. May I sit down here?" Patosh asked, still a little confused by the flair that was slowly overwhelming him.

"Yes, certainly. I have a few points to discuss with you before we get started, so listen to me carefully. These creatures are extremely dangerous. Their intelligence is a million times greater than ours and they can easily penetrate the subconscious of their counterparts and if you think they are on the same floor, think again. These creatures are another five floors below where we are right now and you, Patrick, have already experienced how long the elevator took to get to this floor.

"Indeed, the elevator ride seemed endless. You said it had already killed some of your colleagues? How?" Patosh asked him, already imagining a horror scenario. But Dr. Friegstaaad just shrugged his shoulders.

"We don't know that for sure. They all suffered a fatal stroke, but it must have been agonizing for the poor souls. Part of their brain matter evaporated. Sounds scary, doesn't it? As I said. This one is particularly good at it. The others have a similar ability, but they only spy on you subconsciously, but they don't hesitate to use violence either. We had to kill two of the other variety. They were able to melt the armored steel door with laser beams. Laser beams that they could shoot from their eyes and other sensors in their hands. Pure science fiction. During the autopsy of the two people killed, we only came across more questions, the answers to which are still to come. As I said. We can only keep them at bay with drugs and we'd prefer it if they hadn't turned up at all. One more thing They sense fear. Under no circumstances should you give them the feeling that you are afraid, otherwise they will have an easy time with you. Be confident and consistent. Have you drawn up a list of questions?" the doctor asked

"No. How? I didn't know what to expect. But I'll think of something." Patosh tried to convince him.

"Good... Luisa, here we go. Keep the cameras rolling and record everything....and Patrick. Sometimes they take their time. A lot of time. You'll see."

Patosh remembered all the crime dramas he watched on TV when criminals were interrogated in interrogation rooms and you could watch the delinquent behind a mirror without being seen yourself. That was more or less what was happening here, except that he would be conducting the interrogation unobserved, and he wasn't sure he would have been unobserved, because aliens could see through steel walls. Roselyn had proved it to him once.   Cell 34 brightened up a little, but apart from two chairs, a table and a cot, nothing could be seen. They sat there for minutes and no being from another world was to be seen until Luisa finally gave a sign that the infrared sensors of the cameras were recording something. Smoke rose up like a mist and as if it wasn't already creepy enough, a silhouette appeared through the smoky fog. Patosh thought of the rock band Ramstein. What a performance. But when the smoke cleared, his blood froze in his veins, because what he saw before him would terrify even Satan in hell. If he wanted to describe it, he wouldn't know how.

The shape had no solid form, but the image manifested itself in Patosh's mind as that of a glowing, man-sized insect, its jaws tipped with sawtooth-like blades. It had no hands, but rather hooves. The eyes were covered with facets that glowed metallic green and stared at you continuously.

"Are you ready Patrick?" asked Doctor Friegstaad.

"How can you be ready for something like this?" Patrick whispered and nodded in the affirmative.

"If you want to talk, just press the microphone button and then let go.

"Wow... how advanced." Patosh thought to himself.

But the insect, or the creature, beat him to it.

"Patrick van de Brog from Belgium. Former innkeeper and now unemployed. Divorced but living with someone...oh yes...interesting....more mutants and hybrids... but she's not pregnant yet. Do I detect helplessness and fear?" it said in a deep, synthesized voice.

"What do you call yourself? Do you have a name?" asked Patosh, who seemed to have regained his self-confidence.

"No. We don't have a name on our planet. Not even our planet has a name and why bother with such trivialities? You, however, need names, numbers, letters and so on. We do it all with our senses. But your colleagues there have given me a name. Caligula, isn't it? And they don't even know whether I'm male or female. Being given the name of a madman is pretty insulting, don't you think? Patrick van de Brog?"

"So, what are you now? Male or female?" Patosh asked, unimpressed.

"We don't have genders. Just like the Venusians don't. We are cell dividers. We are neither male nor female. Not exactly socially acceptable for this planet, is it? We also don't need to be compatible with anyone or anything. We take what we need and want and live best in solitude."

"Why are you here? What do you want here on earth?"

"To exterminate you and take over this planet before the Venusians do."

Patosh flinched when he heard this and noticed how the insect creature with the facets in its eyes changed colors.

"Why do you want this What have we done to you to make you want to destroy us and why do the Venusians want to do the same?"

"We don't need a reason. You are so inferior to us, mentally and physically, that you are nothing more than universal bacteria."

"Why do the Venusians want to destroy us?" Patosh asked, clearly more curious.

"They don't want to admit their mistake to the Confederacy.

The mistake they made 75,000 years ago when they left this planet and handed over the leadership to you. You, who can only do one thing. To destroy yourselves. It would be like giving the leadership of your people to the weakest of the bunch. Leaving a ship's cook in charge of a nuclear submarine, if you get my drift. The Venusians went to war in a war falsely faked by the Orion clan and almost lost it. Everything was at stake and only with the help of the Confederacy had they been able to avoid the worst. To unbalance the balance. But you worms, in that time you squandered everything you were given and have a life filled with greed, selfishness, personal ego and worst of all...emotions. The seed of all evil. The Venusians are to be expelled from their seat on the High Council in the Confederacy as they are being pressured by the Orion clan. But Roselyn already knows everything."

"ROSELYN?" Patosh shouted in horror.

"Yes, of course. Roselyn. She's part of the flop. The catastrophe. How old do you think your Roselyn is, Patrick?" asked the cosmic insect, seemingly amused,

"She doesn't belong here..."

"Oh no? What did they tell you? The sex story between KXTLG and Mary Mitchell? No, how lovely. That actually happened, but Roselyn had already incarnated three times.

Every 25,000 thousand years a Venusian is deactivated and usually reactivated through compatibility. But in the last case, KXTLG wanted to sire his little darling into the womb of an ordinary, earthly slave and mated with Mary, which is not unusual. Venusians and others, mate with foreign beings, some with consent, others by force. The house maid Mary Mitchell was abducted against her will and fucked until the lights went out, to use your language. KXTLG inserted the germ of his compatible daughter, who had already incarnated three times, into Mary's womb and lo and behold, the miracle child appeared. But why not in a compatible way, one wonders. Roselyn should be permanently deactivated. She had caused the chaos with the Orion clan and triggered a panic on your Earth. The last incarnation that made her an ordinary mortal at the end was supposed to sweep the whole thing under the carpet, but KTXLK, or Roselyn, made the next mistake. She fled when she learned that the Confederacy had already convicted her. KXTLG was given the chance to stay activated if he caught her and brought her back."

"And what about KTKFK? The new leader? Why did he pardon her?"

Even "Caligula" could not answer this question, because his silence was long.

"You say your planet has no name, but it is located in KROM-57.... " Patosh continued, so as not to waste any time.

"KROM-56." Caligula corrected him

"My apologies. KROM-56. Did you name this solar system, or did the Earth astronomers give it that name?" Patosh asked, hoping to find a contradiction.

"Your astronomers named it that."

"Could you tell me how many light years away?"

"We have no such measurement, but in Earth units it is 59 light years."

"How did you get into this embarrassment of being found by us and brought here?" Patosh continued to ask him, observing the creature closely, because any change in its appearance could indicate whether Caligula was lying or telling the truth. But so far, nothing could be seen that could give such a clue.

"Our vehicles, or spaceships as you call them, are not designed for weather phenomena that prevail on Earth. At least not the version I was piloting. I got caught in a thunderstorm and lightning struck, suddenly knocking out all systems. My spaceship crashed and I survived, also thanks to the medical help of the humans."

"So you are grateful to the people who saved you?"

"No!"

"No? I don't understand that now...."

"We have no emotions or, like you, feelings. You of all should know it by now. We don't know mercy and compassion. If I hadn't survived the crash, it wouldn't be a loss for my clan."

For Patosh, this was already an indication that these species did not take on human traits or habits, as is the case with the Venusians when they stay on Earth for too long.

The Earth energy therefore had no power or influence to make changes in their consciousness and this fact made it clear that they were a dangerous species.

"Do you know Jesus Christ?" Patosh asked, to everyone's surprise.

"Yes," came the short answer.

"What can you tell us about him?" and here Patosh was able to record a change in Caligula that apparently gave the creature quite a headache.

"Why do you ask about this being you call Jesus Christ?"

"We want to know if his story is the one the Bible tells us. What else do they call him in your spheres?"

"Well, he is called KAMRA in the universe, but as I said, we have only adopted this name from hearing it, because we have and know no names.

He is a being of the eighth density and therefore directly subordinate to the Creator. Your Bible is just a bestseller of the time. Published too late, revised far too often, censored by publishers whom you call bishops and distorted in many ways from the actual reality."

"Do you believe in him?"

"What do you mean by believe in him?"

"Do you worship him?"

"No. That's something you do better. He was just a messenger. A traveler like many others. Understood by few and misunderstood by many. "

"Why was he unable or unwilling to protect himself when he was captured by the Romans?"

"You would have to ask him that yourself, but that will probably never happen. You had the chance and, as always, your weakness won out. You are the streptococci of the universe."

"Can you tell us which solar system he comes from?"

"No."

"What about asexual reproduction? What is true about it? His mother Maria....."

"Can we call it a day soon? I don't feel like answering questions like that, even though we don't know how it happened. But prehistoric or a sexual reproduction is the wrong word. You've already experienced what compatibility can do. Telepathic compatibility was more at play in this matter, with someone from eighth density."

"You mentioned the word "creator". What do you mean by that?

"The creation of everything."

"So a kind of God?" Patosh asked, interested and yet confused.

"That's your interpretation. Proof of how little you know. But I can reassure you. We don't know everything either, although we are a million times more knowledgeable than you. That alone should give you and us pause for thought. With experience comes knowledge. We are all here to create experience. Each for himself and in a unique form."

"Is there a paradise and is there a hell?"

"Yes, but not as your Bible publishers would have you believe. We all create our own hell and paradise through the deeds we do during our existence."

"But here I already see a contradiction in your statement. You claim that you have no emotions and feelings and yet

I hear from your last statements alone that you have emotional depths. You speak of a creator, of hell and of paradise, which you can impose on yourself through your own deeds...."

"For us, the perception of these phenomena is different from yours. It happens differently in us. We know no prohibitions, no taboos, no restrictions and this represents paradise for us. I am experiencing the best example of hell right now. Only here did I realize that we, as a species, still have flaws in our genetics, such as your drugs, which render me incapable of fighting. With all our knowledge and experience, you microbes have defeated me. At least for the moment. The same goes for the others behind the Red Door. I will answer no more questions. I am tired and you should leave me in peace."

"I don't have any more questions either. At least not now."

"Watch out for them. They are not your friends. You can't trust Roselyn either. I'm giving you this advice because it's about time someone found out the truth about everything. You know a tiny part of it now. Farewell, Patrick van de Brog."

Back to Connington on the Shyre

General Cooper and the others went into a room where there was an analytical discussion of the event. A so-called briefing. They were all excited about the results, except Patosh. He didn't know how he should behave towards Roselyn, after Caligula's advice, if he ever would see her again. He should not trust her. He was also confused by the different statements from Charlie, behind the green door, Tom, behind the yellow door and finally Caligula, behind the red door. He had a telepathic conversation with Charlie, who seemed to be on Roselyn's side. With Tom, he didn't know exactly who he was and whether it wasn't just a confused "Grey". Caligula seemed to be the most honest of them all, although he was classified as the most dangerous. Charlie and Tom claimed that genetic experiments were done so that the military, under General Cooper, could develop super soldiers, but Caligula was not a cloned result of any earthly experiments. He was an original. You couldn't develop something like that with the available KNOW HOW here on this planet. Yes, surely they would work on such experiments and try to create human wonder weapons, which categorized Professor Farnham and Professor Curtiss as a Dr. MENGELE, because the Nazis were not different, and these two "GENTLEMEN" should take a good look at themselves in the mirror.

General Cooper was simply a tin soldier commanding thousands of tin soldiers under him and very soon he would have the best tin soldiers in the world under his command should he succeed with his perversity.

Patosh was not particularly happy even though he had gained an experience like no one ever would but that would haunt him for life, for he had actually seen them. Aliens who, like humans, wanted to survive and could not be more different in nature and species. He made a decision for himself and heard Charlie calling in the back of his mind. "Play their game...." and that's exactly what he would do.

"Well Patrick. What do you think? You did an excellent job out there and we congratulate you. So if that doesn't convince you, what will?"

"I'll do it. I will work for this institution. But not for free and I mean I want to see money. A lot of money."

"Money doesn't matter to us. So you will sign?"

"Yes."

Patosh knew he was putting himself in a snake pit when he signed the papers. He was initially assigned a low security level until they could build trust in him, which seemed understandable to him. An intensive interrogation followed and no point was left out.

From his birth to his present, his life was turned upside down and compared to what Cooper already knew through the "BACKGROUND CHECK". Disappointingly, Patosh had led a very boring life until the day he rented the caravan and went on a well-deserved vacation. Fate had then turned his life into a rollercoaster ride and placed Mary, now called Roselyn, in front of him. Was this planned by whoever was up there? All the aliens mentioned the "Creator". Who or what was it? A being? A plasma mass made of energy? A light or even the "NOTHING"?

Who knew.

"Now we come to the painful part Patrick. The chip will be inserted and I have to warn you. If you, or anyone, even attempts to remove or disable this chip, we will be informed immediately and the consequences could be prosecution, imprisonment, isolation and in the worst case, elimination. Sign here that you have been informed of this."

After signing the last sheet of paper, everyone took the elevator again and this time the ride went upwards. Again, Patosh struggled to equalize the pressure as the elevator shot up noticeably fast. The corridor that revealed itself after the elevator door opened was now brightly lit and reminded one of a clinic. Nurses, men and women in white coats hurried through the halls and rooms like iron balls in a pinball machine, metaphorically speaking, and when they entered a consulting room, a doctor appeared with an assistant carrying a stainless steel tray. There was some kind of pistol on it and without a greeting or a kind word of reassurance, the doctor ordered Patosh to take off his shirt and lift his undershirt a little. The assistant handed the doctor a disinfectant swab, which was ice-cold to the touch, and without warning Patosh was shot in the right side, where the appendix was normally located. A scream that woke the dead and echoed through the corridors let it be known that General Cooper was right that this would be the painful part and if looks could kill, the doctor should drop dead on the spot, Patosh looked at her so angrily.

"Are you insane? I wasn't prepared for this, you butcher!"

But the doctor only gave him a weary smile and left the consulting room with her assistant.

"So, I think we'll take you back to the accommodation where you can rest. A private jet will fly you back to Luton tomorrow. You can then go back to your normal life and not say a word about this to anyone. But I think that goes without saying."

"Roselyn will want to know where I've been," Patosh said justifiably.

"Tell her that you were taken into custody by the Brussels police for 48 hours for drunk driving. You had a drink after you finished handing over your pub to get rid of old memories and you were caught driving thereafter."

"She'll never believe me..."

"Don't worry. We have everything under control."
General Copper said with satisfaction.

But Patosch knew that Roselyn had an intergalactic
intelligence quotient and that she wouldn't believe such a
lie. He had to think of something else, because he had a
problem. He couldn't get Caligula's words out of his head
and yes, he felt persecuted, harassed and bothered by
him. Caligula apparently didn't need a chip to know how
to track someone, because an inner restlessness
accompanied him and he couldn't sleep a wink as he lay
down on his bed in the shelter. Cramped in mind and
body, he just stared at the ceiling and the pain caused by
the inserted chip was the only sign of life he could feel.

It was already dark outside when there was a knock at the
door and when Patosh opened the door, two Air Force
soldiers were standing in front of it. A sergeant and a
captain, according to their rank.

"We are to accompany you to the canteen and then back
to your quarters," said the captain.

"Will General Cooper and the others be there too?" asked
Patosh.

"General who? And which others?" was the answer he
got back.

The world seemed to be coming apart at the seams at that
moment and the situation couldn't seem more bizarre to
him. He put on his shoes and jacket, quickly combed his

hair and followed the two soldiers to the canteen. There was no General Cooper, no Professor Farnham or Curtiss to greet him and no Michael Robertson to be seen. He sat down at a single table after getting two hot dogs, a Coke Zero and a tomato salad from the bar. He looked around and felt like the main character in a science fiction movie. Everyone around him didn't say a word and just looked deep into their plates as they led the cutlery in their mouths. Half an hour later, the two soldiers appeared again and took him back to his accommodation. At the door, the captain said that he, Patosh, had only three hours to sleep. After that he would be picked up again for his flight to Luton. Of course Patosh couldn't sleep, but he would be able to do that on the flight and so it was that exactly three hours later the two men came back to pick him up. A dark blue Dodge van drove them in front of a parked Gulfstream 550, where he was met by a stewardess.

He got in, but he was not alone on board. A man was already sitting in one of the dark brown leather armchairs and gave him a smile.

"Welcome aboard Mr. van de Brog. My name is John Miller."

Of course it was, because Michael Robertson had the same name when Patosh was abducted and now this stranger was sitting there with the same pseudonym,

"Is that the only name in your repertoire?" Patosh said sarcastically.

"It's simple and easy to remember Mr. van de Brog. I'm supposed to give you this."

Mr. "Miller" handed over an envelope. It contained twenty thousand dollars, a 9 MM Sig-Sauer pistol, a smartphone and various SIM cards. There was also a dictation recorder for him to listen to. The general's voice was loud and clear with instructions on how to use the smartphone. If only the general knew that he, Patosh, had something more sophisticated like a Vybe scanner, which puts everything in the shade. Fortunately, he hadn't had it with him on the day of his abduction, because in the wrong hands, it would have changed the world within hours and he was only now coming to this realization. The consequences would be indescribable.

The jet's boarding door closed, the engines were already running synchronously and the stewardess brought the men coffee and small snacks for refreshment. A short time later, the Gulfstream took off into the dark but starry night and a glance at the sky brought a thousand questions to Patosh's mind. All the stars were shining particularly brightly that night, as if the universe was wishing him luck on his quest, and he wondered how many aliens were taking a vacation trip to Earth at that very moment, because not all of them were coming to explore or to wipe out humanity. There were some like Jonathan, Martha and Fred who were his friends and close to his heart. He thought of them and thanked the "Creator" that there were also people like them. But what place would Roslyn take in his heart now, after Caligula's warning not to trust her? What was real and what was not. Not to mention, this advice came from a species that had no intention of doing anything but wiping out humanity, so why believe it over the person you love above all else?

The jet reached its service ceiling and Patosh was able to follow the progress of the flight on a screen. The route ran far north along the Arctic Circle and it took four and a half hours to reach the east coast of North America. They then continued over Greenland and the rest of the Atlantic. Tiredness caught up with him and no dream, no shaking and jolting could have woken him up and it was only when the wheels touched down on British soil that his eyes opened. The jet taxied to its parking position and as the door opened, Mr. "Miller" hurried out to where a car was waiting for them.

"Good morning, sir. We've arrived in Luton," said the stewardess kindly.

His eyelids were still sticky, his breath smelled of cold coffee and as he slid his hand around his face, he could feel the beard stubble that had grown that night.

"Why did you only wake me up now?" he asked the stewardess, a little miffed, but she didn't let this unsettle her, she just pulled up the table and said.

"There's no need to rush, sir. You were sleeping so deeply that we did not want to disturb. Have breakfast first and then you can freshen up in the washroom at the back. Customs can wait as this flight has diplomatic status. "

"And Mr. Miller? Where has he gone?"

"He's just driving up and declaring everything to customs. Don't worry, he'll be back."

Thirty minutes later, Patosh was already in a rental car and on his way to Bedford. He wanted to stop by William's Red Lion first and find out what had happened during his absence. Roselyn, as much as he longed for her, would have to wait. Too many questions were racing around in his head and perhaps a Guinness with a good friend would put his feet back on the ground again.
His plan came to nothing, however, because Roselyn, Mary and Malcolm Jenkins were sitting in the Red Lion's pub talking to William, who suddenly looked towards the door in astonishment as if he saw a ghost.

"Patrick! Where the hell have you been? We haven't slept for nearly 72 hours!" he shouted with joy.

Roselyn jumped up from her chair and ran to Patosh, who also couldn't wait to hold her in his arms. And yet it was there again. That coldness that had caught up with him once before in Spain when he left her. His body pined for her, but his mind held him back. There was no way he could tell the truth. At least not now, until he convinced himself that it was all more or less just a bad dream. But it wasn't a dream, because he felt a sharp pain.

It was the chip that reminded him to hold tight and at the same time informed General Cooper that Patosh was at home.

"Oh my darling, we were so worried," Roselyn whispered in his ear and kissed him until Patosh pushed her back.

"I'm here now dearest. What do you have to do here to get a Guinness?"

"Coming right up my friend!" William shouted euphorically and it wasn't long before Patosh was telling them the story of his 48 hours in a Belgian jail for drink driving. William and Malcolm believed it straight away, but Roselyn wasn't sure and old Mary was too smart to believe a word of it. But she kept quiet because she suspected something. Something about Patosh had changed and yes, the others didn't realize it, not even Roselyn, but old Mary, with all her human experience, couldn't escape such a change. She just smiled and waited, for time would solve this riddle.
It was several Guinnesses later before they finally drove back to the farm at Connington on the Shyre and despite Patosh's half tipsy state, he kept his mouth shut and didn't say a word about the events of the last three days.

"I've got to have a bath and then off to bed, I'm so exhausted," he apologized. Roselyn ran the bath water in the tub, poured in some bath foam and left Patosh alone with his thoughts.

"Lie down, my darling, and tomorrow you can tell me how Georgette took it that you left her the Golden Jug. You haven't said a word about it.

"I will do that, my angel. You go to sleep soon too, because you look tired Roselyn."

"I missed you and I couldn't fall asleep. The only reason I didn't go to the police was because Mother had asked me to be patient. She was right. As always. Relax now." And after a kiss on his forehead, she left the bathroom. Patosh lay down in the hot water and reviewed everything. From the moment of his abduction to the last second of his arrival, he left nothing out. The almost invisible stab wound where the chip had been inserted was still itchy and had become slightly reddish. But that couldn't be allowed to happen. He would tell her, but first he had to be sure who to trust. Could he trust anyone at all, and how would this nightmare end? He wondered why he had been chosen for such a fate? Why not someone else like Jenkins or some other UFO freak? But everything that went through his mind regarding this matter kept leading back to Roselyn. She was the one who gave him this destiny. He was just the link to her. The door to her knowledge. He had been chosen because he shared her bed, her heart and her secrets. What did Charlie say? The beings in the cell behind the red door were the product of the experiments of a few madmen, like Professor Farnham and Professor Curtiss, and why wasn't he allowed to see the others behind the red door? Was it perhaps because there were no others and Caligula was perhaps just a hologram to fool his senses? To make him believe that there were also bad aliens in space and not just the good ones? A distraction to make him believe there was a danger that didn't exist just to get Roselyn's knowledge and profit from it militarily? But why go to such a billion dollar effort to lie about something?

Was perhaps the moon landing also just a lie? A test of how to lie to three billion people back in 1969 without getting caught? Can this be true and what kind of individuals could carry out such a crime against humanity without suffering remorse and succumbing to moral conflicts? Were humans even capable of such perfidy? The answer came over him like an icy black night fog. No, man could not do it, but aliens could. They, who could not muster emotions and feelings, would do such a thing without batting an eyelid. So did they already have control of Earth, and if so, which of them did it? The Venusians? The Orion Clan? The ones from the KROm 56 solar system without a name? How long could and should he keep this secret and with whom? With Jenkins? Absolutely not. He might want to sell the story for the sheer sensationalism of it, even if he had proven himself reliable and loyal. But for how long? William? He too had been on Venus and he too had witnessed it himself and yet he could one day tell his lodge brothers everything in a drunken stupor, even though he had sworn to keep his mouth shut. Keeping secrets is actually what Freemasons do. But why not go straight to Roselyn with it? Charlie, from the Corantio planet, had strongly recommended it. He was the most trustworthy of all after the visit to the Mojave Desert, now that Caligula could be a fake. Patosh stared into the void, playing with the lukewarm bathwater as he pushed the foam aside. All that remained was Mary. Old Mary, who herself had once been abducted and mistreated. She would understand and support him with advice. She was just as intelligent and secretive, even towards her own daughter, because Roselyn also found out everything after he, Patosh, showed up at the farm after three years and searched for her on behalf of the three foreign Venusians.

What a horror story in itself. Yes, Mary would be the first to know, but not today and not tomorrow. Soon.

Hell is empty and all devils are here

...was this not what Shakespeare once said in his play "The Tempest"? But the thing with Shakespeare was and is also crumbling, because even today his talent is doubted and he is described as the cherry-picker for the work of others. What is still true and what is not? Has man been living in a swamp of lies for all these millions of years or did the lie emerge much later, when man evolved and the devil embedded himself in his intelligence? Who will ever know? Months passed and nothing was heard from either General Cooper or KTKFK from the High Council on Venus. Peace and quiet returned and the scar where the chip had been placed disappeared completely. Roselyn was out shopping that day and Jenkins was with William as he had promised to help him paint the walls of the inn. Patosh was helping Mary in the garden. He mowed the lawn and she tended the roses. Her health improved daily, as if a miracle had occurred and as if the "Creator" needed her for further services on earth. No, he didn't want to take her back yet, because her task had not been completed and therefore the contract with the universe had not been fulfilled. When Patosh put the mower down, as he was finished with it, Mary asked him to take care of the geraniums and the roses and on this occasion, she dared to start a chat.

"What I don't quite understand, Patrick, is why you didn't call us as soon as you were arrested by the police. We would have called a lawyer."

"They wouldn't let me...."

"Stop lying. Drunk driving is not a state offense. You're not a state wanted terrorist where you have to submit to days of interrogation before a lawyer is consulted. What's all this secrecy?"

Patrick was caught out because, as said previously, Mary was not a stupid woman, despite her age.

"All right, Mary. But what I'm going to tell you will knock your socks off. You might see me with different eyes."

"Test me. I know something is bothering you."

"Very well. But we should both sit down for this."

"That's a good idea. We'll both benefit from a tea break. Put down the tools and let's talk."

Mary prepared the tea and brought the typical English egg sandwiches, which Patosh didn't like per se, but he was hungry and thirsty and the break would do him good. After the second bite of the soft bread, he started chatting and Mary listened. They talked for an hour, but there was no sign of astonishment or horror on Mary's face, for she had no difficulty in believing every word he said. She put down her tea cup and said.

"It was good that you kept quiet. But the question is. What shall we do now? How long will that general wait over there and how far can we really trust Roselyn?"

"What? To hear that from your mouth, Mary, that leaves me at a loss for words..."

"Does it Patrick? Roselyn is not the same Roselyn I knew after she came back from Spain. At first I thought she had become like this after you parted, but she shouldn't be able to do that as a half-Venusian. Yes, she has emotions and feelings, but there is the other half in her. The cosmic half that should balance reason and equilibrium. Not to forget, she was a member of the High Council and not too small, but the direct successor to the Head. I know what you're about to say. Circumstances would have changed her, but I say something else happened. Something I can't easily explain and we should include Jonathan in that. He may know something we don't. Roselyn didn't have such a need for my attention and affection before, how could she as the alien she is. Her human half doesn't change that and the vibes of this planet only affect purebred aliens, pardon the expression, but I can't find another term. She has been "grounded" so to speak since birth. She used to be cold and unapproachable and now this Roselyn, who couldn't be more foreign to me. I've been wondering what she's up to for some time now that KXTLG is no longer responsible for her."

"Maybe that's where the answer lies Mary. KXTLG was her power source, her champion, her promoter if you will, and now he's been banished somewhere. She is missing the source that motivated and moved her. She's lost, come to think of it. It would be dangerous to confront her with this new knowledge and that's why we have to keep her in the dark for the time being, as she no longer serves any purpose for Venus and the henchmen of the military only want to enrich themselves with her."

"The one they call Charlie. You said he's from Corantio?"

"Yes."

"Then we can hope, Patrick. Then there's a chance that this Caligula from KROM-56 doesn't actually exist, but that it's just a feint by the general. There is no evil in the cosmos, because that's not how it's designed. Evil only came into being here. The universe consists only of unconditional love and the Venusians represent nothing else. So I can assure you that you have been the victim of a lie and that you have shown understanding and reason by doubting and questioning this matter. You have not been taken in."

"But which lie did I fall for? The general's or Roselyn's?"

Not even Mary had the right answer to that, and as she looked into Patrick's eyes, the little Peugeot drove into the yard that belonged to Roselyn.

"She's back. Let's put a good face on it, Patrick."

Roselyn waved from a distance and carried the shopping bags into the main building. She didn't suspect a thing and just called out, "We're having a barbecue today because I've bought some good steaks and sausages."

"That sounds good, my angel," he said and hugged her tightly. He loved her and he wasn't lying. A truth that at least held true for him.

The days passed and fall arrived. Golden brown covered the ground with fallen leaves from the oak and maple trees that adorned the driveway to the main building like palm trees. Patosh and Jenkins collected the leaves with electric garden vacuums and a cool wind whistled its song to herald the winter that would not be long in coming. Patosh didn't talk much to Roselyn, but this estrangement didn't seem to bother her. On the contrary. If you didn't know better, you thought she would be happy not to have to answer uncomfortable questions. But how long would Patosh wait before he burst his collar? Every day, General Cooper pestered him via the smartphone he had been given and every day Patosh had to put him off with flimsy excuses, but the general would have none of it. Patosh was equally unsettled every day as to whom he should believe and who not. What if the general was right and Earth was actually in danger of being invaded and conquered by aliens and his theories turned out to be pipe dreams and wishful thinking? Why shouldn't extraterrestrials behave in the same way as humans on Earth, with both sides polarized?

Bad as well as good? Naivety would be misplaced if we thought that the universe consisted only of pure love. Nature can also bite and harm or even kill humans, see tsunamis, earthquakes, hurricanes, volcanic eruptions, climate change, etc, etc. What if a blessing today can become a curse tomorrow? Dryness and drought in a steppe can lead to famine, just like a monsoon or a tropical hurricane. See Katrina in New Orleans, floods in Bangladesh, tsunamis in Japan and Malaysia. Everything has an opposite pole, otherwise the balance does not work. Matter and antimatter, light and darkness, love and hate, good and bad is what decides and gives life meaning. People themselves decide which side they feel called to take. Does one want to be a dictator or a priest? Why shouldn't aliens feel the same way, even if it is said that they feel nothing? A life without a goal would be boring and goals can be good or bad, the important thing is to get there. With all these thoughts flooding his mind, Patosh was suddenly fed up and he put the leaf sucker down.

"I'm taking a break Malcolm. I need to talk to Roselyn. Go on without me."

"That's all right Pat."

Roselyn was watering the flowers in the hallway when Patosh grabbed her by the waist, turned her around and kissed her, but immediately after said, "We need to talk."

"Oh dear. What have I done?"

"I don't know," he said seriously, and Roselyn understood that it was going to be a long evening.

"I don't know how to start..." Patosh tried to open the conversation.

"Just say what's on your mind."

"Fine. I lied to you. I wasn't arrested for drunk driving back in Brussels. I was kidnapped."

"I knew it. By whom? By Venusians?" she asked more attentively.

"No. By a General Cooper. I'm also supposed to say hello to you from Professor Curtiss."

"Really? And why are you just coming out with it now?" Roselyn put the watering can down and looked for a place to sit, as Patosh could now see an uncomfortable change in her. She looked unsure and didn't know where to put her hands. Her inner calm had been shattered.

"I could ask you the same thing Roselyn. But I didn't, out of consideration, out of anger, out of shock and above all out of mistrust. I can no longer believe anything that comes out of your mouth. They want me to spy on you and find out what you're up to with us. With us humans, mind you, and this godforsaken planet. I don't mind if a comet comes crashing in here right now, then these lies and this perfidy would be done away with once and for all.

You are no better than us. Here I sit now with a broken heart and all my hopes of starting a new life with you blown away again. Show yourself to me. Show me what you really are, you monster." Patosh screamed so loudly that even Jenkins with his hearing protection and the suction cup could hear it. He also turned off the device outside and moved towards the main building, because he wanted to see what the commotion was all about. Less than a minute later, Mary also met him in the corridor.

"What's going on with those two?" asked Jenkins

"We'll find out in a minute Malcolm."

"How old are you really? How many times have you graced this earth with your arrival? I think you owe me....oh you're here too.....us all an explanation. I should also include William, because he was among us when we were allowed to visit Venus." Patosh turned to Mary and Jenkins. His anger was overwhelming and his veins threatened to burst from his forehead.

"Enough hide and seek Mary. You're partly responsible and should also explain a few things. You're both accomplices in this dirty game, aren't you?"

"What's wrong with you Pat? I don't recognize you." Jenkins exclaimed in horror and tried to calm his friend down.

"Call William, Jonathan and his family Malcolm. They have to get their asses over here because I'm going to tell you all what happened to me. ALL OF YOU!"

And they came. Less than an hour later after Patosh's outburst, they stood or sat in the living room and listened to Patosh's story. William and Jenkins couldn't hide their amazement, but Jonathan, Martha, Fred, Rosleyn and Mary just sat there and listened, unimpressed. Yes, they seemed indifferent.

"So, what have you got to say to me Roselyn, or Mary or whoever you are? I have broken an agreement of silence at this moment that could cost my life, but I can't stand it any longer because I have become a slave. To you and now to the Americans too. Cooper wants to know why you haven't shown your face to continue working with them."

"Because that was no longer possible, Patrick. I saw what they were planning to do with our knowledge and I could no longer justify it. I went into hiding back on Venus and it was only thanks to KXTLG that I was able to regain my senses. More and more you have spread, like a cancer, over the natural and universal glories and instead of using our knowledge to grow in harmony with the divine, you have chosen the ways of the Orion clan. You are destroying and killing yourselves. Everything that is newly discovered through physics and chemistry is not for growth, but for destruction.

Your military and its associated industry is the cancer I am talking about. Albert Einstein, Marie Currie, Werner von Braun and whatever their names may be, had to experience with horror the purposes for which their services and their abilities were used. Then your pharmaceutical industry. Ways to cure diseases quickly and efficiently by natural means are being destroyed and eliminated from the world, even banned with prison sentences. Natural healers disappear, doctors are disbarred and those who speak out about the abuses are silenced. The one Cooper calls Caligula is not a mutant from your evolution. He belongs to the space police, as ridiculous as that may sound to you. He's the last resort when a judgment is passed by the Confederacy.

"Space police? Don't make me laugh. A Robocop is supposed to save the world? Is that what you're saying?"

"Not one. Thousands equipped with technology you're no match for. Yes, your Earth will soon be taken over in cooperation with the Confederation, and unfortunately, the 'aligners', as these beings developed by us are called, will have to be used. They were developed so far away from all solar systems because they have also become a danger to us."

"Oh yeah? Apparently some of them have dared to go so far as to land on our Earth...."

"They're just scouts. Experimental soldiers to find out how long such an operation would take to arrive in light years and what problems to expect."

"And apparently your technology and artificial intelligence is not fully developed after all, because according to Caligula's statement, a lightning strike caused his spaceship to crash. Our primitive aircrafts have no problems with thunderstorms. At least not to this extent. What makes you so sure that even such a triviality cannot jeopardize your operation?"

"We're working on it."

"AHA. So you admit it. You've betrayed yourself now!" Patosh shouted with a laugh.

But the others didn't feel like laughing.

"Yes, I admit it. My last coming wasn't an escape. It was an order that I had to carry out as a member of the High Council. Only interfering with my free will had brought down KXTLG. I presume he tried to stop my Mission out of guilt."

"Free will? Even when it comes to conquering a foreign planet? Is that also part of free will? So anyone can do what they want without having to feel any restraint? You're sick, if you ask me. So we humans are not that self-destructive after all, because we have interfered with the "free will" of some dictators in order to save the lives of other peoples.

How important is this earth really to you that you have to resort to such measures to want to conquer a grain of sand in a desert, because the earth is only a microbe, a plankton in the universe."

"Each planet serves to align and balance the universe and when the planet's time is up, it cools or explodes naturally. Nothing is for eternity."

"And so you are euthanizing this planet here? Have I interpreted it correctly?"

"No. We are taking control because you have already lost it. We're not destroying it, we're saving it. From you."

With these words came the silence that was as unmistakable as a cricket's fart.

"Are you saying that the humans will be destroyed?" asked Jenkins, visibly frightened.

"No. Just modified. You'll get another chance, as you so often do. We are not murderers. We only eliminate those who are not doing their proper duty and have fallen to the Orion clan. Eliminate is the wrong word. They will be taken away."

"Where in God's name?" William asked, beside himself.

"You gave yourself the answer William. To the Creator. There they will dwell and first be returned to second density to evolve again within your 75000 years.

All those who have done harm on this planet are there. They too will get a second chance and a third and a fourth and an infinite chance to re-evolve and understand. All of you have experienced such a cycle. Of course, such a period of time always comes as a shock. Or is received as such, but everything will one day also be erased forever so that it can be reborn again as something new. So you see, there are two sides to everything."

"Why don't you just enlighten people? Why all this fuss? Why don't you just eliminate the Orion Clan?"

"Because they are part of the cycle and part of the balance. If they didn't exist, Free Will wouldn't exist either. The decision of what I want to be, good or evil, would be taken away from me," said old Mary,

"What a shitty game." William cursed. "And pretty perverse of the "Creator" if you ask me."

"What shall we do now Roselyn? I can't go on like this. I have a chip in me and I'm being held."

"I know Pat. You're being monitored by six satellites. There are also drones high in the sky scanning the estate. At least they can't hear us." Roselyn said.

"What makes you so sure? And how do you know all this?"

"Firstly, I can manipulate the chip, but only to a limited extent, otherwise they'll smell a rat, and secondly,

Charlie and I have been communicating telepathically for years. He's our mole. His crash was intentional, as was his arrest. As you can see, my love, I knew everything from the beginning."

"ROSELYN!" screamed Mary, beside herself. "This has gone too far. I didn't bring you up like this."

"You raised a hologram, mother. But I was trained and instructed by KXTLG. I miss him because he understood me. KTKFK will never do it that way, even if his intentions are good."

"And you? What part do you play in this infernal drama?" Patosh now asked Jonathan and Martha.

"Us? We only had our vacation in mind. We came here for a vacation, but the earthly vibrations have taken us over. We have no plans for anything that is being discussed here and would prefer not to know anything about it. Why did you drag us into this in the first place?"

"In for a penny, in for a pound. You've been involved from the beginning, from the moment KXTLG asked you to find me," said Roselyn.

"Yes, but we knew nothing about such plans to conquer Earth. We are simple Venusians. So all this remembering procedure was for nothing?" protested Martha firmly.

"Calm down Martha."

"No, I'm not calming down because I've rarely felt so screwed and I say that as a citizen of this planet. We've been through enough because of you and Roselyn, and Fred, who has a chance of becoming something big here on Earth, won't give in to your experiments. We were brought to Venus to forget everything, only to be reminded of everything again and yes, I have to agree with Patosh here. How sick are we ourselves? I have long since stopped imagining myself to be any better and the more I realize all this, the more I loathe our origins. You're sitting on a very high horse Roselyn and can fall low if your saddle isn't tied tight enough. I want to get out of here and have nothing more to do with you. Jonathan, if you love me, then let's go. Fred get up. We've lost nothing here."

Roselyn tried to stop her from leaving, but Mary held her back.

"Let her go. They have a right to live their lives the way they want to."

As they left the house, the room became even more depressed. They had lost good friends and Patosh was overcome with sadness.

"What should we do now Roselyn? We are in danger."

Starwars is possible.

Patosh and Roselyn had been arguing regularly lately, but there was no thought of a separation Not because Patosh had a chip installed in him to be controlled and even killed outright, but because he cared a lot about Roselyn and she felt the same way about him. But something had to be done to keep a few madmen in Nevada and in space quiet. KTKFK demanded, after what he had been told, an extraordinary meeting of all those involved, on Venus but Roselyn didn't want to go to Nevada to deliver this invitation to the General as a sign of goodwill. She feared that the organization, which didn't even exist on paper, would arrest her. She would disappear like the others. Like Charlie, Tom, Caligula and the rest which Patosh was not allowed to visit. But Patosh tried to persuade her, because Cooper and the professors would listen to her.

"You're under contract with them, why don't you make an effort?" came her reply.

"It's different when a Venusian delivers the invitation."

"You don't know these people and I've worked there long enough to know that their word counts for nothing. They trusted me then, but now they wouldn't let me live in freedom and experiment on me. Call Cooper and ask him to come to Luton with his entourage. Here in England they don't have a detention and transfer authorization.

"OK. I'll get back to him and will be able to give him some positive news. At least an interest exists to be at the negotiating table.

You also try to convince the Head of the Council to move the extraordinary meeting to Connington on the Shyre, I don't think the General wants to go to Venus with his henchmen."

"Neither will be easy. Because both will be stubborn. KTKFK and General Cooper."

"If we don't want Starwars here on earth, then let them get off their asses and compromise. I'll call Cooper on the smartphone right now."

"I'll get in touch with the KTKFK." Roselyn said in response and picked up the Vybe scanner, as she had no use for telepathic communication due to the headache that had been plaguing her for the last few days.

"I SHOULD WHAT???" yelled Cooper on the other end of the receiver.

"You have a choice General. Venus or Connington on the Shyre. Nevada is not holding this trial and I would be surprised if the new head of the High Council will agree to England. I can only say this much General. The likelihood of a galactic invasion is high and I wouldn't get on too high a horse and turn it down. The negotiation must take place in a neutral zone where everyone feels safe. Roselyn doesn't want to go to Nevada because she fears arrest on your part...."

"Oh, what is she thinking? She's already done such good work for us that we would never be so ungrateful. Even if she did behave suspiciously."

"Nevertheless, General. I don't think there's any other option. Unless you would agree to a trip to Venus."

"NEVER! Give me 48 hours to respond. I still have to talk to the others. And you said the whole thing was to take place in this dump? Connington on the Shyre? Why not London or Paris for all I care?"

"Because it attracts the attention of undesirables. It's not in your intcrest, is it?"

"OK. I have understood. 48 hours." And General Cooper hung up the phone hard.

"What did he say?" Roselyn asked.

"He said to give him 48 hours. After that, he'll answer us. What have you achieved?"

"KTKFK has agreed. The farm and the Wellington estate suit him well. He will also appear with his entourage. Two from Venus, two from Corantio and two independent ones who have yet to be selected. It all depends on the General now."

It took less than 48 hours, because after just under 30, the General decided in favor of the proposal to come to Connington on the Shyre. The professors, Michael Robertson and two other deputies from the White House would be there. These last two were subject to the strictest secrecy and were only directly answerable to the President of the United States, who actually did not know what exactly was going on. Not yet.

"Now we just need a date general and if possible the whole thing should happen quickly."

"OK, I'll call you in 48 hours," said the general.

"What? Why do you always need 48 hours to make a decision like that? We shouldn't and mustn't waste any more time General."

"All right, you pain in the ass. Tomorrow night we will arrive in Luton. See that we are picked up. Arrival time and other details to follow."

"All right."

"Oh Patrick, we want to get to you before the aliens do, because I'm not going to let them take away the landing of the spaceship. I need to see it!"

"Well General, I can't promise a spectacle and I don't know the Venusian protocol on this. They might as well land somewhere else and just transfer themselves wherever they want to go. They certainly won't be taking a Taxi."

"You have a sense of humor, Patrick. Tell the Chief that we Americans love a show. Tell him not to make such a fuss."

Once a cowboy, always a cowboy, Patosh thought to himself, but he understood the general only too well, who only got to see the crash sites of the aliens and was never allowed to see a real landing. Patosh also thought that such an experience would be a demonstration of their inferiority to the two deputies and would only reinforce the urgency of a peaceful solution. Roselyn discussed with Mary, Patosh, Jenkins and also William, who were to be involved as part of the negotiating team at the request of the head of KTKFK, the placement of the landing site for the spaceship. They also discussed the distribution of the guest rooms and the planning of the catering. The Americans want steaks, the Venusians rather not. But above all, how can such a gathering be kept secret?

"Just carry on as before," said Mary.

"They 'll find a place to land, because there are plenty of clearings in the woods. The general will get his money's worth. I'm just worried about who the other independents will be that KTKFK will bring along. I have a very bad feeling about that."

"Why mother?" asked Roselyn, and Patosh wasn't sure why this was worrying her either.

"If they're one of the organizers from KROM-56, then they can influence the whole trial for the worse," Mary said warningly.

"They're just policemen...." Patosh tried to contradict.

"They're more than that. They are organizers, which means that their power of disposition can exceed that of the Confederation if we don't reach a conclusion and an agreement. They are the true guardians of the Creator and the universe, so we can only hope that the two independents are not about them."

"Don't worry Mary. One way or another something has to happen and we have no other choice. What worries me is the general's cowboy attitude."

Patosh received the general's arrival details that evening. A civilian private jet was arriving with six people and all he had to do was pick them up. William would do this, as he owned a Ford Transit that could transport such a number of people. But the general was shocked when he saw the Transit. He thought more of a Mercedes S Class, or at least something similar. Squeezing into a Transit van was far beneath his dignity. But he had no other choice. What annoyed the General even more was that William wouldn't stop puttering during the journey.

"Now shut up and get us where we need to go," he shouted at him.

"Of course sir."

The journey was torture for everyone involved, as one roadworks after another turned the highways and main roads into an obstacle course. General Cooper and some of his staff complained about the Ford Transit. It was uncomfortable and smelled of rotten food.

"I mostly use the Ford for shopping. Food, cleaning products, drinks and whatever else you need to run an inn..."

"You run an inn? Well then I hope we're not staying there if it smells just as rotten..."

After this remark, William had no choice but to slam on the brakes and lo and behold, the alliance that apparently existed between England and the USA during the Second World War was nullified during this journey.

"You might as well get out here and walk to the farm, you arrogant lot. If you're used to something better, then Connington on the Shyre is the wrong place for you varnish monkeys. I'm sorry I didn't take the Rolls Royce to transport your pussy asses, but it's next to my Ferrari and the Lamborghini at the inspection!"

"You have a Lamborghini?" asked Professor Farnham, who didn't notice the sarcasm.

"No, of course not, you wise guy. Now, quiet in the brothel, because we'll be there in 20 minutes. So shut up!" William shouted.

There was dead silence afterwards and William couldn't get rid of his grin. What a kindergarten, he thought to himself and shook his head. There were now six men sitting in his transit who were supposed to have an elevated IQ, but apparently everyone was allowed to call themselves a general and a professor these days, which proved that academics were just people and not gods. At last the journey came to an end and the guests were awaited with great excitement and nervousness. General Cooper looked first at Roselyn, who stepped out of the van and gasped for fresh air. His look betrayed disappointment and regret, but to everyone's surprise, a different General Cooper was seen the moment he walked up to her, gave her a long look and a fatherly hug.

"You have caused me sleepless nights Roselyn, but I am glad that you are well my child."

"Good to see you again Freddy. I hope we can make your stay as comfortable as possible," she said with a smile, to which Cooper turned his gaze to William and said, "The journey here has already given us hope that everything that follows could only be better."

William's grin disappeared and he turned and left.

"May I introduce you to Mr. Malcolm Jenkins, my mother Mary, of whom I have told you much, William and Patrick you already know."

He didn't waste another second of his attention on Jenkins, because he didn't like ufologists and conspiracy theorists who proliferated in the media and destroyed any respectability that other potential researchers were working hard to establish.

Yes, General Cooper knew Jenkins, because he was the one who used Interpol and other police forces against him. But Jenkins didn't know that.

"Mrs. Mitchell, it's a pleasure and I wish we had met under different circumstances."

"I wish the same General. Now here we have the opportunity to do it anyway."

"Indeed we do. May I briefly introduce my staff? Professor Alfred Farnham, Professor Richard Curtiss, Special Agent Micheal Robertson, Deputy David Melassio and Special Advisor Joseph Berger."

Mary just nodded her head and asked the gentlemen to follow her into the house. They all didn't have much luggage with them, although there was no way of knowing in advance how long the hearing would last, but it was hoped that it wouldn't take longer than three days. Mary showed the guests the accommodation and drew their attention to the corridor leading to the living room, where they could meet for tea after having showered and freshened up. She then met Patosh, Roselyn, Malcolm Jenkins and William in the tea room, but they had something stronger first.

"My God, what a stiff bunch," said Jenkins.

"Yes, and I'm still surprised at how warmly the General greeted you, Roselyn. Is there anything I should know? The professors, instead, were rather cold towards you." Mary remarked.

"I noticed that too. I would have expected the opposite effect." Patosh confirmed.

"You're imagining things. Control your phantasies, because Cooper always treated me well. To him, I was the daughter he never had after his wife and two children died in a plane crash. The only problem is that you can't judge him when he's doing his job. I never had a good relationship with the professors because they are the ones who gave Cooper false hope and continue to do so. They are the ones responsible for the experiments on the aliens being held, which finally made me decide to leave. KTXLG was sympathetic when he received my report. I now hope that I can convince Freddy of the reality."

"We hope so too. I'm curious to see how KTKFK will behave during the negotiations." Patosh said and emptied his whisky glass in one gulp.

The moment of the pre-meeting arrived and Frederick Copper appeared in civilian clothes that couldn't be more Texan. Dressed in plaid golf pants held up by a belt and a matching silver cowboy buckle, accented with cowboy boots and a western hat, he represented Texas in a style that would blind any British eye. The others appeared in the usual expected attire of polo shirts, jeans or flannels and jackets. Mary could not conceal an amused expression, but the General, who insisted on being called Freddy, took no offense. However, this privilege did not apply to William and especially not to Malcom Jenkins. Mary poured tea in beautiful china cups and handed them each a plate with the usual pastries.

"Nice place you have here Mary. I like this style. Roselyn has already told me that your late husband was an officer in the Royal British Army. There's no denying his taste, my dear," and he looked at Mary with a smile.

"You are an incorrigible flatterer General..."

"Freddy for you. Don't forget, because we want to be friends in this strange game, don't we?" the General corrected her.

"Of course. Freddy. I beg your pardon. Yes, it would be desirable to form what I hope will be a productive and serious friendship between all of us, because there's a lot at stake here. It's hard to believe that only a few people hold the fate of this planet in their hands in this small room."

"I hear you, Mary," said the general with a serious look.

"I know that a lot of things are not going right, but this has been the case for thousands of years and as long as there are no changes that require a serious course, the fate of this earth is bad."

"You have sabotaged it for years, this change you are talking about General." Jenkins intervened loudly.

"You have trampled on the truth and obstructed and prevented coexistence with the aliens to this day, just to keep the energy supply as primitive as before, not to speak of your militarizing attitude.

Whistleblowers like me are persecuted, even hunted down and removed, so don't come to me now with such pontifical slogans."

"We have made mistakes, I admit that. But at the time, the information was withheld for security reasons, to prevent a panic Mr. Jenkins, not to deceive humanity for economic reasons. We were worried, because yes, being confronted with beings from another solar system is very disturbing at first. What do you think would have happened if we had gone to the press with the appearance of the Greys? We would have had to reckon with civil war-like situations, especially during the Cold War. Believe me when I tell you all here that the Soviets had to deal with the same problems back then. They also had regular visitors from space."

"We already know that. But why did they remain technically behind compared to the western world? Our progress was several years ahead of theirs. What would the consequences be if the aliens had chosen the Soviets?"

"Could have, would have. Be glad it didn't happen that way. The aliens recognized the Soviets' intention immediately. Their policy of global and socialist deprivation of freedom through a communist idea and thus the intervention and control of the free will of each individual would have been the consequence Mr. Jenkins.

What do you know. Yes, we have used knowledge to drive our progress, but unfortunately we are not in charge of how this shared knowledge may or may not be distributed. We are dealing with other species at the same time, who know the weaknesses of humans all too well and exploit them shamelessly. Promises that could not be more corrupt and destroy all morals and ethics. Strong politicians with strong personalities, who have also had a hard time in their youth, be it through wars or economic hardship, are more likely to understand what is at stake so that their people would not experience the same, but these men and women have long since died out and a generation of the indifferent and self-loving has followed in their place. I already know this problem Mr. Jenkins, but not all are like this. There are still people out there who see and recognize the deplorable situation, but they are being eliminated and silenced. How much do you know about the Orion Clan?" the general asked angrily.

"Only what I've learned through my years of work, and I thank whoever it is that my work has finally brought me into this circle. Not to mention the humiliations, lies and financial ruin I had to go through to open humanity's eyes, only to be put behind bars by the likes of you. Where are your Men in Black anyway? Why didn`t you bring these assholes to this meeting?"

"We don't work with this department Mr. Jenkins and as I said. The aliens have been visiting this planet for thousands of years.

There are many who take it for granted and consider them more like vacationers. But don't let them fool you. Not all of them have good intentions and to find out exactly what will happen to our planet, we are here. Time is ticking Mr. Jenkins and the last thing we need here are fantasists and conspiracy theorists undoing our years of work. Seriousness is being trampled underfoot and stupidity is winning out thanks to the marketing of false information via social media. Nothing is rose-colored and nothing should take us away from facts, because the surprise and the truth could hurt. I understand that you, Mr. Jenkins, have had the pleasure of being brought to Venus and yet I ask you not to see everything in black and white, because no one can be trusted, not even the Venusians," General Cooper said without mincing words.

 The suffocating atmosphere in the room made it necessary to change the subject and so Roselyn now came into play.

"We have a golf course nearby Freddy. I see you didn't bring your clubs, but don't worry. Dad still has his somewhere. Maybe you have the time."

"Probably not today, my dear. But I wouldn't mind doing the negotiations over a game of golf. However, I doubt it would go down well at the golf club. Just imagine that. A game of golf with aliens," Cooper said with a laugh and everyone joined in. Even Jenkins.

"I think that would be the least of the problems, because the Venusians can change their appearance molecularly." Said Roselyn.

"The Venusians can, but what about the others?" objected Mary, who thought it was a bad idea.

"I think such a meeting should be held behind closed doors," she said, looking at Roselyn.

"I was only joking mother."

"I know that, my child. I've sent our cook home today and for the next few days Freddy. I think a nice roast lamb and roast potatoes would be a successful meal for tonight's dinner. What do you think? I'll have the pleasure of preparing it myself and Roselyn will help me, won't you Roselyn?"

"Oh I agree Mary. I'm sure it will be a delicious meal. How about a whisky now? I'm not really a tea person."

"But of course Freddy. I think we could all do with one." and everyone agreed without argument.

The evening ended nicely and the roast lamb was, as expected, delicious. Here and there they indulged in a sherry or a port and yes, the general was even allowed a cigar at the end.

"I think we'll all be tired and tomorrow will be an exciting day. Who knows which landing site they'll choose, but I think we'll be informed shortly beforehand," said Roselyn, hoping to be able to go to bed afterwards, as she had already been tired for hours.

"Yes, absolutely. I don't want to miss the landing." Said the general.

"Speaking of landing," interrupted Jenkins.

"What do you think about the moon landing, General?"

General Cooper just smiled and said with a poiseness look.

"Why don't you ask the aliens tomorrow, Mr. Jenkins?"

The Arrival

It was early in the morning, around 4 o'clock, when Roselyn woke all the guests with the words "They're coming". General Cooper changed into his uniform, because such guests had to be honored with the best possible labels, even if the aliens themselves wore no clothes and, stark naked as they were, had nothing to hide. The others did the same, with the exception of the uniform, because as a civilian you didn't have that privilege.

"Mary has already prepared coffee and sandwiches in the kitchen," said Roselyn.

"I thought the Aliens were coming. Do we have time for a coffee?" asked Professor Farnham hopefully.

"Of course. They will be here in thirty minutes and there has to be that much time for a short breakfast."

"How do you know all that?"

"They reported it to me. Telepathically. They should have flown past Pluto by now. Have you noted down any questions for the meeting, gentlemen? The High Council will only answer questions once and repeated questions will be considered a sign of incompetence. Also, please avoid questions about Jesus Christ and the moon landing as they did not come here to teach history."

"Oh no? But that's what could be fascinating. I don't think even half of our history is as we've been told and drilled into us. The truth is...."

"The truth is the past Malcolm. Venusians stick to the present and don't cling to the past or even the future. The mistakes one has made in the past are mentally stored but never applied again. So please let's just focus on whether they are claiming the Earth for themselves and if so, what can we do about it, or whether the dangers are even greater and we will be banished from the universe for all time by being eliminated. Also, please do not shake hands in greeting, because this ritual is seen as a sexual approach. Sex is not a sin per se for the extraterrestrials, unlike us, and serves to restore the energy of the soul realm. One more thing. Address him, KTKFK, as "wise one". That is the title of a leader, whether in the High Council or in the Confederation. That's it."

"Where will they land Roselyn?" asked General Cooper with his mouth half full after grabbing a sandwich.

"There's a well-hidden clearing less than two miles from here. A suitable and reasonably dry landing site. They already know the coordinates because I gave it to them. We should set off and William's Ford Transit and my Land Rover should do the trick."

"I'm driving the Land Rover, that's for sure," Cooper said, looking at William.

"So let's go."

Fog hovered over the damp ground and darkness still prevailed, even though it was already 5 o'clock in the morning. They arrived at the spot and it smelled of meadow and flowers and nature couldn't be more beautiful.

Hundreds of birds were already singing and here and there a woodpecker knocked and a cuckoo cried.

Yes, this earth is always worth saving and caring for and preserving for humanity, but for a humanity that is open and endowed with the purest purity of soul. The earth showed itself that morning as the true paradisc. Was this a divine sign that civilizations from across the universe were being brought together so that love and unity could once again reign as it is meant to, or were they just being deceived as the universe also showed its cruelest side several times in the form of crashing meteorites that wiped out almost everything? No one could find an answer to this question at that moment and they surrendered to the freshly inhaled air with all its scents. Suddenly, Jenkins held up his right hand and pointed to the cloudy sky.

"There!" he shouted

"Where?" shouted the general.

A strange light pierced through the thick fog and it became deathly quiet.

The birds stopped singing, the cuckoo stopped screaming and the woodpecker also stopped working. The light came silently closer and closer and changed its colors from bright light blue to a bright yellow. Now you could also make out outlines, but if you thought you were looking at a disk, you were deceived. At least the general, the professors and the deputies were. Rosleyn, Mary and the others, however, recognized the ship. It was the flagship they had seen once before when they were deported, or rather rescued.

The "GALAXIA TITANICA".

Four long leg-like frames were extended, serving as landing gear, and when they touched the ground, what you would think was a door opened. A hole simply appeared in the hull and a metal-like plank manifested from it. But what was that? Jenkins pointed to the sky again and what they now saw left them speechless as more and more lights appeared out of the misty void and more and more smaller spaceships, now in disk-like form as they were usually thought to be, landed. The trees were simply hologrammed away to make way for the estimated thirty spaceships. But back to the flagship, from where several figures suddenly appeared at the bright opening. They all looked the same and from a distance it was impossible to tell their rank or position. The alien at the front must have been the "wise man", but far from it.

The one in front was just a herald. The one at the back was KTKFK and now you could also recognize his rank in the form of a gemstone on his forehead. The aliens in front of him formed an aisle so that "The Wise One" could approach his hosts and how could it be otherwise, General Cooper gave a military salute and adhered to the etiquette that had been drilled into him for years. As briefed, his hand was not extended.

"It's a pleasure to meet you here, General Cooper," said KTKFK "....and if our appearance bothers you, we can assume human form, as you already know."

"That is not necessary, Your Wisdom. That way we can distinguish ourselves, because nothing is further from my mind than a masquerade."

"Very considerate General. May I introduce you to the others on the Confederation board? The Wise from Venus KTGGD, the Wise from Venus KTUHF, the Wise from Corantio who has chosen the name Konrad for this journey, the Wise from Corantio George whose name has also been adapted for your conditions and the two independents who have no names but belong to the group of organizers."

Mary and Roselyn's blood ran cold when they heard this, for it could not mean anything good, and this was confirmed by the appearance of the additional spaceships.

General Cooper, Patosh, William and Jenkins took it as part of protocol, just as presidents do when they go on diplomatic trips with all their security officers, bodyguards, communications officers, hairdressers, tailors, servants, etc. They had no idea of the seriousness of the situation, or perhaps they did, but didn't want to give away any paranoia.

"You have a large entourage at your side, we haven't planned any logistical accommodation for that, Your Wisdom."

"You worry far too much General. My companions do not need accommodation and we hope to get this meeting over with as quickly as possible. I see you are here with your vehicles. We would have come straight to you in the living room, but Roselyn already said that you would look forward to a show on our part"

"And what a show that was my "wise one". We will never forget it I think. Very well. How are we going to manage this issue with the transportation to the farm...."

"Just drive ahead. We'll be there to receive you," KTKFK said dryly, which didn't surprise General Cooper.

He had been in this alien business far too long and had seen things far too often that would have been better left unseen, but an original landing was the highlight of his experience so far. He nodded and said. "I'll see you there."

Still exhausted from the night before, Roselyn, General Cooper, Mary, the two professors and deputies sat on one side of the negotiating table and KTKFK with his own on the other. For Patosh, William, Jenkins and Mike Robertson, another table was set up away from the action, as they could not have any direct influence on the "final solution". But they were allowed to listen to the proceedings.

Bottles of mineral water, pots of tea and coffee as well as cookies and the appropriate crockery were lined up on the long negotiating table, but this was more for the human side, as the aliens would not be taking any of it. General Cooper poured himself some coffee and wasted no more time and started talking.

"OK. We all know why we're here so let's not beat around the bush. You've been in and out of Earth for thousands of years and have influenced our existence, more or less, and not just for the good. My question now is, what do you want? The earth belongs to us and by us I mean the people. You keep sending us advisors and whatnot and threatening us with an apocalypse if we don't do this or that. Let's stop this shit once and for all and talk straight.

The Orion Clan has to get out of here, otherwise the invasion you're planning behind your closed curtains won't help either. We can't interfere with free will by you showing up here and wanting to play God, because let's face it, you're not holy either.

Evil must be fought and that is our main goal, but sending more of your spies, organizers, advisors pretending to be on vacation will not help the cause. If the universe really meant "LOVE" to us then the evil wouldn't exist to begin with and so I don't buy your "love story", see KXTLG who went off on his own and caused chaos in your ranks. You are not perfect either gentlemen.

KTKFK took a while to respond, but a distinct clacking on the aliens' side made it clear that they were conferring among themselves.

"Forgive me for taking a while General, but we are only concerned with giving factual answers to such an emotionally charged plea. We have come and gone from this planet because it does not belong to the human species, as you falsely claim, but solely to the universe. There is therefore no claim to ownership on your part and had you accepted our help back then and submitted to our rules, you too would have had the technologies to explore the universe, make contact with other species and form friendships, vacation in other solar systems without restrictions and live a life in harmony and yes, we also have faults, but we are further densities ahead in development than you are. The universe means balance and free will means being able to decide what you want to be. See the Orion Clan as a test that you have not passed so far. On the contrary.

You have allowed yourselves to be corrupted because you have used your free will to follow the Orion Clan, for a fee of course, to subordinate yourselves to material goods and to exchange money and gold for the wealth of nature already given to you by the Creator. The earth does not belong to you and you all, as you live here, belong to the universe. Your DNA was transported here from far away on this once cold ball and developed into what you are now through evolutionary processes that have lasted hundreds of millions of years. With the only difference that you have stopped learning from nature and growing with it. Technological progress is necessary, but it should be used for the good of all and not for so-called elite groups that are subordinate to the Orion clan. You can no longer save your planet and that's where we come in. The only question is, what do we do with you, since you are a weak species and are not of much use to space. On the contrary, to use your words, you are nothing more than a deadly virus and we are the necessary vaccine. This is getting serious General and I have promised you that this negotiation will be short-lived, because the first settlers for our subsequent takeover are already here. The escort spaceships you have seen are not part of a diplomatic escort, but of the Host Confederation and they will be making preparations for a full Venusian takeover. Prepare the people for something that must force them to rethink and believe me when I say here, it is for your own good.

As you said General, we don't beat around the bush, we act and we have acted. The landings have already begun worldwide as well, including the Mojave Desert and your Area 51. Our liberation begins now. I'll give you some good advice General. Fly back to Washington, get in touch with your president, and most importantly, get in touch with the other dictators posing as heads of government. Make them realize that their time is up and none of the weapons developed here can do anything against our takeover. Part of free will dear General is also to go so far against evil that special measures may be used and as we speak the operation is in full swing. Thank you for the tea and coffee, but we will leave now and wish you the Creator's blessing."

"WHAT?" shouted General Cooper.

"You've got to be kidding me...." shouted Patosh.

"What about the moon landing?" shouted Jenkins, an echo reaching them as they saw an energy source make KTKFK and his entourage almost completely disappear. It sounded more like a laugh. A laugh that said how small humans are.

"You scream for the moon when you could have traveled and conquered the universe. You are pathetic."

And with these last words, the silhouettes disappeared and a strong glow of light confirmed the disappearance of the flagship.

General Cooper and his entourage stood there as if nailed down while Roselyn fell to her knees in tears. Wracked with guilt, she cried, "It's all my fault," and despite Mary's attempts at consolation, Roselyn's despair could not be lessened. Jenkins and William looked at each other anxiously. Only Patosh caught himself and shouted, "Pull yourselves together." Calm returned, but the bewilderment was great. Greatest among General Cooper.

"General? What are your orders?" Michael Robertson asked, but the general was mentally unresponsive.

"General? What are your orders?" Mike Robertson shouted louder and finally reached Cooper, who seemed to feel lost and empty.

"Call the pilots in Luton. Refuel the plane and file the flight plan for Washington DC and you're coming with me. All of you!"

Cooper's smartphone rang and the number that appeared on the screen announced that shit was about to hit the fan.

"Mr. President......I understand.....no I'm nowhere near you. I'm in England......naturally. Tomorrow morning. Will be there." With a chalky pale face, Cooper looked at Robertson and ordered him.

"You stay here Robertson. I need you here as a link. Report back to me on everything that happens here, because I don't think this is the last we've seen. They've freed all the aliens in the Mojave Desert and destroyed the secret facility. Area 51 has been razed to the ground. The president just told me about deaths. How many has not yet been confirmed. Caligula disappeared in one of our uniforms and was recognized in the massacre by some of our own. We are at war."

"As you wish General. I will stay here."

"Mary. We need the farm. It's needed as a base for Mr. Robertson. Can you provide him with everything that goes with it?"

"What do you mean by that? What do you want me to provide him with?"

"Well, house keys. Information about the facility. Everything he needs to be aware of here so that he can operate and stay in contact with us."

"Yes, I understand now. Of course I can do that."

"General. One of the group should stay here because I need someone who knows this area. William should stay here."

"OK. William can stay here in England and support you. Is that OK William?"

"What kind of question is this? I live here and you just take control of us like that, without any legal authorisation? Why can't Jenkins stay here and Patosh? Why not Mary? Isn't Roselyn enough? She got us into all this," William shouted, beside himself.

"I apologize William. Of course I can't just decide who has to come and who doesn't. I just don't know where my head is at the moment and your safety is my consern, especially now that everyone wants to get at you. You know too much and the President's phone is ringing off the hook. China and Russia suspect the USA of strange events that are taking place there. He didn't want to talk about it any further. So once again. I would be grateful if the others would come with me. You too, Jenkins."

"I don't want to stay here a minute longer. I'm coming with you." Jenkins said in a shaky voice.

"We're coming along just as willingly. I'm just looking for Harry and Gonzi." said Mary.

"Who's Harry and who´s Gonzi now?" asked the general nervously, who wanted nothing more than to go to Luton and take the jet back to the United States.

"Our dogs. They have to go with us."

"That's all right, Mary. They can come with us, but quickly. We're in a hurry."

"Is it just the flagship that's left or the escort too?" Patosh remarked anxiously.

"I can't answer that. You take the transit and Jenkins the Land Rover and drive us to Luton Airport. Robertson and William will go back to the clearing and report back on whether the escort is still there or not."

Robertson just nodded and Professor Farnham and Curtiss pleaded with Cooper to fly them to Nevada to the Mojave Desert, but Cooper refused. The President had priority and everyone should be there so that nothing would be left out of the protocol at the White House.

"They will have their revenge on us." whispered Professor Farnham, but no one said anything more. They arrived at Luton Airport and the chaos there was indescribable. All regular flights were canceled and there were police and military as far as the eye could see. Nobody knew exactly what had happened, neither Cooper and his troops, nor the concerned citizens and the respective governments. Several roadblocks had to be overcome and only with great difficulty did they reach the apron where the Gulfstream was waiting for them, fully fueled. One engine was already running as the pilot recognized the Transit and the Land Rover approaching the plane at high speed.

He had also received further instructions from General Cooper via his smartphone and had a good description of the vehicles.

Even before the boarding door electrically raised and closed, the second engine was running and before they could sit down in one of the seats, the Gulfstream taxied to the take-off position.

" November two three five Charlie, you`re cleared for take off ! " came the instruction over the radio and the pilot pushed the power levers forward so that the aluminum bird accelerated and took off in a westerly direction.

Roselyn fell into a deep sleep after allowing herself a brandy to calm her down, but the others stayed awake, because who could sleep after such an experience?

"What now General?" asked Patosh.

"To be honest, I don't know."

"You must have a plan B for cases like this." Jenkins remarked.

"We did, but apparently Plan B didn't work and neither did Plan C." As the general was about to continue, the on-board telephone installed next to his seat rang.

"Cooper here." A long silence followed and Cooper listened intently. With a petrified expression, he put the phone down, unbuckled his seatbelt and walked to the cockpit. One of the deputies, David Melassio to be exact, did the same and followed him.

"How could that phone call upset those two?" asked Jenkins.

"We'll soon find out, I hope," replied the second deputy, Josef Berger.

"You don't seem too worried, Deputy." Mary said.

"Appearances are deceiving madam, but we can't change anything from this plane and why make the pilot nervous with three of us? My gut feeling is that we'll have to land somewhere else," he said calmly, looking out of the window. He was right. Cooper and Melassio returned and argued loudly with each other.

"Could we all find out what's going on?" Patosh interrupted.

"We're landing in Goose Bay," Cooper said curtly and painlessly.

"In Goose Bay Labrador? That's Canadian soil and neutral as far as I know."

"Not anymore Mr. Jenkins. The President is meeting with other heads of state there. Washington is no longer safe and we've been given direct orders to show our faces there."

"What else General? That wasn't all, was it?"

"No. Reports have been received that during the raid on Area 51 and the Mojave base, personnel from several aliens, or organizers, were abducted. Nothing is known about their fate yet, but they are important scientists who had been working on various projects. I don't want to know what will happen to them. The same thing happened in Russia, China, North Korea, India, Iran, Israel and Pakistan. Seems to me that our alien friends are going to draw a line under all the sinful games we humans have been playing."

"What about the other scientists from the European countries? Aren't they developing military projects that don't serve mankind?" Jenkins laughed.

"You must think that's funny, you airhead. The projects being developed in Europe are probably not dangerous and worrying enough for our aliens, but how should I know? I never thought it would ever come to this. All these years I thought we had everything under control, despite the known risks. Only now do I realize how bad we really are. Billions that could have been invested in something meaningful have been wasted in destroying ourselves. Our eyes are being opened, my friends, by the police of God, as macabre as it may sound."

"I didn't know you were a believer General," Mary remarked, pouring herself a whisky.

"I am Mary. Even if I appear to be an ice-cold, emotionless creature, I often regain my inner peace through prayer. I ask him whether everything we are doing here is right and why he allows some things to happen that also give me a severe headache.

I rarely get answers, but I recognize some signs as the language of God and the aliens also speak of a Creator, even if it is different from ours. We have actually sold ourselves and subordinated ourselves to the devil. The greatest torment for me, however, is the fact that there is nothing I can do about it. Too many opinions and too much mental closure have separated us from the natural sources. Demanding proof for everything without allowing belief in the supernatural has turned us into machines. Nothing can be expected anymore without having to pay for it and nothing happens anymore out of pure charity Mary and shall I be completely honest with you? I am glad that all this is happening, because only in this way can we hope that it will finally be recognized how much this earth needs to be saved and how much man can contribute to this. First of all, the evil must be eliminated from the world, but it will be difficult to recognize and get rid of the exact perpetrators of this evil. Those who lead us in this direction must have their heads cut off, then and only then will we find peace."

Roselyn listened, but she kept her eyes closed. The words of her alien father, KXTLG, appeared again. "You must warn them about themselves Roselyn. Free will is being abused and the Orion Clan is becoming too powerful. I am betraying the High Council with my intervention, but I must do it and I need you."

That's how it all began thousands of years ago and reality appeared to her like a hologram. Even then, KXTLG realized where the direction of the humans would lead them, but the presumed insignificance of the matter, in the judgment of the Confederacy, with the excuse of not being allowed to interfere with Free Will, had made things worse. They had allowed too much time to pass and had been distracted by an artificially created star war with the Orion Clan, so that this scum of space would spill its venom on Earth and now it was almost too late to do anything at all. Too late had she, Roselyn, responded to her cosmic father's pleas to leave Venus and go on a secret mission to set the rails of balance straight as she struggled with herself. Breaking the rules was a difficult decision and in the end she appeared as the traveler named Mary. This is how this development took its course and how she met Patosh, who now became an accomplice to her operation through no fault of his own. She had thrown his life out of joint without her wanting to. How could she go on living with this guilt?

The hours passed and the sun set on the horizon.

"We'll be landing in twenty minutes, sir," said the flight attendant as she cleared away the empty glasses and cups

Invisible war

The Gulfstream jet landed in Goose Bay as night was falling and when the plane pulled into the parking lot, two black Mercedes Sprinter buses were already waiting for them. No customs and passport control was cleared and a representative with other agents in their typical black suits and sunglasses (even though it was night already) urged the important passengers to board the buses.

"We are in a great hurry General. The President is furious," he said.

"There's nothing I can do about that." Cooper replied indifferently and just as angrily. They drove off and Cooper briefed everyone to shut up and let him do the talking. They were only to speak if they were questioned and only when he gave permission with a nod of his head.

"He's beside himself. That's typical. When the carpet burns, they react late and blame the others. I still don't know how the situation has developed and what's going on."

"Don't worry General. We'll find out in a moment and yes, you're right. Only one person should talk," said David Melassio, who was already in fear, knowing full well that this president was a man with massive mood swings.

Josef Berger remained relaxed, as he had done throughout the flight, and even smiled at the drama unfolding before him. There is something strange about this Berger, Patosh thought to himself. The convoy, which consisted of two Sprinter buses and two escort vehicles, sped through the country road and drove to the military base called "5 Wing Goose Bay" in Happy Valley, about 5 km away. The gate to the base, which was heavily guarded at short notice, was opened immediately and not a glance was wasted by the guard to even check who was inside. But why didn't the Gulfstream land here straight away? On this military airfield that had everything, including a long runway? The representative's answer was as to be expected. "For safety reasons," which caused Jenkins to laugh derisively. The Konvoi arrived and just before they entered a building, a last briefing was held by the representative.

"You will first be taken directly to the president, as he has some questions to ask, and then we will go to hangar number 7, where the actual meeting will take place. As I said, he's not..."

"Yes, yes. He's not in a good mood, you don't need to repeat yourself man. I'm not either, so we have something in common the president and I. Patosh and the others follow me."

"That's not possible sir..."

"But it has to be possible, otherwise the questions won't be answered. Not because I don't want to, but because I certainly can't answer them all. So don't make a scene here and let us in to see him."

The representative just nodded and opened the door to the room where the US President was engaged in a conversation with other generals and when Cooper entered the room with his entourage, the President arrogantly waved at him.

"So gentlemen. That's all for now. If you'll leave me alone with General Cooper, I'll follow you to the meeting as soon as I've finished here."

The generals of all branches of the armed forces left and some of them saluted Cooper with a pitying face.

"So General Cooper. Now, out with the story..."

"My President, may I introduce you to my group first...."

"No, you may not. I'm not the least bit interested in who they are, because I can't see another unknown face. Who gave you permission to enter the room with strangers in the first place?"

"My president. If you don't take the time to get to know these people your questions will only be half answered. They were there when this all started and I advise you to listen to them as well."

General Cooper said loudly, his Texan accent even taking the wind out of the President's sails as there was swearing to be heard between the lines.

"All right, then. What's going on here Cooper? During my entire tenure, I'm being deprived of things that are apparently not meant for my eyes and ears..."

"It's not like that...."

"Oh no, General? Are you just bullshitting your president? You have constantly put rose-colored glasses on my nose when I asked questions regarding extraterrestrial phenomena and now it turns out that they are not phenomena, but a bitter truth that has been withheld from me, the President of the United States of America and of a nuclear world power. Who do you think you are within your secret society? Your behavior is treason and where do the billions come from? I never signed up for such a budget. I've had enough of you people causing a war behind my back and now one with fucking aliens Cooper."

"What exactly happened General? Was Russia or China attacked?"

"We were all attacked but not with weapons. All the software that makes this world go round, military, satellites, finance, GPS, energy and medical care has been paralyzed.

Hospitals can no longer treat their patients, citizens can't withdraw their money from ATMs, banks have lost all their data and I'm even talking about the back up system and the military is also paralyzed. Yes, there have been casualties, but more from friendly fire caused by misunderstandings. China, Russia and the rest of the world of course blames us for the whole mess. Some passenger planes had to make emergency landings because their entire navigation systems failed and we are left in the dark. Then this..."

The President picked up a remote control and pressed the play button. A strange face appeared, but it was clear to Patosh, Roselyn and Mary who it was. It was KTKFK, who had undergone a molecular intervention to make himself human, but to everyone's amusement not as a man, but as a woman. Cooper and the President didn't think it was funny and a look that could have killed the group he had brought with, instantly froze the prevailing ambience which was only meant for Roselyn, Mary and Patosh. Jenkins, the professors and Cooper didn't initially recognize the figure that began speaking on the screen.

"Who is she?" asked the president.

"Who is it?" Cooper corrected.

"He, or she, is the head of the High Council on Venus."

"Really? And why don't I know that, General Cooper? Is that too high for me? Is that it? Am I not worthy to know what is going on outside our atmosphere? This presumption has been infuriating me for years. Listen to what this creature has to tell us."

"Greetings human of the planet Terrarion, or as you call it, Earth. You may call me Susan, for simplicity's sake. As I'm sure you've already realized, we Venusians have shut down your entire network, which has led to catastrophic consequences on your planet. We have a right to do so, because let's face it, the network is based on our technology and we gave it to you with good will so that you could live your life more easily and happily. However, once again, as in all the thousands of years, you have proven to us that you use our gifts selfishly and self-destructively. We gave them to you so that you would use them responsibly and develop your planet gently and progressively. In this way, your being and your species should also continue to develop so that the next shift can also begin for you. The fourth density, which will make a life without war, without money and without hate possible, but you have not passed the test imposed on you and so you must repeat the third density for another 75,000 years until you and your fellow human beings have understood what is important. Old mistakes are repeated again and again, but not because you cannot learn, but because you do not want to learn and the few who are supposed to guide you only use our technologies for their own needs and for self-enrichment. And although this is already obvious to everyone, the rest of your species is doing nothing about it. We, the High Council and the Confederation, have therefore decided to leave you in your darkness until you come to enlightenment on your own and free yourselves from your darkness together. We will not use force, because we are not authorized to do so and it contradicts our ideology. However, be warned, because the organizers who will witness your development are authorized to immediately transfer subjects who do not abide by the rules and our laws to our punishment planet Centauro Magno. Since our intervention, there are already 1456 subjects on this punishment planet, and the trend is rising. We are not talking about petty crimes, but about offenses that are listed as highly punishable in our galactic code. These are offenses that lead to the destruction of your species and your planet. So do not be surprised if high and well-known personalities suddenly disappear from your public life. Do not look for them, as they have committed serious offenses and have been transferred to Centauro Magno. We too have tribunals and we too can and may judge and believe me, human, we have been following your actions for thousands of years.

So I advise you to use the highest gift you have been given since birth with utmost passion, which is Love. Love will lead you all out of the darkness and if we deem your test passed, we will help you develop as before.

The blessing of the Creator be with you.

Greetings to you.

Susan."

Then the President switched off the transmission and looked at the group.

"So, any suggestions? If yes, let's have it!"

"Are other members of the foreign governments already familiar with this video?" Patosh asked without having asked General Cooper for permission first.

"You are?" came snippily from the president.

"For you, Mr. Patrick van de Brog." was the answer he got back from a furious Patosh.

"Don't you know who I am? Show more respect. I am the president of the..."

"You are not my president. We owe this whole affair to you, so show me the respect I deserve. You have kept silent for years and lied to the world in your typical arrogance and now we have the salad. So please listen to us and get off your high horse. I didn't ask to be here."

"OK. Okay, Mr. whoever. No. The other governments don't know yet, or at least I don't know if they do. They're all sitting in Hangar 7 and were flown in here this morning. Maybe everyone got their individual video, but it doesn't seem to me. And yes, you're right Mr. van de Brog. We must now pay the price for our many years of laziness, but the main culprits are the generals like Cooper on your right, who are keeping all the information to themselves and not letting the President in on it. This already is treason and obstruction of evidence that we could have solved this problem years ago."

"We were only at........," General Cooper tried to intervene, but the angry president would not be talked into it,

"Don't give me stupid excuses Cooper. The people are subject to the President's authority and therefore I decide what is right and what is not.

There wouldn't have been a panic if we had taken the time to inform people about aliens over the years. There would have been a gentle transformation and we would be much happier today. And what about security? That was the point you were trying to make, wasn't it? The same bullshit over and over again, I could just puke with this boring cliché. You can't lie to people anymore Cooper, just so a few billionaires can try out their murderous toys and enrich themselves even more by the state budget they are allowed to recive, which consists of the citizens' tax money. The cold war has been over for over 35 years and we are trying to keep the peace with our neighbors, so tell these morons from your lobby brethren that their time is up. I'm the wrong president for you because I'll take every single one of them by the balls and put them in jail if the Alliens don't, get it Cooper?"

"I'm not in any lobby sir. I don't know what you're talking about."

"You're a pathetic liar Cooper. You disgust me and so do those Dr. Mengeles standing next to you." He pointed to professor Farnham and Curtiss, then the president turned his eyes to Roselyn, Mary and Jenkins and asked.

"And who are you?"

"I am Roselyn. A Venusian from the planet Venus."

"You're joking my dear." he replied incredulously with a grin of helplessness.

"I'm not joking Mr. President." Roselyn said, not taking her eyes off him.

"What is your story in all this theater here?"

"I'm the cause Mr. President."

"So you are. Then you have much to confess to me, I suppose, and I insist that you leave no sin out of your confession, my child.

I want to know what's going on here because how else can I serve the people?"

"I will tell you everything Mr. President."

"ROSELYN!" shouted Genral Cooper.

"One more word Cooper and I'll have you taken away. My patience is at an end."

Then he went to Mary and asked.

"And with whom do I have the honor here?"

"I'm Roselyn's mother, Mr. President. Mary Mitchell."

"So you're a Venusian too?"

"No sir. I am, like you, a human. But I was once abducted without my will and mated with a Venusian. I don't regret it, though, because I got my Roselyn in the process."

"Believe me Mam, my astonishment is never ending and I'm sure your story will give me goose bumps. Where did that Venusian rape you, because that's all it is if you didn't want it Mrs. Mitchell. The result that happened afterwards doesn't matter. Yes, you got Roselyn, but it was still a crime. Where would we end up if aliens infested the earth and impregnated our women? We're not living in the Middle Ages and this isn't England being invaded by the Vikings."

"The mating happened on Venus sir!" said Mary with a smile.

"Too bad. Then we are outside the jurisdiction of this planet. Do you want to press charges after the fact madam?" the President actually asked, not sure if he was being sarcastic or serious.

"Believe me ma'am, I'm so beside myself that I would eliminate every single alien who dares to apply his laws here. We are at war, because our infrastructure is crippled and so is the rest of the world." Then he turned to General Cooper and said without mincing words:

"And we have the likes of you to thank for that. If you had cooperated with your presidents, we might have a better world now and live in peace, but no,.....we presidents are only puppets. Not with me mister!"

He went to Jenkins and you could already tell he didn't like him. Malcolm Jenkins was no beauty. Short of stature with a belly and greasy hair, he didn't exactly radiate a sympathetic aura.

"I've seen your face before. I can't remember where. What's your name?"

"Jenkins. Malcolm Jenkins, Mr. President. I'm a ufologist and have made private broadcasts on MY Tube, even on television. But I've been arrested several times, allegedly for libel and conspiracy."

"Oh yes. Now I can remember. My God, I laughed so hard watching that. Well, I can assure you, Mr. Jenkins, that I'd rather have the likes of you than the gang behind me jerking off while lying to their president. NOT TRUE COOPER?"

he turned to the already dejected general and looked at him with contempt.

"But I still have to criticize you, Mr. Jenkins. A lot of things were made up and lied about, weren't they? You probably wanted to scam yourself the quick money and the Ferraris, didn't you Mr. Jenkins?"

"Absolutely not the case, Mr. President. My reports are based on years of observation and collaboration with other colleagues in my industry around the world. What could not be proven, we have established as a theory and believe me, I have invested my last penny and lost it. I am poor and Ferraris are out of the question Mr. President. I too want to open people's eyes and that's what you swallowed down your crooked throats and for that I got persecuted, interrogated, arrested and it ruined me."

"This is how democracy works Mr. Jenkins. It serves mostly the politicians and all wrongdoings are excused with the slogan "INLAND STATE SECURITY". Well, I have enjoyed your programs at least. And what is your job here now?"

"I slipped in like this. Long story, sir. But I've seen Venus and I think the situation is very serious."

"It is, Mr. Jenkins, it is. Well then. Let's get to Hangar 7 and give the others a fright. I'm curious to see how the Chinese delegation will react. They'll lose their sardonic grins. I'm not worried about the Russians."

An armored bus drove the president and his newly arrived companions to Hangar 7, less than 500 meters away, and yet the bus was surrounded by motorcycles, GMC Yukons and other vehicles filled with bodyguards and other security personnel. Of course, a pennant symbolizing the national flag was waving on every fender of the vehicles and the presidential coat of arms with its eagle was not to be missed either. Several Apache helicopters patrolled the area, creating the ambience of a state of emergency. Hangar 7 was heavily guarded and when the bus and its entourage reached the gates, the US President was first greeted by the Canadian Prime Minister, who assured him of his support in this matter. As expected, things went haywire in the hangar and if you think you were dealing with adult state diplomats, think again. The US President was not only "FLOWERED", no, he was booed by most of them. It couldn't have been more surreal for Patosh and the others, but the US President remained calm and was not intimidated when he reached the lectern.

He waited until calm descended and greeted his rivals in a friendly and diplomatic manner.

Like a chameleon, he had changed from the choleric man he was before to an understanding gentleman.

"Ladies and gentlemen. I thank you for responding immediately to my urgent appeal and assure you all that I was as surprised and overwhelmed by the prevailing conditions as you were. I will be brief. We are at war, but our enemy is more powerful than what we know so far. He is not fighting with weapons but with a technology that we cannot counter with anything comparable, unless you have already developed something that nobody knows about." and he looked at the Chinese and Russian delegations.

"Nevertheless, we can only turn this situation around together, but I will show you this video, which was leaked to me by this enemy."

"We already know the video Mr. President!" shouted a Russian envoy, followed by the Chinese, Japanese, French North and South Korean and others. Some presidents even made an effort to appear in Goose Bay themselves, as the case was considered far too sensitive for them. One envoy was not enough and Russia, as well as China, showed their disrespect by such a measure.

"Well, I'd like to play it again anyway to make sure we all got the same video."

It turned out that everyone received the same video and no one was sure whether it was just a rigged game by the Americans to fool the world once again with a Hollywood comedy. To distract attention from a project of greater proportions that could bring the other powers to their knees. They've lied before and it would have been nothing new, but the idea of using aliens to do it would be downright outrageous. Such a lie would be seen by the world as the greatest insult to its intelligence and it had already been insulted with viruses and vaccines that created a wave of panic, fear, social separation and much suffering. Mistrust is the balancing pendulum of world politics and one should be glad that such mistrust prevailed. People watch each other's backs so as not to miss out on any of the big cake and the Chinese in particular had it thick as a fist behind their ears.

"And who's to say that the United States isn't working on a huge scam, as usual? Which countries will suffer this time?" asked the Russian deputy Ivan Kamarov.

"I assure you, sir, that we are not working on such an absurd idea. The aim of the United States has always been to preserve the freedom and rights of its citizens and also to play a decisive role in world peace. It is with regret that I, as President of a world power, have not been informed of everything and must admit that I have been kept in the dark by my own ranks and to have to admit this here in front of assembled government representatives of the global world is humiliating enough for me and should be proof of my honesty for all of you. The situation is serious and if we do not work together on this matter globally, equally hopeless."

"It is both astonishing and shameful to hear such an admission that the President of the United States is not informed about everything. That he has to rely on the information that is thrown on his desk without being able to be sure what is true and what is not. " the Chinese delegate bristled with derision.

"It's not that trivial, Mr. Luan Han Li. We live in a different system than the one you denounce against your people."

"Oh yes? Our president is informed about everyone and everything to the point and the people are not lied to. We would rather keep quiet than lie to them. Your confession here only proves to us that you are nothing but a recipient of orders. We would never dare to leave our head of state in the dark, that would be treason. I ask myself, who is in charge here? This information withheld from you has led the world to such a situation."

"Oh yes? If China has information about aliens, you have also done little to find a solution. The Russians have at least partially admitted that they have gained experience and even asked us for cooperation, which I would have been only too happy to grant if I had not been left in the dark.

Yes, that's why we have a problem today. Pointing the finger at everyone is not helpful. How can we proceed here without causing a panic that will lead to anarchy? We must all pull together, otherwise this planet will no longer be ours."

"May I then suggest that you force the people who have withheld such important information to speak up and that all scientists also get off their EGO and work together around a table to find a solution? I think this is the only way we can at least build a foundation. You are right Mr. President. We all have to pull together, but how do we start?" Kamarov asked

"That's why we are here in Goose Bay and yes, I will make sure that this silence disappears once and for all. Here I see a real opportunity for global cooperation that requires humanitarian proportions. We must move quickly before more people are transported by the Venusians to this penal planet with all their knowledge and we are left without further details. I ask you all to gather your in-country experts and assign them to come together as a consortium and request this without prior approval from the United Nations, because we don't have time," the President said, looking out into the crowd and for the first time the media and press were not involved in such a meeting, but kept as far away as possible. In the meantime, one piece of bad news after another reached the heads of government. The financial system was on the verge of collapse.

The stock market also collapsed and travel came to a standstill. The world was in danger of being transported back to the Middle Ages and neither radar nor satellites were available to the military. But the worst was yet to come, as spaceships were sighted around the world. Hundreds of them landed for all to see and nobody could do anything about them. They were by no means vacationers from outer space, but battalions of aligners and their leader was "Caligula".

Abyss

Yes, the world was on the brink of the abyss, because before even a start could be made on establishing global cooperation, more and more people belonging to various governments and industries disappeared. The Venusians did not allow interrogations on Earth and shipped corrupt and ruthless heads of state, industrial magnates, military leaders, scientists, financial gurus, human and drug traffickers and many more to the penal planet Centauro Magno. Many presidents who ruled on this planet before and during this global gathering in Goose Bay disappeared along with their henchmen of deputies and corrupt associates who helped them to their thrones in the first place. Surprisingly, the US President was spared, but the Chinese and Russian leaders disappeared completely, as many others did. General Cooper, Professor Farnham and Curtiss and several of the deputies and senators who had not kept faith with the president and had enriched themselves in a roundabout way were also among the galactic prisoners and so there were not many left to build a "foundation" with. Ivan Kamarov, Luan Han Li and other so-called entrepreneurs who had made a name for themselves worldwide and were in the upper elite league also disappeared. The earth was completely freed from the scum and "reset". But this did not solve the problem, because what should one do now? New presidents and leaders had to be elected and new tycoons put at the helm so that a new, pure Earth could be created to appease the universe. Could this be done so easily?

Of course not, because man is what he is. Corruptible, greedy for power, selfish and weak in character.
Patosh, Roselyn, Mary and Jenkins had long since returned to Connington on the Shyre in England and were working as ambassadors with a direct link between the President, the newly elected Prime Minister of England and KTKFK. The internet disappeared and made do with the resources and conditions of the sixties and seventies. Conditions in all countries degenerated and poverty and civil wars were the results of the fait accompli. People should show responsibility again and take nothing for granted, according to the words of the High Court on Venus, and this could only be achieved if the system was reset to its default setting.

New Earth

The years passed and Mary, as well as William, died. Mary from her illness and William from grief, as he also became impoverished and lost his hotel "The Red Lion" to his creditors. He bequeathed his Land Rover to Roselyn along with a long letter assuring her how much he appreciated Mary and the family and how much his life was enriched by them, for who could claim to have been on Venus, even if he told no one? No one would have believed him anyway. His grave was not far from Mary's and so it was easy to visit them both. Roselyn and Patosh married, but remained childless. Their work would never have given them the time to raise any children. Malcolm Jenkins moved to the United States and was called to head the consortium of the "Coexistence with Extraterrestrials Foundation" and no doubt did valuable work, much to the liking of the US President, who was elected for the second time in a row and served his country selflessly. He became a good president. Jonathan, Martha and Fred opted for a life back on Venus, because in the end they didn't like the development, even if they could have made a big contribution. Their vacation turned into a life task that they were unable to complete. Were they not up to this earthly challenge after all?

Georgette was doing well and the "Golden Jug" in Lontzen, Belgium, was flourishing because the Belgians remained true to themselves and were not swayed by the circumstances that surrounded them.

The EU disappeared as ninety percent of its workforce were arrested on Centauro Magno and each country became its own again, but the collaboration to create a better world remained. Wars decreased more and more and people understood each other better than ever, as they reached out to each other again and took away the air to breathe from the corrupt and the uneducable through their newborn love, and thus a new human being was born. The Orion clan no longer had access to this new consciousness and thus lost interest. They left Earth with their spaceships and when this happened, it was also time for the Venusians to withdraw from this planet and let the free will of the new human prevail again. A new progress will come. One that will once again make Earth shine as the most unique star in the universe.

The End

Remarks: